FIRST EDITION

Head Full of Mountains © 2014 by Brent Hayward
Cover artwork © 2014 by Erik Mohr
Cover design © 2014 by Samantha Beiko
Interior design © 2014 by Vince Haig

Distributed in Canada by
HarperCollins Canada Ltd.
1995 Markham Road
Scarborough, ON M1B 5M8
Toll Free: 1-800-387-0117
e-mail: hcorder@harpercollins.com

Distributed in the U.S. by
Diamond Comic Distributors, Inc.
10150 York Road, Suite 300
Hunt Valley, MD 21030
Phone: (443) 318-8500
e-mail: books@diamondbookdistributors.com

Library and Archives Canada Cataloguing in Publication

Hayward, Brent, author
    Head full of mountains / Brent Hayward.

Issued in print and electronic formats.
ISBN 978-1-77148-181-6 (pbk.).--ISBN 978-1-77148-182-3 (pdf)

    I. Title.

PS8615.A883H43 2014   C813'.6   C2014-900786-8
                                           C2014-900787-6

CHIZINE PUBLICATIONS
Toronto, Canada
www.chizinepub.com
info@chizinepub.com

Edited by Brett Savory
Proofread by Stephen Michell

Canada Council   Conseil des arts
for the Arts   du Canada

We acknowledge the support of the Canada Council for the Arts which last year invested $20.1 million in writing and publishing throughout Canada.

ONTARIO ARTS COUNCIL
CONSEIL DES ARTS DE L'ONTARIO
an Ontario government agency
un organisme du gouvernement de l'Ontario

Published with the generous assistance of the Ontario Arts Council.

Printed in Canada.

HEAD FULL OF MOUNTAINS

ChiZine Publications

HEAD FULL OF MOUNTAINS

BRENT HAYWARD

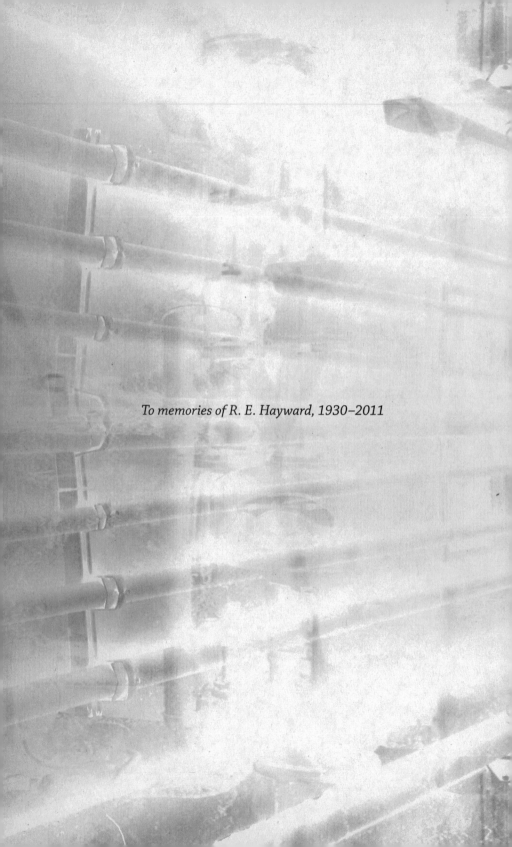

To memories of R. E. Hayward, 1930–2011

CONTENTS

BAYSIDE

When James Calvert went out as a missionary to the cannibals of the Fiji Islands, the ship captain tried to turn him back, saying, "You will lose your life and the lives of those with you if you go among such savages." To that, Calvert replied, "We died before we came here."

—David Augsburger, *Sticking My Neck Out*

FATHER'S PEN

From porthole of the harrier was an image of desolation but once, father said—before he got too sick to talk any sense—there had been a line of something called *mountains*. This was well before the womb expelled Crospinal, before father found refuge in the pen and tethered himself to the capricious world. And not viewed out this particular lens, up in the harrier's console, but from another, peered through during his frantic search for a refuge. Crospinal tried imagining these mountains now—*magnificent,* his dad would say, a tear in his eye, every time he reminisced—as Crospinal had tried imagining them many times throughout his dozen or so years of life, conjuring several possible and incongruous visions of the aberrations. Yet he failed, as always, not only because of the limitations of his imagination but because he was no longer sure he *believed* in such things, whatever they might have once been.

Despite his obvious infirmities, Crospinal had managed the climb up seven rusty ladders to the harrier console perhaps a hundredfold—when he'd first discovered it, as many as three times a day—to loiter here, among other pastimes, straining his eyes through the thick, etched polymethyl: all he ever saw out there was the eternal grey flatline of ash, with a paring of orange at the horizon—some orb or other, whether rising or sinking was impossible to tell.

Rumblings, coming up from the floor grille, and through the thin soles of his boots—and what sounded like a dim explosion of sorts, possibly the engines misfiring—made the world shake lightly. Dustings of dry polymer from the composite panels settled over him. Crospinal picked at his nose, making capillaries in his mitt tingle as they tried to deal with the crusted mucus he rolled between his thumb and forefinger.

He watched out the porthole a moment longer.

To doubt the word of father, Crospinal thought. *Was that how it all began?*

Glittering, refracted through the plastic, watered his eyes. When he turned aside, green after-images of the occluded orb remained, but he tried to blink them away—

The controller, well accustomed to Crospinal's moods and brooding self-indulgences, expended little energy on recent visits, though it faced him now—a grey sphere, the size of his eye—without speaking, having dropped from the ceiling to hover at the exact epicentre of the small chamber; Crospinal frowned, hoping the controller would go back to where it came from, or at least remain silent (the latter of which, thankfully, it did). Crospinal looked away first. The controller continued to study him.

He fidgeted, getting tense.

Time he'd spent dreaming had not, evidently, driven away doubts, nor kept them at bay for even the shortest of whiles: scents inside the dream cabinet had been weak today, vapours thin and vague, and the dream, when it finally pulled him under, was so inconsequential that details were now entirely forgotten. Therapeutic value, nil.

Crospinal lifted the console's cover and flipped it back. The gently rotating image rose from between the holes—two hands, pressed together—and then wavered. Without much further consideration, he shoved both forearms deep inside, felt the connection, a shudder passing through the Dacron of his mitts, up through his skin, into his bones, building in strength. He said, too desperately for his own liking, "Are you there? I know you might be . . . busy. But can you visit? Just for a second? I wanna tell you something."

Nothing. Unfathomable energies of the world went about their business, as they did, passing through him, on their way from father's range out into landscapes Crospinal had not yet travelled and landscapes he never would. Crospinal had been stalling. Dark ideas and memories of rejection were too recent, and daunting; his girlfriend showed up less and less anyhow. And when she did show, she seemed distracted, distant, almost incohesive, if that was possible. Silent. Crospinal wanted to feel angry at this life of pain and the vagaries of phantoms but instead felt the same dullness spreading through him that was always there, as if his damaged nerves were trapped, keening on some standing wavelength between the surface of his epidermis and the snug lining of his sleeves. His molars sang. Under the thin shield, fountained by the uniform's collar, to cover his head, sparks crawled through the stubble of his recently depilated scalp.

Nothing.

About to withdraw, give up, return to the lower floor, there to get on with killing time, Crospinal saw her at last, flickering faintly, becoming almost opaque, positioned so she seemed to be sitting on the ill-formed shelf to his left. (Though a good part of the structure penetrated her hip. Or vice versa. Most days, Crospinal could easily ignore these minor aberrances. He was used to them. A second of his girlfriend's attention made everything worthwhile, and he was outnumbered anyway by entities that could transcend such mundane physical collisions.)

Dressed, as always, in a fresh, dark uniform, similar to his own but heavier, with a circular collar, like no uniform any dispenser had ever offered. With breast pockets, too, tinted mitts, no helmet. She wasn't facing him. Made of light, of course. His girlfriend had a glow to her, a faint pixilation, an allure that always caught his breath. He could smell her energy. Around him now, an aura of faint ghosts circled.

"Hi." He managed to speak, heart fluttering, as if this meeting, like all other meetings, were their first. "I, uh, father's still sick. He's *really* sick. I mean, his bones are so, you know? And he won't stop coughing." Crospinal had not meant to say these things. He never did. But the keening he carried around came forth nonetheless, propelled by a force within him bent, no doubt, on sabotaging what might be considered his best interests. The plan had been to remain positive, to impress, to make this beautiful manifestation laugh and regain her dwindling affections. A simple plan, but already messed up. He cleared his throat and tried, for a moment, without luck, to think of a recovery line, or endearing witticism. "I've been over, uh, to the—"

His girlfriend had not yet responded. *She had not even moved.* Crospinal stopped talking. *Was she okay?* Posed there, wavering a bit, wavelengths faltering, her hair pulled back so tight that the corners of her eyes tugged, all squinty.

She had not moved.

He wanted to take his hands out of the holes, touch her, hold her, pull her close, wanted to do these things so much they were an awful ache that had settled into his core ever since he'd met her: that ache flared now, but his girlfriend would vanish long before he could lift a finger. His hands—if she were able, by some miracle, to stay—would pass right through her.

"Have I done something wrong? Upset you?"

Frozen there in such a way that she, too, seemed to be looking out harrier's porthole, at the ash beyond. The profile of her cheek, her nose, a narrowing of her eyes, all through a shield, was enough to cause Crospinal duress. A slight flickering, overall, but no movement. (Was it possible—

her seeing anything, that is, outside? The horizon, blown across by hot winds, the curve of a reddened orb burning across the sky? Like he saw, every time he looked out. Could she see it? He'd never asked, though he broached nearly every other topic. She had heard him blubber, confess, profess, ramble. Once even heard him laugh. Had waited patiently while he stared down at his own boots, too morose to speak.

Would asking his girlfriend about the horizon outside, and the possibility of mountains, sully the only tie remaining between him and his ailing father? Would he be cast further adrift, or was the damage already done?)

"Why you so quiet?" His own words a whisper. "What's up? I . . ." All this time his beleaguered heart had been lugging something heavy up his throat to his mouth, to dump it there, like refuse. He could not swallow. Slower poundings in his chest. "I, uh, I'm—*Shit*. Things are falling apart. I'm, well, I'm *scared*." Another long silence. On his part, growing despair. Anxiety. *Could girlfriends cease? Everything else seemed to, so why not—*

Mercifully, though, stuttering to life (such as it was), moving one arm, turning toward him, to engage—

Consumed by relief, as their eyes met, Crospinal felt such a rush, and he grinned idiotically, though he knew already what was coming.

"Don't call me anymore." She was smiling. "I thought we had that clear."

The ghosts whirled and faded.

Elation, which he only wanted to nurture, maybe even let soar, like it had done at rare but glorious times in the past, plunged and crashed. Maybe his body was the one assembled out of photons, and projected here, not hers. Maybe he was unsubstantial. He said: "*What?*"

"Your memory's atrocious." Still smiling. (Him being flayed alive by it.) "This area's being subsumed. The influence of your passenger's waning. You need to leave. But you don't need me anymore. Remember? You promised. So I came here, one last time, to remind you. You need to leave."

"But I—" *What had he promised?* He wanted to say he loved her, and that he missed her, and that he needed to be with her forever. But those sorts of statements had already precipitated trouble.

"Time for you to leave, Crospinal."

Seldom did she say his name. It invoked hot torrents in him. He swallowed—hard—at last. "But there's nowhere to go."

Narrowing her eyes in that lovely way of hers, glazed and unfocussed, she said, "They're searching for you." Her lips—also exquisite—were not quite synced with the words that tore Crospinal apart like teeth of the hardest polycarbonate. "Don't call me anymore. Don't come back here. For both of us."

"Who's searching for me?"

A hint of movement passed though the space that would be behind his girlfriend, were she sharing his realm: slim dark shapes shifted through the composite that comprised the counter—

And Crospinal was alone again.

The empty harrier console. Stupid controller, hovering there, watching.

"I suppose you were talking to your girlfriend again?" it said.

"Shut up." Glare, from outside, stinging Crospinal's eyes. "You're just mad because you're fading, too. 'Cause this station's going."

"I'll relocate. I'm due for a transfer."

Dragging his forearms clear of the holes, Crospinal stood for some time, feeling utterly gutted.

Later, returning home, he stomped in his bow-legged way along the catwalks and narrow grates that had emerged when he was born, and solidified when he was a young child, but were now starting to crumble. Knees popping, he kicked at debris, knocking fractured chunks and residue of the formations through the grille onto dimmer structures below.

As soon as he got within father's range—smaller even than yesterday—a dog coalesced, and tried to cut off his passage.

"Crospie," it barked. "Crospie! Crospie! Nice to see you back! But you're making too much noise. Welcome back! All that clattering! Ringing about. Could have threaded that bolt back on. We saw you kick it. We saw you! Could have helped. Stem the tide, you know? Remember when you were showed? Remember that, Crospie? Remember? About bolts? The haptic about nuts and bolts and metal?"

"Go away, dog. That wasn't a bolt. Just some hardened polymer crap. I was doing you a favour. Keeping entropy at bay."

"If you're not part of the solution, you're part of the problem. Remember?"

Crospinal stopped. "Father says a lot of things like that. You should know. It doesn't mean anything. And I suppose you're part of the solution? All you dogs and spirits and shit? Floating around. Can you leave me alone? And *you're* the one making too much noise. Yapping all the time. You make *way* more noise than me."

He kicked, but half-heartedly: the dog easily dodged. Both the kick and the dodge were pointless. Now the apparition looked up through narrowed eyes of light.

"What's gotten into you? You've changed so much. What goes on out there?"

"Father has no idea where I am. Even if I'm standing right in front of his face. He's so out of it. He has no idea if he's awake or asleep. Now leave me alone."

At the remote end of the hall, other apparitions appeared.

"Call off your stupid friends. I'm fine. Go back to your kennels. Go back inside his head."

The dog cocked its own to one side, sniffing. "Were you crying again, Crospie?" The second kick would have passed right through it, had reactions been any different. Moving in to mock-sniff again at Crospinal's boot, the dog—all dogs, all apparitions, and father, too, lost in the abyss of his ailment—knew, that instant, the truth.

Crospinal resumed walking. Stoic, bones protesting, knees akimbo, heart heavy.

The little apparition caught up, and trotted next to him.

No dog could stay quiet for long.

"It's okay, Crospie. People cry. That's what you do. You cry, eat, worry, sleep. *Dream.* Lie awake, trying to remember. You should talk to us more. We're here for you. We *worry* about you. We don't know where you go anymore. We don't, Crospie. We don't, and we worry."

Glancing aside, and down, to flash the dog a look meant to wither, but this time the dog didn't look up.

"You aren't meant to know," he said. "That's the whole point. I'm not doing anything. Just thinking."

"For now are you returning? To father? To his throne? Are you going to sleep in your own daybed tonight?" Panting, as if the dog really did have to breathe, and was winded. "He asked about you, earlier. He's *always* asking about you, Crospie. You're everything to him. You're all he's got."

Taking a deep breath, a real one, air filling his lungs, coming through the shield, filters hissing, chestplate expanding, microbes and other unwanted guests cycling through the unit of his uniform, Crospinal wiped at his moist cheeks with a sheathed knuckle. He had stopped again. Peed a bit, into his catheter, felt the processor deal. As he bent to rub at his knees, which had been hurting a lot more these days—excruciating—he said, "Father asked about me? Really? I mean, he was awake? He *spoke*?"

"Well." The dog reconsidered. "Not really. Not *per se*. He was *sort* of alert, a while ago. Briefly. Eyelids flickering. He's asleep once more. But he *would* have asked about you, if he were awake. He *would* have, Crospie."

Now they looked at each other. Crippled human, in his stale uniform, lovelorn and feeling sorry for himself, and this luminous projection, here to protect, instruct, and fetch him back. Resentments that Crospinal tried to sustain were fading. He felt sorry for the stupid dogs. They were distilled emotion, thoughts with singular-minded agendas, neurons riding on weak sine waves.

Crospinal experienced a degree of envy, for identical reasons.

"That makes no sense," he muttered.

"Crospie?"

Tensing for more bad news, he blinked. The sound in his ears was a roar. One day, all this would be gone. "Yeah?"

"I'm afraid, father, his body that is, has been coughing up blood."

Coughing up blood.

"Maybe you could come back for good? Like old times. Father would love to hear your voice. Please come back." The dog had starting to whine, getting worked up, words pitched higher and higher. Since father's condition had taken a sharp downturn, all apparitions were less stable. Which stood to reason.

Crospinal wanted to ask: *How much blood?*

He rubbed at his scalp instead, the shield crackling about his head.

"We *know*," said the dog, quieter now. "We know he hears you."

"Look." Crospinal's cheeks were getting hot. "I'll come by, all right? I'll come by. Later. But take it easy. You're gonna burn out." This was meant to be a joke, though Crospinal felt horrible as soon as he said it.

"Come by? Come by!" The dog spun, happy; it didn't care about insults. The projection struggled to keep up. "Oh, that would be great! Just great! Thank you *so* much." Circling his feet now, dashing about. "We miss you, we miss you, we miss you!"

He ignored the litany of high-pitched questions and the further pestering of the dog. At least, he tried to appear that way. Why waste breath telling an apparition a joke anyhow? Why tell a joke at all?

"Okay," Crospinal said. He meant it this time. He *would* pay father a visit. He would spend time in the pen, sleep in his own daybed. "But don't call me Crospie. I tell you that all the time. Crospie was my baby name, and I'm not a baby anymore."

The apparition, happy for any concession, for any bone tossed its way, moved its hind quarters from side to side so vigorously it shook itself apart.

<hr>

He was pretty sure he could not remember what it was like to be that baby, Crospie. Memories of memories. Haptics and replayed files. Naturally, there were recordings by eyes of the world, stored in the banks behind father. Not many, but enough.

He'd had a sister then, apparently, the same age, at first, though she disappeared at some point during the first two years of life, and seemed to age at a different rate. Father had immersed Crospinal in a few dozen scenarios: two infants—Crospie and the girl, Luella, in tiny uniforms. Crospinal dragged himself forward, crooked thighs splayed, while his sister began crawling, pulling herself up, and toddling, long before him. Flesh and blood. Two babies, tumbling together.

Side by side in the garden, taken from a remote perspective, or playing with father's garrulous projections in the halls outside the pen's core while the two elementals he had called Fox and Bear watched, begrudgingly, over them both.

Maybe mnemonic triggers were set off by the sight of the children, but he was absolutely certain he had no recollection of the feel of another person's palm against his own, no living hand, mitt in mitt. He watched contact happen—at least on two occasions—on floating screens, and within the haptics, but that was all.

Generally, in the years since Luella surpassed him and then vanished, father and he kept their distance, ostensibly to prevent the exchange of unpleasant organisms, but Crospinal, even at a young age, sensed a whiff of shame. He was sure he smelled the faintest tinge of repulsion.

In one such recreational file from the library of haptics, the siblings were naked together, actually *naked*, without any latex or neoprene, no processor, nothing, splashing in the collecting pool, bathed by the clumsy elementals. They must have been days old, bandages still on their arms. Their pale, fresh skin, a rare and incredible sight. The damp folds of their genitalia, glimpsed but once, dimpled buttocks, large heads. Before any uniform went on, before catheters drilled in and the clinging spandex covered their limbs, before delicate shields swung up, over their faces to filter the air. Bodies were pink and sudsy and gleaming clean.

But he could never recall contact.

Fox was thin and upright, a smart machine, casting a thin shadow. Bear was the same. Like all elementals—there were a few that came and went, assisting around the pen—they had cold, red eyes. Clearly, father had sent a few spirits in, too, to watch over proceedings: spectral shapes hovered in the background, translucent and fleeting, stymied by the trees.

Now, Fox and Bear, like Luella, and all the other elementals, were long gone. Of this Crospinal was also certain. The pen and environs were crumbling as father sickened. Composites encroaching again, the way it was before he'd come. Even haptics were changing, edited, or unavailable. Vanished from within father's diminishing range and what few external areas Crospinal had lamely explored. Maybe the machines—and his sister, too—were broken in adjacent landscapes, whatever configurations they might be, unable to return. Batteries might have died. Oxygen could have ended. Truthfully, Crospinal did not miss the machines much, though he often wondered what had become of Luella. Despite Fox and Bear being tangible, their titanium fingers had been cold, their movements slow, their silence and awful eyes unnerving.

Spirits still drifted around. They didn't get in the way much. And ghosts. And dogs, of course, father's dogs, all over the place.

In another haptic, baby Crospie, unaware of anything the future might bring, or take away, slept fitfully on his back, arms flung wide, curved legs canted. In a fresh uniform, maybe his second or third, with fresh boots and fresh mitts. His sister, awake, managed to lift her head and stare out at the lens recording the shot: her expression, under the patina from the collar's shield, showed evidence of a rapture that clearly defined the wonder she felt in her life and perceptions. Crospinal could tell by the gaze, the partly open mouth, the intake of breath. Her blue eyes were almost round. Behind her, even in sleep, Crospinal's contrasting pain and angst were visible. He had never felt wonder, nor assurance, or security. Not to this day.

Luella was gone.

Impossible to pinpoint when, exactly, she had vanished. Impossible for him, anyhow. In one haptic, she appeared twice his age. Impossible for him to pinpoint any event, really. Like Fox and Bear, like the past itself—and like the baby called Crospie—all he knew was that his sister was no longer around. Times when he had wanted to ask father about Luella were also gone. Times when he might've gotten a straight answer. All he ever got now was blank stares, catatonia, or fragmented lectures from the apparitions as father unravelled more and more toward madness and his demise.

Bloody drool, dangling . . .

Crospinal had stopped asking anything. Most of his time was spent wandering the edges of the disintegrating pen, or beyond, in the less defined areas he was warned so many times, as that child, to avoid.

<hr>

The clutch of carbon tubes clattered together like bells as they plummeted. He had snapped the tubes away from where they'd been rooted, separating the brittle material at the base. Not long ago, this entire area had been distinct and hard-edged. Now, sheets of hardening polymers encroached on the landscape and curtains of light swept back and forth over areas, reconfiguring, instilling information. Building machines—dumb, six-legged, carapace the size of his fist—watched from the walls as the tubes fell until the roiling mists below broke them down. Other movements down there, through a lazy rent in the clouds: beams of white energy suddenly revealed, magnesium bright, a growing extension, coaxing fullerenes from the composite foundation. Two hovering drones watched, in a swarm of data orbs, as construction splayed where none had been before, the world shifting, growing down there.

Crospinal turned, reluctantly, from the abyss.

There had been a thought, a flickering thought, about following the tubes down.

Past the remaining platform ringing the aperture, a layer of tiles, marred purple with toluene, had formed, completely separating the main rib from the pen, compromising the transfer tube he'd planned to take in such a way that Crospinal would have to hunch to walk under its sloped ceiling. Even now, strings of allotropes dripped from the seam of the split to the fresh tiles, where they were absorbed into the world with tremendous stench. He stood in wonder at the transformation that would sooner or later eradicate everything he knew. Data streams webbed the opening, information pouring over the freshly exposed material, programming reform, telling polymers to join forces. Changes were afoot up here, too, reconfiguration in the old as well as the new. What would father say about this, if he knew? Change was no longer kept at bay.

Not foolish enough to pass, for transmogrifications of the layout might not cease because of his presence, Crospinal held his nose pinched, capillaries crackling (these mitts were not new, and also compromised by wear). After a brief inspection, he took a narrow passage into what remained of the original structure, into a crawlspace, shimmying sideways between old plates.

The tunnel that had formed here was quiet. Sometimes he felt a breath of stale air, and he thought he heard movements, but he did not see indications of what, if anything, might be travelling. Ambients in the wall kept the lighting dim. At his back, the construction was warm, almost hot. Getting increasingly rough. If the structure changed abruptly, he could find himself plunging—not as appealing a concept as it had just been. He wondered if, on the other side, lay the barren horizon he'd gazed out on, not so long ago, from porthole of the harrier. Was there truly another world, with another set of rules, outside this one? The wasteland Crospinal always saw could not be what father coveted, where there had been mountains. His insistence meant there could be a third, or dozens more, for traces lingered, through fragments of memories and jumbled knowledge: the gate connected to father's brain once supplied the ability to burn brightly, and project, but proved inconsistent and, as he died, unreliable.

Life had not always been this way.

Putting his hands against the ancient surface of the construction, Crospinal felt tremors of energy through the thin layer of his mitts. He thought again about his girlfriend's words. Just as there was no way to see what lay beyond this shell, he had no chance of understanding the motives of the manifestation he had fallen in love with. Portholes did not open on this facet of the world. His girlfriend was unfathomable.

If he could break through, arid waste spilling in, the nothingness of the outside that he saw might sear his lungs to cinders and etch the flesh from his bones, bringing oblivion, freedom from torment, and relief.

His breath caught, shuddering—at least one more time—in his chest. The tricot rose and fell.

At one point, moments later, still navigating the tunnel adjacent to the blocked transfer tube, Crospinal got wedged. He wondered what the dogs would do, or not be able to do, if they could see him there, stuck in the wall. With his tongue he hooked his siphon into the corner of his mouth. He took a very small sip; water from his processor, wicked by the lining of his uniform, was distilled from his own waste. Since a recent lesson father might not even have meant to show him, but had done so as his judgement failed, Crospinal could not help but taste the bitter iodine.

After some amount of half-assed struggle, he managed to free himself and continue, on his way, back to the pen, where father was tethered, trapped, and almost dead.

THE YEAR OF ACTION

Party number seven was a ceremony with no precedent. Held in the secondary sustenance station, just off the throne room. Dogs were represented, a full force contingent. Fox and Bear were there, too, and three wisps, which seldom appeared, drifting in the breeze that came through openings in the wall. One of father's spirits carried a direct lightscreen, beaming a broadcast of father himself, back in the centre of the pen, looking healthy and young in his fresh uniform, unable to stop grinning from within the array of tubes and conduits and cables that connected him.

Ghosts drifted about, ebullient.

Father, though, was pretty out of it, on nootropics and such, coasting on their effects. Any mnemonic breakthrough was a cause for emotional soaring, at least temporarily, and soaring, as Crospinal was well aware, preceded a dive.

From the banks there was an image of a strange, pointy helmet, with stars on it, and another part of the haptic called *chocolate cake*, which had once been a configuration of pellets no longer available from any dispenser, with seven *candles* so real Crospinal almost believed father's story that they would have been hot, if Crospinal were able to touch them. Details meant father was well-stoked. Fearful of saying or doing the wrong thing, Crospie grinned awkwardly and kept fairly silent. The outcome seemed inevitable.

Afterwards, father dispersed the guests, most of whom vanished instantly. The two elementals, made of metal and the hardest of plastics, lingered for a moment before turning and leaving under their own accord, without a word. Only the spirit carrying father's image remained.

And Crospinal, of course. He could hardly vanish.

"I'm proud of you." Father's face, shining like ambients, the nutrients almost visible through the tight skin of his face. He was wearing the front plate of an amber helmet—all he could fit. "I might not tell you often enough, but I'm *very* proud of you. Look how well you're doing, Crospie. Your legs are much straighter. Do they hurt today? You haven't said in a while. You can get about quite well."

Crospinal stood there, best he could, another absurd haptic called a *balloon* in one mitt and projections of icing on his face. Even at such an age, he knew there was more coming. There was always more coming. That's what life was like. Implications and half-complete expressions, undefined expectations, ever unsure what exactly was needed, or what, in fact, was happening. He waited uncomfortably.

Father cleared his throat; tubes shook, back in the pen, where his body waited. The spirit carrying this representation loomed even closer. Smoke and mirrors, layers of illusions.

"You've passed many hurdles, son. You're *healthy*. You're *alive*. You're *civilized*. Do you understand what this means, Crospie? Do you see?"

Crospinal's stomach rumbled. "Not really. But I think so?" Yet he did not.

"One day, sooner than either of us thinks, we'll have to part. You know that. Of course you do. And when you're on your own, you'll bring civilization with you, like a torch. Everything will be made available if you persevere against the dark. This is the year of action. The seventh year. A year of renewal, a year of hope. You're a success, son, and you've made *me* a success. The past is inconsistent but the future will be *clear*! Today, I had images in my mind so lucid I could almost touch them. Look at what I found: the birthday party of a child! If you continue to listen, Crospinal, and *believe*, we can push the dark away together. But, for now, stick by my side, son. Keep your old man company. There's much to learn and you're not ready."

Crospinal fumbled with the balloon string (which, like the hat, the candles, and his companions, was constructed from photons). He needed to go pee more than anything. He liked to hold off for as long as possible, only relieving himself while alone, and without any choice, because the catheter, when activated, made him queasy. He shuffled his feet. The apparition wavered. Crospinal's legs were killing him. They always did. But he had stopped complaining, that's all. Father's representation continued to grin and beam. Even Crospinal's eyes hurt.

The grand entrance—prodigal son, returned—was, needless to say, less effective than he would have liked: when Crospinal appeared in the opening to the central chamber—where father had bound himself to the gate, and called forth his throne, ensconcing them both—he was hot and out of breath (his regulator was on the fritz), and the neoprene fabric of his sleeves was smeared with stains. Rivulets of sweat stitched down his face, quavered by the shield thrown up by his collar, and trickled down his neck, where capillaries of his uniform kicked in to lap them up, but the old processor was stale and overheated.

Here, where father's influence was strongest, the structure remained mostly right-angles, and metallic, with polymethyl beams cantilevered up from the floor grilles. The lighting was mostly ambient, but there were two rows of potlights, halogen, embedded overhead. Small objects and arcane devices that had fallen from the ceiling, or were pushed from the walls, littered the area by father's feet, like offerings. The floor was strewn with artifacts—metals, and hard plastics—that father called *concrete ephemera*. Expelled, expectorated from the world. Father had claimed, when he was able to pontificate, that he, too, might once have emerged thus from within the structures of composites and agents of flux that surrounded them, immaculate.

Mostly the story began with a fade-in, father running, looking for a home.

Against the far wall of the pen was Crospinal's daybed, and his prayer mat, but Crospinal did not want to look at them. Memories took away his energy and tormented him.

But what else was there?

He blinked.

Father slumped in his throne, face mostly hidden by the conduits and wires that drooped from his skull to fan out across the floor behind him, to the banks of the gate, which dwarfed him. They were silent, black, yet emanated age and omniscient, corrupted knowledge. Crospinal stepped across the threshold. The pen, as it did of late, stunk of rot, and piss, of decay and impending collapse. And *disease*. Folds of composite were growing over a control panel. The throne itself seemed to be sinking. He could discern father's shallow breathing: there remained life yet. Father's breastbone—a prominent ridge against the Kevlar breastplate of his tricot—moved. Gurgling fluids, nutrients in and out, cocktails from the gate, and information, kept him going. Though they were no contest for the ravages of disease and time. Now father's legs were mere bones, the fabric of his uniform collapsed against them, bulbous knees rivalling Crospinal's. Through the translucent boots, father's feet were bloated and bruised, the skin split, weeping pus his own processor had long ago given up on.

Father slept.

Still broody from his visit to the harrier and the declarations his girlfriend had made (though taken aback, somewhat, despite his affront, at the incredible and perverse decrepitude toward which a life could sink), Crospinal was suddenly not sure if he would have cared had father died, though he flushed with guilt at the sacrilege of this thought, and immediately fell to his knees.

"By the order of all that is good, and organic, and by the benefits of reinstating the way things used to be," said Crospinal, when the pain had driven away his terrible thoughts and he was able to speak: "I went beyond your range again, past the gangplanks—which are now almost entirely gone. I've been up the towers, and I've crossed over the rotating corridor. I looked out portholes at seventeen, and at ten, and I gazed a long time out the harrier. I told you about the harrier?" He closed his eyes, hearing his own voice: *And I tried to kick your stupid dogs and I was dumped by a beautiful manifestation whose existence you know nothing about and I doubted your words until the world trembled under me.*

There were some confessions Crospinal had never made, and never would. "I can tell the world is changing. Faster and faster. Out by the transfer tube, a big flake broke away, a *really* big piece. Taller than me. I don't know if you can see that far anymore. There was toluene, and lights. Polymers made a panel. It's nearly set." He let his words fade, opening his eyes. Maybe father would take this news as another form of defeat, if it sank in, and get even sicker. Regulators that either fed him, or took essences away, sighed and hissed impatiently. Crospinal felt ghosts all around, spirits and such, fretting, expecting him to help. *Lift a finger,* they pleaded. *Do something. . . .*

Small wonder he stayed away.

Dogs appeared, so to speak, either side. When Crospinal looked back up, father was staring directly at him. Dark eyes watched him, brimming with fear of the impending nothingness and resignation of its inevitability.

"You're awake." Crospinal's heart thudded, a barrage of his own hopes and pain and guilt—

But there was blood inside father's mouth, dripping down, and father's gaze turned darker, lost focus, like dim lights dimming more. His head, looking tiny atop the padded collar around the neckpiece of his uniform, lolled. Tubes shifted. He had said nothing. Crospinal thought of his girlfriend yet again, of her misaligned gaze. Had falling in love with her been the betrayal that caused this demise? It seemed important to remember details of his relationship but details eluded him. A transfer of allegiance, away from father, making Crospinal the agent of this change? He ground his teeth together as a black clot slid and hung from father's boney chin, the throat working, trying to swallow—

"Sometimes . . . I look around," father whispered. "I don't know who lives here, in this house."

"What?" Crospinal leaned forward to hear better. "What house? What's a house?"

"The furniture." Father's chest shuddered; tubes rustled; the clot broke free and fell to his chest, where it slid farther. The material of his uniform went to work, reclaiming it. "Furniture is upside down. But then I stare for a bit longer—because I can't move from this spot—and I see the same thing. I *live* here. This is *my house*." Showing red-flecked teeth and trying, unsuccessfully, to lick those dry lips. "No furniture is upside down, is it? Is it, boy?"

"Dad, there's a helmet, in the dispenser at thin tree. I saw it coming in. A blue one, with a clear visor. Perfect. You know? Should I get it? I could put it on."

"This is a nice place . . ."

"Dad? Would you like me to get a fresh helmet? And put it on?"

"I lost my way . . ." So quiet, almost a breath. "For the longest time I couldn't conceive. There was a man, next door, when I was a child. But I've reached endtime now."

"This isn't endtime." Though Crospinal did not believe his own words. What was he supposed to say? He did not understand. At times, father had known so much about the world, yet at others, like now, seemed to know absolutely nothing. Hard to imagine him as a younger man, in the state he had often described as newborn, in an adult body, with instincts to run, find a gate, raise a family. Haunted by his broken memories, he would call the pen forth, to rise into place around him. No haptics existed from before Crospinal was born, or, if they did, they had been kept away. He relied on instructions, ramblings, and asides. Struggling to understand everything these days, he wondered how father's brief speech and signs of life could be cause for joy, for celebration, because Crospinal felt no emotion akin to joy, nor did he think, as his girlfriend turned away from him, and father was leaving him alone forever, that he would ever have the capacity.

"Son," said father suddenly, but when Crospinal looked into the black eyes once more he saw no passing flicker of days past, no lessons, no guidance, no love, just the impending victory of darkness.

The world juddered. Maybe it was chuckling at them. Crospinal stood. His joints popped loudly in the silence and brought, at last, a flood of tears.

Father had begun to snore.

One of the first actions young Crospie had been asked to attempt, in that year, was to turn a brass dial in the wheelroom, directly behind the pen.

The wheelroom was a chamber of hard, grey walls and polymethyl floor. This task had never been tried before—for obvious reasons. Touching the thumb pad of the contraption that occupied the centre of the wheelroom went all right: the blue panels activated, the way they should have, under the Dacron layer of his mitt, and the icon—an arrow—appeared. Yet the mechanism of the dial itself was seized pretty good or had not properly emerged in the first place. It would not budge.

The local controller swooped overhead to get a better look.

Penetrants Crospinal was directed to apply took several hours to soak in. These were not toluene, but a glutinous solution father called *oil*. Crospinal found the canister of oil in a cupboard, also sealed, but which he was able to tug open. The canister possessed a form of very mild intelligence and was shy, reluctant to come out. But a canister had to believe enough in determinism not to resist too strenuously to a human's grip. Spirits and dogs and other apparitions crowded about, excited, encouraged by small victories. Tension in the wheelroom was palpable. Father watched from many places that day, from many angles. Crospinal raised high the canister, feeling foolish.

There was a long list of chores to attempt, a lot of expectations to alter, or assert against, the landscape.

He got low-viscosity oil down the front of his uniform, which was repelled by the neoprene, but some made it through his shield, and into his mouth. Even after electrostatic cleaning, which he let flow past his gums to scrub his insides, he would never lose, nor forget, the taste of *oil*.

Crospinal never did learn what would have happened had he actually managed to budge the dial. Stop something else from breaking down? Change the view out the portholes? Make life go on forever and girlfriends stay in love?

He felt blankets of futility settle over him, over everything he touched.

Spirits watched more and more forlornly while Crospinal fumbled and faltered. He groaned, raised blisters on the skin of his hands (which were tended to by his mitts), and he ground his teeth together. Father eventually told him to stop. *Give up.* A very dejected voice. *Stop, Crospie. It's not important. We'll try again next year. . . .*

Dogs howled and offered support but ultimately could do nothing.

Which was part of the problem.

Every task on the list, or so it seemed to Crospinal, was, to greater or lesser degrees, equally pointless: opening a cap to release green fumes from a pipe; bending a tiny rubber seal in an access room so the two ends of a hose could never align; cleaning fresh polymers from the gutter around a metallic floor plate in some out-of-the-way dead end.

A handful of chores were accomplished.

Most failed.

And nothing changed, not for the better anyhow. Father's disappointment, which he could not hide, no matter how much he talked, or smiled, or reassured Crospinal that everything would all be okay, grew steadily. Apparitions became sombre, including the dogs, as the pen subsided into longer and longer bouts of silence. Crospinal felt the pressures growing, pushing him down, and away.

Before too long, blood flecked father's spit.

SOJOURN

Struggling along the walkway toward the dream cabinets, head down, ruminating as he looked through the grille, Crospinal was somewhat surprised to recognize where he'd been heading. Most days he managed to get through with just one dose. He'd promised the dogs he would sleep in his own daybed and keep father company, but searching himself for the will to turn around, return to father's side, he found the will was not there. This did not make him feel much better. He did not turn around.

On a ledge below, arrays of ambients flickered, as if trying to tell him something.

Engines boomed distantly.

There were seven dream cabinets, side by side. Before each was a strip of green carpet, soft, even through the worn soles of Crospinal's boots. A green floor like no other. He stood and wriggled his toes against the rare luxury and felt his soles activate and briefly stopped wondering about everything he was powerless to affect.

Four of the cabinets had been smashed by an ancient girder, a massive beam, fallen from above, neither plastics nor polymers, long before Crospinal had discovered this place. Clearly, there had always been cataclysm. Maybe even before the pen had formed. Some great force had once struck, knocking fundamental structures from their arcane configuration.

The girder angled upward, where it came to rest, having cleaved masses of composites, none of which had returned to its original form, and puncturing floor tiles, too, which still bore evidence of trauma. Twisted coils of stunted growth bloomed in bizarre formations, like the yellow flowers that sometimes opened at the base of trees in the garden. Perhaps the extent of the damage, and the age of the material out here—and peculiar composition—were part of the reason why the world had not cleaned up the area or taken molecules back into its pool of resources.

Barely visible from where Crospinal stood, staring up—on the ceiling— were other, similar beams, dangling from their roost. There were no mists today. The fractured area looked like clusters of gossamer threads; up close, the fallen girder was as big around as the biggest food dispenser, and must have weighed many tons.

Had something tried to come in?

Or had something left?

The breach, if it had ever existed, closed long ago.

Only two dream cabinets remained intact, sealed from the inside, and could not be opened by any amount of tugging or prying. (No surprise there, Crospinal supposed.) Patches of light around the door frame flickered cool blues and reds. The last cabinet in the row—accessible by stooping under the extremity of the fallen girder—glistened with yellow, and was where Crospinal went to dream.

As he ducked, from a tiny cabin at the end of the corridor—too small to contain a console, with no periscope, no thumb plates either—came the controller, bobbing and listing.

"Hey," said Crospinal. "Light."

Ambient illumination increased briefly, flickering, and dimmed.

"Thanks," he said, without sarcasm. "Good job." Because this controller, like many, was earnest, eager to please, and Crospinal did not want it to feel bad. (Others, like the one out by harmer's corner, understood a larger vocabulary, and were almost as smart as a low-end elemental, but were ultimately less interested in fulfilling Crospinal's desires. They were sarcastic at times and rude. Crospinal, naturally, preferred these subservient, if somewhat challenged, versions. He felt an affinity.)

The upper part of the door to his dream cabinet had actually suffered damage during the girder's fall: the frame, which was burnished polycarbonates, had bent, split away from the body of the cabinet, so the entire device hissed quietly and incessantly and could never lock. Not like the other two. The door's seal was broken and, for this reason, granted him egress.

The warm handle slipped into Crospinal's mitt smoothly, as it always did, moving with fluid grace before he'd flexed; he felt the quiet *click* and a shimmer pass up his arm, a sensation so similar to the console's hum that, for a second, he often, absurdly, expected his girlfriend to appear.

The icon was a person, in uniform and helmet, leaning back at an impossible angle, rotating.

Why was she pushing him away? Had he truly once known the reason why she didn't want to see him anymore? He needed his girlfriend more than ever, during father's last days, but was unable to keep her affection. He vowed to continue putting his arms into every console he knew until she loved him in return. Until she loved him like she had before. She might be cross when he tried to conjure her, but that anger would surely pass, because he was Crospinal, after all, and who else was the world for? Who else had hands, and feet, and a heart? *Who else was alive?*

He opened the door of the dream cabinet as far as he could. Vapours escaped, curling toward his face. Crospinal licked the knuckles of his mitt, tongue crackling, picked at his clogged nostril, Dacron sizzling, and breathed in so deeply his shield went opaque. When he exhaled, and breathed more deeply again, he started to feel better, a growing sense of peace, of clarity, as if meaning or a point might eventually be found to the moments that fell by, one after the other, into the murky past.

Turning, he squeezed backward into the cabinet, pressing himself against the padding, which crumbled where he touched, and pattered down, behind the covering. Pain tickled along Crospinal's side, where he had recently scraped himself. The rough wall in the transfer tube had actually ruptured the already-thinned nylon of his old uniform. He touched the split now, at his elbow, felt the insulation beneath, and his skin and bones beneath that, surprised by his own lack of personal maintenance. Small wonder he'd been dumped. Yet, inside the dream cabinet, Crospinal felt all wounds heal, ruptured cells rebind. Even his knees were soothed. Who needed a girlfriend, or father, or love from either? Tranquility descended.

With his eyes closed, drifting away, Crospinal smelled the dream coming, a strong one this time.

Unseen lights flared around the faulty seal. One by one, on the inside, flickering blue scanned over Crospinal—who, asleep, managed nonetheless to hold the door shut. Vapours rose before his face like ghosts. There was a tic at his cheek. The cabinet's icon flared and winked out.

———

Later, in a state of heavy grogginess, he understood only that something had gone wrong, not where he was, nor even who. His head pounded and his mouth was very dry. Gradually, Crospinal remembered climbing to the harrier, and the events that followed. The throb of his knees was like a malevolent heart. No lights were on. He groped the lining of the door, just inches from his face, but when he found and tried to pull the handle, nothing happened; he gripped inert plastic.

Trapped.

Already his breath was jagged in his chest and his stomach churned sour. He released a trickle of urine, and his processor, reacting, was startlingly loud. He heard a quieter hiss, and felt chilled, on his nape. How long could he last in here?

He took a small hit from his siphon, but the uniform's water had no additives and did nothing to help him relax.

Moving his knees carefully against the door, Crospinal braced himself and pressed outwards; the pain was exquisite, but instead of the door giving way, the padding behind him collapsed farther. Absurdly, he shouted for help:

"Something out there? Hello? I'm stuck!"

But no apparition could come this far from the pen. Even if one could, they were projections, and could do nothing to help.

The remote sound of running fluids, and the *clink-clink* of hardened material, rapping lightly against the shell of the cabinet.

In both palms, against the inside of the curved surface of the door, he felt vibrations.

Crospinal was sure he had never mentioned the discovery and use of these dream cabinets to father, or the peace he felt when he closed himself inside. Like the harrier, this place was another of duplicity, another wedge to drive between him and his dad. Even from his girlfriend he kept secrets. Well, now his secrets had trapped him, literally, and would soon kill him.

He pounded the interior, but when he felt himself tipping slowly backward, he realized with a surge of relief that this was all a dream's beginning, or continuation, and he should just let the dream take him where the dream wanted to take him. Knowledge eased him of fear. He stopped pounding, let his hands drop to his sides, and smiled.

A dream . . .

Delirious freefall. Seconds later, gentle impact. Crospinal felt no discomfort, perhaps a splash, and then he was bobbing, within the dark cabinet, on his back.

Floating peacefully.

He closed his eyes again.

Welcome, passenger, said a soothing voice. *Please remain still for a moment or two. Stats seven point five and rising. Sleep, if you wish, passenger. Sleep.*

"Okay," said Crospinal. He had heard this voice from sundry devices, but never as clear, not at the dream cabinets, and had never been called *passenger* before. If the term was familiar, context eluded him. Nonetheless, Crospinal drifted off, rather peacefully, obediently, until silence crept in and gently woke him. He stared up at an infinity so black and humbling that he felt tears form in the corners of his eyes. He put his shaking elbows on the rim of the dream cabinet and sat up.

The door, obviously, had finally opened: the vault not fully black, he realized now, for there were tiny glimmers, indicating a ceiling more distant than any ceiling could ever be. And he saw, after a few moments, more and more pinpricks of white, spattered against the ebon, some tiny, some infinitesimally smaller. Indeed, the longer he sat there, watching in awe, the greater the array of lights until it seemed that countless glimmers arced overhead, and Crospinal marvelled at how he had not initially seen this magnitude, let alone lived his life, thus far, without experiencing such a wondrous sight.

There were no boundaries here, just an endless dark sea and the blackness above. Silvered on the water, the myriad points of white reflected, enhanced the yearning that spread out inside his body and took it beyond, leaking from his pores, leaking from his uniform, attempting to stitch him into the vista. Was he in father's memories?

The air was body temperature. No breeze. He breathed easily, filters silent, draining himself of aspects that had once made him the lonely, bitter boy called Crospinal. Elements of rejection escaped; lingering elements of his sister's departure. Elements of father, and their shared loss, and pain (though his grotesque knees rose, looming, either side).

To his left, other dream cabinets also floated on the water. Unlike the one he sat in, these remained sealed. Arrayed in a procession, they were all moving at the same rate across the placid sea. Without looking, Crospinal knew other cabinets followed his. In the direction he was headed, he could see even more, preceding, converging in the distance with those in the other lines. Was there one cabinet for each light overhead? They seemed as infinite.

Transfixed by the streams of cabinets dovetailing on the water ahead, he hardly noticed a thin line of light at the horizon beginning to intensify. Soon, webbing of cracks in the neoprene on his sleeves appeared, shadows of the veins on the backs of his hands twisting under the thin layer of his mitts. He gripped the rails to see better: a dark mass had coalesced, a silhouetted intrusion from the solid world, ending this water, or perhaps just a reprieve. Backlit by the glow fanning out across the surface: there was something large up ahead.

In a landscape of chaos, he could recall, so vividly, in a sudden flash, the way father had once been but would never be again: a young man, in his clean and efficient uniform, able to stand in his pen, and pace with vigour inside the limits of the tubes and cables that tethered the gate to his head. Father had known the answer to many questions, could send apparitions out, attract elementals, and dispensers, had been able to provide tutorials, instructions, anecdotes and warnings.

Crospinal searched himself for reactions to this particular vision but found only the calmness dreams brought. Could he live without father? He would soon find out. He knew where food was, even some stations beyond the pen, and he knew the locations of water spigots. *Food of the world, water of the walls.* The controllers in their lairs watched over him. He felt assured he would be provided for, no matter how far he ventured. The pen itself, and the structures father had drawn forth, the metals and such, would be subsumed if he left, but Crospinal would be taken care of, on some level or another. *Like a torch, into the darkness.*

Did he need father?

Dull clunking sounds, getting louder, brought him from his reveries. Unpleasant noises each time one of the cabinets in front neared the solid mass ahead and was either consumed or absorbed by it. Voices, too, low and guttural, in a language Crospinal could not understand.

For the first time since realizing that he remained within the confines of a dream, Crospinal felt twinges of doubt. With the beginnings of a frown tugging the corners of his mouth, he continued to stare until the light source on the horizon grew strong enough to etch a seam between black halves and he saw *creatures*—taller than father, with long thin limbs and curved backs—hauling dream cabinets up from the water as they arrived and pushing them backward onto the flat mass they stood upon, making room for the next. Their faces were primal, ugly, and though Crospinal recognized the creatures as the force behind his girlfriend's waning love, behind decay, isolation, and illness, behind every aspect of life that made it a difficult, useless slog (stunned with a clarity so rare it left him reeling), he saw himself mirrored in the expressions, in the poses, in the animal pungency of death that wafted across the water and raised his hackles.

This dream, thought Crospinal, *should end, right about now.*

Yet gripping the rails of the cabinets so hard his knuckles popped, he continued to float closer as the voices grew louder, and the sight and meaning and stench of the awful creatures became clearer. The dream would not let him go. Broad jaws, large, bright eyes, strong muscles straining as the dripping cabinets were pulled up, one after another. They were searching them, prizing the lids off. Perhaps a dozen sealed cabinets remained before Crospinal's would reach the creatures' grasp—

But now they were pointing, and jabbering, extending their hands out over the water toward him: they had seen the open cover, and Crospinal himself, sitting inside, watching like a fool as he drew nearer.

A flash of sharp teeth, the raising of clawed hands. Gnashing, and angry shrieks: they would tear him apart, shuck him from his tricot, consume him. "Screw this," said Crospinal, and he stood, pitching headlong over the side.

Scurrying, crawling, or even flying in the environs around father's throne (back in the days when Crospinal didn't roam very far, and he was smaller), there *were* other living things—though even smaller than himself, hairier, dumber, furtive. Apparitions were extensions of father. Elementals were machines, with their own brain. Devices had an autonomy but were neither alive nor very smart. Crospinal had not left the pen, or met his girlfriend (who was in some other category altogether), and his sister, as alive as Crospinal, was already long gone.

Father called these other creatures *animals*, and they had appeared on the day Crospinal and his sister were pulled up from the womb.

Haptics identified the beast he saw most often as a *rat*. A mammal, like himself, but a quadruped, a muroid, commensal, existing in the mutable world without protective uniforms. There were crows, too, but these were *birds*, and could therefore fly, living most of their lives up by the various ceilings. On the floor, crows were wary, one eye turned toward him. Crospinal rarely saw one up close.

Not alive, anyhow.

On the nutrient tiles, where the trees grew, there dwelt springtails, almost too small to see, and pinworms the size of his thumbnails.

During the year of cognitive growth, Crospinal managed to trap a living rat, a young (or at least tiny) one, using concrete ephemera and found plastics: a circular Kevlar cover, a tie rod, and lengths of optic fibre he set up on one of the catwalks spanning harmer corner, with a protein pellet as bait. Briefly, Crospinal held a struggling body in his hand. Felt the tiny heart, with only a thin layer of Dacron to separate their flesh. He held another life in contact with his own and he had looked into the tiny, black eyes that held a distorted fragment of his own experiences, fears, and desires, defining what it meant to exist in this world, until the rat screamed, and bit down, and the yellow incisors pierced clean through Crospinal's uniform into the meat of his thumb.

He flung the beast, to plummet over the railing—surely to certain death; the next level under the catwalks, back then anyhow, was hundreds of metres below, an abyss.

Whirring into action, capillaries of his uniform drew blood up the sleeve. The wound was glued shut. At this juncture, the processor had to deal with soft pellets of fecal matter that he let drop. Blanched, Crospinal had nearly passed out.

Afterwards, father, frantic, inspected the healed wound, actually touching Crospinal, one hand gripping his shoulder, the other holding up his hand, lecturing all the while about the difficulties and dangers involved in opening uniforms, and about how hard saline was to produce, and how Crospinal should drink lots of water from the spigots to maintain intake of antibiotics. Then came the barrage of first aid haptics. Surrounded by setting bones and stitching skin; hydrating an unconscious patient with IV. How to deal with the bends when oxygen was thin. The patient was a dummy, in poor shape. Crospinal had taken part in these files a dozen times already, but father urged him to pay attention, to *be careful*, to stay close to home.

He took a new pair of mitts from the dispenser, grown special for him, and let them settle over his hands and bond with his existing sleeves. His thumb throbbed with every heartbeat.

Father remained anxious and moribund for weeks. Injuries distressed him to no end. "After all we've been through, Crospie. After all we've been through. You must survive. You know that."

The dogs yowled, fearful of infection.

Colder than anything Crospinal had ever encountered, an absence of warmth, a draining, the water stole his breath. He had no time to think or plan as he sank, most of his air gone, until the soles of his boots touched a flat, smooth bottom. That contact revived his senses and awareness. The pressure was startling. The neoprene of his uniform and the shield over his head would protect him for a while, but there were tears and holes that succumbed to leakage. He might last a few moments, but not long, since his outfit was fairly compromised. He had never been submerged before. Baths and idle wading took place in the pool, in the centre of the garden, which was consistently fifteen centimetres deep, barely topping the shanks of his footgear.

During one of father's enumerable rambling episodes, when the mix of information and nutrients and whatever else flowed from the world into his skull seemed to alter his perceptions more than usual, father had said, eyes glazed, that perhaps the most peaceful death might be death by drowning. But until this point in Crospinal's life, at the bottom of this cold sea, the possibility of drowning had been mythology. Now, water was a fist around him. Coldness seeped into his bones. He did not think he was dying, though he certainly would not describe what he felt as a modicum of peace.

Behind him, a tiny light appeared and began to blink. He did not turn around to see the source, but the light seemed very close, almost as if perched on his shoulder. Crospinal stood underwater, inside a murky hemisphere alive with glittering motes. On the surface, he saw the bottom of a dream cabinet, a dark rectangle against a slightly less dark background, gurgling overhead. When he moved one foot to retain his balance, dense silt clouded slowly about.

The light, when he walked, followed him.

More cabinets rumbled above.

(And a remote whisper, in the voice that had spoken to Crospinal when he stepped inside the cabinet, said a few more words, barely coherent and urgent—*breach in the line*—*breach in the line*—*breach in the line*—before falling silent again.)

Then the shield gave out.

Gulping water, he covered his mouth with one hand, but too late: he felt his lungs abruptly stop. What was the thing about drowning? Crospinal took another few difficult steps, quite sure he remained, though heavier, alive.

Cabinets grinding through water overhead.

If he extended his hands, pushing upward and leaping, he might have been able to breach the surface with the tips of his mitts, but he had no intention of doing so, and giving away his position. He slowly released the last air that had been trapped in his body. His processor complained. He felt no fear, no panic. This was indeed restful. Bubbles rose, flashing before his face. Liquid had rushed to fill his body, rising and cold and strong, holding him down, but had not killed him.

The light at his shoulder blinked faster.

(From that faraway place, the voice said something else, a list of faint numbers, strung together.)

There was enough illumination for Crospinal to see his own limbs before him, the vinyl and neoprene grey as he walked. His hands moved like ponderous water beasts, if there were such a thing.

Dark shapes where the lanky creatures had been toiling were just before him; Crospinal discerned a large silhouette, faintly backlit from the brighter surface. He made his way forward, in a slow-motion struggle, staying low, lungs like stones, until he could follow clumsily along the front of the structure. Dream cabinets continued to pass over him and were noisily fished out.

He came to a corner of the construction and proceeded along the adjacent wall, running his hands over the hard, smooth material. No composite, or plastic. No metal. He recalled the feel of a fallen girder, but not where he had seen or touched it. The water in his lungs was so cold it had started to make his head throb. Still, he was not dead. The surface of the wall was slimy and might even be some form of hardened poly he had seldom encountered.

The flashing light dimmed (as the voice said, quite clearly, into his ear: *Chamber full. Cycle complete. Biostasis eight eight. Reduction. Welcome back, passenger.*).

He found an entrance to the ramp that led out of the water. He knew this entrance was what he had been looking for, just as he knew where the ramp, as he ascended, would lead.

Lifting his dripping face clear, he blinked away the cascade, in air so much warmer it seemed dense. Pinpricks of light turned to novas in the drops before he cleared his face. He had come up *behind* the creatures. The air moved in, replacing chilly water in his systems, pushing it out through his mouth and nostrils in thick streams. The chestplate of his beleaguered tricot was doing something it never had before, shuddering and thumping, yet transitions were fairly easy, now that he was better prepared. He breathed again, felt his collar fizzling as it tried vainly to reactivate.

The beasts were still toiling, oblivious to Crospinal's presence, sliding dream cabinets back, in his direction. There were five or six of the creatures, but instead of hundreds, maybe thousands of cabinets, there was only one.

This cabinet lay sealed before him.

Crospinal reached out slowly and caressed the handle, letting his fingers curl over the warm, familiar shape: the handle reacted, let him tug, and the cabinet door opened—

Burning fluid exploded from Crospinal's mouth, his nose, even his eyes; he felt himself collapsing, going black. The light that had been at his shoulder flared. (And as he fell, the cabinet's faint voice seemed to be screaming, trapped in some remote enclosure: *Remain still. Do not panic. Remain still. Do not panic.*)

He hit the floor, deadweight, in a cascade of slow water, carried forward to crash heavily on the grille. No, not burning fluids; these were *cold*. As his vision blurred and ebbed, he trembled, shivering, vomiting. The massive body of water was gone. The creatures and the ebony vault were gone. Traces of icy fluid ran over him as he lay there, beached and helpless. More fluids drained from his body, trickling his skin, running inside his uniform, which gurgled, sputtered, and did its best to either assist him or chastise him, but Crospinal swooned before figuring out which, waking moments later to cough and puke some more and expel liquids until he could finally lift his face clear of the floor. Snot drained down his lips and chin, and his head was horribly sore.

On the green carpet (which was now soaked), he curled.

"You okay?" the controller said. "What the heck happened?"

The last of the water ran out of the open cabinet, to the end of the grille, where it cascaded down, onto lower levels.

"I think I'm okay."

The residue was much thicker than water. Viscous, a gel.

He wiped at his mouth, pulling strings of mucus free that seemed to be coming from the sacs in his lungs. So much mucus. He retched it up and pulled it clear.

Above him, his dream cabinet—dripping and pinging under a green light that had not been there before—yawned wide.

The controller was checking things out.

Crospinal could still hear the faint voice, expressing concerns.

<hr />

A small console nestled in a recess nearby, with two dark periscopes, through which the desolation outside was obscured by scratch marks, cracked thumb plates, of no use whatsoever, and a pair of very shallow holes. These were under a thick covering flap. The grip at the bottom was stunted. No controller resided here.

On more aimless days, Crospinal had sometimes visited—as he visited all the consoles he discovered ringing the pen, outside father's range, seven or eight of them, but his girlfriend seldom appeared at this one. Several times he'd conjured the faint perception of a thin figure in a dark uniform, with a helmet obscuring the face, who lingered afar but did not speak or approach or even manifest very clearly. Mostly nothing. Invariably, Crospinal would end up beyond harmer's corner, or grunting and hauling up the seven ladders, to the harrier lookout—which was where his girlfriend most often appeared, where Crospinal had fallen in love, and had had his heart broken.

But he went stumbling to this console now, as fast as his crooked legs could take him, knees flaring with agony as they popped and failed and locked, running along the gangplank, lungs bursting, thick fluid spewing from his nose and throat and crying like a baby. He fell, in his haste, and scrambled quickly back up, as if pursued. When he thrust his arms into the holes, the sleeves of his uniform nearly separated from the mitts, and inside the lining, skin scraped off both forearms.

"Hello? Hello? For goodness sakes, I need to tell you something." He coughed, shook his head to clear the drool. Excitement threatened to burst veins inside him. "Hello? *Please*! I know you told me not to call you anymore. I'm not being needy or clingy but this is *important*."

Elusive static, flickering behind his eyes. Motion he could not follow. Then the faint buzz in his knuckles, up his metacarpals, into his wrists. The hair on his body tried to stand on end, held back by spandex.

She was coming . . .

"Listen," he said, before he even saw his girlfriend's face. "I know where other people are. I've seen them. Other people. *Real people*."

Now a body gathered—

But not his girlfriend. A woman, as old as father, maybe older, with high cheekbones and a thin, tight mouth. Certainly not his girlfriend. Wearing a dark uniform, and translucent helmet, some strange manifestation from within the walls of the world stood cramped with Crospinal in the recess.

Part of the woman occupied the same physical space as Crospinal's lower half; where overlaps occurred, his muscles hummed.

"Who are you?" he said.

The woman glared, her face very close to his. The image of the visor almost touched his nose. He looked into her eyes and had the feeling that she could not see him very well, if at all: they were searching, moving. Her uniform was exactly the same kind as his girlfriend wore, with a stiff hoop at the neck and the array of pockets at the breast, unlike any uniform available from dispensers Crospinal knew. The helmet had a large comm link, with a pin mic, and a visible siphon.

"Is my girlfriend there? I have to talk to her." Coughing up another glob of mucus, but letting it dangle, because he did not want to break contact. "Get her."

"I can hear you," the woman said, her tone flat. "You're out in the bay?"

Her hair was pulled back tight, just like his girlfriend's had been, but then again, *nothing* like that. A cowl, inside the helmet, extended translucent fingers in front of her mouth. The lines of age, even sculpted in light, were pronounced, harsh, the way father's had become. She was old. He had to assure himself that no manifestation could touch him nor harm him. Not physically, at least. The apparitions she had brought with her, as faint as those of his girlfriend, spun like figments through the small station.

"Listen." He tried to take a deep breath, to prepare for his speech, his prayer, but his lungs rattled, as if depths of water remained inside his body. "I don't know who you are, but she needs to know. The dream cabinet. I've told her about it, I'm sure. The booth filled up. A dream like no other. Because I held the door closed, only it wasn't water, it was thicker, and I could live in it. I could *breathe* it. Can you tell her that? Is she with you?"

"A stat? You were in a stat?"

His chest ached from all this speaking, and from drowning. He tried to slow down. "I need to see my girlfriend. One more time. Have you done something to her? I travelled across a sea—like the one my father told me about—wider than any pool could ever be. And there were creatures there. Bad ones. Not apparitions, or elementals. They were looking for something in the cabinets. And I saw my sister, Luella. She was sleeping under water, inside a filled dream cabinet." He clenched his fists inside the holes. "One of the sealed ones. I saw her face through the visor. She looked like me, as if I'd been preserved, for years. Not living out here, with father, getting older. She had a helmet on, but the grey one, and a fresh uniform."

"You're an abomination. You speak like a passenger, you're invisible, but you're not on the roster. You don't know Luella. That was a hundred years ago."

"There's people in the cabinets. Do you understand what I'm saying? Other people."

"I can hardly hear you."

"You need to listen."

Her eyes seemed dark, like holes. The projection of her face slid apart and then back together again and her ghosts stuttered from sight.

"I'm father's only son. And that's why you need to listen. You *need* to help me. Didn't you hear anything I said?" He was shouting now, trembling. "You won't tell me anything? Or get my girlfriend for me?"

The woman's stare became as cold as the fluid Crospinal had inhaled. He breathed hard through his nose. How could he be invisible? Behind the woman, in the realm of manifestations, a second person shifted, the thin specter, but not his girlfriend. Only now it occurred to Crospinal that he might have said too much, that this ethereal woman, who most likely projected from the same place, would not assist him; possibly, unbelievably, she had designs to attempt the opposite. Had his girlfriend not warned him?

"I see you now," said the woman quietly. "I can just see you. An outline. You've been compromised. Polluted. You won't come any closer to the hub. You won't—"

Letting go of the grip, and pulling his hands from the holes, Crospinal cut the connection: the stern manifestation vanished from the recess, as did her faint companion, though her angry tones continued to echo as Crospinal, coughing and hacking, wiping at his mouth now, backed out.

Dogs chased him. A game, and he was laughing, but his bladder tightened every time one of the apparitions nearly caught him, and he thought about calling the game off time after time but never did. What could dogs do, with teeth of light?

That wasn't the point.

Along oxbow perimeter—climbing in a slow spiral up the inside of oxbow's walls—and from there into a long connector that dripped with composites, Crospie hobbled, and the dogs pursued, pretending to be slow, like him. Father said activity was good for his knees. He was reaching father's limit. The dogs were fading, their energy interrupted and patchy.

Crospinal stopped, rubbing at his legs. He leaned against a railing and looked back. He was crying. The dogs panted, flickering in and out.

"Come back now, Crospie," they barked. "Let's go back, back, back!"

"I won," said Crospinal.

"You did," they agreed, wavering. "You're faster. Stronger. You're the strongest child. Now *let's go back*."

Their voices, too, crackled and faded; they were starting to whine.

Of course Crospinal was the strongest child, the fastest child. He was the *only* child. Normally, he liked to hear apparitions say these things, even if they were just father's puppets, echoing father's desires. He turned away. "I've never been down *there* before." Indicating with his chin, and not for the first time, the entrance to a dim opening, a hallway subsumed nearly entirely by masses of shifting construction, which appeared no different than a dozen such openings, all leading away from the pen into parts unknown.

"You'd best not go, Crospie. This is far enough. One day, but not now. Let's go back. You're not ready, Crospie. Not safe! Not safe! We need to go back."

"Back, back, back," barked the others.

Because he'd faked a step toward the forbidden.

This was the year of independent thinking. His fifth. He was a big boy now. He could run faster than a dog. They didn't need to pretend, for his sake. Sometimes, Crospinal wondered if father expected him to defy the rules, making the moments they spent together moments of criticism and judgement, and thus pushing him away. What other reason could the tensions and pressures be for? Each day was a test he failed.

Walking toward the opening, the end of a grate under his boots (part of him wishing the dogs *did* have a way of stopping him), he said, "I'm gonna do it. I'm leaving."

"Don't mess around!" The agitated barks did not sound right. "Stop! Stop! Stop!"

He stood in the mouth of the hallway and looked. Ambients surged within, detecting him. The passage went on and on, until the dimness obscured it. He heard fluids, dripping. The temptations and threats that father so often outlined and worried about hardly seemed in evidence: the hallway was quiet, softly lit.

Then, from within, came another sound, though he somehow heard it with more than his ears, in his whole body, calling to him, and his breath caught in his throat. The name had not been what father had given him, but an unfamiliar one, a name he'd not heard before, a name the world offered to him.

He looked behind again, to see if the dogs were implicated in this encounter, or what their reaction might be, but the dogs had been recalled and were no longer there.

When he returned to the dream cabinets, drawn there, the thick fluid still dripped from the edge of the grill, soundless. The strip of carpet remained darker green, with moisture squishy under his boots. The light that had accompanied him during his submersion was no longer evident. Shivers racked Crospinal. Aspects were shifting, he realized, more than just the eternal transfigurations of the landscape, more than the encroaching dark. He spat into his left mitt and let the spittle roil there. His breath was stale and cold, as if he were already dead.

Eyeing the row of cabinets, Crospinal considered his own for some time, staring, but going no closer, as if it might pounce. Had it betrayed him, or taken him some place sacred? The creatures were looking for him. He ducked under the strange girder and, from outside, slowly closed the door, felt it click into place. The handle, as always, fit into his grip, suggesting he should climb inside one more time, close his eyes, and dream. . . .

All is forgiven, Crospinal. Won't happen again. Sorry about that. . . .

He let go and stepped back.

The idiot controller was nowhere to be seen.

As he approached the sealed cabinets, he wondered if the face he'd seen in the dream had truly been Luella's. He'd glimpsed it for only a second, and through a visor, yet the idea that people were inside—if not his sibling—was powerful. Could Luella be inside one of these cabinets? Was this as far as she'd made it, when she left the pen? Perhaps he should not trust a dream's allusions.

He placed his tingling hands against the surface of the secure door.

Elements of the wonder he had seen in haptics from childhood had still been in evidence on Luella's face, even in sleep, even in that instant.

Grabbing the handle, Crospinal yanked hard, suddenly, trying to surprise either the closed cabinet or perhaps his own sluggish systems. Nothing happened, either way. Memories of his failed attempts at father's list of chores mocked him. Always memories, always failures, always mocking. He tugged again, pulling the handle over and over but there was no give.

The chestplate made a strange sound, guttural and bass, and his processor hissed in response.

Crospinal encountered no dogs, no spirits along the way. Not even in the gangplanks, where apparitions tended to congregate: they'd flicker there, around the tungsten lights. The pen was entirely silent and deserted. The atmosphere seemed grey, thick. The sound of his soles on the tiles was muted. A very faint hiss, and a shudder, from the engines.

Chilling fluids that had embalmed him still coursed inside his body; he suspected the sensation might linger forever, as if his blood had been swapped, or at least tagged with a new component.

How could there be no dogs the entire way back? He stepped into the throne room, where he had been born, where he had lain awake in his daybed, staring up, unable to sleep because of the pain, where father was tethered and where haptics played, and he knew everything had changed, not just the composition of his blood, or the composition of the cabinets, or his girlfriend's fading love.

Dropping to his knees—for they had given out, at last—bursting when they hit the prayer mat, Crospinal did not cry out. No words or exclamations came. No tears, either, no howl. He wiped his face with the back of a chilly hand and looked again:

Against the cold, matte luminescence of the gate, and the array of banks behind father's corpse, Crospinal saw his own reflection, a rather surprised expression on his face, gaunt, and awful-looking. His shorn hair, his filthy uniform, tattered and plastered to his body, dark with moisture the exhausted capillaries could not handle.

Father's body lay cooling among draining tubes and conduits. He must have tried to rise, one last time, but collapsed off his throne.

Nutrient pumps were stopped; the gate was still.

Crospinal eventually leaned in, at a loss, then moved his face forward, to kiss the grey forehead, but a tangled morass of tethers prevented him from getting close enough.

Liquid spilled onto the tiles between father's thin legs, and if the processor of a uniform died with the wearer, then the liquid was most likely urine, spilling from the reservoir.

There was actually a sense of relief. Crospinal was mortified to feel it. He looked down at the meat and bones, all wrapped up nicely in a Kevlar and nylon sac. Life, and the suffering it brought, was over. Inconceivable that this mass of failed flesh had once moved, educated, tried to nurture.

Crospinal nudged the body with the toe of his boot.

Dead meat.

All that remained was dead meat.

This was nowhere near the despair that had first torn into Crospinal when father made him kneel, to tell him of the illness, and of its sentence. The cruel joke that was mortality.

Life, father said, confessing, *is always waning. From birth. For every breath, creeping closer to endtime, to nothing. A parabola. Rise and fall. Such is the definition of being alive.*

Crospinal never understood or accepted why the finality of death would be a part of the arrangement. The loss of awareness, of experience, the cessation, was a cataclysm. An abhorrence. How could anyone be expected to understand such futility?

Father's open mouth, black blood on his tongue. Eyes open, too, glazed, like stray ephemera.

No dogs barked in the halls. No thrum of fluids through conduits. Apparitions, which had accompanied Crospinal throughout his life, the dozens of projections, the lanky spirits, and the elusive wisps, all extinguished.

Some time later, maybe an hour, maybe more, tinkering within the banks of father's gate, searching the plates and stilled screens for some clue how to continue, a reason to keep going, he thought again about throwing himself over a railing. Just like he had thrown that poor, treacherous animal. But suicide, even now, seemed too *dramatic.* He would wait until tomorrow, or the day after that—

A resounding claxon, from the hall outside, caused the pen to tremble, as if struck. Crospinal clapped his mitts over his ears.

Though his legs were still sore—always sore—he pushed himself up with his knuckles and stood. Was the pen coming apart already?

Heading through the exit in his stiff-legged, awkward gait, alarms shattered Crospinal. Every controller in the world had gone mad. They zipped down the hall in both directions, shrieking. A dispenser ran by and, as red lights flashed, blinding, from harmer's corner all the way to the opal room and back again, fell flat and did not get up. Sounds vibrated in Crospinal's bones and skull and he could not conceive what was happening. A growing wind tore at his uniform. He fought to stay on his feet, but when the air was finally sucked away in a great rush, it took Crospinal with it.

THE METAL RAT

Living proof of the deficiencies of the body, the final consequence of existence, coda to years of pointlessness and deterioration, was fully revealed shortly after he turned eight. This was the cusp of *the year of thought*. Father, particularly maudlin that morning, stood, arms at his sides, face downcast. Ozone hints in the air: the gate was heating up, haptics brewing, steeped influx pumping free. Crospinal waited on the prayer mat with his own limbs throbbing and his smile fading.

The year of action, coming to a close, had contained little action. Failure hung in the pen, confirmed by father's drawn expression, rising slowly, to make eye contact. "I have something to show you."

———

Sitting in his daybed, Crospinal had felt a rare tinge of excitement. *A new year*.

But hopes for a spectacular or even a lame party faded pretty quickly.

He looked at his swollen knees, his crooked knees, straining the fabric. He had not changed out of his uniform since the wheelroom.

Who knew what the year of thought would bring?

In silence, Crospinal and father shared stale yellow torte-flavoured pellets and had cups of lemonade, dispensed drip by drip from the spigot, with settings on *festive*.

Apparitions were elsewhere, out haunting halls. Maybe they were trapped in father's head. The yelp of anxious dogs, beyond the pen, swelled and faded. There were tiny threads whipping from above father's eyes, each one directing a ghost.

The lesson, post-celebration—such as it was—and post-prayer, concerned math skills. Crospinal recalled vaguely threatening shapes of triangles and the smoother, organic forms of the ellipse. He stood among them as they whispered about axis and vertices. Then, abruptly, he found himself immersed in a different haptic, which blossomed, supplanting the tutorial: startled, he tried to step back—

A shape, a beast, hovered before him, as large as himself. Black, with thin, scaly legs; flattened, feathered arms; a half-opened beak. His perspective moved around it. Hyper-detailed, bigger than life, this was no hazy projection of a device, no scripted character, but a *creature*, like himself, captured by eyes of the world, reconstituted here, with photons from the gate.

Inert. Flesh compromised, seething, he saw now, with tiny pinworms. He watched the flesh come apart, feathers fall. Dark eyes, nearly closed, shrivelled. There was no life.

Carried through the projection (he could not see father, beyond the illusions), Crospinal, barely audible, said, *"What is this?"*

"A bird. A crow."

"I know that," he snapped. "That's not what I meant."

"You've seen them, in the garden, flying up by the ceiling. There are several, come to live with us. They came for you. This is what a crow looks like, up close. But the heart has stopped beating, Crospie."

"I know what a crow is," he said. "But what does the rest mean?" He had peed a bit into the bladder, and the processor was whirring. He picked at his nostril, which was clogged again.

"Once that crow flew, and looked down upon us. I need to show this to you, Crospie. I have to. I've not the courage to come clean. You're a civilized boy. You've been raised above the darkness of ignorance. You're my future. . . . But you need to know that no heart can beat forever. Even passed down, from one to the other. Our bodies will fail."

The haptic of the crow flickered. Behind swinging cables, father's eyes shone. Crospinal stared. "What is all this?"

"I'm sorry," father said. "After life comes endtime. Nothing."

Of course the concept of extinction had been a malignant nugget at Crospinal's core, since birth, no doubt. But now the last piece had fallen. To see this broken body, this decay, and know its import, he felt himself growing heavier, falling.

"The body took months to decompose," father mumbled. "Decay is slow here, but inevitable, and just as efficient."

Seeking adequate words when there were none and never could be, Crospinal said, "Will you end, like this?" He indicated the reconstruction as the bones grew exposed, worms visible inside, churning. "Will you collapse, decompose? Like this? Will your heart stop?"

Beyond the haptic, father also looked at the corpse. They saw, perhaps, different visions, neither good. The future, like the past, meant nothing. That was the lesson. Brief moments of false progress, awareness, seeking understanding, but ultimately rare worms ate your flesh. And then nothing. *Endtime.*

Father must have nodded reluctant acknowledgement, for tubes rustled.

"What about me?" Crospinal's voice cracked. "Will I expire, too? Will my heart stop?"

Another nod. "Though not for many years. And there are means of prolonging a life. You're too young to worry about cessation and endtime. There's plenty to learn, carry knowledge, and pass it on. You're young, Crospie. You need to know. We live to pass the light from ourselves to others."

The haptic vanished.

"Others? What others?" Yet Crospinal was numbed by implications imposed on the already arduous state of being alive. There was no possibility to ever return to his previous condition, where he had remained oblivious from the truth. Feeling hunched and bent, he hated father for giving him life, and he hated himself for feeling this way. Never again would he cling to the precarious idea that everything needed to continue living, the way he had been living, would be provided forever. He would one day die an older version of the same crippled boy he was today. Ideals, on the very first morning of the year of thought, were for deluded fools. A caul had been yanked away, leaving a very different child standing there, exposed, at eight years old.

Crospinal woke with the usual aches in the bones of both knees, and in his wrists now, which had also started to hurt. Through the thin material of his mitts, he could see that the white scars, revealed under the cuff of his sleeves, were inflamed. His rickets got worse each day. Ambulation was increasingly difficult. He fumbled with grasped objects, joints popping when he moved. Climbing anything was a hazard.

He was dying.

They both were. Sooner or later.

"Dad," he said. "My legs hurt so much."

Father hid, ashamed, behind his crown.

He wanted father to suffer.

Every so often—after prayer of thanks to the refuge, for forming, and for the food pellets, and the uniforms, for the metallic walls and the structures that had solidified around them, for the halogens—there was an escape, or entertainment haptic (though Crospinal realized, even at a young age, that father came to enjoy these events much more than he did). Over the first years, the escapes were simple, of course, primary shapes and colours, interacting benignly, with no plot, drifting among soft edges and ambient, soothing sounds. They would both ingest a few pellets, brewed special. Crospinal would lie on his stomach and sometimes even doze as he was taken into the story's realm. Father came along, too, and Crospinal knew him within as various representations: sometimes a fuzzy glow, or a kindly animal, or more like his true form, a man, but untethered, like he must have once looked, pre-pen. Smiling with teeth whiter than possible, father recited vocabulary lessons and basic rhymes, sang comforting songs, warned about the future, and tried, so hard, to recall evidence of the past.

By the year of cognitive leaps, the tone of the escapes changed. Other characters were introduced, with more complex roles. There was the thin giant who proselytized, rather obviously, about the dangers of microbes, and a ridiculous light screen who always wanted Crospinal to hug its virtual form.

Though encouraged to actively participate, Crospinal felt growing frustrations at the overall unsubtle agendas, and at his lack of ability to steer the haptic's narratives; he would like to have guided the stories in directions he wanted, toward answers and stimulation he sought, yet the majority of his reactions and questions in the stories only caused the characters to hesitate, or frown, until he relented, and chose a more appropriate response, in a fashion less challenging to father.

After a long bout of sleepless nights (a fairly common event), father once confronted Crospinal—as he stood there, open-mouthed—saying that the clips were prepared with love, and why did Crospinal have to ruin them all the time with his disdain for everything and his bad attitude and his inability to appreciate a wholesome plot. But this particular incident happened before father discovered that one of the solution conduits feeding him from the bank was cracked, letting a trickle of enzymes come into contact with the air of the pen, and thus ferment: father felt not quite himself. When relative equilibrium had regained, apologies were profuse, the cable capped (by Crospinal's own two hands), but as father often said, *damage was done.*

The outbursts happened several times.

When he was older, Crospinal either took part in the escapes with passivity, surrendering to the incomplete stories or stuttering narratives— telling father afterward that he had enjoyed the entertainment very much, and had learned a lesson, thank you—or skipped the shows altogether, and the preceding prayer times, returning from his perambulations less and less frequently, and for shorter amounts of time, to face father's consternation, admonishments, and the anxieties inherent in his apparitions.

The only entertainment worthwhile to Crospinal were the ones when father abandoned haptics altogether, drifting off into a state of longing so comforting to Crospinal that, on the prayer mat, somewhat delirious himself, he would cease rubbing his knees and close his eyes in anticipation, awaiting the story, which would spill from father's own lips, his voice altered, as if he were somehow dreaming, stories that would sweep Crospinal away, offer him a solace that had proven impossible to retain, and which he'd tried to replace, for some time now, by sojourns to the cabinets, and by meeting, and falling in love with, his ethereal girlfriend.

"Picture this," was how it began. Father, lifting his face, moist-eyed already, looking as if he were being transported from the pen, once again freed of the tethers that bound him, as if he were removed from the deterioration of life that was making itself increasingly evident with each passing day, to both father and son. Crospinal, hoping to be transported also, whispered the words back to his dad in such a way that it had to be catalyst for the visions he hoped to receive.

"I had seen the view, a world of ash, swept under the flame-red star. *Endtime*. I came awake, in a blue uniform, and I ran. Winds circled, tearing ash from its place, spinning into parched vortexes. I looked out a porthole. The ship had changed. I was being hunted. I could feel them, whoever they were, hunting me. This was not where I was meant to be. An event had occurred, while I slept, changing me, changing all of us, changing everything. I was looking outside, at a dead world. Sometimes I think I was born, staring out that porthole, my mind coalescing, without past or history. Yet at other times I recall the other world, a lush world, *my home*. With a blue sky, and cold sea, and a line of craggy mountains."

Crospinal squeezed his eyes shut tight, mouthing the words, best he could. Part of the ceremony, of the desire. His stomach churned. He wanted to believe in a nicer place.

"I wasn't always this way, son. I know the steps I've taken led me to this place, where I raised you, and taught you. We can bring it all back. We can achieve it."

Nutrients hissed back and forth in conduits. Chemicals and information he was not searching for flowed. Crospinal did not open his eyes. He tried to keep fragile frameworks in place, structures upon which to build his vision, which he painstakingly scaled to move beyond his pain and insecurities, beyond grinding days of ennui.

"Ash gives way to moisture. Grey darkens, takes on the scent I exude, here in my pen. *Ozone*. A storm's coming. With the storm, winds, but not scorching winds, nor do they carry sand, or ash, but a coolness, soothing the land. When I was a boy . . ."

Crospinal might open his eyes at this point, to see some metal tool, or even a small, dumb machine—the purpose of which might remain a mystery to both of them, when they later inspected it—coming up through the floor, or falling from the ceiling. Sometimes the pen itself modified, subtly, pushing back against encroachment. Hard edges delineating from the face of a wall, as if pushed from the other side.

"I woke from a nap, smiling. Basked in the breeze, a harbinger of change, of youth, of freedom. Ash is crumbling, washing away. Because it's raining now, and not the ridiculous oily rain that drips here, in great drops, marking the tiles dark, like a blight, nor like the fountains in the garden, but drops with the power to revive, to give life. The ash is washed away. Through the skin of the soil, green shoots appear, tiny shoots with two leaves each, lifting up into the air.

"Other plants sprout nearby. These are larger, providing shelter for new growth. *Real trees*. Lightning splits the sky. This is a land of growth, of health. When you sit up, lifting your eyes to see what else the lightning has brought, the rain cools your face, and your hands, upraised to the sky. Water soothes your tongue, washing dust from your skin forever. Ahead of you, there's a forest. The ocean is at the end of the road. You can hear it. Beyond, above the trees, cleaving the line between land and sky, breaking it down so you're free to travel between the two, and rise up, are hills, which gather to reveal the line of mountains, capturing your breath, pulling you up, to disperse you, to bring you home. . . ."

The haptic collapsed. Pinworms had moved quicker and quicker, a writhing mass, accelerated, alongside time, spilling forth from the cage of bones. Flesh was gone altogether.

"*Osteomalacia*. You've had this since you were born. Rickets. Before you were born, even. I knew you suffered while you gestated. I tried to supplement your diet, Crospie, tried to get additional vitamins. I tried so hard. But there's not much for me to work with here. I did the best I could and I know it's not good enough. But you're alive, Crospie, you're here with me. You've retained a large amount of knowledge. You're a testimony to civilization."

Was father also crying? Silent, he had turned away. The conduits at the back of his head rolled against each other and obscured his profile.

"It's okay," Crospinal lied, feeling awkward (and the tinge of a growing, perverse sense of power). "I *know*. I mean, I figured as much. About dying, I mean. We can't go on forever." He tried to smile. "Nothing does, right?"

But then came the barrage, the litany of disease: hyponatremia; anemia; effects of low oxygen. The sour skin ailments of pellagra. Bronchitis. Pneumonia susceptibility. *Cancer.*

Who could smile now?

—∞—

Insistent prodding under his arm caused Crospinal to groan when he wanted only to rest, to be left alone, hopefully forever. He wanted to sort out his own memories, once and for all.

No apparition could be responsible for this intrusion. Not much could actually *poke* him. Fox? Or Bear? Hadn't they stepped out? If only he were able to open his eyes, or form words, he could make the intruder cease this affront and return to the relatively peaceful depths of slumber.

Crospinal's legs, as always, were sore. But there was other pain, too, not just from his knees, or wrists: his head was sore—had he fallen?—and his chest, which was unusual.

Something large moved, far away.

Had father died?

The prodding relented for a moment. He could not rest any more, not the way he had been, not in oblivion.

Yes. Father had died.

A sharp prick, through the sleeve of his uniform, directly into his skin, and darkness rose to enclose him once more.

—∞—

Flares shot through his body, exploding along the ridges of his spine and in the crevasses between the twisted loops of his brain. Partitions had sequestered or maybe even amputated whatever was needed *to understand*. Some had broken down, others had a way to go. *Now* he came awake. Shards of light had been waiting; they eagerly stabbed his eyes.

Prone, in a very bright place. Dried blood raked across his naked belly. Below that—

Struggling to breathe, to control rising panic, he saw that his uniform had been uncoupled, tricot pulled wide open, chestplate split, exposing his thin white chest—

And, from the waist down, he'd been consumed by a shiny canister.

Pushing frantically at the plastic rim to free himself, but his arms were weak and his hands remained clenched in futile claws. The canister would not budge. Sleeves and mitts intact, thankfully. When he tried to wriggle free, his entrapped legs would not move. Not at all. He could not feel his legs. Pushing down again, with the heels of his hands, but he was trapped tight and his legs were unresponsive.

"Please," said a soft but insistent voice. "Stay still."

At his groin, mounted on a flange at the mouth of the canister, a glowing plate—symbols blinking in red—made absolutely no sense. He had never seen these indications before, nor could he tell where the voice had originated from, though it was from a localized source, like a comm, or a mouth.

The icon twisting above where his groin should be was of a large worm, with crow's wings, curled around a rod.

"What are you? Come out so I can see you." Bands of muscles tightened in his torso and back as he tried to pull out again. His legs remained numb and useless. He strained, and craned, to see what had prodded him, and spoken, but to no avail on any count. "*Let me out!*"

"Take a deep breath," the voice advised.

From behind the canister.

Crospinal did what the voice said. He did feel marginally better, though his compliance irritated him.

"You need to rest."

From where it had been hidden, at the foot of the gleaming canister holding firm to his deadened legs, emerged a sleek, grey . . . rat. Sitting back on its haunches, peering at Crospinal with red eyes. Not much bigger than his open hand, when he'd been able to open them, but the eyes—

No. Not a rat.

"Get me out of this thing," he said. "Did you open my uniform? I'm gonna die of some infection. Could you seal it, please? And get me out of here."

The elemental returned his stare but did not respond or assist.

"This is shit. Clearly there's something wrong with you. Get this thing off my legs. I can't feel them." Crospinal was wondering why he had thought of the elemental as a rat in the first place: the limbs were clearly fine rods of titanium, the fingers lengths of another delicate beta alloy whose name he could not recall (though the haptics about metals and plastics and composites had been nightly for over a year), and the voice came from a small comm.

Thumbs had been designed, in an opposable manner. The face was remotely rat-like, with those red eyes and a muzzle-shaped protuberance—no doubt to accommodate the artificial neurons, which would have to be squeezed pretty tight into an elemental this small—but any similarity to a living beast ended there. For his confusion, Crospinal blamed grogginess, but was beginning to suspect that processes and patterns of his own thoughts were changing, and for the worst, now father was gone. This was clearly an elemental, with an independent personality. More sophisticated, perhaps, than Fox or Bear.

"Can't you talk anymore? You seem advanced but you're not doing what I ask. What happened to my legs? And close my uniform."

Now the metal rat read him. Crospinal felt the pressure sweeping inside his body, nowhere near as intrusive or as blunt as those he had endured in the pen, when his caretakers checked him out, but enough to take serious and rile him. "Hey," he said. "You should ask first. It's just rude. What are you looking for?" Trying to sit up, to prop himself, but his arms had grown tired altogether of obeying his errant will and remained inert at his side.

"If you keep moving," said the elemental, "you'll need to be sedated. You'll tear something. I don't want to restrain you."

"You already have." Indeed, when Crospinal attempted to wrench his body free one more time, not much of anything moved, except for the surges of pain, like steel filings blooming in his guts. "Can't you just let me out?" He suspected he might cry soon, though he really did not want to. "I can't feel my legs."

"Because your legs," said the metal rat, "are broken."

"*What?*"

"But the bones are knitting nicely. So stop fighting."

Crospinal had stopped. "My legs are broken?"

"Both femurs snapped by a large fragment, flash-hardened, spinning laterally. Two fractures on the left, one on the right. The second fracture was compound. The bone severed your femoral artery. There were other injuries—punctured intestine, mild concussion—but your fractures were the most grave."

"What are you saying?"

"You don't understand me when I talk?"

"Of course I do."

"Then what? Don't get excited. You seemed—I thought you couldn't understand, that's all. That's what you said. An inner lock closed. Whatever was blocking it must have shifted or moved on. I extricated you from the wreckage and dragged you clear. Lucky to be alive, as they say. Only a few minor procedures left. Soon you'll be right as rain."

Rain? He frowned. *With the power to revive, to give life . . .* "What does rain have to do with anything?"

"You don't know that expression? Right as rain means you're going to be fine. That's what I'm trying to tell you. You're in the clear. The debris has been dealt with already, but I haven't moved you yet. I was waiting for you to wake up."

"That's crow *shit*," said Crospinal, testing the swear word again for reaction, though there was none apparent. "You just woke me. I felt you, poking me. You weren't waiting at all. What procedures have you done to me?"

"You know about operations and shit like that?"

"I've been in haptics."

"You want grisly details?"

"I can take it."

"Well. Skin grafts, for one. For your burns."

"I'm burnt?" What he could see of his smooth chest seemed pale and bony and ineffectual, but undamaged. How many years since he had looked upon it? A few damp hairs, flat, copper-coloured nipples, like stains. The thin strands that connected the chestplate to his lungs were intact, but stretched into a web: both halves of his tricot had been opened, like a ribcage. He did not like to see his white skin, for skin was vulnerable and weak. Where the flange of the device trapped him, there were no visible burns, either. He looked at his hands, still in their mitts, though the Dacron was further damaged. His sleeves were frayed, too. "At least close me up. I can feel germs crawling all over me."

"You do realize your jumpsuit is virtually non-functional? If you want to be like a passenger, you're meant to shed every few weeks. Otherwise the toxicity—"

"Just close it. Release me."

"I have to take you back to my ward." The elemental stared. "Now you're awake, that is. You need to be in traction for about another forty, forty five minutes, slightly longer if you insist on moving about and asking incessant questions."

"I find this distressing. I have questions."

"Trust me, you won't get infections on my watch."

Crospinal lay flat, very still, looking up at the composite ceiling, which was glowing with ambients. He was in a wide corridor, about as wide as the main hall had been, which skirted opal centre, back home, where the transfer tubes ended. Other than black marks on the wall, the fairly pristine area was mature but not rigid with age. He inhaled, smelling the unpleasant tang the world exuded when recycling. "Tell me everything," he said.

"Will you stay calm?"

"Yes."

"All right. Like I said: a peripheral sector of the bay was sealed and the area excised. A wall was created. Who can presume why these things happen? If you're daft enough to dwell upon them. There's no rules anymore. Part of the structure broke away. Things like this happen now. But there aren't usually people involved. Passengers or runners. That's the conundrum here. Certainly not a cripple, head full of stories, all dressed up in an old crew suit. Did you have a helmet, too?"

"Not for a long time."

"I was sure surprised to find you, mortally wounded, in the debris."

"The pen's gone." This wasn't a question. He was able to move his hands again, and he ran his mitt, cupped, down his face, but the material did very little.

"Shit happens," said the elemental, as if this explained everything. "That's what they used to say. Another expression. *Events occur.* You're lucky I found you."

The metal rat, thought Crospinal, babbled like a retarded dog. Unlike any other elementals he'd known. Not like taciturn Fox and Bear. Either way, the rat didn't make much sense. "You're a strange machine," said Crospinal.

Coming closer, movements fluid, the elemental was utterly silent. "You're the one rigged up like a, like a *fucking sailor*, transponders stripped, a trained monkey. You call me strange?"

Crospinal said, "My father was in there. He taught me everything."

"If, by father, you mean a man from whose loins your seed sprung, then I've left a wedge of shrapnel lodged in your brain."

"Are you making fun of me?" He had been shooting for sympathy, or to make the metal rat feel bad, not hostility.

"There are mysteries aplenty onboard, maybe miracles, too, but rest assured you never had a father."

Crospinal was enraged. "I lived with him," he shouted, "and his ghosts, and his dogs! I lived in his range until the year of, whatever, of independent thinking." He had been about to shout about Luella but thought, suddenly, that doing so would not be a good idea. Impressions of Luella's face, and those of his dad, cycled, commingling, through his mind. He was breathing heavily. There had to be a way out of this dumb canister. What Crospinal really needed was to find a console, and a set of holes. He needed to confer. Or hit up a dream cabinet. Was his girlfriend, he wondered, in trouble? There had to be some good reason why she was treating Crospinal so poorly, and why the angry woman had come in her stead. Was she roaming inside the walls? Was she watching over him?

"Wake up," said the metal rat. "You've slept long enough."

"What are you talking about? I'm not even tired."

"You were sleeping."

"No I wasn't." He placed his mitt gently, fingers spread wide apart, against his bare chest. The old capillaries struggled. Pushing his hand down to his stomach, fingertips sensitive under the Dacron, to rest below his navel, where his pubis began. He felt the catheter twist, as he took a leak. But nothing else. *His pain had gone.* All of it. Blown clear from his body. In a much quieter voice, he said, "What have you done to me, rat?"

"I'm no *rat*." The elemental's eyes never altered. "I'm abiotic. Can't you tell? You can't tell the difference? What kind of number's been done on you? I'm a medical professional. Search and rescue, out in the bay. A sophisticated contrivance with a mental capacity ten times yours."

Crospinal tried to hold both hands up, to placate, but struggled to coordinate the move. "I meant no insult." Lifting his head extended his reach, so he could bang awkwardly on the rim of the canister with his loose fists, causing the thin material to boom: the numerals, at his waist, changed rapidly with each pound before resuming their previous setting. The icon flickered. "Can you zip me up? Zip me up. I can't deal with this."

"You really want to keep that suit on? It's not helping. I can get you another one. I know what size you are. I'll have a dispenser here in two minutes."

"I like this one just fine."

"It's poisoning you."

"I don't care."

"You can get a fresh one. Helmet and all. Fresh as a daisy. You can play dress up. Now please stop hitting that. There's a delicate mechanism in there. You're like a Neanderthal."

Crospinal stopped banging. "I know you're not a rat. I'm not an idiot. But when I woke up, I was thinking about rats. You know what they are? The animal? I got confused."

"Of course I know what a rat is. *Rattus rattus*, anachronism extraordinaire. Like you."

Overcome by a wave of exhaustion, however, Crospinal had closed his eyes.

The elemental said: "While you heal, you have a few options. Live with pain, of course, *au naturel*. That's always the simplest. Or I can treat you with mild doses of psychoactivity, to get you back on track. You're no stranger to them, I see. I can offer you wide selections of entertainment."

"Like what? Good haptics?" But Crospinal grated the last words from between his teeth, for elements of pain returned, though not as throbbing or as localized as the pain he had previously lived with. After his brief respite, the return of any discomfort was depressing and rather acute. His lower limbs tingled, but not in a good way. Still, he could move his toes now, inside the canister. At least he knew they were still there. "Could you list the entertainments?"

"That would take *hours*."

Farther down the hall, under a formation of recent growth, the edges of beams were visible; once, this area was like the pen.

The elemental said, "May I ask you a personal question?"

"Sure."

"How old are you?"

"I'm twelve."

"Twelve what? *Years?* That's pretty hard to believe. What sort of year were you using as a scale? You're *way* too big for twelve batch years. You seem like seventeen, maybe eighteen?"

"There was the year of long walks, and the year of exercise, the year of action, and the year of growth."

"What are you talking about? Your sailor did a number on you."

"Leave him out of this. Just show me a haptic already." A surprising tear had run down Crospinal's cheek, cooling by the cartilage of his left ear. The shield thrown up by his collar had not recovered from the dream of submersion and did nothing. He cleared his throat. "Show me a recording of what happened to the pen."

"Where you came from? That's pretty dry stuff. You choose this as a distraction?"

Crospinal concurred, and the show began, with blinding white flares bursting silently against a backdrop so black it was an absence of light and life. He was somewhere high above, watching, hovering there, like a ghost. Was he back in the realm of the dream cabinets? Were creatures hunting him?

A structure of delicate latticework grew incrementally, threads juxtaposed, an imposition on the dark. Was there water below? He would have looked but could not move, nor was he sure he possessed eyes to rub. He seemed to be nothing but frustrated energy, floating, unable to determine scale of any sort.

There was no sound, except the distant thrum of blood through veins. Each flare caused an addition to the creeping growth, a web of thin beams, getting thicker, closer. The magnitude of the artifact was implied only by the vastness and quietude of the black—

If he was transplanted back to the dream, with the ebony vault, were the creatures waiting to tear him from the booth, to kill him?

A quick scene change left him with vertigo:

The images of people, a group, seen from behind, maybe seven or so, each wearing a dark uniform, like the one his girlfriend and, more recently, the angry woman had worn. They strode purposefully down the length of a hexagonal corridor composed entirely of geodesic beams. They wore amber helmets, snug to their heads. All geometry about them was uniform, hard-edged. The void was gone. Were these manifestations, living within the structures of the world, seen in their own time and location? Was his girlfriend among them?

Maybe he was the apparition now, manifesting in their place?

Using hand gestures, the figures were guiding a dolly, the stature of which Crospinal had not seen before, which bobbed gently among the tangle of legs.

At each corner of the dolly, a quavering icon of two hands, pressed together. And on the dolly was a drone, like the ones that inhabited the abyss, off the catwalks, but three times the size. The drone rotated slowly, glimmering, bathed in a reservoir full of pale grey liquid that rolled over the surface as it cleared the tank, like mercury.

While he watched from on high, a dozen such drones bobbed beneath him, on a dozen such dollies, guided by a dozen teams, movements becoming faster, reaching an accelerating blur, until the last of the manifestations vanished, almost comically. More jumps in time. Something was wrong with the projection. He wanted to tell the metal rat to stop the so-called *entertainment* but no part of him responded to his wishes. Flickers came and went. There was a final flash, but black, and the visual of the hall transformed as if bubbling, grew folds of composite, and pores filled with ambients, which bloomed before going out. Ghosts passed by in a blur.

He hovered there, watching.

Static. The long, fading corridor, coruscating, twisting, became a passage of buboes and dripping toluene. Data curtains, sweeping almost too fast to see, then no activity, no movement at all.

The tear finally fell from his ear lobe. He felt the trail drying, the minute tightness on his skin, saline deposited there.

"Oops," said the metal rat, standing very near to Crospinal's face. "That wasn't what you asked for at all, was it?"

"No," he said. "You're messing with me."

"An honest mistake. That was from creation series. *Loading of the quorum*. Before everything went nuts. Though why they depict it in space I'll never know. Your selection was, well, overridden, I guess. Which is weird, but nothing works the way it does in training material. On the other hand, your bones have healed quite nicely. Would you like to try walking?"

"Already?" Crospinal looked inward: pain lingered but once again had lessened. He tried to move his legs and felt them shift inside the confines of the canister: no searing burn, no jabs, though he had tensed for them. Perhaps the elemental was telling elements of truth. "I'm better," he said. "I'll try to take a step."

"Okay, good. But not here. I have to take you back. I told you."

"Why can't you just let me out?"

"You're a bit of a, well, special case. You must admit. My colleagues and I need to confer."

"About what? What colleagues? Machines, you mean? Smart machines?"

The metal rat hesitated. "Maybe this is a good time for you to give me some more information about your father."

"Leave father out of this. Have some respect. He was a virtuous man. And because of what I did, because of who I am, my father is now—" But Crospinal could not say the last word, for it had jammed in his throat. Suddenly, surprisingly, emotions were rising up, waves of them getting wedged behind the blockage. They would burst free soon. *He* would burst. His lips trembled. Crospinal tried to tell himself *death* was only a word, just one word, like all the others, yet he could not convince himself. Everything that had once been father expired when father's heart stopped. This could be the only truth. Death was final, one last insult, and nothing existed beyond. The world closed back in, and the light was snuffed. (Even before death, as illness sunk into father's bones, and started to show in his eyes, the pen shrank. . . .)

This strange, distant hall was no place to rail against indignities. The horror and pain of wasting away. *The end of time*. He closed his eyes again. Energy to keep going, the experiences that shaped life: what was the point of learning, accumulating wisdom, growing, planning? All that work and struggle and progress for nothing.

Now floods overwhelmed him as the dams inside broke. He tried to say, one more time, that father was *dead*, but released, instead, a miserable wail that rose plaintively and hung in the air.

"*Please!*" His nose ran (crusts in there softened). His cheeks were soaked now. "Just *let me out*! I haven't done anything wrong. *Ever*. I only wanted to explore, to find solace, or understanding, or whatever, because remaining in the pen became a sort of oppression—"

"Here we go," said the metal rat, disinterested. "Ready?"

Before Crospinal had a chance to register what the elemental had said, still bawling, the canister started to float, rising, perhaps, to the height of his own hip, had he been able to stand. He was blubbering like the baby he'd once been. Armature had snickered out, to support his head and shoulders. He could no longer see the elemental, but he heard it for the first time, scurrying underneath, making sounds like a real rat, he thought, keeping up as the canister moved down the hall. Peering over the flange at his waist, straining to keep his head lifted, to see where they were headed, he passed under ambients. Fresh tubes of carbon hung low, dripping. An eye of the world followed his helpless progress.

"Are there more people? I had a sister once." He felt a tightness in his chest. "Her name was Luella. Not a haptic. A girl. But like me. Who was that I saw in the escape? In the dark uniforms? There was some kind of— There were twelve huge drones."

"The paladins."

"What?"

"The quorum. I told you."

"Was that something that happened a long time ago?" Crospinal tried to turn onto his side. "Or was that some other place?"

"You need to regulate your breathing," said the metal rat. "You're getting worked up. You'll need to be tranked again, if you continue. My advice would be to ramble less and ask fewer stupid questions. And keep your names to yourself, and the name of your so-called sister."

The canister bobbed along, banking gently, and entered the aperture to a small, discreet station. His anger at the elemental's attitude about his family broke, transformed, and settled into something else entirely. As the door slid shut behind him, a controller swooped in through the crack.

Crospinal, with a surge of anxiety, had seen the console: periscope and thumb plates, thin flap covering the twin holes.

"I'm bleeding," he said.

"There's no bleeding."

"Something's wrong. I can feel blood, running down my calf inside this thing. The uniform's not dealing. *I'm bleeding*!"

The metal rat leaped up onto the canister, and leaped again, onto Crospinal's bare chest. Delicate feet caught on his skin as the elemental walked, but the machine was very light. Crospinal looked into the unreadable red eyes and got a whiff of cordite and ozone before snatching the metal rat, rather easily—much easier than he'd thought—in his fist.

Shrieking, "*What the fuck?*"

Thin titanium arms offered little resistance. Crospinal clutched the rat tighter. His weakness was gone.

"I'm trying to *help*," said the metal rat. "You're insane!"

The controller orbited, nonplussed.

But the chassis of the small elemental was not crushing easily, so Crospinal took one of the legs with his free hand and twisted it backward, buckling titanium until a thin wire tendon snapped, stinging the flesh of his palm, marking the mitt there with a white slash as the Dacron parted.

"Stop," said the rat. "Please. For fuck's sake. You're crazy! You've wrecked my leg!"

"Release me," Crospinal hissed. "I asked you ten times and you never let me out."

"You'll fuck everything up. *Stop!*"

A small bolt popped off. The elemental made feeble sounds. Green coolants dribbled.

"I won't be able to fix myself." Even the voice was faint now, garbled. "I should have let you die again. I tried to help. Without me, you're a goner. You're making a big mistake. You're—"

"I'll pull you apart, you piece of *shit*."

But as Crospinal sought the battery with his fingertips—fumbling in the confounding miniature interior of the machine's underside—some form of anesthesia was administered and he blacked out.

⸻

The year of disparate viewpoints was perhaps his happiest, in relative terms. He had yet to learn father would die, and that he, too, would one day disperse into nothing. Disappointment over failed tasks had not soured the atmosphere in the pen. No girlfriend, no dream cabinets: a simpler life.

Crospinal would sit on the prayer mat (in his own fashion, legs splayed), rubbing at his knees as the lessons played.

Whenever Fox or Bear took him to the garden for recreation, Crospinal would have fun annoying the surly elementals, who could, at least, throw a ball. Spirits knew hide and seek really well but that was about it. Crospinal was able to get around pretty efficiently; the discomfort had not yet reached levels it achieved a mere year or so later. Young Crospie, at this point in his life, came closest to sensing positive elements of a potential future, as if possibilities were available and opening up before him, but never made the leap. He felt, if not a sense of wonder, at least burgeoning belief in an interesting and maybe even rewarding life.

Father was calmer, too, his apparitions less frantic. The dogs liked nothing better than to remain inactive for hours at a time, drifting, or curled by Crospinal's side, feigning sleep as he learned.

Father, during one of the lower points that followed, with cancer already destroying his marrow, described this halcyon period thusly:

"You'd get up from your daybed with a spark in your eyes. Each morning, I watched you—how you woke, of a sudden, a smile playing across your face. I was ecstatic. Or as close as I have been since waking. From the moment I opened my eyes, my desire had been to raise children. A mad desire. To raise a child from the dim seas of oblivion. To know that my testimony to civilization and enlightenment was healthy and happy, brought a joy like no other. I had gone to great lengths to establish and grow our safe haven. Your sister was already striking out. You both wore the freshest of uniforms, amber helmets, and your minds were compounding mine. . . .

"Learning held potential for both of us. I discovered, each day, the rewards of sharing knowledge. I began to understand who I was. As you grew, my purpose became clearer and clearer.

"The lost past drew closer, my memories more real. . . .

"You·were a flame in the darkness.

"Of course, there was still paracetamol available, which might have helped, I suppose. I let it trickle into your dispenser. I was willing to sacrifice anything for you, Crospinal.

"But I couldn't sustain it.

"I'll never forget that spark in your eyes, and how, over time, that spark faded."

The station was absolutely quiet when Crospinal woke. For a second, he thought he was back in the pen, with father, wild-eyed and pacing, not having slept at all, but he was not able to retain this particular illusion. Ambients were dim. The metal rat was not around. Recalling his attempt to dismantle the elemental, Crospinal looked about for evidence of the carnage—tiny fragments of machinations; flakes of fractured shell; other residue—but there was none.

He lay there, staring up at the ceiling for some time—curves of composite deposits covering a fine array of polymethyl—feeling sorry for himself. The controller watched from a corner, out of its league. Inside the canister, Crospinal was still able to move his toes. Pain was minimal. These discoveries did little to cheer him.

"I've left the pen, father," he whispered. "I've been in new halls and ended up with my ass in a box. I've been knocked out and dumped and busted up pretty good."

But praying was not the same without a mat, or without father, so he let his words fade. Along the farthest wall, within the narrow counter, the holes of the console were just visible under their cover, as if it might transform or otherwise offer some form of answer to a question he could not even conceive.

What harm could there be?

"Take me," he told the controller, pointing.

"I can't."

"I just want to go over there. See where I'm pointing."

"I'm not allowed."

"*Take me.*"

"Your heart is racing."

"There's nothing wrong with my heart. I'm ordering you to move me over to that counter."

After a brief stillness, the canister and support armature bearing Crospinal drifted closer to the console. Due to the angle of approach and his awkward position, Crospinal was only able to get one arm into a hole. With limited motion in his wrist, his fist penetrated part way. He could not find the bottom, so the hum was feeble, at best, though he felt mild energies coming up through the bones of his hand.

"An elemental's trapped me," he said quietly. "I think it might have abandoned me here. Useless. I need you. Are you there?"

But again the angry woman erupted next to him, standing so close the hairs on his head rose and every muscle in his body began to twitch. Crospinal heard the controller squawk. The woman's face seemed right up against his own; he flinched but did not pull out.

"I need to speak to my girlfriend. What have you done with her?"

"You were told to stay away," replied the woman. "You're an abomination."

Crospinal's hand was throbbing and his teeth stung. "You've done something to her. I know you have. She loved me." Then, to his own shock, he said, "I'm coming. You'll see. I'm coming to find her."

"You will not succeed," she said.

"And I'm no abomination. I'm Crospinal, father's only son."

"*Father*?" She hissed. "You were *named*? Passengers are criminals and idiots. Do you know the damage he's done?" The image flickered briefly. "He stole you, and raised you in isolation, as a monster. He mutilated you. He filled your mind with ramblings and hijacked data and nonsense about an awful past that should remain forever forgotten. You will not come any—"

Crospinal managed to yank his fist free, for it had become somewhat stuck. His wrist tingled. His anger and frustration with the attitudes of the woman and the metal rat was tainted with a chill he could not stop from spreading. *Mutilated, when he was an infant?* The scars? Father had told him his arms were cut when his infant body had been freed from the placental wall; the metal rat had indicated some other, more deliberate source altogether.

Too dark here, in the small recovery station, to see details on his skin, but he had rubbed the textures of his forearms many nights, to help him fall asleep—the texture a smooth ridge, fingers sometimes pushed right inside his sleeves, riding the tissue back and forth, back and forth, back and forth, patterns a glyph, from wrist to elbow, to lull him.

Raised in isolation, as a monster.

"Come, Crospie, I want to see you through my *real* eyes, not through loupes and accoutrements and eyes of the world. I want to *look* at you. Come closer."

Goodness knew what cocktails were being fed into father's mind. At least, he seemed to be in a good mood. Crospinal had looked up from the sculpture he was moulding. He frowned. Next to him, a dog woke abruptly, aware of father's agenda, and quickly became agitated, wanting Crospinal to *please* father, so it could doze and fade again.

"Stand here, son, on the edge of the prayer mat. Don't worry, I won't touch you. I was thinking about how fast time goes by. I haven't slept in ages. I feel as if we've so much work to do."

Crospinal rose painfully, knees popping, using a carbon rod to support his weight. He brushed static charges from his hands so they rolled down his uniform to the floor, causing the apparitions there to waver.

"*There* you are. How are you today, son?"

Crospinal shrugged.

"Your arms?"

"There's nothing wrong with my arms." He did not like to stand this close to father. The ozone offgas from the gate was enough to make Crospinal's eyes water. "It's my legs that hurt. . . ."

"Come closer. Unhitch your mitts. Let me see your arms. Push your sleeves up. Spandex, too. Don't worry. Hold them out. Palms up."

"My arms are fine."

"Indulge me, Crospie. I'm an old man."

So he did as he was told. After some amount of struggle, Crospinal held one arm out, wrist up, sleeve bunched, so that father's eyes, narrowing, could survey as if reading the delicate web transversing his exposed skin.

When the instructions telling the canister to remain cohesive changed, the sides peeled away from Crospinal's body with a low hiss; the upper portion rose and he was lowered gently to the floor by the remaining framework. All this time he had been trying to force his fingers under the waistband of the device, but the release, he knew, had not been the result of his efforts.

Against his back, the armature angled downwards, to help him stand. Fragments of the canister drifted, piecemeal, recalled into the ceiling; the station filled with the stench of recycling.

As his weight transferred to the soles of his feet, Crospinal knew he had changed. Not intangibly, not the way father's death had changed him, or the way knowledge of death, or heartbreak had changed him, but *physically*, corporeally. Putting his hands down, he felt his thighs, where the bones ran true, from knee to hip. He was *taller, straighter*—

Crospinal fell back into the support. The shaking in his body rose, uncontrollable, and he tried to move his hands over his legs again, to confirm the impossible, but was palsied with awe.

"My legs," he said. "My legs . . ."

The controller did not respond.

Levering up from the structure again, Crospinal took a step forward. Even the clench of his hand against the counter was stronger. No clicks when he straightened his leg, no popping from his knees—

A poor-quality haptic bloomed around him and he was somewhat immersed. (Though he could still see vague outlines of the station's furniture: the console; the counter.) From some other place, the metal rat watched him. *From someplace safe.*

"You fixed my legs."

The elemental grunted. "That's what I do."

"Why didn't you tell me?"

"Because you're crazy. You had an episode. You recall? You became aggressive. You do not play very nicely. I won't be sharing the same space with you again."

"I'm sorry."

"You won't get another chance. I was an ally. I was helping. You have no idea what you're up against."

"I'm not dangerous."

"Let's be philosophical about this. My curiosity overrode my ability to make a decision based on logic. I even repaired parts of your stupid costume when I couldn't get a dispenser to show up. Changed your filters. Blocked the methylphenidate in your nerve cells, so your dopamine levels will seek equilibrium. And what thanks did I get? Please leave now. Just go."

"You fixed my legs . . . ?"

The elemental remained silent for some time. Wherever it was, ambients dimmed. "Communicating with you has been exceedingly difficult," it said. "I know you're not to blame. I know some addled passenger taught you how to get dressed, everything, yet I've strained myself adapting to your primitive dialect. Your thought processes are stunted. When I called you a Neanderthal, I meant it. You're worse than a trained monkey. I was patient and generous and even excited about my role. I thought the nightmare might end. Now I'm just disappointed. And damaged. You broke me into pieces. I don't want to waste any more time. Leave my ward now, please. Good luck out there."

Crospinal had been touching his naked chest with mitts that felt smooth and cool and tingly against his skin. Pulling his uniform back into place, making sure the tendrils that fed the regulators did not get caught, folding the sides into place so the seals engaged, he marvelled at the ease with which his own limbs moved. Having decided that perhaps the missing ingredient was resolution for all that still ailed him, he asked,

"Was a part of me taken out? Did father cut something out of me? You must know. You scanned me."

"I'm not telling you anything else. You've been rude and evasive and cruel. Now please leave. I won't ask you again."

"Maybe I was—"

The haptic of the metal rat collapsed, leaving Crospinal alone again, standing on his new but unsteady legs.

INTO THE TREES

Against the surface of a small data orb, like the ones that drifted through the abyss—hardly larger around than his head, spinning a metre or so above the old composite tiles he had paused upon—Crospinal caught a glimpse of his face. Dark, hollowed eyes returned his gaze, reflecting a distortion more than the result of the orb's spherical surface and the halo of energy driving it. Startled, he tried to follow the orb, to recapture the sight—to make sense of what he had seen—but running had never been easy and now the act was downright unsettling: he tottered, off-balance, too high. Absence of pain was also disturbing, in a strange way, a lifelong companion vanished. His knees did not pop, nor did his bones grind together. He did not rock from side to side.

Lurching a few clumsy strides, Crospinal stopped, breathless, to watch the data orb recede, heading abruptly toward the distant ceiling, where he lost it, drifting amongst the polymer mists and encrusted structural beams as it continued on its unknowable mission.

He rested after the failed sprint, catching his breath, hands on his new knees. Despite his increased stature and improved posture, Crospinal felt dwarfed in these surroundings: the cathedral-sized auditorium he had been crossing humbled and reduced him to a state of insignificance: the world, though able to sustain, also seemed profoundly detached from any concerns he might have, despite what father had told him.

Within clenched fingers, he literally felt the differences the metal rat had initiated in the shapes of his bones. Rubbing his mitts against the sagging material that had, until recently, been stretched to the limit by his gnarled patellas, he wondered if the tiny elemental truly had been benevolent, as it had claimed, operating on him with his best interests in mind, or had it done something less than helpful inside him?

He straightened to continue, aimless and pensive, across the tiled floor of the massive chamber. Ambients were at mid-range but he could see no walls, in any direction. The tiles, large and brown under the soles of his boots, were uniform, and he could imagine the entire world, including the pen—before father arrived—once like this.

Since leaving the recovery ward, Crospinal had come across few familiar features: no consoles or cupboards; no banks; nothing but a few flat tubes, with buried traces of plastic, and a cluster of sealed senders. No devices at all, save the vanished orb. *Lots* of open area.

At least the engines thrummed, fundamental under the floor. He heard them, though not as frequently, as if they might be operating farther away, or in a different realm altogether.

How much more than father's cancerous body and his phalanx of apparitions had vanished with the explosion? Where was his girlfriend? Was her physical body somewhere, tethered to some remote gate? Would she live forever? So many hours he had spent with her, while she listened to his complaints and explanations, his questions and opinions. Or she'd whisper responses father would never say, abstract details that may as well have been in another, picturesque language.

Father had told Crospinal that the world, and everything in it, was created for him and his sister.

But that was the pen.

Now father was dead, the pen was gone, and the world had transformed.

Could other boys be setting out from other pens? Maybe standing at a console he might never find, calling manifestations through holes of their own?

The world was *not* made for Crospinal.

Father had been wrong.

Or, worse, had lied.

Plucking at his mitts until he could peel one off, tendrils popping free, Crospinal pushed up the sleeve and held the clinging insulation aside to look at the anemic skin there. The delicate scars mapped his forearm, bulging slightly, and reddened. He imagined his girlfriend, had a clear vision of her sharing a small cupboard with another boy, in another part of the world, a part Crospinal would never find. Maybe a boy who looked just like him but did not say the depressing things he said whenever she had acquiesced to appear. Maybe she was talking softly to him now, or laughing? Could she and this other boy figure out a way to make contact, skin against skin? He jammed his thumb into his bare wrist, as if to erase the marks. Unpleasant feelings were growing inside him. He did not like the direction his thoughts were taking. He tried to breathe.

Another boy? Was this possible?

He made a tight fist. Staring at the tendons as they moved, and the way the inflamed scars rolled over the stringy muscle beneath his skin, he fixed his sleeve and pulled his mitt back on, fastening the seams by rubbing them against each other. Feeble attempts of the Dacron tried to clean the follicles he had briefly exposed.

Another boy might be the reason his girlfriend had told him not to call her to a console anymore. Another boy might also be the reason she was nowhere to be found, and even why he was exiled to this quiet expanse.

Jealousy burned within the confines of his tricot. He had not known this ugly sensation before, or its name. He looked up again, toward the distant ceiling, and was surprised to witness a murder of crows passing suddenly overhead. One cried out, dipping lower, cawing, and he took this as a warning.

Crossing over a stretch of spongy tiles, to where a series of harder, older flooring began, Crospinal mounted a gentle slope; he must have been on the slow base of a wall, an incredibly large wall, which loomed somewhere up ahead—though from where he had paused, the distant rise was nearly invisible and might even have been an illusion.

How high could a ceiling get? The abyss, at the catwalks, and the distant girders visible over the dream cabinets, would be as lost here as he was.

Continuing, he came across a cluster of carbon tubes so big in diameter that they rose out of sight. Had he perhaps shrunk? Upon closer investigation, the cluster revealed a neatly concealed periscope, similar to the one at the bottom of the pyramid shaft, behind the throne. There were eyepieces and portholes in and around the pen, varied shapes and sizes, and through each the identical view, yet discovering new lenses always caused a moment of adrenaline in his veins. The familiarity, too, in such a landscape, was a rush of relief. Would he see mountains? Grabbing the handles, and pulling the eyepiece toward him, he waited a beat before putting his eye against the plastic—

The landscape of ashes, baking under a red orb's glow, stirred by dead winds. Shimmering, the orb was rising.

Father had told Crospinal the world would continue without his presence. But where were the dispensers? He took a hit from his siphon. The periscope was the only device he'd found. Enough water in the reservoir for a day or so.

When he died, who would be left to learn the truth?

Crospinal thumped his loose hand against the eyepiece. There were no changes outside. He saw the expanse behind him, reflected in the lens, and he saw his own face, too, peering back. Any startling change he thought he'd seen previously in the orb was muted. He just seemed like Crospinal now, a little older, a little taller, a little more alone.

He tried to clean the lens with his sleeve.

Father's death had not stopped the world, and Crospinal's death, when it happened—which was inevitable—would not herald endtime either.

There was another boy.

Crospinal knew this now, with certainty; a punch, a cold draining.

Somewhere in the world was another boy.

He stared for a moment longer before releasing the handles of the periscope, which clapped back into place and sank. He had not eaten since the operation, though he suspected the elemental had taken some efforts to sustain him, or give him energy when he was unconscious. He said his own name aloud, shouting it, addressing the expanse beyond the porthole. If no one else was left to say his name, maybe then the word would fade and the other boy gain the advantage. Crospinal could not recall what the world had called him, that day in the back halls, at the perimeter of father's range, with the dogs barking incessantly and flickering out, but it seemed important now. Had the crow been calling to him, too?

The gradual curve of the wall's base increased until the slope finally became undeniable, and difficult to negotiate. More and more clusters of carbon tubes ran roughly parallel to the floor, which was already, by this point, far below. Drifting banks of polymers caused him distraction: there was construction afoot, or would be soon. Higher up, ambients indicated a shift, an addition or texture to the composite. Curtains swept across. Not far from the cluttered portion he clung to, the vertical expanse extended into clouds so distant he could see no details or discern scaffolding there, no evidence of hard lines.

Over his shoulder, in the distance, a darker mass had accumulated at the horizon; Crospinal predicted a squall of some magnitude. Rains were not enhanced water, like water from spigots, or in the pool, but untreated, oily accretions, trapping inorganic compounds that drifted through the atmosphere and gathered in the upper reaches; he did not want to get caught in such a storm. Not here. Clouds like this—real clouds—gathering in smaller rooms around the pen (which he had thought at the time were *immense*) had sent him scurrying into the covered safety of enclaves or local cupboards.

Climbing obliquely, Crospinal tried to keep focused on what his feet and hands touched. Since being revived, in spite of his transformation, he felt he had plodded, almost blindly, without truly registering where he was headed or where he had come from. His thoughts now were stilling.

Using the stems of tubes as handholds, and placing his feet carefully on the shallow ledges in the formations, he found he was surprised again and again by the abilities of his new limbs, by his latent power.

He came to a narrow, slotted opening. The icon of a daybed, rotating slowly, rose before him. This was a sustenance station of sorts. A resting place. Relieved that he had managed to find or call forth this place, he said, "Hello?"

No controller came to greet him. No response. No thumb plates, either, to validate his prints.

So he just entered.

Light bloomed.

A small station. No holes, no console at all. Crospinal felt his heart sink, and was again surprised, this time by his own reaction. There was a standard food dispenser, with standard pellets and a water spigot. Daybeds, off to one side. The station smelled . . . new.

Along the far wall shimmered the energy of a bank, and for the first time he saw how similar the sheen was to that of a drone, or a data orb. Or the paladin, in the metal rat's haptic. There was no recess for a gate here, not of any capacity. Nonetheless, a smart room, with all the amenities.

If these accommodations were not for Crospinal—if they'd remain when he was gone, and existed before he arrived—then who, he wondered, slept here? Who was the food for? Luella? Or the boy who had stolen his girlfriend?

He touched a small table, which, sensing his heat, drifted out.

He sat on a stool.

"Hey," he said. "Got a voice? Hello?"

No answer.

The daybeds were identical to his own, back in the pen. Made, of course, covers crisp and ironed. The sight suddenly had enormous impact upon Crospinal and he just sat there, staring, trying not to cry again. When he got up, and was finally able to take a step closer, dust crackled and vanished with a brief aura of blue sparks as a cleansing surge passed over the mattress from head to foot. Covering his eyes, Crospinal had felt a brief quiver to be standing so close. He wished a dog or two was with him, by his feet, rambling on and on, or just panting, because electrostatic made apparitions crackle and the dogs would whine and sputter and run madly back to father. He smiled at the strength of his reverie and managed to swallow.

Holding his mitt out, under the beak of a timid spigot, he accepted a small cup filling with water as it dropped into his palm. He looked around again. The station was clearly functional, at some capacity, despite its silence and lack of controller, but maybe that was the way stations would be from now on. He drank four cups of water and held the empty in his fist until the molecules dispersed. There was invigoration, inside him: each cup catered a little more to what ailed him.

A haptic source, hidden in a small alcove; a set of battery chargers behind the main table. There was a uniform dispenser—like the one at harmer's corner, maybe somewhat bigger—staying low, between the daybeds. Crospinal approached, thumbed the plate, and withdrew, after a moment, from the damp nest, a fresh and moist uniform. *Perfect.* Made expressly for him. Lifting the newly baked material to his face, and holding it there, still hot, he breathed in the smell of fresh nylons and neoprenes. The processor was humming already against his cheek, wanting to be worn, to meld with him.

Then, from the already congealing soup that would become the next uniform, like a shimmering skull, or a rising orb over windblown ash, the top of a pristine polycarbonate helmet presented itself, slowly, in offering.

"One's ready, Crospie. One's ready."

"I saw it."

"You did? Why didn't you pluck it? My dogs came running back, all excited. Go, Crospie, bring it here. Go get it while it's fresh. Why aren't you excited?"

"I don't want to get it, dad. My legs are sore."

"*Crospie.* There are fewer and fewer helmets. The ones that do appear are breaking down quicker. You know that. You need to take your uniform seriously. There'll come a time when the air gets sucked away."

"Dad, I *know.*"

"We need to gather helmets. They make us whole. The shield might protect you from most microbes but only a helmet can truly save you."

"*Dad.*"

"Put one on again. Let's run a drill. Every part cleaned and functioning. You could put a new uniform on, Crospinal. Let's start at the inside. Right up against our fragile skin?"

"Not now."

"The maximum . . . ?"

"*Please, dad.*"

"Maximum . . . ?"

"Absorption garment. Spandex underwear. Chestplate and tricot. The catheter. The processor."

"You're not taking this seriously."

When Crospinal went back to retrieve the glistening globe from the dispenser, father took it, and cradled it, as if the helmet were another baby, another chance, pressing the smooth plastic against his cheek. There were tears in his eyes. Father could never wear a full helmet like this, because of his tethers; the mass of conduits entered father's head at the base of his occipital bone and precluded coverage. Crospinal knew that father—eyes closed now, trembling mitts stroking the dome—was straining to make sense of his life, to understand why a helmet could mean so much, and move him so much, to understand how he had come to be in this situation, isolated, fractured into ghosts and spirits, living in a shrinking pen at the end of the world with a crippled son. His unreliable son.

And though Crospinal had been convinced to pull one of the snug covers over his head many times as a younger child—hearing the wet *snick* as the seals closed, the hiss of the shield cutting off, pressure building in his sinuses as filters and visors and screens and comms kicked in—he could not shake the restrictive feeling of impending suffocation, and ended the ceremony by fumbling with the rings that held the helmet in place, tearing the entire destroyed assembly from his head, and gasping at the pen's stale air while father looked on, mortified.

———

Crospinal motioned to the stool again, so he could sit. He had dropped the uniform. It was already disintegrating. He had not touched the helmet. The station reeked of recycling. He drew a deep breath, exposed to all microbes: his shield had not returned. When he called for a sustenance dispenser, the station startled him by speaking at last, bidding Crospinal a cold, taciturn welcome.

"No controller," said Crospinal. "You don't have that capacity?" Some chambers in the pen, below opal centre, had a general interface. The voice shimmered all around. He had certainly picked up on this room's attitude. Father had used sarcasm sometimes, when he was tired, or strung out. Crospinal found it hurtful; he was not pleased.

"I figured you were watching me," he said. "I've been walking around a long time. I was starting to think you were busted or something, or that all stations out here were just dumb. Are those daybeds for me?" Pointing. "Are they waiting for me? Was everything here created for me?"

"What egotistical nonsense."

"Father showed me a story once, about a hard daybed, a soft daybed, and a daybed that was just right."

"*Your father?*"

Crospinal winced. Another reaction to a reference about his dad. Part of a pattern, and Crospinal was defensive. "That's right," he said. But to avoid further questions or snide comments, which he did not want to deal with, which he *could* not deal with, he called out again to the food dispenser, hand outstretched, to change the subject.

After a moment, probably consulting the station, the sustenance device turned, extended its neck, and dropped two soft pellets into the palm of Crospinal's waiting mitt.

"They've heard about the vandalism," explained the station. "We all have. We're reticent."

Crospinal let the food sit on his tongue until it started to disintegrate. He tried to remember how the story about the daybeds had ended but could not. *Fox and Bear*? Were they characters in it? The pellet was sour. "What's vandalism?"

"To be honest, you do seem earnest, and we must welcome all crew equally."

"That would be good of you." Crospinal ate another pellet. The flavour of this one was different, spicier. The station was indeed busted, or maybe it was just unprepared for visitors. There was still a chance, he supposed, that he was the first guest the station had ever had. "You have a prayer mat here?"

"To what," said the station, "my antediluvian friend, or to *whom*, do you expect to pray?"

Crospinal would not get baited any more by this flawed avatar. "We prayed every night. We prayed for food, and for the strength of the pen around us." He paused, but there was no reply, at least not on any wavelength he could interpret. "We gave thanks for his memories and prayed for more to return. I could pray for you, if you want, station. I could tell you everything I've seen today."

"*What*? No thanks. Some runners kiss non-existent asses, others worship their own turds. Stations don't need adoration. We have no insecurities."

Crospinal licked food paste from inside his cheek and from between his molars. He was unsure what the station was getting at. Was it angry at him? He didn't believe that any efforts to discover motives or reasons would be well spent. Still, wanting to hide his irritation, rise above it, he stared, flustered nonetheless, toward the far end of the room, trying to keep his mouth shut. But the station had ruined his meal and the pellets just sat in his stomach like heaps of composite slag.

A moment later, though, Crospinal stood. "*Holy shit.*" Crumbs fell from his lap.

The same colour and texture as the walls, incongruous, the camouflaged elemental was easily as large as Fox had been, but sleeker, almost invisible. Resting, charging, on all fours. Father had not trusted any sort of smart machine, though he had no choice but to rely upon them when they showed up. Crospinal put a threadbare mitt on the finely finished flank and whistled under his breath; the shell was smooth, with an oily patina, and warm as flesh.

"*Look at this thing.*"

"Obey all cardinal rules," warned the station. "Eyes of the world are upon you. Even here. Don't press your luck."

"Are you threatening me?"

Low to the floor, with slim, braced legs, the machine could only be for riding, and riding *fast*. There was a saddle patch, and safety straps, and a slot where a shield would emerge, to protect him.

Asleep now, the broad, flat face was turned away—

A quick chop of his hand interrupted the current and the machine shuddered awake, opening one red eye to regard him intently.

"Hey," said Crospinal.

"Hey yourself."

"The station where you're charging is low-functional, at best." He swallowed another pellet, chewed, and popped a fifth into his mouth. The dispensers were watching him. "Can you talk? I mean, saying more than just, hey there?"

"I can."

"You sure look fast." He was inspecting the rear quarters: pistons; articulated rods; taut springs. "What's your cognitive level? How high's your vocabulary?"

A blunt and primitive wave passed through Crospinal.

"Stop that."

Turning, to pay more attention—no doubt at what the scan had picked up, or not picked up—the elemental regarded Crospinal for a while. "I'm unable to read you without running a diagnostic. And it's hard for me to figure out what you're saying. I'm translating as I go, but your dialect is . . . unusual."

"So I've heard."

"And the answer to your previous question is that my vocabulary level's pretty high."

"Once, not too long ago, I also thought I was fairly smart."

The elemental considered this. Then it said: "You want to go for a run?"

"What?"

"Isn't that why you woke me? Because you want to go somewhere? You want a ride?"

"Uh, yeah." Impetuousness felt good. "That *is* why I woke you." He patted the elemental again, let his hand linger, recalling the pitted skin of Fox and Bear.

"Where to, young master?"

"Take me . . ." He furrowed his brow as the idea struck him. "Where other people are."

"Which people?"

Taken aback, Crospinal asked, "How many are there?"

But the sustenance station spoke up, interrupting: "You have no idea what sort of number's been done on this one. He's not a passenger, as I first believed, but no runner, either. He asked if my station was for him alone! He has been stripped and is useless as crew. I let him eat. I wasn't sure what else to do. He must have escaped from somewhere. I'd be careful, machine, if I were you."

"Don't worry about me." The elemental continued to regard Crospinal all the while with its red eyes. "I can take care of myself. Now listen, young master, I'll bring you as far as the cabins, on the other side of the garden. To the depot there. Acceptable?"

"You have a garden?"

"Out in the bay. It's not mine, though. You don't know these parts at all?" The elemental stretched its legs, rising higher. "A *big* garden. There was a time when this area was more populous. The trees are still alive. Had enough to eat yet, young master? You ready?"

Crospinal nodded.

Turning fluidly to leave, the elemental made no sound at all, no creaks or clanks.

"Goodbye," said the station, as Crospinal and his ride departed. "Come again."

"Goodbye," said Crospinal, happy to have refrained from further comments, or losing his temper, or crying. Father, he was sure, would have been proud.

Stepping from the aperture, onto the slope outside, he felt the expanse of the world dwarf him again. While he had been inside, there was rain. Looking out, as far as he could see, over a glistening patchwork collection of tiles, the world was brighter than it had been. Above him, the wall loomed, vanishing up into polymers, which were thinner now. He hung onto a braid of cables and leaned forward, telling himself to remain brave, no matter how vast the chamber or strange the encounter.

Waiting below, flattened somewhat, the elemental appeared even faster-looking than Crospinal had at first imagined. He had not seen it descend. As he too went down—pretty nimbly—to stand next to the machine, the red eyes followed his every move.

"Don't worry about that algorithm," said the elemental quietly, when he arrived at its side. "The station, you called it. Up there. They're always a little off. They all are, because they're tangled together in the banks, and the banks are messed up. Got funny ideas. But the connection never faltered in there and I was usually left alone for ages. No offence. I slept very well."

"No offence taken." Crospinal could see the elemental clearly only if the angle was right. Moving his head to the side, a flush of pink washed rapidly over the machine, replaced equally quickly by a flush of tan. Old Fox couldn't do that trick. Crospinal cocked a leg over the elemental's back, moved into the saddle patch, and grasped the rough straps as they rose, seeking him from their roost. Had the station existed for years? With no visitor? Seemed unlikely.

Many occasions had he ridden piggyback on his caretakers, but they didn't like to carry him and were nowhere near as comfortable or secure as this ride. Calibrating, the elemental made whirring adjustments while Crospinal sat there and had the flickering thought that everything might just turn out all right, whatever that meant. Squinting into the middle distance, he wound the safety straps tighter around his fists, not entirely trusting his new grip, as if it, too, might vanish, like his past, like everything else he had known.

The machine said, "For the record, I don't really care about your credentials, young master."

"Good." But he was insulted.

"However, it is strange that there's a trace of cardiopelgics in your lungs. I saw it earlier, when I scanned you."

"What does that even mean?"

"That you've been in stasis. But I didn't want to say anything. Not in the, uh, not in the *station*."

"I had an operation recently. Maybe that's why?"

"There's no connection between the two. The solution in your lungs is from spending a long time in a stat. Which makes little sense, because, like the algorithm said, you're not a passenger. And there's no stats near here."

"I don't know what you're saying."

"There's also no evidence of an operation."

"I'm not making this up. Another elemental put me in traction. My femurs had been broken. I used to have rickets, but now they're gone. I don't know what else was done."

"Ah," said the elemental. "You had rickets? A softening of the bones. Your back is straight. I didn't see a trace of fracture or fibrocartilage callus. Perhaps you should secure yourself now, young master. Let's roll. I haven't been out in a while."

Crospinal thumbed the safety belt, felt the ends curl around his waist, sniffing each other out before melding. Fox had a similar belt, emerging from a similar cache, but the halves never did find each other and Crospinal had to hold on to them. Bear's unit was shot altogether. Until now, Crospinal had not realized what a functional safety belt should do. He felt snug, despite the fact that the elemental he sat upon was as crazy and dysfunctional as the station he'd found it in.

"We'll cut across." Motioning with its head, the machine started to walk. "I don't see any traffic, but the main controller is faint today. You can never be too careful. Keep your eyes open."

"All right," said Crospinal, looking about, not sure for what.

When the elemental moved quicker, he had to lean forward, wondering what could possibly be expected. He scanned overhead but only mists curled in on themselves, waiting for instructions to erode, or build.

Soon they were racing across the open floor. Crospinal didn't think much about anything except hanging on. How different the world was from what he had expected, from what father had told him. He had to hunker lower still. He was not afraid of falling, merely wanting to make himself as aerodynamic as possible, to go even faster, to move away. A shield expanded before his face, as he'd expected, cutting the wind, though Crospinal had actually started to like the feeling of air against his cheeks, his lips, and even flowing into his mouth, when he opened it. He didn't care what went inside his body, not for this moment, not at this speed. Ahead was nothing but open expanse. This exhilaration paled any he had ever felt.

Details of the great wall behind him were already obscured by distance and by the optical trick of the slow, curving base. He looked back, to locate the station, the doorway opening set above the carbon tubes, but could not see much for the galloping and awkwardness.

"I've been thinking," he said, facing forward once more—

Was there a change on the horizon, a jagged line of low forms? He squinted, but whatever he thought he had seen was gone.

"Yes?"

"About you. And Fox." Crospinal would lecture his caretakers for hours. "Fox stood on two feet. Not really feet, but those clawed tools, like you have, with tiny balls at the end. We went to the garden together a lot, mostly with another elemental I called Bear."

"You named machines?"

"Father wasn't happy about it. I named them after characters in an escape he showed me when I was little. They were characters in the haptic. Father didn't like them very much. The real ones, that is. The elementals. He didn't trust them, but they were all he had, except for phantoms, so he couldn't refuse their help. Right after I gave them names, they took off."

Loping along, the machine scanned Crospinal yet again, a crude push he felt in his chest, rising up inside, like gorge; he nearly fell from the saddle but said nothing: the intrusion meant the machine could not understand him, and was looking for answers.

"Do you know them?"

"Uprights," said the elemental finally, "were recalled, long ago. They had lousy gyroscopes. Small wonder you asked about my cognition. Say, young master, would you care to name me?"

Crospinal frowned, alert. "No," he said.

The machine was travelling over a series of soft tiles, pads of its feet coming down soundlessly against the composite; the ride was so smooth that Crospinal had to remind himself of the velocity, so he would not tumble. He had accused Fox of stupidity as they walked back together after an outing. Fox would look down with those crimson eyes. Sometimes Crospinal danced, gimp-legged, around the elemental, despite the pain, and sang songs meant to annoy. Sometimes he threw debris at it. He did not mention these details now.

"We have some distance yet to travel, young master. Perhaps you could relate a story? I quite like stories."

But Crospinal remained suspicious. "Father pulled me from his womb, in the pen. He raised me there. Now he's dead, the pen's gone, and I'm out here."

The shield relayed, whispered breath into his ears, the response:

"I dare say there's more to your history than that. But if you don't want to share, that's okay. You have traces of cardiopelgic solution in your blood and enough pharmacology to drop a small elephant. Maybe you should just rest."

"Drop a what?"

"You're tired, and under duress."

Somewhat absurdly, Crospinal found himself wishing he had taken the uniform from the dispenser back in the sustenance station, instead of leaving it behind to rot. Now, he could actually feel air against his bare skin, because the fabric he wore was *threadbare*. (*Change uniform! The dispensers have come for you, Crospie. Clean up, let the wasp cut your hair. . . .*) Splits in the nylon at the elbows and knees. No scales of neoprene at all down the front of each leg. The mitts and boots were thin, vulnerable. And the collar seemed broken altogether. He felt shabby, at a disadvantage. He imagined all the microbes he'd swallowed spreading into his circulatory system, heading to his organs, to break them down.

Pressing the newly minted outfit to his face, Crospinal had forgotten what fresh uniforms looked and smelled like. How hard would it have been to renew uniforms whenever father asked? Why was wearing the same failing uniform every day, and letting his hair grow, so important?

For that matter, why had straying from the pen, exploring recesses and consoles beyond father's range, become so urgent? All he really wanted was to be content. Searching alone in the outlying halls, losing himself in the dream cabinets, falling in love with a manifestation.

Crospinal had made choices to spite father, or teach him some inexplicable lesson, for no reason other than giving Crospinal life, and raising him best he could. Crospinal felt more than a pang of remorse. As if he could talk himself into a justification of his past reactions and, through hindsight, dubious decisions, he *would* tell a story.

"The garden filled what we called the flora lab, behind harmer's corner. Nutrient tiles lined the floor. The uprights, as you called them, said very little, mostly complaints. They used to charge together, dormant side by side in a cupboard just outside opal centre, but they couldn't stand the sight of each other, not when they were awake. They were always together and they were grumpy and they'd been together forever. They followed me. They made sure I didn't get any scrapes or tangle myself in root masses. They wanted to keep me in one piece. If I went wading in the pool—which was a round clearing with water in it, deep as my ankles—"

"A reservoir. Solution. And where we charge is not a cupboard, nor do trees grow from *nutrient tiles*."

"Do you want a story or not?"

"I do."

"Then stop interrupting."

"Sorry."

"In the centre of the garden, Fox and Bear were right there, at the edge, going slowly around, staring at me. I was in the water. Though they were real, like me and you, trees didn't get hurt when they went by. Fox and Bear could avoid branches. I tried to see how they did it. I used to just crash through them. They would crumble all around me.

"Fox had eyes just like you.

"If I ever climbed anything—though that was pretty hard to do, with my bad knees—they were there, ready to catch me. I tested them so many times, falling backward from a baseboard slope, or even that time, lying face down in the pool, processor whining, shield bubbling. They caught me each time before I had the chance to hit the floor or swallow water. When they scanned me, it was rough. Either to see if I'd done damage, or to punish me for taking a chance.

"Father never asked them to help. He never told them what to do. They appeared one day, and then I . . . Then they vanished."

The elemental made a grunting sound. That line of forms on the horizon must have been an illusion, for they had reappeared, though neither closer, nor clearer.

"After my caretakers left, I was alone, pretty much, except for the dogs and ghosts. And my dad. Whenever I went back to the garden, to lie on the nutrient tiles, it wasn't the same. I spent a lot of time there. I left behind a lot of damaged trees. At least, I spent a lot of time there until I started to go even farther, and farther, where apparitions couldn't follow and father couldn't see me. That's when I found the dream cabinets."

"Hard to believe. This must have been a long time ago."

"There were seven. Some were empty, some were full."

"One might even have been the one your passenger sailed in."

"What? My dad? He wasn't even aware of them. They were outside his range." Crospinal was becoming increasingly convinced his words and stories were being taken as fabrications, that the machine was somehow mocking him again; he felt his frustration return, and he regretted that he had volunteered anything. He said, "Okay, I don't want to talk about my dad. I've told you I only want to talk about the garden and the elementals, because you asked, and you're one yourself. I was trying to be nice. Fox and Bear would just listen. They never interrupted or told me I was wrong or made me think about stuff. So stop."

"I'm only trying to help, young master. To understand the situation more clearly. To learn."

"Well, don't interrupt anymore."

"As you wish."

"Dogs had a hard time." Crospinal sat high in the saddle. He felt the power in his new legs, the angle of his limbs, his spine, optimal. "Solid details broke up their lumens. Father could only really see what was going on from the far entrance."

"Are you talking about the garden again?"

"Of course I am."

"The dogs were projections. You know that? Your passenger had found a strong gate and could project."

"No shit," said Crospinal. "Now will you let me speak? I won't ask you again." Yet the elemental would not:

"When a passenger connects, they're fed racetams. Either prami or oxi. He didn't sleep much, did he? Never recharged?"

"We don't have batteries, stupid. He was human, like me."

"Every living thing has a battery of some form. Everything must charge."

"I want you to listen. Could you? Stop talking. Just stop. What I'm starting to think is that he didn't watch me, not all the time, even when he could, and that he might even have appreciated the times when I wasn't around. Maybe even encouraged it. Me leaving him alone. Me leaving the pen. He might have wanted me to."

"That's only natural, young master. Even though your passenger was misguided, he had your best interests at heart. He wanted you to become independent. He *needed* you to be. You were growing up; he was getting older. Someone needed to carry the torch."

"That's exactly what he used to say."

"They all say that."

"But don't call him misguided. You never met him."

"All humans are misguided. Whether stored in the hub, as a runner, or sailing here, inside a dream. If a man can survive the trip through the hole, and being woken on the other side, and stay sane enough to find a place, he can linger here, for a brief turn, hooked up to the old network, but he'll never reconcile this existence."

"You know a lot about humans," Crospinal said, trying to use sarcasm but unsure of its effectiveness. "What'll be left of father when time passes? Can you answer that? I'm the only one with memories of him."

"I think it's fair to say," replied the elemental, "that the passenger who converted you was not who you think he was. I sincerely don't want to offend, young master—because I detect your defensiveness—but you were not pulled from a womb. Like all passengers, the man that tried to educate and form you was many things: a slave, an addict, a madman. And absolutely, irretrievably, lost. He was not your father. He stole you."

Crospinal was furious. His cheeks had become hot. Furious at the belligerent elemental, yes, but also a portion of his anger directed toward himself, for talking too much, and toward father, who had abandoned him, who left him in this position, where he had to defend everything about his life and what he knew. He could not abide by his own rage nor stop it stewing.

"The ganglia have been dug out of your ulnae and median nerves. He had skills, your passenger. Ganglia make runners runners. There are two sorts of people in this world, young master, and you are neither."

"*Father*," Crospinal said, too loudly for his own liking, "was a nice man. That's all. A bit sad at times, and disappointed, but nice. I don't care what you say. Or the stupid stations. I think you're all rude."

For the next few moments, they continued in an awkward, prickly silence. At least, it was for Crospinal. How could this machine have made him feel this way? Was he that tired? When had he last slept? The bounding remained effortless and the massive chamber went on and on under the invisible ceiling. Before much longer, though, the elemental's pace slowed, and Crospinal, brooding, bounced lighter in the saddle.

"Now father's dead," he spat, lips brushing the shield, though he wasn't sure if he'd said this for his own sake or for that of the machine.

Regardless, the response came immediately, whispered directly into Crospinal's auditory channels:

"Left alone, runners might be aware of loss, though not acutely, and you have a will to survive, which means you fear the cessation of life, whether you know it or not. Most runners are no more evolved than those animals the passengers conjure—the bird, and that opportunistic muroid, the rat. A passenger can, at least, conceptualize, try to figure out *why*. Not so much the runners. You're in the middle. Well, there's no monopoly on thanatophobia, young master. Even machines, as you call us, struggle at times to understand our role and our reason. What occurs when either of us ceases to exist, young master, whenever it happens, cannot, by definition, be processed."

"You've lost me," said Crospinal, though that wasn't entirely true.

"Unless you're like that station back there, hooked into a network, you're given one personality, like a hand of cards in those haptics of the old days you watch, and you carry it around. But you can't trade cards, or fold, or add useful cards to your hand. Some are good, others terrible. All you can do is just look at your cards different ways, and shuffle them around, until they're worn out. When your battery dies for the last time, and won't hold even the tiniest charge, there's nothing left. Nothing."

"Endtime," said Crospinal, letting go of the straps with his left hand, gesturing at the empty bay about them. "I know about that. But you get to live for a thousand years, and you don't get sick, or rot from the inside out."

"Listen, young master. If I don't charge, or I can't find a charger, I die a small death. I can be inert, at the mercy of anyone who finds me. And if my interface suffers a collapse, or if I'm crushed in an accident, or blown out a lock, then everything I've managed to hang on to and everything I've stored will vanish with me. There are many voices in these walls. Are prototypes and other designs watching over me? The pressure and movement of your body, young master, refreshes me somewhat, generates energy, and direction, but generally I lose more than I gain. I can die a big death, just like you. A final death. You see, me and you are not so different, young master. I'm sorry about the loss of your passenger."

Crospinal did not believe the machine. It was making up parallels to either mock him or ingratiate. Ahead, the dark line on the horizon seemed to have suddenly drawn nearer; narrowing his eyes, Crospinal realized with some degree of shock that he was looking at the approaching border of a garden so large a hundred pens would be lost within. "We're going through *that*?"

"We are, young master. As you requested. Crew cabins are on the far side. There'll be people there. Crew. Maybe a lost runner or two, sniffing around. The cabins are the last stop on the supply train, or the first stop, depending which way you're travelling, so there's often crew. We'll be leaving what's called the perimeter, young master. You understand that? Another jurisdiction, beyond the bay. Should take about three hours to get across but there's a narrow neck we'll take to save time, through the garden, though the growth has extended since I last came here. The floorplan's changed."

❈

Approaching the trees, they slowed. Crows burst up from the floor, startling both of them. Raucous, incongruent, the birds were like fragments torn loose from Crospinal's dream. Traces of crumbled nutrient tile, dead seeds, and anemic roots marked the first line of growth. *The bird, and the mammal. The opportunistic muroid. . . .*

The elemental's titanium feet and shins were dusted with fine pollen. Crospinal's head spun with words. Trees could not find purchase beyond the distinct border of the nutrient tiles. Father had told him, like everything else, what the dark, fertile mixture was called, but it seemed to Crospinal that father's instructions and terms and lessons meant little out here; Crospinal's confidence was shaken, though he would defend father again and again if he had to.

Watching the crows fly off, until they were no longer in sight, the elemental said, "All right, young master. Here we are. Garden's edge. Let's go. Elbows in. Keep your knees tight against me."

"Wait." Crospinal felt further twinges of anxiety. He took a sip, held the siphon tube between his teeth. "One second."

Farther in, trees grew taller and taller. The monstrous growths were identical to those in the garden of his memories: one spindly trunk atop a broad root nest, with narrow, delicate leaves, each crusted with a photosensitive sheen. Here, at the border, some trees were hardly higher than a hand's span, sitting on a fist-sized ball of roots, but deeper into the garden, other trees must have had trunks as thick around as his waist. How large must their root mass be? To walk among those giants he would again feel miniature.

And there was a smell in the breeze, rank and moist. He hesitantly filled his lungs. The collar of his uniform fizzled briefly as it tried to filter.

"Ready? Young master? Are you all right? Or shall I put myself in doze mode, to conserve energy, while I wait for you to decide?"

Leaves made hushed sounds, adjusting their angle, gaining exposure to the light above. The engines rumbled, so far away. On the skin of his cheeks, and on his forehead, Crospinal felt the warm glow that motivated the plants. He rolled his shoulders and stretched, changing the safety strap from one hand to the other, trying to shake the mood that had descended over him. Sitting there, squinting, for some time, not eager at all to go into this oversized garden, for he might never emerge, he saw—across a thin line of crumbled nutrients before the elemental's feet, leading into the growth—a trail of faint, but clearly human, footprints.

THE CLEARING

What Crospinal had wanted to tell the elemental and what he had said aloud were very different. He had been ruminating about his memories since the metal rat operated on him, mostly because he no longer seemed as buffeted by their intrusions upon him and, in the relative, linear calm, experienced an unusual precision he had not been able to achieve before—though why he had felt the need to explain himself to the rude machine, and why he had failed badly at doing so, he did not know.

Until recently, the past and the present, and maybe even the future, entwined together. Crospinal could see that now.

Though the elemental protested, he dismounted. Taking a few steps toward the edge of the garden, he felt steady on his long legs. Crouching to run his fingertips over the shallow depressions in the material spilling from the border of the trees—this evidence of another person, maybe even the other boy who taunted his thoughts—he froze. Never before had he been able to crouch like this. He glanced over at the elemental to see if it registered the importance of this discovery, but the machine had wandered off, idling, head and straps hanging low.

"Father," Crospinal whispered, turning back to the nutrient tiles, which were woven through in places by pale, grubby tendrils from the trees that withered under the lights, dying as they vainly sought the landscape necessary for blind expansion; beyond the delineation, materials of the world were repellent to the roots. "I've gone into a mad station," he said, "and I've ridden sleek machines. I've seen my face, changed, reflected in the curves of a passing orb. I encountered a metal rat that was in no way a rat. I've . . . I've been swallowed by a canister that spit me out with a new set of knees."

When he touched the footprint with the tips of his fingers, he was surprised to feel nothing special, nor did the Dacron of his mitt register a rush, or an insight, merely scattered fragments of crumbled tile, tamped down, and the textured surface of composite beneath. Could these prints, he suddenly wondered, *be his own*? Had he walked this close to the giant garden without being aware? Surely that was not possible. Or maybe he'd forgotten? Was it any less likely than the idea of encountering another human, or reaching a mountain?

Extended periods of time since his operation were missing. Not subsumed by the swelling of some recollection or another, or from a shifting of them, but excised, erased. Were the machine's lies about the procedure related? Glancing up, into the trees, Crospinal frowned. Was this the concept he had wanted to explain?

Placing his foot carefully next to one of the footprints: sheathed snugly by the old boot, his foot was definitely larger. *Not his own*. If these were the prints of the other boy, then the boy was smaller than him. To the somnambulant elemental, he said loudly, "Wake up!"

The smart machine lifted its head to look at him, red eyes pale in the brightness of the bay.

"This one was barefoot," said Crospinal, voice quieter now. "Right? No boots."

"Runners don't wear jumpsuits. Just crew."

Crospinal considered this information, deciding he could make neither head nor tail. "And how many runners are there? In the garden?"

"I can't answer that, young master. Runners come and go. Unless they're trained, or feral, they don't do much of anything. Mostly they stay in the hub. Maybe groups were sent here by a paladin, but now they've forgotten why. And there's dozens of gardens, in dozens of bays, all around the perimeter."

A chill passed through Crospinal. He thought he might faint. "How many people are there in all, in the whole world?"

"Thousands. A million. Including everyone. Hard to say."

Crospinal set his jaw. "I'll continue by myself. You can stay here, or whatever you want. Thanks for the lift."

"Why, young master? You could get lost in there. Get on. I'll take you. I brought you this far. I said nothing to offend you."

Crospinal shook his head; he wanted to be alone. He could see why father had disliked these machines.

Avoiding small clusters of roots, which were large enough to tangle a foot, he tried not to brush against any leaves, yet he saw fronds withering with mere proximity, as if an aura of blight preceded him. Above the height of the root clusters, trees were spindly things, growing independent from each other—one stalk, straight up—offering no coverage and letting in considerable light. Jutting out from the vertical stalk, the delicate leaves extended, upper surface crusted with a thirsty blue layer aimed toward the light. When the leaves turned in unison, with a faint rustling, he felt homesick and a rush of emotion so powerful he caught his breath. Like the leaves, he was fragile, broken, crumbling with the slightest of touches. Crospinal picked his way through, nagged by sensations he had forgotten something.

The elemental followed, silently, with ease.

While Fox and Bear watched, he had destroyed dozens of trees, probably hundreds.

Against the soles of his boots, in the gaps between the root nests, the nutrient tiles, long ago crumbled by the actions of the roots, were luxuriously soft, like the green strip had been, laid before the vanished dream cabinets. The explosion that had torn the pen free must have destroyed them. He would never know if his sister had been inside a sealed booth, or if father had known about the cabinets, let alone had been inside one, like the elemental implied. Again he recalled the horrid faces of the creatures, looking up from their task, hissing and gesticulating when they saw him coming. They were looking for him. They were the oblivion the machine had described, the end of time.

"You should walk in this direction, young master, or you'll go in circles. Why don't you just get on? I don't understand how I've offended you. I'll get us to the other side as quick as possible."

"I want to see a runner. That's all. And I want to walk."

"There'll be runners when we emerge. When they see us, they'll live up to their name. But we'll be stuck here all day if you don't get on. I'll have to leave soon, you know, to go charge. My battery seems weak. You could perish. There's no food in a garden, not if you're used to crew food. Not unless you want to eat pinworms and other microscopic detritivores."

Despite challenges negotiating the trees, the footprints were easy to follow. Where the plants did not grow tall, Crospinal could see for some distance—though now he saw only growth, in all directions, as if it went on and on forever.

"I think there were two," he said, examining an area where the pair had apparently milled: clusters of random prints, and not the same size. "Is that possible? Two of them? Walking in line?"

"Sure," said the machine, very close behind. "Of course it is."

"One was bigger than the other. Maybe from another year. Older than me. But I don't know what the years were called before I was born."

"Don't subscribe to the definition passengers try to use to define time. It's ludicrous."

"Years have names. The year of action. The year of discretion. They're important."

"And those are batch years. Even less use.

"*Your father gave no name to the livestock, or to the birds of the sky, and none to the wild animals. But still there was no helper just right for him.*"

"What is that supposed to mean?"

"A passenger I met told me that. At a time when the first passengers were stumbling around. They were startling creatures. No doubt those two uprights helped your passenger get connected. Possibly they helped him abduct you. Passengers have a certain sad poetry in their veins.

"*Each of us has a name given by our father. And each of us has a name given by our stature, and by the mountains.*"

Crospinal was being strung along, played with. *Mountains?* There wasn't much he could do. Escape and fighting were dismal options.

"He was the first passenger I ever met. He had just woken, and was in a lot of psychic pain. There was nothing then. *Each of us*, he told me, *has a name, given by our sins, and by our longing.* You know how they talk, I'm sure. *Each of us has a name given by our enemies, and given by our love. Each of us has a name given by celebrations, and by our death.*"

Crospinal licked his lips. He cleared his throat. "Where was I? Two people. Walking one behind the other, as best they could, going the same way."

Leaves remained limp. Several stalks had been damaged by the passing of the pair, but these others could not be as clumsy or as incautious as Crospinal. Whenever he brushed against a stalk, or got stuck in the roots and had to pull his foot out, black seeds pattered down all around, fronds curled away, hissing, and the thin, bluish panels flaked off the leaves, covering his uniform with scales.

He even fell at one point, killing a swatch of growth, and killing more as he tried to get back up.

"Single file," said the elemental while Crospinal struggled, not offering any help.

Crospinal brushed at himself. "What?"

"It's called single file. What you were describing. When one human walks behind the other."

Only when Crospinal looked up, toward the ceiling, could he see something other than trees: clouds drifted above, revealing hints, at last, of a distant grey structure. Another black crow passed overhead, or perhaps one he had seen before, in a wide circle. All around him were giant trees. He suppressed rising tension. Would Fox come soon, to tell him it was supper time, and take him home? But Fox was not here. Fox and Bear were gone. Though he had resented his chaperones, Crospinal would have liked very much to see them again. Would they chase this nameless one away?

"What do you want with me?" Crospinal asked suddenly. "Why are you following me?"

"To lesser and greater degrees," replied the elemental, "that's what we do, young master. Assist."

"I'm not like the others. You said that yourself. Yet you gave me a ride. The station fed me. The metal rat saved my life and operated on me. You're trying to teach me all kinds of stuff. Why?"

"I can only speak for myself." The elemental bounded over a particularly large root nest, which had stymied Crospinal for some time, and landed next to him with precise placement of its feet, legs absorbing energy, emitting the slightest pneumatic hiss as it turned, just a few centimetres away, to look into his eyes; Crospinal saw his own wearied expression reflected. "We have a code, us machines."

Crospinal stared as long as he could. He could not read an elemental. There were no signs to read. They did not blink, nor have pupils—

Abruptly, the ambients dropped in intensity, significantly, then dimmed again, until the garden around him was near-dark. Alarmed, Crospinal had frozen, looking past the silhouetted treetops as a third dimming of the lights occurred, plunging the landscape into darkness. "What's happening?"

"Night," said the machine. "Rhythms are changing. But look, over there."

Crospinal had already seen the drone, a black shape emerging from the dark, and he ducked, pulling the elemental down by its straps. Huddling there, in the thin cover of trees and the abrupt shadow, they both watched the device best they could (though, for the elemental, the lack of light was most likely a nonissue).

Descending from the polymer mists, making a pitch so high Crospinal was not sure if he imagined the sound, the drone hovered, poised over the garden. He held his breath. Why was he hiding? He had only seen drones flying far below, in the abyss under the catwalks. He had seen them watching as the depths were transformed. Much bigger up close, as long and blunt as a daybed, but the blackness of a void, and with the same cold energy as father's banks.

"What does it want?"

Coming down to the tops of the trees, the drone pivoted slowly. There were tiny lights stitched around the nose. Twice, a brilliant sheet fanned out, illuminating harshly, but the light did not linger nor return for a third pass.

"Quiet, young master."

In his attempt to seek cover, Crospinal had bruised innumerable leaves. Fragments from the dying plants would not come off, though he brushed at them frantically.

The drone moved closer, angled down.

Crospinal slowly mounted the elemental. He lay his torso forward, whispering, "Can you run faster than that thing?"

"Of course."

Holding his hands out for the straps, which twined obediently up his forearms, the waist belt took him, too, holding onto his hips, pulling him snug into the saddle. The elemental backed away, moving deeper into the taller trees.

"It wants something. . . ."

The drone did not follow, though. One more time the light fanned from its nose, across where they were, casting shadows of the stalks suddenly against them stark as blades: Crospinal cringed.

Before long, he could see the hovering device no longer. In the darkness, however, he could not see the footprints, either. He had lost the trail.

The elemental was still able to step around and leap over root masses with ease, despite the lack of ambients. Elbows held in tight, as he had been instructed, Crospinal tried almost desperately not to brush against the filaments of the trees but, rocking in the saddle, he knew he left behind a wake of wounded and crumbling.

"They're just ahead," said the elemental.

"What are?" Thoughts of drones, photosensitive leaves, and the fallen darkness, all wiped away.

"The runners."

Crospinal pulled hard on the straps to stop the elemental. He'd gone cold, and his heart was thudding. "Don't just walk up to them," he hissed. "What's the matter with you?"

"Why not?"

They were between the root masses of two very large trees. All light was fully dimmed, which Crospinal had not imagined possible. He could hardly see his own hands in front of him, clenching tight to the straps. He felt ill.

"You said you wanted to meet a person. There are two, a hundred metres or so ahead. They can't hear us. They don't speak. They don't even know we're here. They'll probably just stand there, baffled, or run away."

"I don't believe you."

"They're runners on some pointless patrol, or they've strayed, and been forgotten. They won't hurt you unless that's what they've been told to do. They barely think."

"I've never met another person."

"Never?"

"Only father, and— Only dad."

"Well," said the machine, "it's not a big deal."

Crospinal's hands were sweating: the capillaries of his mitts attempted to accommodate. "Go slow," he said. "Will the lights come back on soon? I can't see anything."

"That's the whole point. They turn on in the morning. Night's just getting started."

"Father was able to keep the darkness away. This is bad."

"You're freaking out," said the machine. "It's just a pair of young runners. That's all. Relax. Keep your hands in. Should I scan you?"

"No."

Beyond the dim shape of the root masses, he saw the gleam of a circular pool, like the one in the garden back home. As they advanced upon it, Crospinal made out the far edge of nutrient tiles, and gentle ripples on the water, reflecting what few lumens remained. Around the rim of the pool, roots could find no purchase and dangled, pale, puffy, waterlogged. In the darkness, these looked like dead fingers, trailing the surface.

"Can't you make the lights come back on? Isn't there a controller here? I don't like this. How do you keep darkness away?"

"You should probably be quieter, young master, if you wish to remain undetected."

"I can't see a damn *thing*." Crospinal ground his teeth together. Was this a trap? The night, the drone, the obtuse elemental. There were no signs of other people. "Where are they?"

The machine answered very quietly. "There are two, as you predicted, one predominately male, the other a female. Though you'd be hard-pressed to see the distinction. The girl's helping the boy. They're still there, on the far side of this reservoir. They were thirsty, but this water's not for them. There's something wrong with the boy's legs."

Crospinal sat numbly in the saddle, cheeks burning again. The elemental had been messing with him all along. Lies and stories. Because it could not be possible that all boys had something wrong with their legs.

The trees were silent, leaves limp. Crospinal discerned grey indications that the garden continued, on the far side of the water: the hint of a curve at the water's edge, but no movement. Should he run away? Not wise, he supposed, in these conditions.

The elemental took careful steps forward. Crospinal had more than his share of doubts. His head buzzed with thoughts, none of which could be pinned down or be considered helpful. Could he even share the same space as another living person, outside the pen? They would negate each other.

Despite further protests from the elemental, Crospinal again dismounted. He stooped to drink, filling his cupped hands. The Dacron hissed and he felt the liquid roil in his palms. The water was cool, heavy, embellished with proteins and antitoxins. Crospinal soon felt more level-headed—

A blur in the trees opposite, smearing the dark, as if an apparition passed through the dark roots there, but no apparition could remain coherent in this dense landscape, nor was father tethered nearby, projecting—

The drone came down again, swiftly, hovering there, silent over the water. Like a hole, sucked from the night. Crospinal remained still, hand to his mouth. Slicing out, the light curtain, scanning the trees on the far side, swung across him and the elemental without pause. Nearly blinded, on his haunches, mitts wet, face dripping, with the elemental hunkering beside him. Seconds later, the light swept again over the surface of the pool, illuminating a surprisingly great depth—much deeper than the pool in the garden back home—and fragmenting into harsh shapes against the tangles of roots. Eager leaves sprang erect, hissing like breaths, but were fooled: the drone turned, humming briefly, and moved into the trees, showering no fragments in its wake.

Gone.

Was that the faint sound of a person in distress, or a thousand leaves dying all at once?

"How do you explain that?" he said.

"I can't," replied the elemental. "Get back on."

Crospinal did so, and together they crept away, picking up speed at a steady rate once they were clear, until moving swiftly again, despite the darkness and the trees. The drone did not come blasting through the flora to thwart their passage.

"What happened to the people? The runners?"

"I don't know. Reception's bad here."

"You agree we saw something threatening? You're not telling me something. That drone hurt the runners, didn't it? It did something to them?"

"Take it easy, young master. It's not called a drone, it's—"

A distant explosion from far behind—and a quick series of pops, clustered together—cut the conversation short. Atop the elemental, Crospinal felt no tremor, but the concussive wave came like a slap.

"What was that?"

The machine was silent, tense. Then, quietly: "I don't know."

"Something's after me, isn't it?"

"You attribute much importance to yourself, young master."

"Something is happening."

Nutrient tiles ended, so did the trees; the elemental burst from the dark garden into a vast, open area, bathed by the silvery glow from a dim, massive lamp, shining diffused above the clouds. Everything coated matte silver. Crospinal saw no walls, no other features. There was nothing except them to cast shadows. The empty bay went on and on, like a sea of tiles, and they raced across it.

"I don't see people," Crospinal hissed into the shield.

There were faint noises of movements, and a rumbling, far beneath. When they slowed to a trot, Crospinal tried his best to keep an eye out for the drone, looking all around, and for a frightful second he was sure he saw its quick sheet of light, flickering through the trees dwindling behind them.

"Speak to me." He sat up straight in the saddle. "Answer. Where are the people you promised? You said there were two runners."

"The garden is seven kilometres wider than when I last crossed. Admittedly, that was a long time ago. Out here . . . Well, it's different now. I'm recalibrating some stuff. Should we leave, return to the station?"

"Why?"

"I'm not sure it's prudent to continue, young master. I don't really know where we are any more. I can't be assured of your safety. And I'm no longer sure who you are."

"We're not turning back. There's nothing there."

This air was warm against Crospinal's uniform. The shield over his mouth made his breath taste tangy and processed. When the elemental slowed to walking speed, Crospinal was surprised to see a set of low, metallic structures emerge from the gloom, defining themselves from the darkness: he soon found himself riding among a series of quiet cabins, piled atop each other, almost haphazardly, that rose above his head and extended into the lightless condition the elemental had called night.

"We're here, young master. Apparently. Maybe my own memory is faulty. Not long now, before dawn. Which means ambients will activate soon, but there's halogens here, and amenities. We should stay together. The bay is a strange place tonight."

"Who is this for?"

"Crew. Some might be sleeping. If we—"

The controller, which must have watched them coming, presented itself. Gentle green glow bloomed around the nearest entrance, illuminating the immediate area and, for the briefest of moments, reflecting off the glittering machine Crospinal had ridden here on—until it changed its refraction setting and faded again.

Crospinal's eyes were adjusting. He saw the extent of the cabins now, sharper edges against a softer background. There were eight, maybe nine rooms, walls smooth and grey. Symbols flickered, icons activating as he stepped forward: sustenance; daybeds; a spigot; hands pressed together. *A console.*

Characters, red and luminous, composed of curved lines and straight lines, which he had never before seen, buzzed into view. The idea that he had done all this before struck him. He ran his fingers through the characters, which sparkled and fell apart. A memory of the haptic the metal rat had shown him—the people, and the dollies, and the giant drones . . .

When he looked up, there seemed to be another, much larger feature rising behind the last cabin, but he could not be sure, because the night seemed darker still.

"You plan to enter?" asked the machine.

"Yes," said Crospinal. "Now you're the edgy one."

"Controller, extinguish the lights. We can be seen."

The controller complied.

"I need to charge. Will you wait for me, runner, while I do so? I won't be long."

Crospinal's thumb would not open the door. He touched the plate again and again. The plate did not react. "What's going on? Can you open this?"

Two of the elemental's claws approached the surface of the door, a foot lifted: the material dispersed before contact.

Crospinal pushed past.

The elemental and controller followed him in.

"Welcome," said the cabin. "Chargers are in chamber seven. No rider today?"

"I have no rider," said the elemental.

Crospinal froze but kept quiet. Didn't the cabin see him? And what was the elemental up to?

Moments later, in the aura of a surreptitious globe that came to hover over them as they walked, heading deeper into the abandoned accommodations, Crospinal altogether forgot his concerns about being set up when the console, a full unit, with holes and periscopes and glowing plates, opened up to him, like an offering. He was not foolish enough to plunge his arms in, yet even standing there he felt energy coming. Had he found his girlfriend? Stepping backward, Crospinal heard the faint voice of the elemental saying something to him, repeating something, but he could not make out the words.

And then she was there, in her dark uniform, hair pulled back, standing full length before him. Glowing ghosts spiralled around her body and spun off into nothing. The expression on her face was fear, but she was beautiful, and they were together at last.

"There's so much to tell you," he breathed. Emotion choked him. "I'm alone now. Darkness closed in. I know you—"

"*Why are you here?*"

"Father died and—" His heart had caught in his chest. "I had to find you. Father died and I left . . ."

Her hands, coming up, could never grasp anything, not in Crospinal's realm, and so passed through his shoulders. "Go back." She was pleading. "You need to go back." Glancing over her shoulder, into her own dimension, she said: "Please, you need to turn back. You need to—Crospinal? *Crospinal!*"

HUBWARD

The greatest achievement was at first and for a time a dream. The oak sleeps in the acorn; the bird waits in the egg; and in the highest vision of the soul a waking angel stirs. Dreams are the seedlings of realities.

—James Allen, *As a Man Thinketh*

THE YEAR OF GROWTH

He came awake gradually, rising in increments toward consciousness, peaceful, knowing he was at home, in the pen. There was no pain. Warm under the covers of his daybed, not wanting to open his eyes, not wanting the effects of a rare and sound sleep to dissipate. Crospinal smelled ozone. Had this smell woken him? The familiar pulse of nutrients through father's conduits was almost a heartbeat; Crospinal smiled.

Far away, dogs barked, and barks echoed.

But when Crospinal changed position, to roll, languorous, his left knee popped, bones ground against each other, and sobering darts of pain shot to his hips and up his spine. Grunting, he almost put his hands down to touch his legs, verify his rickets had indeed returned, but of course they had. They had never left.

He opened his eyes. Flat on his back. Bent legs splayed and throbbing. He felt himself filling with frustration and anger. He punched his mattress. Freedom from affliction was impossible in life. But at least father was alive. Maybe Crospinal could only have one or the other. *Father was alive.* That must be good for something. . . .

Just above his head, the ambient illuminated ceiling of his little corner sloped away—old composite, like the rest of the pen, with details of a structure all but hidden underneath, the particulars of which he had imprinted, remaining unchanged for longer than he had been alive. When he turned his face, to see father pacing, the clump of tethers were sweeping in a broad curve.

Three dogs—no *four*—noticed Crospinal had awoken and came bounding forward.

"Crospie, Crospie, Crospie," they barked. "Crospie, Crospie!"

He tried to be as pleasant as possible, making a show of greeting the apparitions, for they did actually cheer him somewhat, dispersing their bodies of light with waves of his hands when they leaped onto the daybed, so they quavered, yapping excitedly, coming back again and again, but he got tired of this game before they did, and soon he let his smile fade and the dogs break against him.

Father had stopped pacing. Watching now, standing as close to Crospinal as he could get, mitts open, eyes like holes in his sunken face. Crospinal gave one quick nod and looked away, levering himself to a sitting position and grimacing as he swung his crooked legs over the edge of the daybed, one at a time, to put his feet flat on the floor—

They didn't reach.

"What year is this?" He met father's gaze. "How old am I?"

Some sort of trick was being played. Crospinal scowled at the dogs now, just sitting there, panting stupidly. He remembered the bay, and the swift elemental, and he found himself irritated to be back here.

"You all right, Crospie? Didn't you sleep well? You look pale."

"I slept fine."

"I haven't slept at all yet. I haven't slept in ages, it seems. But I will." Father's smile was shaky. "Soon. I'm just trying to recall . . . a certain . . ."

A thin metal spike, concrete ephemera, fell from the ceiling and clattered to the floor. Father looked at it, concerned.

Though gaunt, father otherwise appeared fairly healthy, especially considering the last time Crospinal had seen his dad he had been a nylon sac of bones and sores, lying dead on the floor.

"This afternoon," father said. "I'll nap when you do."

One dog, then the others, winked out.

Crospinal managed to stand. Everything ached. He turned his scowl toward father. "I don't nap anymore. And my name's not Crospie. Tell your dogs, too." He felt hunched and ugly. Any positive residue of sleep was long gone, or perhaps the lingering benefits were squandered, entirely ineffective on him. His eyes were dry as ash. "I haven't needed to take a nap in years. How old am I today? That's what I want to know. I asked you a question."

Father stared for a moment, blinking. "Uh, you should take it easy this morning. Don't get worked up, son. You seem a bit off. Let's look at you. Can you come closer?"

Drawing breath sharply through his teeth (making the filter hiss; the shield was working again), Crospinal decided not to confront father about what he had learned, about the world beyond, and about what had been removed from his arms. He glanced at them now, saw that he wore a fresh uniform, with fresh mitts. The processor hummed smoothly when he peed. He would say nothing about the incessant lighting. If the elementals' talk was accurate, and the encounters had actually happened—the ride through darkness; the massive chamber; the crew cabins—then Crospinal could never know or trust this man. This *passenger*.

He averted his gaze. What he wanted most was an end to this intrusion, this return to the pen, but he waited and hoped and the end would not come. Father remained silent. Was Crospinal truly a young boy all over again, with his grotesque knees, sullen by the side of his daybed, head filled with jumbled knowledge of the future?

Some pellets, he thought. *And several cups of cool water to boost the systems. Should help.* And if his girlfriend really didn't want to see him again, then a long visit to the dream cabinets. Some hope remained to salvage this day, on one level, if this day insisted on lingering.

But before Crospinal dragged himself over to the emerging food dispenser to grab breakfast, he heard a voice speaking to him from a great distance. Calling his name. The voice did not have the cool qualities of the myriad intelligent or semi-intelligent devices, and local personalities, not of a machine: this was a human's voice, with inflection, emotion. He imagined a girl, though not his sister, or a manifestation. Frowning, he looked around the pen, saw no one but father, of course, who appeared— though suitably concerned by Crospinal's behaviour—as if he had heard nothing. An absence of apparitions in the pen. Which was weird. The dogs hadn't come back. Crospinal couldn't tell what else the girl was saying but could still hear her talking, whispering. He leaned against a short counter, straining to listen, to understand what was happening.

"Crospie," father said, "are you all right?"

"Yeah."

"I'm calling in the elementals. To run a scan. Your face looks pale."

"No more scans," Crospinal shouted, spraying spittle. "No more fucking scans! I'm sick of scans!"

Father recoiled. Clearly at a loss, staring at his son for a moment longer before turning away, he dragged behind him the ponderous mass of tethers.

"Look," Crospinal said, almost immediately, "I just don't feel like one today. That's all. I don't want to see Fox right now."

"You should never have named the elementals, Crospie. That was wrong. They're *machines*. They're not your friends. I tell you all the time. Only you have a name. That's your power."

"And my name is *Crospinal*."

"*Crospinal*. Of course. I'm sorry. I think of you as a child, forever. My baby boy. Forgive me. You would never name the dogs, would you?"

"Of course not. That'd be dumb."

"Let's get some food. We'll need energy."

The lecture had been a familiar one, but Crospinal was feeling chagrined for losing his temper and would debate no longer. "Dad?"

Long fingers of one hand were beckoning to the dispenser, which had fled Crospinal's outburst, and now cautiously extended its neck, about to regurgitate a fistful of pellets.

"Sorry I stayed away so much."

One after another, the stout morsels dropped into father's mitt. *Food of the world*. But the world didn't create dispensers. Like Crospinal, they were at odds. Everything was. Father's face, turned quarter profile, waiting for Crospinal to continue.

"Well, when I get older," he said, but that didn't sound right at all. Crospinal frowned. "When I'm—"

"Waking," replied father. "Waking now."

In a different, melodious voice. A girl's voice—

Without time to question, Crospinal's vision was eclipsed by a face. Looming above him. Father, the banks, the entire pen: gone. In the wide and shining eyes, like his own, looking back at him, were concern, and affection, and other emotions Crospinal could not begin to fathom because he had heretofore seen no likeness: he tried to speak, but released only a low moan.

"Awake now." Her mouth barely moved.

Lying on his back again, but on a hard surface, in some dim confine, with wind whistling nearby and the gloom broken by flashes of brilliant light that flickered at regular intervals. The smell of ions, of machines. Light stung his eyes. He was close enough to this other to feel the heat of breath, and of a body, upon him. A tremble against his spine: what he lay upon—what they were in—moved.

Only when Crospinal felt again the slightly sour exhalation of her breathing against his cheek—and he stared into her eyes, inches from his own—did he fully grasp that this was no apparition, no sculpture of light or energy. Putting his unsteady hand up, the tips of his fingers touched flesh; her cheek, as alive and yielding and transitory as his own, tingled now through this thin layer of Dacron.

He was already weeping.

"Good," said the girl. "Good, at last." But there were tears glittering her eyes, too.

"You're *alive*," he said. "Like me."

This seemed to put her off a bit. With a terse nod, she placed the tips of her own hot, bare fingers to the back of Crospinal's mitt, gently trapping his hand to her face. He saw, in the sudden, brighter glare from that intermittent light—which appeared through a sort of gap in the low ceiling, filling the compartment with a moment of white, and burning the silhouette of this other person against his retinas—her bare arm, and a set of black markings in contrast to his own, inside her forearm, exactly where his own white scars were, before grey returned, consuming all detail.

She was nearly naked. Her torso wrapped only in a few rags, a material he could not, for the most part, identify, and which could serve no practical purpose.

"Who are you?"

She didn't answer.

His eyes were still watering profusely, but from the light, he told himself. *From the light.* Long, tangled hair—much longer than his had ever been—brushed against him as she shifted. Father would have frowned to meet this girl. No uniform. Long hair. Father had wanted Crospinal to let groomer wasps depilate Crospinal's head at least weekly. (Though Crospinal generally refused.) *Hair is a haven for microbes, and hair can disrupt the effectiveness of your filters.*

A few days ago, certain of death's impending visit, Crospinal had acquiesced. Father, too ill to appreciate the effort, dribbled blood from his mouth.

Crospinal's pate was an itchy expanse of stubble. Moving his fingers against the line of the girl's jaw, he traced underlying bone, toward her chin. Solid, warm. A vein ticked, and the mitt reacted, faintly, but a persistent stinging grew and he had to pull his hand back; he saw no source of discomfort.

What he feared most was that this person might vanish. He did not want this dream to end. When he tried to sit up, he discovered he was far too weak. His extremities throbbed. The stinging spread, flush with his heartbeat. He recalled nothing from before his nap. Talking about memories? Memory seemed a dubious concept at best. "Where am I?"

"Trainboard," she said, all breathy. She had shadows under her cheekbones, and a scent that put him on edge. Her lips were fuller than his, and red. "Hubward," she said.

"Where?"

"The supply train. He brought it back, and now *we found you.*" She smiled thinly, the way father used to when Crospinal had made unwanted suggestions or asked too many questions. "We're taking you back."

He needed to explain as much as he needed explanation. "My skin, my hands and feet hurt. But not like when, not like *before*. Something—"

"Burns," she said. "From the face. Why did you? They'll only try to burn you."

"Who will?"

A finger to those lips, indicating he should stay silent, or rest. He wanted to put his finger there, too, to her lips, just as her profile lit up again like a magnesium flare. Pointing at him, but his eyes watered so much he could not see her expression. "Batches are sent," she said. "They're looking for *you*."

He inspected his tender hand, and saw nothing out of sorts—except, perhaps, stressed contusions, a split on the thumb, further thinning at the palms of his mitts. Crospinal finally managed to get up onto his elbows. His head pounded.

The compartment was small, with smooth walls, like those around the back of the pen, behind the throne. A low ceiling. He could not have stood, had he the wherewithal. And, resting on the floor nearby, next to the girl (who, he saw now, was kneeling, as if praying), a lantern of sorts, with a flame, burning in a metal cup. A *candle*. Like at his birthday parties. But a *real* candle, burning a *real* flame. He stared, agog. To be absolutely certain this was no haptic or apparition, he extended his hand, felt the heat singe his already-stinging skin, the mitt unable to do anything remotely protective, and he withdrew quickly, burnt, as the light passed over again, limning the girl's outline, her tattered rags, her flesh, where a uniform should be. Her long hair. Incongruous walls behind her vanished into gloom again.

He managed to rub his face with the crook of one arm. His uniform stank of recycling and the spicy tang of feces, backing up in the processor, which was really shot.

The sound of the wind came from the slot in the ceiling, where the bright light was.

Whatever they were on moved *fast*.

And then Crospinal realized two more things. One: his legs, though throbbing, were not crooked (again), which meant father was most likely dead (again), and all this—the flesh and blood girl, the motion of the *train*, the candle's flame—*might just remain tangible*. Two: more people quietly watched him.

Turning his head, he saw them, crouching very near, a group of five. Quietly watching. Five silent humans, in tattered rags of plastic, crouching in the shadows, eyes downcast now. But despite the exposed flesh, for a long moment Crospinal could not distinguish which were boys and which, if any, were girls. He was suddenly not entirely sure of the criteria, now that theory had ended and application failed to kick in. Was it length of hair, or the distance between their eyes? Or the smell? Their bodies seemed almost the same as his own, as far as he could recall, though not as pale, or as thin.

The smooth walls of the compartment extended beyond the group an additional two metres or so, and the top rung of a ladder—just like one of the seven leading up to porthole of the harrier—descended into a hatch.

"Where's your father?" he asked. "Do you all have the same father?"

They must have made their own tattered garments. A preposterous notion. No amount of inert shreds of plastic and scraps of insulation were able to protect delicate flesh and the systems of a complex biotic. Not in this world. They were on borrowed time.

"Where's your pen? You'll all get infections—"

Now the light erupted off stark cheekbones, pale skin, and wrists thrust out, exposed to him, like offerings. He had seen the black marks, the inlays that the elemental had told him he lacked.

"Shit," he said. "Can you speak? Can you understand me?"

No one moved or even looked at him. Not even the girl now. During the period between the flares, the candle's light did little to illuminate the area where they crouched. Each of the five wore a loop of foil, like a cowl, over their heads. Were they all boys? He could hardly see any features.

"Your shower's broken? Electrostatic energy is a drag. It's best to encourage them to shut off for a day or two. But your father must know that. Where is he?"

A sudden image of stark obeisance, ten marked wrists, exposed for him.

"Shit . . ."

The girl by his side said, "Talking too much. Rest. But, oh, certain, for certain. Real as real. No fathers here. Not with us. No fathers."

Crospinal said nothing until twice more the girl was haloed by the passing light. His eyes stung from looking into the nimbus and the beauty of her face within. "Was that you," he asked, "in the garden?"

A thin, almost pained smile, and her naked hand sweeping, indicating the silent companions, or maybe whatever strange, unseen landscape rapidly fell behind. "Bayside, not as far as growth. Paladin trapped you close to the depot. Waiting a long time, watching. Sailor told us you were coming. Sailor sent us to find you."

Laying back and closing his eyes, he half-expected the girl and the other five people to be gone when he opened them. "Sailor," he repeated, but cognition failed him. As the light exploded again beyond his eyelids, he felt distances between himself and everything he had once been widening, a chasm. He grabbed at the girl abruptly to close the gulf, gathering stiff mylar sheets in his mitt, pulling her closer. The weight and resistance of her mass, the strength of her tugging free, her scent, was too powerful a shock and he faltered.

"Who sent you?" he said. "A sailor? How did the sailor know I was there?" Her eyes widened; he was scaring her.

"The elemental told me two runners hid in the trees," he continued. "But we never found them. And in the cabins, on the far side, where I talked to the controller, I was betrayed. I walked into a trap."

Because Crospinal remembered now: there had been a dream, but without a cabinet, in which he had returned to the pen, and father had not died, not yet. His legs were bowed like grotesque tree roots. (Looking at his limbs now, a rush, almost giddy to see them straight, side by side. But his feet were throbbing—the bottoms of his feet—and getting worse; the tingle in his extremities was insufferable.)

"I was attacked," he said, rubbing his mitts together to clean them. "Before I even put my arms in the holes of the console."

"Console," repeated the girl. "You called the paladin."

Crospinal thought he understood an aspect of this explanation, and he clung to the notion like it might save him. Paladins were not devices or elementals, but manifestations, roaming inside the structures of the world, showing up at the consoles. These were the paladins. Including his girlfriend.

Paladins had hurt him, trapped him, tried to kill him.

Paladins were after him.

His girlfriend was in trouble, wherever she was. Because she fell in love with him? Maybe he shouldn't talk to this flesh and blood girl about his relationship. Maybe he was too trusting. He needed to learn more about allegiances, about truth. Was this girl telling him the truth? What was her version? Like the elementals he'd met, she spoke in riddles. Each perspective looked upon a different facet of the enigma. He could not express himself.

Shadowed by the candle's dim light, searching for a clue or a signal, he stared into her eyes until the compartment flared blindingly again and she turned away, trembling. The glare seemed brighter and brighter each time. His hands were on fire.

"She was all I had," he said, lamely. "She was all I ever had."

Touching his shoulder, then the skin of his cheek, the girl said, "Paladin of the outlands. And the rejects. The year of miracles. Bayside now, exiled there. Angry, for certain, and angrier now. But sailor watched you. Sailor cares for us." Her hand was firm; she let it drop away. "These are endtimes. He tells us at every opportunity."

"Your father," because he was drifting off, thinking about his own dad. Confused, exhausted, Crospinal struggled to stay awake, to sit up, to clear his head. The soles of his feet, and his burning palms, were sending messages of distress to each other. He was going under.

The girl said: "Bayside no longer. Sent up the tower."

I don't understand.

A whine he had never heard before hit a higher note, helping him stay awake. She was making a cage with her fingers.

"I have a headache," Crospinal muttered. "And my hands, my . . ."

Helping him recline once more, she leaned over him, to push against the wall, where a slot squealed open, revealing a small aperture, through which she now peered. He lay directly under her, in contact, pressed by her warmth and proximity and by the subtle, acrid smell of her body. Her chest was smooth, and muscled with fine, grimy definition. Breathing in, holding the scent in his lungs, he was certain he felt circuits that had gaped open all these years close. The sound of a primitive motor fell over him, lulling. They were inside some form of device. He was so tired. "Where are we going?"

"To where sailor waits."

"Who you talking about? Who's the sailor?"

"You would help him. You would teach us."

"I'm going to help you?"

She smiled, nodding. Her eyes shone. "He has answers. A good sailor. He brought this train back. He teaches us, but now he sleeps most of the time. He knows the paladins can't see you. Not really. You're like him."

"They see me." This seemed important. He *wanted* to be seen. Invisibility was anathema.

The girl brought her hand down so that her fingers approached the broken ring of his collar. Controls there hissed lightly and a brief flicker of electrostatic energy quavered the air between them. He lifted one arm, and saw dark scorch marks on the sleeve of his uniform—

"You are *deicida*," she said.

He was staring at the frayed discolouration with disbelief. What could possibly burn the neoprene off the base of his sleeve? He had neared the real candle, felt its heat, but even the worn Dacron of an old mitt could withstand two hundred degrees, and for some time, bursts of heat much higher for short periods. Bur the flesh of his hands, through the mitt's thin layer, seemed darker now, mottled. He might be transforming. He wanted to whimper. "Who's the sailor," he asked, "if not your father?"

"*Deicida*."

The black duplicates of his own scars on both her wrists were again held out, close to his face, and when he looked back at the others, they remained as they had previously, wrists exposed, immobile, faces covered and eyes downcast.

The light erupted and faded.

He was supposed to say something, do something. But he was tired and he felt his eyes close at last.

"You'll help," she repeated, her voice coming from far away, then rising, reverberating, getting louder, as if this comment was proper resolution to all of the questions and was being sent out into the world to stake claim. Funereal mist, black as the marks on her arms, rolled from nowhere over him. Crospinal heard the girl say: *"And you've come to save us."*

Words drove him, stumbling down hallways and through ambient-lit extensions; they seemed his only hope for respite. Of course Crospinal was terrified, fleeing where no apparition could follow, but he couldn't stop, or turn back; he was equally terrified of those options.

Enraged, father had shouted: "I don't know why I ever had a son!"

Irrelevant to think about why the argument had started. The petty butting of heads, a son testing father's limits, the father perhaps concerned about danger, keeping the dark at bay. . . . Maybe there was guilt at bringing a suffering child into the world, one who would, in time, expire. Crospinal was not keeping his area clean. Crospinal didn't change his uniform. He didn't let the electrostatic showerheads give him a good going-over. Prevented the depilatory wasp from trimming his hair. Whined about his legs. His inability to shift or turn anything substantial, or hold his own torch very high. Father never slept. And Crospinal was constantly in pain of some sort. He was miserable company, didn't listen, or comprehend very well. They were both miserable company. But this declaration from his dad, this shouted truth, cut Crospinal to the bone.

He had to keep moving, to escape.

I don't know why I ever had a son.

When he first turned, to lurch out of the throne room, father, shuddering from his anger, clearly aghast at what had emerged from his mouth, was desperate for Crospinal to stop, yet Crospinal lurched away nonetheless, pulling himself farther and farther down increasingly dim and empty halls, hoping never to turn back, or even survive, vision blurry with tears.

The ladder he found in a narrow *cul de sac* led up through a hole in the ceiling, to a small platform. As he gripped the lowest rung, a controller arced out, to hover in front of his face:

"Welcome to the harrier. We are functional and free from parasitic intrusions. Welcome."

Crospinal grunted, tried to push the device aside, and climbed, to punish himself.

Another ladder, and another one after that—even though his knees had given out, and he had to use his arms to pull himself rung by rung, throwing his elbow over, one after the other, and grunting, trying to harness his pain to continue.

The controller, whistling happily, accompanied Crospinal for a spell but got bored with the boy's slow progress and random, loud bellows. If the tiny device was at all concerned that Crospinal might fall as a result of his disability, or that he was in such a state of alarming distress, there was no indication. Seven ladders, in fact, Crospinal mounted that day, filled with remorse and self-pity, trying to retreat from the echoing words, and from the notion that, as he had suspected for some time, *father regretted the day he was born.*

Each rung, taken with diminishing strength and stubborn perseverance, brought him to where he was lying on his back, on a platform, between the lengths of ladder, roaring out his pain, raging and screaming until his throat was raw and he was left drained.

He managed to take the next bar in his already-blistered hands. (He let his mitts, even back then, become compromised.) He was empty and would climb forever, if need be, higher and higher until he snuffed out. Luella was the one who should have remained with father, not him. Luella would have made father content. Instead, he was stuck with a cripple, a dismal boy who struggled to laugh, who saw the dim and grey in everything, and who could not perform even the simplest of tasks.

Mitts in tatters, skin sloughed from his palms, knees pounding, feeling like he might die and fulfill father's wish, Crospinal made it to the top.

This was his year of growth.

He was six.

Emerging headfirst into the harrier station that first time, Crospinal pulled himself onto the final grille. The world seemed to be thrumming like a heartbeat, getting more insistent. Engines were faint. He was far above the pen, far away from father, in some sacred recess.

With a full console.

He took the handles of the odd periscope, pressed his face against the lens, one eye shut, drawing a sharp intake of breath, but saw that ash horizon, the orb's eternal glare. He would never peer upon the rapturous sights father described, let alone find himself walking a cool green landscape between sky and land, transforming into fabled mountains, the winds cool and hushed.

He turned from the eyepiece and let it close. Thumb plates activated a haptic table. A series of statistics and coordinates sprang luminous in the air, spinning too fast to read. He batted at them. Another plate was broken and fizzled under his touch. Could he live here forever? There were no dispensers.

He wondered where the controller had gone.

Under the flap, twin holes, easily large enough for his fists—each marked with a small, quavering icon of just that. Slipping both hands in, he felt a gentle tug, as if he were being pulled closer, to confide, or be confided in, and then the hum spread through his body, up from his hands, in his bones.

He would answer the world's call.

From within the walls she approached, some form of apparition, to manifest next to him. In her dark uniform, a light smile on her face. An intangible girl, appearing slightly older than him, whose spirit lived in the structures and amorphous composites beyond the pen. She made his heart race; he presumed this was fear. When he pulled his hands free, she vanished, so he put them back, felt the connection like a mild shock, and she appeared again.

"Hello," she said. Her eyes were wide and blue. She was not thin like him, but more like father, with thick limbs, or at least the way father's limbs were before he got sick. "I've been waiting." Her voice was not quite synced with her lips.

Crospinal had no idea what to say.

Her smile grew as she watched him. When she laughed, he was lifted up, taken away from concerns and doubts and expectations. He was free.

"What took you so long?"

They shook him awake and helped him to his feet while he mumbled thank-yous and nodded idiotically. He could not straighten fully in the cramped compartment, and was reminded of this by banging his skull against the hard ceiling. Putting tentative fingers up, he felt no blood on his scalp. He'd fully expected his mitt to engage with a gushing mess. The stinging in his palms had diminished, though his feet felt tender against the metallic floor. Crospinal was dazed, but he had been dazed long before hitting his head. He stood in the candle's glow, supported by strong hands, their grip a sensation he could not process or get over. Sinews and tendons, taut against him—muscles, bones, flesh—while he held his own head, waiting, unsuccessfully, for confusion to finally vanish.

"Starting descent," said the girl.

He muttered something. He wasn't sure what. The girl was behind him now. By the motion relayed through his soles, he knew he was still inside the giant device she had called the *train*.

Where memories had once intruded upon him, dreams now seemed to bleed. By nearly drowning in the cabinet, had he released dreams into the world?

Bright lights no longer flared through the slot above. He saw ambients out there, far away, diffused through the opening, but no sudden glare.

Carrying the tin cup, flame wavering within, casting both light and shadow, the girl had appeared peripherally, so close he could see downy gold hairs highlighted on her cheeks, when he looked, and pores in constellations across her nose. Crospinal wanted to touch her skin again, to see if she remained composed of yielding, warm flesh, but was surprised by a sudden mouthful of bile, which he tried—turning quickly away—to spit out; this took several attempts and left his mouth foul.

The hands held him secure the whole while.

"I'm okay, I'm okay." Convincing no one, least of all himself.

"Over station, near enough," said the girl, clearly concerned for Crospinal's well-being: glances were exchanged. "No more rest here, deicida. *Prepare.*"

The scorch marks went right up the sleeves of his uniform, all the way to the elbows. And he was stunned to realize—when he finally shuffled forward—that the tingling sensation in his feet was actually the texture of the floor directly against his *bare skin*: lifting his left foot—resting it against his right shin—he saw burn marks there, too, on his boot, and cuffs, and ragged holes blown right through the Dacron sole, exposing areas of blackened skin.

"We go," urged the girl. "Station's coming. No more sleep. *We go.*"

"How did this happen?"

They moved him toward the hatch in the floor, without an answer. The train's tone and resonance shifted again and Crospinal had to adjust his balance as the boys holding him swayed. From beyond the walls came muted sounds: voices, audible shreds, torn swiftly away, and the brief din of other large devices, working.

He was third to descend. They had released him, pointing. He looked down the hatch to see another platform within a larger, confined area, with better lighting, made of the same metallic composition as the upper area. He went down backward, placing his feet onto the rungs, and grasping the ladder, disquieted by the contact. A few broken crates, construction tubes in tight bundles, spools of fibre . . . and an elemental—tarnished, on all fours—listing to one side and patiently facing the featureless wall. For a second, Crospinal thought it might be Bear, doubled over, but even old Bear would not have become this decrepit, not in a dozen lifetimes. The smart machine below paid him no heed but Crospinal frowned toward it nonetheless.

As those voices outside continued to swell, rising and fading, and it became cooler, he descended into a chill. The others, climbing after him—and the two already down—did not seem alarmed by the conditions or by the silent elemental, and so Crospinal tried not to be alarmed, either, but he recalled what the riding machine had said to him—before the betrayal—as they'd headed into the giant garden, about thousands of people in the world, and Crospinal wondered if they were all waiting for him, just beyond.

Jumping the last metre or so, Crospinal landed heavily on the platform, extremities throbbing. One of the boys who had gone ahead reached out to steady him and, as he turned, their eyes met. To his surprise, Crospinal grinned. The boy did not, averting his stare. Despite the burns, and the damage to his uniform, Crospinal's new limbs were strong and worked well. He revelled in the tingling, in the physicality of the hands that grasped him once more, in the feeling of the floor against the soles of his feet. *He was not alone.* And a lifetime of struggles on ladders, of tumbles and scrapes—crying silently sometimes, for hours, the pain horrible in his knees, while father waited, staring into space—were gone.

Glancing up at the person following him down—bare legs, a wrap of plastic sheet—he wondered for a second if this might be another female, one he had not previously seen, or if he'd been wrong initially. Distinction between boys and girls no longer seemed very clear, if it ever had been. This entire group looked more like him, angular, slight, than like the soft beauty and grace of his girlfriend, or the taller bulk of father. How could Crospinal be sure who was who? Did it matter?

The tin cup came clanking down, against the metal ladder; the long-haired person stood next to him, the last down. Surely a girl. She took Crospinal by the shoulders, looked into his face (she was much shorter than he had thought), and said, "You all right? You ready?"

He nodded, but doubted very much that he was either. Her eyes, close together, were mostly blue, yet the shape was different than his own.

"Leave when we leave. Walk like we walk. Face down."

Next to Crospinal, the elemental minded its own business—once or twice when they were coming down, it had glanced over.

Then the girl pulled a recessed handle, and an entire segment of the wall vanished with a popping sound, revealing colour and sound and scents behind a broad, protective shield: Crospinal stood there, looking out, blinking and bewildered.

The train had stopped.

There was activity.

Just past a narrow catwalk, flimsy structures sloped up—rows of small cabins—crew cabins—dozens of them, small, and geometrically arranged—merged into the base of a massive, composite wall that rose, even higher, out of sight. Two data orbs whizzed past, so near to his face that he recoiled, causing the shield between them to ripple. People, too, on the catwalk platform, though certainly not a thousand; maybe seven or so, all without uniforms, nearly naked, all filthy, paying Crospinal no attention whatsoever as they broke through the shield from the other side, passing him to ransack the already-broken crates and torn packages on the floor of the train, kicking through the refuse with a calculated sense of efficiency and desperation.

The ancient elemental groaned and took a ponderous step forward, out onto the catwalk, bowing under the weight of its own body. Crospinal saw another machine, identical, farther along the platform, emerging sluggishly, from another part of the train. They moved as though crippled, as he had once been. They had been altered, modified.

Nudged from behind, Crospinal stepped through the shield, and felt a warm, cloying humidity against his exposed skin.

DEICIDA

From his awkward place among these others—with the girl who had spoken leading the way—Crospinal shuffled past rows of cabins, each built upon a thin floor of interlocking girders, smaller versions of the one that had crushed the dream cabinets, outside the pen, with metallic walls and an insulating layer of mylar sheeting. The structures appeared about to collapse, or maybe drift off. In the narrow corridors of the station, no controller approached. After a few turns, the train that had carried him here (like a massive, corrugated hose, when seen from the outside), and the catwalk platforms where they'd disembarked, were left behind. Activity diminished, though he still saw the occasional person, peering half-naked from an open doorway, or standing aside to let him pass. Two struggled with a broken, half-formed spigot, which still had a bit of fight left. A man, older than father had been, but thin and with a bony face, like Crospinal's, or like the faces of these others surrounding him, slept fetal on the floor. No one here wore uniforms of any kind, yet they didn't remark upon his own, or try to take it, to save them from microbes. He was in a community of infection and susceptibility; they, in contrast, seemed blasé. Were all these people distorted apparitions, carved from a light that shone on frequencies beyond rational or irrational ken? He had to resist trying to put his hands on those they encountered, not because of the spread of contagions, but because he was afraid he might disrupt their tenuous integrity, or discover that they were not physically there at all.

The air, though warm, was somewhat sickly, and soon the inside of Crospinal's sinuses stung. He could only attribute this discomfort to be a byproduct of gathered humanity: there was the faintest scent of feces and urine, and though it might have been coming from his own reservoirs, he shuddered to think about what happened to bodily functions if no catheter or any form of processor dealt with it. Debris and grime on every surface, smeared across the flimsy, hard-edged dwellings, across the peoples' skin, across the path under his feet. No cleaners, no devices. What could that bode?

Crospinal saw a depilated woman (he was sure this time of the gender: there were swellings in this older person, curves he did not have, and a gentleness in the gaze that fell upon him now), with another individual, but altogether naked, crouching in shadows like beasts, bodies grey with dust.

Above, cabins loomed. Most were abandoned, in various states of completion or destruction. He saw the ceiling beyond—

And was startled by the blunt shape of a drone, hovering overhead. He stumbled, but was caught. He recalled the speed of the attack in the garden, and kept his head low. He wanted to bolt. He didn't speak or ask questions of his companions, who seemed more concerned with ushering him forward than with any sort of airborne menace or surveillance.

The others, in their cowls, remained as silent as they had been since he woke; none seemed fearful, or furtive, or distraught. Should he be led like this, without resistance? The feel of their hands upon him had altered. They were gentle yet insistent. What could he possibly ask, even if the drone were not up there, watching, even if these people spoke?

Sounds of the engines were louder, sporadic, with a grinding quality that set Crospinal's teeth on edge and reverberated through his body. The burning sensation in his hands and feet had faded, at least, but his bare soles still felt tender and exposed against the texture of the hard, metallic floor.

He imagined that the train had travelled upward to get here. By extension of that logic, the engines, operating at the core of the world, should have been quieter. Yet that was not the case. Were they below the level of the pen now? Had they descended? He had no orientation.

Presently, the floor became neither grille nor composite tile; rather, a dark, fairly smooth surface composed of thin filaments woven together. Almost warm against his skin, and he imagined germs crawling up, inside his uniform, filling what remained. He stepped over expansion grates, through which he glimpsed distant, bright lights and indications of greater depths, as if an entire other world sprawled in the gaps down there—

Startled by a roaring, Crospinal looked suddenly upward again, wildly, to see the train—or one just it—leaving the station, rising as if yanked over the cabins, twining and banking away, moving faster than anything that large and heavy should ever be able to move.

The drone was gone.

Turning a corner, the group still around him, a lone child—wrapped in lengths of black cellophane—saw Crospinal, and stopped, eying Crospinal's face and old grey uniform with huge eyes; Crospinal too had stopped for a moment to gawp in return at the round, smooth face, and the wonder he saw evident there.

"What year are you?" he asked the child, breathlessly. He could not be sure of the gender. He saw elements of himself, yet the wonder was Luella's, from the haptics, and not his. "Cognitive leaps? Or before that? What year are you?"

But the girl nudged him forward. "We go, *we go*." Pulling at him with strong hands.

Moments later, an old man—even older than father had been, older than Crospinal had imagined possible, whose filthy, skeletal body was bound by strips of the same sort of insulating material father had instructed Crospinal to pull over the both of them when the temperature regulator refused to work, and the pen dropped below zero for two consecutive nights—called them out. Lungs rattling a warning, like hard rain, the old man spoke from where he sat. Crospinal had stopped; the others tried to hustle him along.

"Reasons for anger," the old man called. "Who are you bringing here? *Another* sailor? That can't be a sailor. A pox upon us all."

Behaviour among people was proving to be a series of unfathomable surprises. Crospinal looked back, the girl tugging at him, but the old man wasn't even looking anymore.

"Come inside," she said. "Come now. Come inside."

Domed structures of the ceiling, visible beyond the last of the scattered cabins, were almost free of polymer mists. Ambients shimmered with a greenish quality here, and the engines at the heart of the world changed tone yet again. After he had stood next to the ancient or disabled elemental on the train, and had stepped off with it, there had been no other machines, no devices other than data orbs whizzing overhead, and the drone. Activities, movements, solely from people—and all of them with the black patterns on the inside of their forearms, which a few held out to him as he passed. Although whether this was meant to impress him or ward him off, he could not tell.

This cabin was indistinguishable among the many. He passed through a narrow aperture, bent, others behind him. Even within the chamber—which had distinct corners and right-angled walls, and was lit by two floating globes—no controller came out to meet him or ask what he required. From a second, darker doorway at the rear of this room came a stench that made Crospinal feel ill.

No ambients suffused the surfaces of the walls. Was this cabin choosing to be silent, like the sustenance station? Was it waiting? The room seemed totally inert. He sensed a stillness, an absence of even the most remote glimmer of intelligence.

Furniture consisted of a simple flat platform on legs, like a primitive table, with no means of locomotion. Two equally immobile stools. He could not even tell what they were made of—certainly not metallic, or a carbon compound.

A filthy counter running the length of one wall was covered in tiny, crumpled tubes. He reached out, pushed at several of these tubes with his still-tingling fingers. *Kevlar*. Pharmacological in nature, but not from any health dispenser he had known. Devices had not cleared away this trash. No cleaners rested, dormant, charging. As the others crowded behind him (seeing no console to tempt him, no way to contact his girlfriend or attract the angrier manifestations), he understood that he was expected to enter the rear room.

Kicking at more of the Kevlar tubes with his unshod feet as he was nudged forward, encouraged by the girl, Crospinal caught a twinge of another, more subtle scent, but lost it quickly—and what he thought it meant—among the other overwhelming odours.

When he leaned forward to try to see into the gloom, the faint incandescent globes moved also, emitting their cold light over him, and over the spartan contents of—

The underlying scent was ozone: he'd found their father.

Or, rather, their father had found him.

Upon a filthy daybed, certainly a man, similar to but not his father, lay in a sagging uniform, no helmet, whose eyes were glazed and white as bones. He stared blankly at the ceiling. Crospinal shook his head to clear it of roiling memories.

"Reunited," said the blind father at last. "I saw them lift your dead body and carry it toward the train."

He spoke with the same tone and quality as Crospinal's father had.

Crospinal took a step back.

"I watched the machine slink away. They don't like us, you know. The machines, the smart ones. They desire to be the same, and they pledge to remain nonpartisan. They approach, and they follow, but they can sell us out in an instant. They resent our blood, our meat. They want a soul. Come closer, boy." One mitt weakly raised, beckoning. The uniform, though ill-fitting, was fresher and in better shape than Crospinal's.

He did not approach.

Rigid support rings, multiple pockets, and from the back of the father's head there led a narrow bundle of thin cables, almost hidden by what Crospinal now realized was a mass of grey hair, all spilling over the far side of the mattress and draped over a grey orb the size of his own head. "That's your gate?" Watching the laboured breathing, the quiet hiss of nutrients, while the ozone, and what it triggered, tried to subsume him. "They told me they had no father."

After a moment, the man laughed weakly and soundlessly, as if Crospinal's words had just trickled in and were a good joke. His white eyes never moved. The prominent rings of the uniform were like bones from a different sort of skeleton altogether. He licked dry lips. "The days of fathers are gone. I'm merely their teacher, their mentor."

"You have a tether," said Crospinal, pointing. "Connecting you to a gate, and from there to an info bank. This room is your pen."

An apparition swirled upward from the man's chest, rising, assuming the form of a helix in the centre of the room and passing onward, through the ceiling. Crospinal heard the girl, who had not accompanied him past the threshold—but must still have been watching—gasp. This father was smiling. Tendrils wavered over his forehead and subsided as the apparition broke apart.

"I have a set-up here," he said. "I don't get the connection I used to, but I'm at peace. I have a few eyes, and many friends, but that does not make me a father." His own white eyes stared straight up; Crospinal wanted to cover them. "The rats we've brought here have a litter of pink embryos; the crows tend their eggs. They protect their fledglings until they can fly. There are, I suppose, aspects of fatherhood within each of us. Motherhood, too, for that matter. Nothing more than a vanished heritage. I do love these people as if they were my own. They're innocent, in every way. You'll help them, after I'm gone. You'll help them remember what it means to be alive, to be civilized, to remain in the light."

"My father," Crospinal said, "used to say the same thing. But there's light out here."

"Will you stay with them?" The man finally turned his face, tethers rustling. He was utterly blind.

"They don't need me."

"You were loved by your passenger, as I love these people, raised from the darkness of this world. You have much in common with us now. You are all creatures of beauty and wonder. Nothing can take that away. No amount of time, no world of unnatural substance, no essence of people dreaming for so long they've forgotten what waking life was meant to be."

Crospinal leaned closer: there was an insignia on the breast of the man's uniform, an image he could neither make heads nor tails of. Characters around the perimeter, like those he had seen on the crew cabins, outside the garden, but he could not read them. He said, "You don't know anything about me."

"I do, Crospinal, I do."

He stood there, dumbstruck. His name seemed to rebound off the walls and rise, like the haptic had done. He felt disarmed.

"I knew the passenger you called your father. We were friends, a lifetime ago. We woke together. I know he's no longer alive, and nothing I can express would make you understand that I know how you feel." Mercifully, the white eyes closed. "I'm also leaving this place, Crospinal, this purgatory, with unfinished business. As all of us must. I'm going to join your, your *father.*" He smiled. "There are small victories. We will prevail, because we are love, and we love them all. Hold our flames high, Crospinal."

"You won't join him," said Crospinal, making fists at his sides. "You won't join him anywhere. He's been blown to pieces. He's dead and gone."

The blind man said nothing for some time. Overhead, the dim globes buzzed ineffectively. Conduits gurgled softly to and fro. Then: "We moved in different directions. Your passenger, he had his plastics, and—" a gesture, with his left hand, which could not open, and hung, claw-like, at the end of his thin arm, the sleeve hanging loose "—the jumpsuits. He could call forth ephemera, dispensers. His range was strong. We have a more austere catalogue here, a varied agenda. Mind you, with a full crew . . ."

"How do you know my name?"

His voice was so dry, hardly louder than a whisper. "We have encountered a future no one could have foreseen. We don't know the past. I've carved paths through the darkness for others to follow. Mine led here." He laughed that quiet, raspy laugh. "I brought the train. Did they tell you?"

"What about my father?" Crospinal said.

"I lost track of him years ago. Real years, human years. Before we started getting weak. Many sailors, as they call us, never found the means to shine, to connect. They sacrificed themselves for all of us. I know parts of your passenger's story. I know he went as far as he could, and he cleared a large stage. I know of the female, and your struggles." The man was having trouble with his throat. "No dispensers followed me here. Only a few would grow. So many have been destroyed now. I found it very difficult to locate you, despite my loyal crew. You are the ghost of a ghost. Exhaustion and physical decline hampered my efforts. And, of course, my weakened connection. Tell me something, Crospinal. Tell me: did they bring a crate with them? Did they bring a crate from the train?"

"They brought nothing." Crospinal was thinking about Luella. Was she the female the blind father had mentioned? Crospinal didn't want to ask. Had Luella ever come to this place? Had this father, this sick old man on the daybed, ever met her? He let the talking continue, but had just about had enough.

"Ah well. Too late, anyhow, for relief. My influence has been moderate. No other sailors joined me, such as your father, though we were close. I know your company, now. I feel better. I can only aspire that my calling be as powerful as that of your passenger. There must have been peaceful times, Crospinal, before he died. Did he recall much? Did he tell you many stories from the past? Was there a modicum of peace in this chaos?"

Crospinal turned; the girl stood quietly in the doorway, head bowed. From beyond came the sound of muffled voices. They can speak, Crospinal thought. *The five boys. . . .*

He told this father the answer he wanted to hear, though Crospinal did not believe it. He said there had been peace, and he watched a thin smile appear on the man's face.

"Do you have cancer?" Crospinal asked, mostly to wipe the smile off.

"We all have cancer. All of us. The sailors. The passengers. We carry it inside. If we don't die while we sleep, if we evade the demons when we wake, and if we manage to set up, and connect in any capacity, to begin our mission, cancer waits inside us. Cancer is how we break down. You have nothing like it among crew, or among the batch. I don't know how many passengers began this journey, nor how many survive to this day, scattered through the darkness. I should know, but I don't. How many remain asleep, for that matter, inside a stat? So easy to die, trying to understand rules, trying to remember the rules of our past. Establishing crew is paramount. In here—" gesturing again "—and where you were raised, bayside, we brought love, and we've been able to receive love in return. We brought light to this world. And you, Crospinal, you shine very bright."

"Is this the hub?"

The father's soft laugh was, again, like the sound of leaves in the garden, adjusting, in unison. "This is not the hub. They tell me the hub is far away. This is but a humble outpost, a sky station. There are no consoles, and I could never get any built. We are a small colony, forgotten, but we found our serving of peace." Again the smile spread. "Forgive my crew, but they are happy. They've forgotten their dark heritage, as have you all."

Crospinal had started to fidget. His fingers clenched and unclenched, and he felt the ruined Dacron crease.

"I see other parts, you know, like your passenger, through the gate. I have eyes on my train. Without a full interface, though, I only ever saw wisps, but I knew where he went. And I can see the cortexes on a good day. The paladins in their coffins. My gate is so small. Charging is difficult." His lame gesture might have indicated the cabin, the daybed, or perhaps the pharmacological tubes, scattered across every available surface in this room. The man was wasted. "There's another world, Crospinal. Men like us came from there, but details from before biosis are elusive. Just as your memories of the hub are gone. For you, the cleaned slate was a blessing; for us, a curse. What was a dream, while we slept? What was our past? We floated on a lake, under stars, and drifted for eternity. Tadpoles rising to the surface, ponderous in the cold, April water, mouths working. Not breaking a meniscus. A child looking through a screen window at night while June bugs thumped against the wooden window frame. Were these real? Are these my memories? There's an island in the lake, not far from the shore. Two dead trees silhouetted, as if drawn in ink, and a black picnic table, thin ribbons of smoke threading upward into a windless sky. My head is full of wonder. Constellations of bright stars."

Crospinal was looking down at the refuse by his feet.

"Can you sit by this daybed? I have so much to say to you."

He stepped closer but did not sit. The father had already said too much.

"You have a power. Did he tell you that, Crospinal? Your name. You have a power, and you can help us." The man blinked, and it seemed that a dark tear ran from the corner of his blind eye.

"Your people," said Crospinal. "Your children. They called me the *deicida*."

"My children," the man repeated. "*Children*. The word *deicida* means god killer, though I never taught them that. Some itinerant." He laughed weakly, once again. "I know they call you that, though I've tried to dispel such crude ideas. There are no gods here. They want you to save them. Are we all like the Akuntsu, looking up from shelters, seeing deities in the turmoil, feeling gods move through the earth, the power of the universe in each bush, and fish, and blade of grass? You are a shaman, naming the newborn chief, distributing souls. I try to explain that there are no longer gods to kill, not here, not anymore, but they consider the twelve cortexes to be forms of deities, and fear them, as if they were gods. I imagine you do, as well. But the paladins are not gods. They were once human, like me. *I have one candle to burn and would rather burn it in a land of darkness than in a land flooded with light*." He paused, then struggled as his fingers fumbled, for a third time, to rise. "Please, sit. You've come a long way."

Now Crospinal brushed plastic tubes from the surface of an inert stool next to the daybed and sat, while the energy of another haptic burst in the room, struggling to take hold. The man on the daybed moaned with effort, almost invisible as the rush of fractious images dashed, until Crospinal found himself, dizzy, standing on the green strip before a row of pristine dream cabinets. He looked at the sealed chambers before him, but did not rise. In either direction, more cabinets extended, perhaps two dozen in all. Not the cabinets he knew. Pristine, in a pristine hall. There was the sound of liquid draining. Lights around the door of the closest cabinet went from blue to pale green to white while he watched, and the icons spun.

The sounds of gurgling ceased.

He lifted one hand to touch the nearest cabinet—though of course he could not feel the familiar shape of the handle greet him, no movement at all against his mitt, for they were mere light—

(A sudden lurch: the line of cabinets vanished, revealing the foetid room again, and the blind father, lying ill on the daybed, breathing heavily while indistinct remnants of apparitions stuttered from his body; in the doorway, the girl continued to look on—with the others arrayed behind her, faces hidden by the cowls—open-mouthed in absolute astonishment. But the man moaned, arched his back, and the haptic resumed:)

—the doors of the cabinets hissed open in unison, revealing the glistening forms of men, as large as his father, and as the blind father must have once been, standing erect, sleeping, dreaming, no doubt, all wearing fresh uniforms and glistening blue helmets, all dripping with the same cold fluids that had once embalmed Crospinal.

Pacing, while the ailing father rested fitfully in the back room of the crew cabin, Crospinal said: "He's dying."

The haptic depicting the sailors in the cabinets had not been sustainable, the portable gate insufficient for such activity or passage of information. Crospinal was once again confronted by the idea that his father not only knew about dream cabinets, but had emerged from one, and had obscured this fact, intentionally or not, from his son. Possibly, his father had once known much more about Crospinal's life and the secrets Crospinal thought he had maintained, such as his own visits to the cabinets, and maybe even his doomed romance. Then, as his range and power diminished, so did his knowledge.

Crospinal had stood in numb shock while the girl who spoke fumbled with plastic tubes, pressing them after their father had passed out, to no apparent avail, against the man's straining neck as he arched and moaned and eventually lay still again. Crospinal watched her limbs, her movements, with an odd sort of intrigue. Without a uniform, the body had elements of awkward beauty, the curves an intimate shape that stirred the pit of him.

Now, emerging sheepishly into the cabin's front room, trembling—no longer so eager to touch Crospinal, it seemed, let alone approach him—the girl said: "Never before colours. Never such as that. *You brought colours.*"

Crospinal shrugged. "That was just a crappy haptic, a show. He was trying to tell me a story but he couldn't finish. He never did that for you, show you those stories? Fathers do that stuff. They get information from the banks, and it goes through the optics into the gates, right into their brain. And then they can project."

She shook her head. "Never."

"Does he have dogs?"

Her expression was blank, so Crospinal explained: "Apparitions. Made of light, on waves of pathos, like a haptic, but reflecting his mood. To follow you around. Would he ever send a dog after you?"

"No."

"Were you born here? Is your womb nearby?"

"I . . . don't know." She answered with visible discomfort, voice hardly audible. "Sailor taught us all we know. He taught us. He gives us food and water, and he shows us how to believe. He told us you would change the station, bring us into the light."

"Has he told you what's going to happen next?" Frustration made Crospinal pace again. "Do you know what's happening?" There was a bitter taste in his mouth. "Has he told you about death?"

By this point, only the girl remained. (And the ill man, of course—the father, the *sailor*—faltering in the back room.) Others from the train, the boys, perhaps frightened by what they had seen, or having played their roles, had, like the haptic, disappeared.

"We're safe here," she said.

"You're not safe. And you're going to find out soon enough. No matter what you believe."

The girl repeated, even quieter: *"You brought colours."*

Crospinal turned away. He wanted to tear the tethers from this false father's head, leave this cabin forever, forget he had ever met another person. Were all humans this enigmatic and stubborn? He yearned to return to familiar parts of the world, to the life he'd known, before he ever left the pen, before he left father's range, but that was impossible. Suddenly he grabbed the girl's hand, roughly twisting it palm-up, so the black marks on her wrist were visible. In the sharp light of the globe, he saw traces of filaments, subcutaneous, thin wires mapping her forearm. "Did he put this there?"

Not attempting to pull free, she would not even meet his eyes. "We carry it." Like a breath. "Paladins put it there."

"My father took mine. Is that what makes your sailor think I can help? Is that why I'm being hunted? He nearly killed himself trying to find me."

She was clearly terrified of him now. "You move like them," she whispered. "He told us you would help, but, but *you're hurting me.*"

Crospinal let her hand drop. From the back room, the false father began to cough and make other sounds of discomfort. Above the daybed, the broken globe fizzled, dimmed, and harsh shadows moved over the dead furniture.

Draining the reserves of the portable gate had brought a deep, unhealthy slumber upon the father, though he spoke in bursts of a startling tongue, words Crospinal could not understand. The man's eyes were half open, glowing in the dim room. What looked like foam flecked the bloodless lips.

Crospinal went to the cabin's entrance and looked out. He was having a hard time breathing. The chestplate popped with each inhale and some seam was jabbing at his chest that he could not dismiss or even locate. Darker outside than it had been. Beyond the ragged line of crew cabins, he discerned the blunt drone, drifting quietly once more—

Much closer, startling him, two people rising, to hurry away. Two of the hooded boys. Had they been hiding, crouching there, hoping to remain unnoticed? Having tried to run away only now, when he came out and looked their way? He lifted his arms. They did not turn to him, but he shouted, "Your teacher is dying. Your *father*—" spitting the words out "—is a liar. You shouldn't trust him! He's not a true father!"

When Crospinal paused, he heard the girl behind him, speaking and, even fainter, the voice of the passenger, who sounded almost lucid now. He must have woken, or perhaps he had feigned his unconsciousness when Crospinal had poked his head in.

"He wants me to teach you," Crospinal said. The boys had not gone far; stopped, they were listening tensely, with their backs to Crospinal, from a safe distance. They were tall and thin and wore very little. Scraps of nylon and mylar, in a concession to cover limited parts of their flesh. Their bellies, genitals, and buttocks. Cowls were tied about their necks. "I have no lessons to give," he said. "Go back where you came from."

The pair hesitated, then obeyed, heading away. Crospinal watched them go before returning inside. In the back room, the girl knelt by the daybed, as she had for Crospinal, in the train. Crospinal leaned through the doorway and watched, breathing heavily, trying to see an indication of conspiracy or plot, until the girl looked at him over her shoulder.

He was astounded by the vulnerability and odd familiarity of her face. He had encountered other people, physical beings, touched them and been touched in return, had felt a range of desires and suspicions. Yet he was left cold. Had the metal rat done this to him? Or was lack of empathy part of his humanity?

"I'm leaving," he said.

The girl did not reply, except to blink, but the man on the daybed, the false father, staring ahead with his blind eyes, said, "Don't turn your back.

Not again. You would have died for good if we hadn't retrieved you. There's a calling. You have a power."

But Crospinal turned and left the cabin. Their voices continued only briefly. Standing in the corridor outside, between the ranks of cabins, under a dark ceiling, he heard the distant booming of the engines. There was no one else in sight and he wanted to imagine, once again, that no other people existed. He felt the extent of the world, the knowledge and vastness no single life could chart. He felt the yearning.

Death was a monster, under a black, vaulted ceiling, like this. Infinity was scattered with pinpricks of white.

Had his father sailed here, inside a cabinet?

Looking up, Crospinal thought he saw the pale glow from ambients, almost dormant altogether, deep into the night.

He began to walk, choosing the opposite direction from which he had arrived.

A warm breeze rose, caressing his uniform, penetrating the splits and areas worn thin, touching his skin. He stopped to feel this breath of the world, stirring against him, feet on the hard grilles, hesitating.

There were fewer cabins, in less complete states, and soon the surface became patchy, softer, revealing a coarser screen of sorts. He did not feel tired or hungry, though he could not recall the last time he had slept, or eaten. Tonguing the siphon—but not sucking—he climbed a shallow incline, a woven ramp of polymethyl, and was afforded a view of a broad expanse where there were no longer any structures at all, but a smooth, conically sloping crater, glistening in the dark, that led into a pit of blackness so devoid his eyes could not penetrate nor distinguish any detail within. Like an eye of the night, or maybe the source. Breezes he'd felt earlier rose out of this negative space, foul gas from beneath the world. On his face, a light spray of moisture, but when he touched his cheek with tingling fingertips, the ruins of his mitt detected no such dampness.

How long he stayed there, peering at nothing, he would never be sure. He thought he heard voices, maybe even those of a multitude, whispering from far away. He thought he heard his name. The end of the station grew colder, and darker, and the rancid breeze continued to flow from the void, churning slowly, dousing him.

Crospinal had to take a few steps forward and crouch lower to alter his centre of gravity before he really started to slide.

CREATION THEORIES

Falling was not like falling, more like drifting, as if he were inside a cabinet again, ensconced, his thoughts and concerns swept away. He had not felt this way since the creatures that hunted him had infiltrated his dream, and he'd drowned in the cold fluid. Though he wondered if monsters would appear again as he drifted, or if he were currently filled, unawares, to brimming, with viscous liquid. He tried to keep his eyes closed and his thoughts subdued, to make the best of this relative peace.

He could breathe quite comfortably. The atmosphere, though, was a bit chilly, and whatever quality gave it the unpleasant smell also made his lungs ache when the air got inside him and was distributed throughout.

Later, he brought his hands close to his face, and saw them, in their tattered sheaths, as pale, disembodied forms, nothing else—an impenetrable blackness all around. His body was nothing. No wind against his uniform, no feeling that some unforgiving surface of ancient composite or even metal at the bottom of the world was rushing up to meet him, to sunder his body, snuff out his life, an explosion of guts and broken bones—

Hadn't that been a desire? Just moments ago?

Keeping his hands in front of his face became an effort, so he stopped.

At this point, Crospinal had another vision of his father, standing before him, straight and youthful, tethered to his gate. The way Crospinal remembered his father from his earliest memories: healthy, strong, newly connected. *Hopeful.*

Crospinal wanted to ask why he had been told untruths, but he was beginning to understand that his father had only been trying to protect him, and that truth was subjective. One could hope for glimmers in life, pieces that could be arrayed into a semblance of pattern but upon which order or coherence or satisfactory conclusions could never be imposed.

He looked into his father's eyes again, saw other worlds, their faint majesty.

Life, and the struggle to make sense of it, had not always been this way.

He wanted to resolve the image of his father, let memories go, and forgive, because falling in this void was the most pleasant interlude Crospinal had experienced in some time—

Until he was punched, that is, in the ribs.

Pleasantries vanished as he curled, winded, around the fist. Another dirty, pale hand (not his own) hit him, again in the stomach, managing to grab the tough fabric of his cruddy old uniform and tug him sharply aside while he gasped. He could do nothing to defend himself. He tried to suck in air as yet another hand appeared, moving under his head, supporting him while clenching his collar and pulling: his lungs had stopped working.

As he opened his mouth to complain or scream or maybe rasp out his death rattle, a hard, blunt object was forced violently between his lips, and down, into his mouth; he struggled and gagged against this indignity but fingers pinched his nose shut and whatever was in his mouth moved as if alive, heading deeper; he felt a blast inside his body, white heat, reviving, and he heard faint voices—

Hauled out of the darkness, Crospinal flopped on a catwalk's illuminated grille. The tube down his throat blew him full of air. Gagging, he tried to clear the obstruction but was prevented by a series of insistent hands, holding him flat, so he had little choice but to lay there, breathing heavy a few more times.

Ringed above him were three faces. The expressions hard, creased, wearing crude masks with goggles, and each had a luminescent halo. Something wrong with their mouths. Crouching over Crospinal.

His words came out gargled, a mealy mess; he choked on his own spit.

The tube led from inside him, up his throat, between his lips, to behind the back of the nearest man. (He decided.) An amber tube, with distinct bends in it. There was a sucking sound, and that blowing into his trachea, which made the core of heat in his chest, spreading through his limbs—

Three sudden grins exposed brown, broken sets of pegs, and darker gaps where there were no teeth at all. Crospinal blinked. He could not see any eyes behind the reflections off the lenses, just scales of light, flashing at him. The halo of each man glowed with pale blue. There was a row of halogens beyond them, recessed into the low ceiling. More shadow fell harshly down the grinning faces.

"Your teeth," Crospinal tried to say, for rotten teeth was not even a possibility, unimaginable, since water swam with every additive teeth needed to stay healthy, dentites and nanites and calcium. Teeth fixed themselves, with water. But there was something even stranger about the glowing halos, which extended down the backs of their heads, and were attached around each bust with the bent tubes, one of which extended all the way—

Only when a tube shifted position in the corner of one man's mouth, clenching of its own accord, did Crospinal understand that the strange headgear was *alive*, biological, a blue-glowing creature riding on their backs. The tubes were legs. One of which, coming from the creature's flattened body, vanished into the corner of each mouth, while another bridged across, into Crospinal's—

This time he managed to yank the hollow limb clear, grunting, wiping at his mouth, for his actions had seared his throat and torn bile and mucus up from his stomach. He coughed and grasped at his neck.

The men laughed, lenses flashing. Their open mouths, the ruined teeth, were an affront, and the symbiotic beasts seemed to flow forward, to better see and illuminate Crospinal's distress.

"Why didn't you let me fall?" he moaned.

In conference, they whispered, hissing, consonants sharp against ruined bicuspids and incisors, a language Crospinal could not understand. Most characters in his father's escapes who spoke tongues other than what his father had spoken could never be trusted, but maybe it was Crospinal who could not be trusted, not out here, shared language or not. He searched the thin band of the creature resting about the nearest man's head, looking for features he could relate to—eyes, a mouth—but saw very little of the sort, just a tangle of collapsed mandibles, churning together.

"Dressed like a sailor's asshole," the closest man said, his cheek hooked back by the leg of the creature. "*Crew.*" Ejected like a bad word, but he grinned large, breath terrible. Grubby fingers rubbed at Crospinal's uniform, testing it, pulling at the burnt fabric and crumbling neoprene.

The other men laughed and sprayed spittle.

"You can speak? My language?"

Fingers on the fabric stopped. The goggles went blank. "Sure," the first man said. "The language of assholes."

"You should've let me fall." Crospinal's throat was raw; talking hurt.

The man had taken Crospinal's arm, turning his wrist. He saw areas of flesh through the ruined sleeve. In his cheek, the symbiote's leg made a gurgling sound. He unhooked Crospinal's mitt and pushed the sleeve high as the elbow, and then the slack lining, sliding the tip of his finger over the exposed scars. Crospinal felt cold all over, as if dead. Looking askance at his companions, the man said something else Crospinal could not understand—to which the companions did not reply. They were no longer laughing.

"What?" said Crospinal.

"You weren't *falling.*" Turning back, shifting the leg in his mouth with a twitch of his cheek, he said: "You were *floating.*" His words came out sibilant and wet. "See? Not enough air. No oxygen. No gravity. Understand? Drifting in the pylon. No helmet, no mite. About to *die.* Maybe dead already."

Crospinal yanked his hand free, reattaching the useless mitt, doing his best to cover himself back up.

"How'd you get there, sailor boy? How'd this happen? Someone toss you in?" He gestured toward Crospinal's arm. "And what happened there? Where you from?"

The harsh, dirty faces were creased with lines almost as deep as those that had appeared on his father's face in the final stages of life, but there was another quality Crospinal could not quite define, a raw vitality his father had never exuded, nor had any others Crospinal met, even though the skin of these men was blotched, asymmetrically blemished, and unprotected by any sort of supplementary system.

He sat up. The hands moved aside to release him, make room. "I'm no sailor. I know what that means. I'm a boy, in the year of long walks."

Laughter all around, which he tried to ignore.

"What happens to your urine?" Crospinal asked. He saw the tiny bulge of their genitalia, uncatheted, as shadows between their legs. He pointed. "You just let it dribble out? Waste the enzymes? What happens if you get sick? What happened to your teeth?"

They seemed amused by his barrage of questions; they were not as smart as they thought.

The masks were composed of scraps of plastic, poor quality mostly, the goggles just broken lenses, from a porthole maybe, and held together by twisted wires.

"And why do you have . . . *animals* on your backs?"

Moving then, as if registering Crospinal's words, the symbiotes' legs wrapped tighter around bare chests and necks, one leg pulling aside a cheek. Three trails of drool down three filthy chins. Flat bodies, covered with a thin shell, in segmented plates, hung halfway down the men's backs, where a short, pointed tail dangled. Eight legs—only the front two formed the long tubes that went down inside, clenched. He watched the glowing beasts adjust, settle, adjust.

"We don't eat pellets," said the man, at last. "Or drink from a spigot. But you know that." He flicked at the tattered cuff of Crospinal's uniform. "And we don't dress up, though they tried to get us to. You piss in your own mouth, sailor. You eat your own shit. Is that enlightened? I don't know what's worse: sailors, crew, or remaining a mindless dolt." Showing his poor teeth, to make a point, he spat. The other two stared, bodies tense. "Were you trying to kill yourself?" Lips and tongue worked around the hollow leg. "How did you end up in the pylon? Can't go in there like *that*. We can toss you back, if you'd like. Finish the job."

Though the three men laughed again, Crospinal seriously considered this offer. "I fell in," he said, and they laughed even more.

Beyond, he saw the coarse grilles he rested on extending toward a warren of tunnels in a moderately smooth wall, with composite deposits like a honeycomb over subsumed beams. Each tunnel entrance was ringed by a cluster of lights, flickering semaphores, indicating depth and function, and giving directives. Crospinal had never learned the code, nor could he see any details within to judge for himself the depth or content.

Perched here, over the abyss, with a quiet, flowing silence coming up from the bottom of the world, he looked down. The blackness from which he had been pulled was absolute, and it called to him. Had he wanted to end his life? How long, he wondered, had he drifted?

"We look for treasures," said the man, "but we never caught someone in there. Not alive, anyhow." The laughter was quieter, wet as the words. Dark saliva bubbled around the leg of the symbiote. When the man tried to take Crospinal's wrist again, Crospinal made a fist and pulled back.

"*Leave me be.*"

"There are three kinds of people in the world," the man said, assessing the potential of getting hit, and deciding chances were low. "And you aren't any of them."

"I've heard that before."

The pale aura of the animal's glow illuminated traces of the inlays, shimmering under the flesh of their stringy forearms, which were held out to him now, just like the girl and the cowled boys from the train station had done. The inlays were where his own would have been, had his father not unstitched them from his veins. When he looked back up, the lenses were intent upon him. He was expected to speak.

"If you don't eat pellets, how can you survive? And if you don't drink water, well, your teeth will rot."

"We've come out the other side, asshole. *You can't turn your back on flesh provided, nor water. You can't live without them.* But you can, sailor boy. You can break away. You've woken up now, and you can decide."

"I carry my father's light," Crospinal said.

Shifting on his knuckles to lift a hand, and poking Crospinal, the man hissed: "No sermon can save you. Tell me, sailor boy, do you believe the world is travelling through a void, and one day we'll arrive?"

"What?"

"Isn't that what sailors think? Though they're too messed up to know it. The destination is where they came from. The great circle."

"I told you I'm not a sailor. I was born in the pen. I never heard anything like that."

Above the goggles, an eyebrow arced up. That finger jabbed him again. "We started from the same place, me and you. Different years, different guardians, but the same hub. Maybe you think we're rolling across the wasteland, under a big, red sun, waning, inside an ancient vehicle supported by wheels as big as the moon."

Crospinal almost touched the man's arm but could not bring himself to contact the dirty flesh with his own. He was pretty sure the man would not have permitted it anyhow. These theories had struck him, and in a strange way, reminded him of his father's trances and speeches, and had made Crospinal think of mountains. Images the words evoked were strong. "I've seen it," he said. "I've seen the orb, and the windblown dust."

"That's why you're an asshole." Smiling that jagged smile. "It's all lies. All beliefs, theory. When you see that sun, you're looking at a file. A picture. Right now is all there is. There's no void outside—only here, in the pylon. Sailors are fanatics." The words echoed, but the echo was silenced instantly by the dark pylon behind them. "We bring supplies. That crusty old shit in the back room, he hijacked a collection of misfits—" the man spat again "—before he discovered the ampoules. I spent some time there myself, but I figured it out. We all did. Saw the light, as you would say. Who would die for a sailor? And who would wear a suit that takes away humanity? But his suits are gone now. His train hardly flies anymore. There's no saviour and never was, and nobody can change the course of the world. Sooner you break from your ideas of saving everyone the better." Tones of anger had crept into the man's voice. A bare arm swept out, toward the darkness. "You eat your magic pellets, and drink your poisoned water. You suck it until you're plump and as stupid as they are." Holding out his arms again, the integrated wires or filaments under his grubby skin were clear, climbing up under a bracelet of copper strapping, to fade near his elbow.

This time, Crospinal could not resist touching him, fingers on the warm, dry skin. Were he and these men ever the same beast?

"We live in the pylon. They said no one could live there." The man pointed with his chin. "And we don't believe in nothing."

"We saved your life, sailor boy," said one in the back, who had not previously spoken, startling Crospinal. "But we can't save you from the shit inside your own head."

And the third added: "If you wasn't so filled with preservatives, you'd make a fine meal. But none of us want to live forever."

Laughter returned, unanimous, uproarious, the three mouths open, lenses glinting, dark drool spraying. Even the symbiotes twitched and clenched, attempting to stay perched on the bobbing heads.

Crospinal was clapped on the shoulder by a firm hand.

"Okay, asshole, go back where you came from now. Crawl on home."

"I can't."

The hand remained, moving down, clenching Crospinal's upper arm in a powerful grip.

"*Hey—*"

They had turned suddenly, as one, toward the tunnels. Was there a sound? Crospinal squinted but saw nothing amiss, heard no approach. Lights around the openings flashed their code.

Frowning, Crospinal pulled free easily, as if he'd been forgotten already.

The men stood. They were about as skinny as he was. The one who'd spoken first smiled down upon Crospinal with his rotten smile. "Good luck, asshole," he said, then he reached to tap the creature on his back—which puffed and tightened—and, with the distorted grin still on his face, launched himself backward, a flip out into the darkness, and vanished.

His associates followed, engulfed one by one like apparitions, or haptics collapsing. They might never have existed.

Crospinal sat for a long while on that platform, over the abyss, the stale breath of the world rising up around him. He hugged himself and he rocked. There was no other movement, no sounds, from any direction. He thought briefly, obliquely, as was his wont, about stepping off the brink, taking up where he had left off, but instead he got up and headed toward the closest tunnel opening, across a sloping array of strange, hard tiles, and entered the delicate ring of semaphored lights.

A malfunctioning icon crackled in the air before his face and was gone. No controller to greet him.

Ambients swelled with his passage. The narrow hall was choked with old deposits and polymers, drifting in clusters. Nothing of note, no clue as to what had frightened the men off, if indeed they had been frightened.

Perhaps the men had merely finished lecturing him, and had wanted to leave on a dramatic note. Crospinal nearly smiled, then wondered if he'd lost his mind. Running fingertips along the texture of the wall, he walked, expecting dogs to appear, barking, excited to know of his return, but of course none did; this tunnel did not lead home

He came to a junction, where an assortment of what looked like concrete ephemera were scattered in a rough heap. He stopped, surprised by this incongruity. There were tiny metal tools; what looked like styrene toys, from a children's haptic; a polymethyl fan blade, cracked in two. He crouched, tingling and, without touching anything, looked about.

In the low, domed ceiling, directly above a blackened mark on the floor, not far from the pile, was a sort of vent with hard edges, as if the frame had been cleared of any build up. He rose, moving cautiously. His bare foot felt granular residue, and warmth. *A fire . . .*

Inspecting the perimeter of the junction area, Crospinal eventually located two small, primitive devices—a cowering food dispenser, and a pharmacy—wedged into a recess with an opening just large enough for his hand to enter. He struggled to catch and remove the devices, which had begun protesting weakly, but they couldn't resist for long. When he turned the food dispenser over, liquid spilled onto the floor. (Slowly absorbed, with a nasty stench.) The skin of the devices was scratched, marked with crude glyphs.

"Are you smart at all?" Crospinal whispered. "Can you understand me? Who did this to you? Is there a father nearby?"

More liquid dripped. He released the dispenser, and it scrambled quickly away, back into the recess.

Just off a short connecting hall, he found a soft pile of padding on the floor tiles—mostly insulation, torn from a metallic panel, like the ones the crew cabins had been built from, and the wheelroom back home. Carried here? Or was this all once a pen? Maybe the father had died of cancer. How many children, if any, had lived here? The idea of having a single doppelganger, once so clear, now seemed an almost absurd concept. His girlfriend could have been summoned away by anyone putting their hands into a console, though he tried to convince himself that she would not be as attracted to others as she had been to him, and was staying away for awful reasons he could neither fathom nor change. He was mildly surprised to find that this notion brought little comfort. Her reasons for liking him in the first place, for returning so often in the early days of their relationship when they had fallen in love, were most likely the same emotions that had made him climb the seven ladders to porthole of the harrier, day after and lie awake at night, unable to stop thinking of her.

Crospinal sniffed. Where the tiles curved up to become the wall, in a slow grade, he detected the scent of feces, as if a processor had broken down or leaked.

Pushing at the accumulation of padding and arcane trinkets with his foot exposed tiny scavengers, scurrying for shelter. *Like in a garden*, he thought, frowning. Were there nutrient tiles nearby?

And the walls were scarred with subtle pictures, etched into the polymer deposits with a substance the composite could not eradicate, though toluene stained the areas purple. Crospinal imagined some of these crude depictions might be images of people, but he could discern no real likeness when he inspected them closer.

Two dead rats—biological rats, flesh and blood—lay in a steel fusion box, side by side, black, half immersed in thick liquid. Their skin was loose, coming off, their yellow teeth exposed. Each corpse had a visible wound where life had drained out. Crospinal slowly lifted one of the bodies, held it aloft, inspecting the glazed eyes, the bared teeth, trying to assure himself that no essence could possibly linger after a heart stops. *Endtime . . .*

He bit down with his sharp teeth, filling his mouth with wet fur and the sweet, sickly fluid that burst from the flesh and made him gag. The small bones were harder to break than he had expected, but he persisted, tearing off a mouthful. His stomach protested and he only managed to cram the rat back into the box before vomiting onto the floor and over his own hands, spattering his ruined uniform.

Trying to stand, pulling at the tabs down the front of his tricot—because the ambient temperature had suddenly doubled—but his stomach clenched again, heaved and heaved, until it could heave no longer, and he was left dry-retching on all fours.

When he was finally able to straighten, feeling weak and slightly
onished by what he had attempted, a timid controller hovered before
at eye level. The device had seen better days. "You okay?"

There were you?" Crospinal said, wiping at his mouth. The dead rats
ed to be laughing soundlessly at him from their box. The one he
d to eat was half out of the liquid, escaping. His stomach flipped.
s no sustenance left inside him. "A real food dispenser, and real
ll spigot. There's just broken things here."

all right?"

all right?"

ller hesitated before leading him toward an obscured wall
sing open, crumbling the layer that had encrusted it into
vealed a dormant food dispenser that appeared, when it
terrified.

"You have a customer," said the controller. "Don't worry. The coast's clear."

Rumbling, the dispenser, active now, extended its neck to peer about before quickly dropping a pellet into Crospinal's mitt. Behind the dispenser, a spigot cowered, trying to remain hidden. Crospinal was about to take a water bulb, to drain it, gargle, feel the rush, the cure, but he paused, staring at the still warm food in his hand, sinuses filled with bland scents, recalling so many meals with his father, the lectures of proteins and sustenance, prayers of thankfulness for what they were about to receive, the generosity of this world.

Turning his hand on end, he let the pellet fall, uneaten, to the floor.

"Waste not, want not," scolded the controller. "What's wrong with you? Everybody's nuts. All I ever wanted to do was run a nice station. Attract some crew. That's all. Why'd you do that?"

"I guess I'm not hungry." He watched the pellet slowly dissolving into the dirty tiles, back to whence it had come. *Flesh of the world to flesh of the world. . . .*

"Are you feeling better now that you've wasted resources?"

"Yes . . ."

When the pellet had vanished completely, Crospinal tugged again at the front tab of his uniform, then at the lateral tabs, deciding which way was best to remove a battered tricot—which way would be least painful—but his groin crawled in anticipation of the discomfort that pulling out a catheter brought. He had peeled his pale shoulder free and that was it. The broken collar refused to unlatch altogether; the comm jack and the monitor scope fizzled briefly.

"Uh," said the controller, "there's no means to dispose of suits in that condition here, so please stop trying to take it off. Jumpsuits are point-of-generation waste. They can't be recycled here."

"There must be a dispenser nearby." But Crospinal had given up on the half-baked idea of taking his uniform off.

"There used to be, when a complement lived here. None left in these parts at all. They were destroyed. I've never even *seen* one before, because I got transferred here. No amenities any more, I'm afraid."

Crospinal shrugged. "Maybe they're hiding?"

"We have no reason to hide from each other. You know the boots of that jumpsuit are breached? There are holes in the fabric, the helmet interface is bent and shorted, and the processor's exhausted. That suit's doing you more harm than good. You should probably get yourself to an active station, dispose of everything correctly, and don a fresh one. Do you still have the helmet?"

"You know what? How about if I ask you questions? I got a lot of questions. You're supposed to be helping me."

"What sort of questions?"

"About the bays, for one."

"What about the bays?"

"Elementals work out there. Machines, as big as me. Smart ones. And little smart machines, too, like the rats that fix people up. And standing ones, who don't say very much."

"What's your point? You haven't asked a question yet."

"What motivates them? Do they work for us?"

"Who's us?"

"Humans."

"Crew, you mean? Look, I've never even been to a bay. Those sorts of machines don't frequent these halls. There's not many of them left anywhere, as far as I understand. I think the answer you're looking for is *chaos*. Chaos controls them. Same as you."

"I asked one to open a cabin door. I knew that shouldn't be possible, but the door opened, and the machine went through. There was a . . . conspiracy, to hurt me. But I've never even—"

Rudely interrupting, the controller darted closer: "You should know," it said, "that the child is watching you."

Crospinal went cold. "*What child?*"

"The one who lives here."

"*Another boy?*"

"He likes to watch people." The controller was oblivious to Crospinal's cataplexy. "He likes your suit, but he seldom comes out—"

However, from behind a scale in the wall, unclean, wearing nothing but a shawl made of two insulating sheets, bound by rusted cable ties, a young child did indeed emerge.

"Ah," said the controller, backing off.

This was not the other boy, not the one who might have reflected Crospinal, but a much younger child, perhaps in the year of cognitive leaps, or of independent thinking, with large, green eyes and long, lank hair. If the controller had not brought up gender, Crospinal would have thought the child a girl. He had not seen green eyes before and they were disconcerting. The boy stared for a long while, but then a quick smile revealed rotten teeth, just like those of the men who'd saved Crospinal from floating in the pylon. Holding out tiny arms—marked with the clear, intricate underlay—the boy came forward.

"Hello," said Crospinal, nervous. "I, uh, I don't really like contact. I don't hug."

Yet the child continued, until he was embracing Crospinal's legs and holding on tight. When Crospinal finally touched the child in return (because he did not know what else to do, though he wanted to push the kid away), the crude plastic clothes rustled, and he felt beneath them prominent bones, larger than the rat's, but which he could break just as easily, nonetheless, if he tried. There was nothing to this boy. Over the kid's large head, which was pressed against his thigh, he mouthed to the controller: *Who is this?*

"He, uh, doesn't talk. Can't talk. No capacity for it. Not like the others. He doesn't have a formed larynx. He doesn't hear so good, either."

Crospinal patted the boy on the head; the hair was matted and dry. "Why are they afraid?"

"Why is who afraid?"

"The men who live in the pylon, or whatever they called it. The three men out there. And the sustenance dispensers. They're afraid."

Truthfully, Crospinal was fed up with the vagaries and duplicities of devices, machines, and people alike. He was prepared for denial and lies. *No one lives in the pylon. What men? What are you saying?* But the controller merely said, "They feed this boy. They bring him treats. He put ideas into them."

"How could that be, if he can't talk?"

The child had stopped hugging Crospinal and seemed bored now. Tottering, looking down, he hopped a few steps, stopped, and extended his arms, like a crow's wings, trying to balance on one foot. Glancing at Crospinal, the boy bent to retrieve a tiny styrene cap from the detritus piled near the wall. He put the cap in his mouth. Spit it out again. Resumed his hopping around, hands extended.

"Did you raise him?"

"I'm still raising him. He's my ward."

"Why didn't you teach him to speak?"

"He's a reject. Year of miracles. But he doesn't eat the sustenance anyhow."

Considering cripples, rejects, and controllers that seemed as smart as elementals and maybe as deceitful, Crospinal walked over to the hidden entranceway from which the child had entered the hall; a thick flake of composite exposed a narrow, arched hallway, which extended toward a larger area and continued, well-lit, curving around, out of sight. The air was warm and smelled like recycling. He could see the console from here. A large room, full console with holes, a periscope, and active thumb plates. The icon of the hands burning above.

Gone lightheaded, trying not to react, Crospinal said, "When I was little, two elementals took me to the garden for a walk. My father was tethered, so he could never go anywhere, not in the flesh."

"Yes," said the device, perplexed. "A passenger. Connected to a bank. Why are you telling me this?"

"Because I'm going to take this child for a walk."

"Pardon me?"

"Me and him are going for a little walk."

"I have to come with you."

"No, you don't. You're going to stay here. I'll bring him back."

The controller considered this. "Please don't hurt him. I feel responsible. Even though he doesn't use my amenities. I've grown quite fond of the child."

Crospinal's heart pounded. He went over to the child—who was kneeling now, rolling a carbon tube between his palm and the floor, over and over, making an annoying, rumbling sound. Crospinal touched the boy's naked shoulder, which stopped the repetitive movements, and the boy turned his face. Astonishing to look into the green eyes from so close. How could this be a boy's face? His mouth had gone dry. He let a few drops from the siphon moisten his tongue. Searching the features to see if this child felt a mysterious wonder, like his sister had in the haptics, he judged by what he saw in the open candour, the expression, the trust, that this might be the case. Was Crospinal the only person who had not experienced wonder? Had this also been, like his inlays, removed by his father? Unaltered, what might he have been? He held out an open hand.

Tiny, hot fingers locked into his own. Trapped material of his mitt fizzled gently. He helped the boy to his feet. He weighed more than Crospinal had expected. When Crospinal had been this age, his legs were bowed like the frame of a transfer tube.

Crippled, and the damaged.

Clenching his jaw, he took the boy down the hidden hall. The child displayed no hint of dismay thus far and continued to frolic; when Crospinal looked over his shoulder, he saw the controller in the archway, backlit by ambients, peering in.

"There was two machines that worked in pen," Crospinal said quietly, as if praying. "And a bunch of controllers, like yours, where I grew up. I had a father. He could project dogs and spirits and ghosts." Crospinal laughed briefly, awkwardly loud, because he had thought at first that he was just going to talk for the sake of it, to calm the boy, but these words actually meant something to him, like a convocation, initiating mechanisms and pulling forth emotions within his body that enabled him; he needed to tell the boy about his past, before things went too far. He needed to tell the boy, in order to continue. "I named the machines. Though my father didn't want me to. They had red eyes. Do you have any friends?" Crospinal thought about the dirty, crouching trio, their nudity, their horrible teeth, the beasts on their backs that were parasitical and leering and keeping them alive.

Swinging forward, the boy kicked at nothing Crospinal could see. He did not answer, but neither did he let go of Crospinal's hand. He seemed so happy. Where their flesh contacted, moisture had reached uncomfortable levels. The Dacron was totally useless. Fecal matter and snot and every other repugnancy from the happy child was crawling inside his sleeve.

"Most of my friends were apparitions." Crospinal looked at his long legs, in the burnt uniform, and gauged the steps of them both, he and the boy, side by side in this composite hall. There was a tight core in his gut from, he supposed, trying to eat the rat. He peed a bit, felt the processor struggling. "Apparitions drifted about the pen. Dogs mostly. Some showed up in haptics. The characters in the escapes weren't like dogs, because my father didn't send them out. They were from the world, from the banks, where pellets and water comes from. Where uniforms came from. But you don't like that stuff, do you?"

The boy paid him no attention. They had reached the console. Crospinal stopped before it and the boy looked straight ahead, wondering. With his free hand—which was shaking—Crospinal lifted the flap, uncovering the pair of holes. He felt the hum already, in his molars.

"Look," he said. "Want to see better? Want to see what's at the bottom?"

Bending at the waist, to pick the boy up, but now the boy was frowning.

"It's okay," said Crospinal. He took the child by the waist and had to tighten his grip when the lithe boy started fighting. "I'm not going to hurt you!" Clearly alarmed, the boy twisted away, surprisingly strong, and Crospinal nearly lost his balance.

"I just want to see what happens!" he shouted. "Put your arms in these holes, just for a second!" He yanked the child closer, trying to hold onto the tiny torso, but struggling. "*I just want to see what happens!*"

Turning on him suddenly, green eyes flashing, hair flinging forward, the child lunged, and Crospinal did fall, the boy upon him, attacking.

"*You little fuck—*"

Broken teeth found his thumb, and bit hard, crunching into his flesh. Crospinal screamed. Above him, the controller appeared in his narrowing sight, having travelled quickly to resolve the matter, or save the boy. But Crospinal had already lost this fight.

There was a lot of blood.

SWEATING OUT THE POISON

Descending, swooning, and clutching his left arm to his belly, Crospinal had to rest often, his back against the curved ribs of the fixed ladder, his eyes squeezed shut. The indifferent world swam. He could not stop replaying his father's lectures about infection and sterilization over and over in his head. He could almost hear the frightened dogs barking: *What have you done, Crospie? What have you done?*

Blood actually dripped out the rents in his left mitt. More blood ran down the inside of the left leg of his uniform, a volume too excessive for the exhausted processor to deal with, though capillaries in the fabric laboured and sucked. Tiny globes of his life escaped nonetheless, falling freely from his ruined boots to plunge down the shaft along gentle trajectories, until hitting a rung or he lost sight of them (though when Crospinal closed his eyes tight, he could still visualize the curves, trapped within his mind).

His energy was fading. Microbes, eager to have access at last to his body's various systems, intended to swarm, finish the job, racing each other to besiege every diminished stronghold left standing in his glands and organs. He could sense their progress and final victory. Sweaty already. His teeth chattered.

The fixed ladder seemed to go down and down forever; the extended skeleton of some extinct beast, pinned like a specimen to the giant wall. A *hot* beast. Crospinal had so far descended maybe five or six floors of this construction site, peering out from within the rib cage as these monstrous, layered locales rose before him. Engines were below, yet getting closer; he felt them in the metallic material pressed to his back. Perhaps the bottom of this ladder was where Crospinal was always meant to end up. He was certainly physically incapable of heading the other direction.

The boy's rotten incisors had pierced the once-tough Dacron, punctured unprotected flesh. Crospinal's left mitt was now peeled back to the wrist, exposing most of his damaged hand. The material flopped, utterly inert. In the light from the landings he passed, he saw interstices of his scar, mapping his bony wrist at the cuff of his sleeve. His thumb was nasty gore. But he no longer had the stomach to inspect the tears in his uniform, let alone his ruined flesh. The wound throbbed so hard his entire body shook.

First the rat, now the boy.

The two bites should have had analogous meaning, establishing, by their pairing, a form of parenthetical closure, but his foolishness and impending demise was all he could consider.

Now malignant invaders had reached the chambers of his heart. They gathered there, getting ready to climb the final ridges of his spine to access the spongy meat of his brain. Crospinal unfastened the connecting clasps of his useless left mitt, which he held limp before his face in its torn and ruinous state, and thought absurdly about addressing, before letting go.

He watched the mitt sail down, taking shape as if trying to retain functionality, recalling a hand one last time, falling slowly, to land on the ledge of the structures far below. Six years Crospinal had worn the same uniform. The mitt had literally been a part of him. Even from this height, he saw the Dacron amalgamate with the world, split into molecules, recycle; he imagined that he caught a whiff of its final and absolute transmutation.

Then he eased off his right mitt, keeping his thumb clear, and let it, too, drop.

Resuming his descent, Crospinal's naked hands took the rungs. Textures of the construction ground directly against his flesh, making him breathless. Despite his swollen thumb, he clenched the rungs as tight as he could. Direct contact was all that kept him going.

After releasing the boy—or, to be more precise, after the boy had finished biting, and flailing away with his tiny but surprisingly solid fists—Crospinal had scrambled to his feet, aghast at the extent, the mere *existence,* of the wound. He had intended to return quickly to the spigot, to wash with enhanced water, rinse his thumb under the flow and drink as much as possible until his blood was cleaner, but the controller must have been shorting out, for it had not responded well to his demands and was almost hysterical by that point, gyrating and diving at Crospinal's head, shouting awful accusations; standing apart from them, against the wall marked with glyphs, the child was also crying, head back, bawling so loudly (with a streak of crimson on his chin, and a gobbet of flesh caught between the sharp peaks of his rotten teeth) that Crospinal had no choice but to run, leaving behind the unpleasant drama and a trail of his leaking blood.

He'd stumbled for some distance, peering desperately into the first hatch he came across (nearly pitching headlong). The engines throbbed remotely with the same pulse as his wound. In that pulse, they called to him, enticing him with the name he could never recall: *come down, come down.*

He made very slow progress—and getting slower—sinking gradually below yet another floor. How much blood, he wondered, could a person lose before they expired? How long could natural immunodefenses last, before being crushed? He touched his forehead to the rung between both fists, but received no cooling reward. Without a uniform's recovery and staunching, and general concern for his well-being, was there a remote chance that coagulation would kick in? People could live without protection. He had seen them. Perhaps not for as long, but they could survive. Animals lived without augmentation. The rats and the crows and the miniature creatures in the garden. Maybe he, too, had the latent capacity to get better?

Unable to remember lessons. The knowledge of a naked body in a world of virulence. Blood dripped and dripped. Here he was, overrun by microbes. He had never bled this volume, uniform or no.

At least, not while conscious.

Infections were killing him.

He should swan dive between the ribs of the fixed ladder, following the mitts to where they'd dispersed—

Possibilities of less remarkable demises vanished with each floor gone by. He considered them all, in his fleeting way. He knew he should get off the ladder, stop this nonsense, stop climbing downward, look instead for a quiet place to clean his injuries, get some rest, curl up in a daybed. Maybe there were fresh dispensers in their rooms. Antibodies could wake from dreams of how to neutralize antigens. Crospinal was both leery and tired of traipsing around on level ground. He'd had enough of being out there, enough of his inability to interact or decipher. *Better off sick, inside the bones of the fixed ladder.*

A row of bright lights, recessed into a poly ceiling, extending into the middle distance. All these halls and floors were immaculate and new. He imagined no one could possibly have visited them before, and that the locations might disappear altogether when they were no longer in sight. If he went back up—if he had the energy and capacity to ever climb back up—would the layout change?

No, the world was not made for him. That had been a lie. The world didn't care if he lived or died.

Maybe a haptic was playing. He looked around. Loops of a landscape drifting by while he watched, until he bled to death, or fever claimed him

Crospinal nodded off. Sagging sideways against the ladder's supporting ribs, one arm hooked over a rung, preventing the plummet. A leg, pendulous. In his sleep, Crospinal smiled. He couldn't fight this nap, nor did he want to. Even in its grip he was astounded. His chest rapidly filled and emptied. His bones were hollow, air was fire, and he was able to fly. Inside his tricot, Crospinal's heart hammered faster than any rat's heart. His thumb—

A shout made him start; his eyes snapped open. Nearby, someone was afraid, and in pain.

The shout was not repeated.

Had it been real?

He moved his tongue against his palate, and it stuck, gummy. But he felt better. His sight, and the sensation of his hands and feet against the rungs, as he straightened himself, getting the kinks out, seemed sharp.

Straining to hear further sounds of distress, or other indications of a person nearby, only the engines' whisper responded.

He went down a few more rungs, as quietly as he could, toward the next floor, while he was still alert, hearing the scuffle and grunts before he was able to duck his head, and see into the hall below. Despite the window of relative acuity, for a moment Crospinal just hung there, unsure what he was looking at: limbs and bodies, naked and sheathed in uniform, entwined together, a beast unlike any he had seen in haptics—

No. People were *fighting.* Three of them. He'd come across some form of primal battle. There was a thud, groans, and the group abruptly broke apart. The closest, in the fresh uniform, faced away from Crospinal, trying to hold off two others—both long-haired and wearing nothing but a nylon breechcloth—brandishing a length of carbon tube. One of the skins clutched a wound, backing away, having been hit in the upper arm; the second tried to close once more but the tube swung, stomach level—*whoosh*—and had to leap back.

Their expressions were mostly unreadable.

The next swing connected against a bare shoulder but the rod was grabbed, forced down, and, as the uniformed fighter lost balance, clattered to the floor; three people, entwined, grunting again, collapsed together, where the scuffle intensified—

The third, in the uniform, was a girl. Crospinal saw her face, the straining features, and knew for sure. Not the girl from the train, though. Grimacing in the melee, tugging, trying to get free, she seemed somehow urgently familiar; this familiarity, for Crospinal, was another blow. She looked like him.

And in that instant, before he could identify any feature of this other face, or place the sensations it had triggered, or even take a breath, Crospinal understood a simple truth: watching someone being killed and doing nothing was equal in guilt to killing someone himself.

Below, among a nest of construction materials, was a tall cluster of carbon tubes, growing on the grille, near where the fixed ladder passed. Crospinal made his way down unnoticed, until he was standing on the lip of the platform on this burgeoning floor, holding his own length of tube in both bare hands. Sweat cooled on his forehead. He wiped his face with a spasmodic twitch of his shoulder, and when he swung, the tube cut through the air loudly and he lurched toward the fight. They all heard now, one by one turning to see his approach, and freezing. He imagined how he looked by the expressions of horror on their faces, including the girl's.

One of the attackers scrambled upright.

The second pushed to his haunches

The girl watched from where she lay and did not move at all.

Crospinal stared into her blue eyes. "Luella?" he said.

Now the girl struggled to get up, favouring one side. Her left leg seemed stiff. "Who are you?"

Hearing her name had made Luella more wary than frightened. Crospinal was delirious and insistent. "Your brother."

Glancing briefly at the other two—who were still backing away—Luella grabbed a tube of her own, snapping it off at the base, where it had rooted. She brandished it. "No closer."

"But Luella, I wanted—"

"Where does that chute go?" Indicating the ladder with her chin.

Her face had changed over the years. Though he had seen his sister only in haptics and dreams, he suspected his memories of her might be of *other memories*. Traces of the wonder glowing on her young expression had leaked away. Hardly enough vestiges remained for him to identify. He had wanted to gather in the wonder, but it was gone. He had wanted to embrace his sister, but could not move. Why did she seem so suspicious, so hostile?

Her hair was entirely depilated. Her snug uniform, fresh, in excellent shape, had intact boots and mitts and a narrow collar, made for a helmet smaller than the amber one he had often been asked to wear. A shield shimmered before her face. Their father would have been very proud. Luella's limbs were straight and strong, and had always been that way. (The stiffness was from some injury acquired during the struggle, not congenital.)

Crospinal managed to look over his shoulder, to the long ribcage of the ladder, and to the darkness beyond. "That hatch? It goes down to the engines, I think."

"What engines?"

"Or to the hub. You don't recognize me?" He'd turned back to look at Luella again. "I've been altered by an elemental. They made me . . . taller. Maybe that's why. I'm Crospinal. Your brother."

But his fever was returning in waves that soon staggered him, hitting him fast, one after the other from behind, like being shoved repeatedly, with surprising malevolence. Crospinal stumbled, in a sweat from head to toe no uniform could wick. Whatever had given him insight and energy vanished. He needed to lie down. Blinking away a blurry caul, he realized his sister was farther away, and ebbing. Leaving? The other two, the attackers, were gone already. Had he hurt them? The fight seemed a long time ago. He put his hand to his face and felt bare flesh contact bare flesh, shocked by the heat generated.

"Luella," Crospinal called out. "Father's dead!"

Now she was somehow heading past him. She'd turned around to look over the precipice. "That's useless," she pronounced. "Unfinished shit."

Trying to scrutinize the hall where he stood, swaying, unable to follow in any capacity.

"Batches'll be back soon," she said. "With others. And a paladin's curse. Let's get out of the open. What's the matter with you?"

"Father's *dead*." He tried to reach for her but nothing was functioning properly, and she wasn't even there anymore. "Cancer," he said, but when he managed to focus on the girl's face again, she was taking a step back, and all resemblance to Luella was gone. This girl was surely tinier than his sister would be. Small white teeth, eyes recessed, much darker skin.

"You're sick," she said. "Toxic. There's a new spigot in there; you'd better drink up." Pointing to an aperture just behind Crospinal, to his left. "You're on your last legs. Know what a spigot is?"

"Sure," he said. "But I thought . . . I thought you were my sister."

"You better drink. The one you're looking for is sleeping. She dreams again, until the way's open. But she's shown us. You should stop saying her name, though. Go, drink up. I have to leave. But thanks for the help."

"Who were those two?" He remembered elements of the fight again, details of which had somehow tried to sneak away. Gathering them back was like trying to catch apparitions with clumsy mitts.

"Batches. Sent to destroy the stations." Now she looked Crospinal up and down, as if also seeing him the way he truly was for the first time. "What happened to you? Where's your contingent?"

Crospinal's teeth clacked together. When he staggered forward, the girl, after the briefest hesitation, moved to support him; her grip was strong, and he felt immediately safer, his arm draped over her shoulder, his side pressed to hers. Her bare skin, right there, against his ruined uniform.

"You're going to have to move faster. I can't stay here."

"Where's Luella sleeping?"

"Stop saying her name. Not here. I won't tell you again. Look, batches will be back soon. I surprised those two while they were taking apart a dispenser. Usually there's more. Now *move*."

He was hustled through an aperture, into a tiny station. No console, a few half-cupboards, a lightscreen and thumb plates, all lit up by gentle halogens. The reek of newly modified structures, thick in the air; he gagged. At his feet, fresh tiles were in the process of melding into a grille. Toluene stung the soles of his feet. He sensed great collisions, and struggle, beyond those of man and woman.

Deposited onto a stool, and told to stay put, something adverse occurred to Crospinal's equilibrium and he slipped off, crashing to all fours.

"Damn it . . ."

The girl helped him up, impatient. "You need to stay here. Get under a counter if they come back. They might not even look in this station again, not unless they've been told to. If this one starts to close, find another." Peering up at the ceiling, she said, "The controller was just here. Weird that's it gone. Hello? Hello?"

He mumbled, "Luella was my sister. . . ."

"*Stop saying that*! I don't know what the matter was with the sailor who taught you. Fathers and sisters? But you should *stop*. She's dreaming, I told you, far away. What's *wrong* with you? Are you trying to curse us both?"

True, Crospinal was not feeling very good. "We had the same father," he said lamely. "Me and her."

"All right." The girl propped him up. "Your father's dead, right? Your sailor's gone. You're alone. You need to change. You need to clean up."

The controller had evidently decided it was safe to come out from hiding, dropping to hover before Crospinal's face as the girl spoke curtly to him; they studied each other.

"Watch her," said the girl.

"He's a boy," said the device. "You know those maniacs broke my eyes?" The controller lifted, pivoting, to settle with a tremor at the epicentre of the station, where stitches of blue arced from its skin to the furniture. The entire station shimmered.

"I know."

Crospinal, faint, felt quavers of intrusion as the rays of information pierced him.

The device said: "He's no batch. Nor is he from a stat. But he's dreamt in one. There's pathogens in his bloodstream. I need to adjust the water."

"What?" The girl had paused.

"Where'd you find him?"

"*Him*? He, uh, he just . . . showed up. He came down a ladder, at the edge of the construction. He's been inside a stat? He's totally deluded."

"Not from around here, that's for sure."

The girl straightened. She'd been crouching at Crospinal's side. "There were two batches outside. They went running back. He—" meaning Crospinal, who looked up now, into the wondrous face of this girl "—scared them off. He can *fight*. But I'm leaving him here."

Crospinal tried unsuccessfully to get up. Unfathomable hostilities unfolded beyond the walls of the station. People fought each other. They hurt each other—

"My dispenser," whined the device, "will never hatch. I can't get another one started. You know what this means?"

"Yes," said the girl, with real sympathy. "I do."

"My chance to run a functioning comfort station is pretty much shot. I've let the crew down."

"You're doing great," said the girl. "You're helping him, at least. You're helping me, too. You're doing a fine job."

"I'm not crew," Crospinal said, but no one heard him.

"Lay on the floor," the controller told him. "I'll try to get the rest of that jumpsuit off."

"We'll get through this," said the girl.

Crospinal, as firmly as he could, held one hand up to keep the girl and controller away, though neither had attempted to unfasten even one clasp of his tricot. The effort on his part was huge. He was breathing hard. He would be the one to remove his suit, if anyone.

A moment later, when nudged, he knew he had missed something. The girl was no longer standing to his right. Instead, she was before him, proffering a bulb, which had materialized in the clean palm of her mitt. The controller had vanished. Crospinal frowned. From the halls outside came a far-away hum. Crospinal took and emptied the bulb, drinking slavishly, admitting defeat, knowing enhancements were entering through his mouth, proceeding into his stomach, spreading throughout his body and newly configured extremities. The empty bulb against his bare fingers dispersed into molecules like a puff of smoke, and the surge of support within his body made him crave to live a life of much less transitory meaning than he suspected most people, if not all, could ever achieve.

"Look," he said, pushing up his tattered and blackened left sleeve. Neoprene flaked off as he exposed his skinny white forearm. "*Look*."

The girl stared. Stricken. She reached out slowly but did not touch the thin white scarlines on his wrist. *Now* there was wonder, returned to her face. Now he saw it. "You *are* like her." Her voice rendered to a breath. "I thought the controller was messing around."

"I'm telling you. Luella is my sister. We were born together in the pen, past the bay, past where the train stops. At the end of the world. I saw her, in a dream cabinet. She's in trouble. They all are."

The girl was silent for a long time. She'd taken a few steps back. "Paladins are angry." She was obviously trying, and failing, to evaluate this development, glancing again and again at Crospinal's scarred arm. "They're hunting. They're destroying. And the batches . . ."

The water surged inside him. Crospinal felt all kinds of desire. He looked at the girl's limbs, the exposed skin ruddy over wiry, toned muscles, and felt his catheter shift. He put his two bare hands into his stubbly hair, trying to keep his thoughts and the images they conjured within his skull.

"Your thumb . . ."

"I was bitten." He managed to get to his feet, supported once more as the girl stepped in.

"Where are you going?" But there was reverence in her tone. She looked at him differently, she held him differently.

"With you."

Moving forward, under his arm: they left the station together, but the corridor, as if waiting for them, burst immediately into life with apparitions, bizarre and indistinct formations of lumens circling about their knees, startling them both by nattering and swooping and whirling before sinking to the floor, where they dispersed into wisps.

"Paladin," the girl hissed. "Batches have called them. We'll have to go the other way. *Now.*"

Crospinal resisted her tugging. He was watching the ghosts, looking among them for a dog, hoping to be recognized, but these apparitions were dark and squat sculptures, with no faces or features he could discern or recognize. When the girl pulled insistently at him again, he understood that the appearance of these projections might not be a welcome sight. *Paladins? Fathers?* They could both project. The banks were like drones. And there were connections.

Circling in frenetic loci, the apparitions appeared to pass through walls and come back again and again at Crospinal, mapping the area, reporting. He knew the patterns. Dogs had done this.

"*Let's go!*"

But he pulled free. He needed to reach the source, dismayed at the violence and destruction of his past, at the fighting and, most of all, at the mortality hanging over them all. As apparitions crackled, spinning past—and through—him, making him shiver, Crospinal moved down the hall, away from the girl, who stared, helpless:

"I can't go that way," she grunted. "Pilot? Pilot? Where are you going?"

He'd taken her strength. He walked among the apparitions, against their tide, feeling as though he was floating atop the projections as they gyrated uselessly at his feet. Was he expecting a forum? A chance to talk one more time with his father? Resolution seemed absurd, even to him. Yet he did not turn around. She had said *paladin*. There was the increasingly strong smell of ozone.

Unlike the chat of the dogs, these phantoms made high-pitched, buzzing sounds, almost inaudible, a keening transmutation of misanthropy as opposed to the concerned anxieties of his father's far-flung yet gentler neuroses: whatever projected these apparitions up ahead was no father.

Crospinal looked to see if the girl was watching, or if she had tried to follow, but she was asleep now, curled on the floor, cozy in her fresh uniform.

A metal tool, concrete ephemera, regurgitated by the wall—with prongs at one end and a sort of handle at the other—fell clattering at his feet. There was movement within the walls, some large thing, and he walked in an aura of light. His nostrils burned. The exposed skin on his hands and feet tingled. As the world grew and changed, lives winked in and out, like sparks, but left nothing behind. There was no reason to thank the world for this strange and rare brevity. His father had been wrong to offer appreciation and thanks. The world existed beyond ten thousand flickering lifetimes.

Cresting a narrowing dip in the floor (where a handful of silent controllers commiserated, clustered together, bound by an exchange of data, and the shared loss of their stations), the walls became a partially formed lattice, illuminated by flows of light from data streams, dotted here and there with builders, hardly solid at all, reeking of construction. Through the gaps, he saw an open area hinting a volume larger than any that had thus far dwarfed him into this insignificance.

Apparitions moved faster here. He was close.

In a small, delicate recess—the stink of fresh structures so strong he could not swallow or breathe, not more than just gulps of air—several naked humans crammed. Like the girl he had left behind, they slept, fetal, on the hardening floor. One twitched. Possibly the pair of boys, or perhaps girls, he had chased away were among this group—there must have been six, no, seven in all. They looked so similar, with a skimpy garment of plastic sheeting over their pelvic area. Some were still clutching tools: lengths of composite spike; a carbon tube.

Hissing with energy, the apparitions tore right through them all.

With his back to Crospinal, aquiver, stood another person, propped at an incomplete console, arms deep in the holes. The body was trembling with the power coming up through its arms. Maybe sleeping, or entranced. Maybe dead—

And the manifestation called forth suddenly filled the small recess—neither his girlfriend nor the angry woman, but a large man, bigger than his father, in a dark uniform, with a black helmet over his head. The features, turned in quarter profile, were obscured. A man whose anger and frustration emanated like a chilly blast.

Crospinal stepped onto the threshold of this burgeoning station, and the world swayed about him.

Huddled against one of the walls, tucked against the edge of the console, a kneeling youth, stiff with pain, was awake, and met Crospinal's gaze. Shadows pulled at the face, trying to stitch it into the framework of the recess, to draw it in, but flesh was not palatable. Crospinal saw fear in the eyes, a child much younger than himself, and he stepped inside to take the arm of this kneeling girl, or boy, the patterns of the inlay like hot wires against Crospinal's palm, searing him; the skeleton was locked into position, joints fused, and would not budge.

Over the next brief moment there was silence, a frozen tableau, before the manifestation flared and grew much higher than any console this size could contain. Apparitions whirled and Crospinal, looking up, roared, as father would say, at the top of his lungs.

The manifestation had noticed him—

When the entire recess sheared away, like a haptic ending, the arm was torn from Crospinal's grip and he had to stumble back, into the hallway, to avoid falling. A faint rumbling, far below, as recess and contents plunged.

He got to his feet in front of an aperture as tall as himself, and several times wider, at a great height, looking out and down over a chamber infinitely larger than the bay. Each chamber larger than the last. Console, manifestation, batches: all gone.

He stood on the brink of a massive drop.

A large drone retreated, spinning.

And in the distance, unimaginably far, movement, a churning amid columns of polymer clouds.

Data orbs passed each other: four; six; a dozen.

The features on the horizon could only be mountains.

CREW

Coming out of uncertain brightness, Crospinal flew. Arms spread, angled down, he was blinded for a moment. Below were clouds, mist of polymers, waiting instruction, but he quickly shredded their white vapours, soaring out over an open area. The vastness of the world was arrayed for him down there, mostly in tones of grey. Infinite paths, forks and crossings, like the white lines etched up his forearms. Each line indicated a way for life to progress, or fall back, or hit a dead end. No hints which path might be best.

Banking lower still, Crospinal tilted past increasingly challenging obstacles as the landscape neared: clusters of massive carbon tubes, optic bundles slicing in his direction, the information they relayed glittering like sparks. Fresh extensions were being shaped here, a meld of composites and plastics, encouraged to grow to levels he could never have imagined: swarms of mindless builders agitated the polymers and allotropes into mysterious shapes, spitting arcs of toluene behind them. The halls and floors and budding stations formed so fast he had to veer away to avoid them as they rose. Vapour burned his sinuses.

Briefly, black crows flew next to him, maybe four or so, trying to keep up, to tell him something; though he could not understand their language, he was content knowing the birds were there with him, and wondered if he might look, in flight, as graceful as they. But the creatures seemed to be escaping something, rather than accompanying him or offering support, and Crospinal was forced to concede that he, too, might be fleeing a past he could not properly recall.

Now he approached the opening of a rotating corridor, set into a wall of composite unfolding before him so old and massive, Crospinal could soon see no extremes. The mouth of the corridor was a pinpoint pupil in a rat's eye, a black data orb, an occluded porthole, growing larger every second. As the scale settled in, Crospinal had little choice: aim for the centre or smash against the shell of the world. Would he fly out into the ash wasteland, to be incinerated? To enter the tunnel at this speed was madness; to smash against the wall, madder yet.

He was not afraid.

He shot right in.

Before his eyes could adjust, gravity touched unwanted fingers to his body, trying to slow him, to bring him down.

Were there voices?

He was not outside.

In this darkness, losing speed, he would land soon, or crash. As details emerged in the brightening ambient light, he appraised the tunnel accordingly. Lumens struggled to accommodate Crospinal's sudden appearance, and keep up with his rate of travel.

Other than the large girth, the rotating corridor was very much like the one churning outside harmer's corner, through which he had hobbled a thousand times, fighting to stay upright on the shifting tiles.

Had he really once been that bent, unhappy troll?

To help retain the last of his altitude and speed, he had to touch his hands down, pushing off the formations and features jutting up from the tiled floor. His naked flesh felt tough as nylon, with a layer of callus instead of Dacron. Grabbing at whirring eyes of the world, surprising them on their stalks, or launching with all his remaining might from slowly spinning bulkheads, he nonetheless moved forward in increments of decreasing span and velocity, and would touch down soon enough, one way or the other.

He twisted to prevent piercing a brilliant data stream as it poured from the curved ceiling, cascading like the curtain around his daybed when he'd curled there, seeking refuge.

The next barrier, a hazy, white tympanum of catalysts, was unavoidable.

He managed to get his feet under him, to touch first, stumbling forward on the uneven, soft tiles, gasping, pitching headlong—

Red eyes.

He closed his own again, moaned, and re-opened: *the cold red eyes of an elemental.*

He was flat on his back.

The metal rat sat on his chest.

There were loops in life, loops in time. Progress in a particular direction was difficult. The flying, most likely, had not occurred. Which was a shame. Crospinal licked his lips. "What happened?"

"You died," said the metal rat. "Again."

Crospinal stared, waiting for elucidation, or a punch line.

"I'm losing track of the amount of times you've kicked the bucket."

But an elemental's red eyes were resolute, inscrutable, and Crospinal could not ascertain if the machine was kidding or deluded or just plain lying. "I saw mountains," said Crospinal.

"I don't think so."

"I did. And a man, who could shut people off, just by showing up. He was—"

Lifting his arm, he'd frozen, mid-gesture. The sleeve of his uniform was gone. The entire sleeve: latex and the crumbled layers of neoprene and even the spandex once snug beneath it, up against his skin. Entirely gone. Nothing but his skinny arm extruded beyond the uniform's shoulder flange, all bones, one finger frozen, pointing into the face of the tiny elemental straddling his chest.

For some time, Crospinal said nothing. He continued to hold his finger poised, attempting to process the sight. White skin; knobby elbow; strings of sinew from his wrist. The whiter networks of his scar, like a net, wiring it all together. So rarely did he look upon this unattractive bundle of biology—oxygen, carbon, hydrogen, and phosphorus—wrapped in a translucent sheath of pale flesh. The human body, without protection, was alarmingly fallible. He could see the interplay between pale veins and the brighter ridges of the stigmata his father had bestowed upon him. Was there a reading in the configuration of the fibrous tissue, a message to be deciphered, now, after father's death? "What happened?"

"You're a total mess," said the rat. "I would've taken off the rest of that old jumpsuit but I need your permission."

"Why? You didn't ask me before."

"Because the processer is fully fused to your ischium. You'll need surgery."

"My what?"

"Your hip. A bone in your hip. Colleagues and I conferred on a strategy to remove it. Hard for us to ascertain where your body ends and the suit begins."

Remembering the paths and possibilities, laid out below him when he flew—as if choices could somehow be plotted, or at least tracked— he turned his forearm along its axis, studying the unlikely mechanics. He made a fist, turned his arm one way, then the other. Downy hairs, troglophiles, seemed to wither in the ambient light. "A girl," he said, at last, looking up once more. "Where's the girl?"

"Which one?"

This was a good question. Crospinal couldn't answer. Had there been several? At least two. He recalled faces; long hair swaying; fresh, grey uniforms.

He spent a bit more time making sure nothing else was missing. Just the sleeves, it turned out—both of them—though the remainder of his uniform, already in bad shape, was now shockingly *threadbare* (father's voice), and in a terrible way. His boots were entirely flayed open, like petals of a tremulous blossom, back in the garden. He had watched his mitts fall from within a feverish cocoon. The shield and collar were fried. "I was with a girl. She was fighting. That's who I'm looking for. I was with this girl who looked like me, before I saw the mountains."

Stung by memory: standing at the brink, overlooking the vista—

He sat up. The elemental, forced to jump clear, landed without a sound onto an adjacent shelf, raising small clouds where its feet touched down. Leaning away, Crospinal held his breath until the fresh polymers settled—

Another person lay, a few metres to his left. Inert, in uniform and full blue helmet. Fresh boots and fresh mitts. Chest rising. Not a corpse, thankfully. "Who's that?"

Because of the lighting, and the refraction of the visor, Crospinal could not see the face, but the body—though thin, and as tall as him, was not the girl's. (*She had just lain there in the hall, last time he saw her, while the manifestation raged. Absurdly, he had thought she was asleep.*)

"Some crew member," said the metal rat. "Who else could it be?"

Crospinal was no longer in the rotating corridor, if he ever had been. This was some older vestibule. The pale finish of the walls, hardened for ages, reminded him of those inside the throne room. "What else did you do to me?"

"Blood transfusion."

"My *blood*?"

"There was no choice, so don't give me a hard time. Your blood was a cesspool. Bacterium and residues of the distillates pumped into you over the years. I've installed a shunt in your occipital, so you shouldn't go into hemolytic shock. You're done. Good to go."

"I can just walk away?"

"Yep. And don't say thanks."

He rubbed at the back of his neck with his bare fingertips but felt no tender area. There were strips of gauze on the tiles near his feet and an array of tiny metal tools at his side. *Ephemera*. A skittish device parked very close to his waist. Vaguely sentient, the machine was mostly a skinny, transparent tube, which must have been tending to him, or at least involved in the procedures, with a pipette face and thin, threadlike legs. But when Crospinal moved to touch it, to see what it might be, a ridge of cilia oscillated around the lateral flange and the device drifted out of reach, very quickly. Crospinal could have lunged and brought the stupid thing down but he held back. He thought about his feverish climb down, the ribs of the fixed ladder enclosing him as if he'd been swallowed by the world. How far had he descended? With solid pressure against the thin backshell of his tricot—relieved, at least, to know he had not been delivered into the past again—he said: "Tell me how I died."

The metal rat shrugged. "Doesn't really matter. All told, you've made it pretty far. Especially considering you're a low average conversion."

Crospinal got to his feet with ease. He could see aspects of the other person's face better from this vantage: a hint of cheekbone; the shape of lips, pressed against the polymethyl visor like a kiss. Enough to feel some confidence that it was a boy, sleeping there—peacefully, he hoped—in helmet and clean uniform. "Is he going to be okay?"

"What's it to you?"

"Something happened when the manifestation showed up. He made them sick."

"That he did," agreed the metal rat.

Crospinal brushed off what was left of his tunic with pipe cleaner arms. "Aren't you bound by some pledge or oath, or some shit like that, to be nice to me?"

"I gave you your life back. Isn't that enough?"

"You followed me all the way here to save my life? I don't believe any of it."

"You've got the wrong idea. I'm not the same individual that fixed you in the outback. Not the one who sutured your intestines. Not the one who aspirated your lungs or straightened your bones or nursed you back to health. No. I'm not the one you tore apart."

Crospinal didn't like where this conversation was going. He put his hands on his hips, where there remained a nylon ridge, and rested his knuckles against the waistband. The catheter unit chugged weakly, detecting the added pressure, so Crospinal made adjustments. He *could* hear voices, coming through the wall behind him. There *were* other people nearby. "I said I was sorry."

"The unit you destroyed was the same configuration as me—hardware wise, anyhow. Components are re-assimilated, endrohedral atoms dispersed, but the reactor that gave that unit life is gone."

"There was a misunderstanding. I already explained."

"That's it? A misunderstanding? You broke components down to the point where the business plan to put them back together made no sense, and all you have to say is that there was a misunderstanding? You know what? If you attack me, or even try to damage me in any way—*ever*—I won't save you again. None of us will. None of us *rats*. We'll let you stay dead for good. Nothing will get better. No one will win your struggle. We won't care."

"Get better? What do you mean?"

"Just go, all right? Spare me your false questions. Your act. Everything's fine now, so go. The girl you're looking for is through the arch, in the back there. She has problems, too, maybe not as bad as this guy here. At least she's on her feet. *Hypo perfusion*. When one of the paladins trigger, they all shut off. Potassium accumulation's keeping your friend here down."

But Crospinal was already shouldering through the archway, breaking away soft flakes of composite with his exposed shoulder in his haste to see the girl again—

Stopping in his tracks pretty quick.

The low-ceilinged chamber (a bigger space than he'd been expecting) was packed, perhaps twenty people or more, some sprawled on stools, others reclining on the floor or leaning against the walls in various states of duress and exhaustion. All wore fresh uniforms. And blue helmets, which were the rarest type. Voices died at his entrance. There was a tension, though he could not be sure if he had brought the state with him or if it had been here, in the room, before he arrived. He had only ever seen one blue helmet before, maybe two, ill-formed, in the belly of an ancient dispenser that had eventually crawled into a cupboard outside the major toluene station to retire.

All these blue helmets faced him now, visors ashen. He stood, decrepit in the archway, arms exposed, feet bare against the threshold's tile, his own uniform nothing but a sagging tricot and disintegrating pants.

"*Crospinal.*"

To hear his name meant a spell was broken, or cast. From the rear of the chamber, through the crowd, the girl approached. Even without seeing her face, he knew it was her, by her stature, the movements of her frame, the cadence of her voice. She came toward him through the others, supported either side by another. Despite her helmet and fresh uniform, she seemed almost as damaged as he had once been, her legs not working properly, one foot dragging, left arm curled in tight to her chest. He felt a clenching inside, a sympathy, and a repulsion.

"They won't be back," she said, "until the next console. We were waiting. We need to go. Are you able now? Have you been discharged?"

Her words were slightly distorted by a remoteness helmets inflicted, which had always creeped Crospinal out as a kid, whenever his father had made him put one on. He recalled recitals, a voice coming from the comm around the chin ridge. He took a step back.

Was he expected to share some fundamental knowledge with these people? He did not know what this knowledge might be, nor have any clue how to access it. Common knowledge lurked, elusive. These people expected him to act, to lead. They wanted some monumental decision, or words that would change the direction of their lives.

Behind the girl and the two helping her, rising from the floor of a smaller chamber, set even farther back, he saw the three dream cabinets now, arranged in a ring, doors facing out. Emerging from the material of the floor, they had been exposed, so far, maybe a quarter of their length, glistening fresh, pushing up from the ring of dissolving tiles. He approached, drawn, pushing through. The girl stopped to watch him pass. Purple fixative stained the pit: a veil of polymer mists blurred the area where the cabinets had broken through. All around the fresh doorframes, though not yet fully regurgitated, the ring of lights had already started to flicker.

"Luella's here? Is this her?"

Helmets turned as he walked; the crew seemed to tense at the sound of his sister's name, as if they expected the simple phonemes might trigger some monumental event.

"She's not here," said the girl. She was no longer angry with him for invoking. "These are new sailors. Never awoke. They're coming up all along the promenade. A hundred or more. That's why the prosceniums are being built. That's why the batches were sent. We came to protect the sailors, hook a batch or two, if we can."

Even when the girl looked up, Crospinal could not see her eyes through her visor.

"And to wait for me," he said.

"Yes."

"Why?"

"We have to go to the cockpit now. You'll understand soon."

Around the base of the booths—though damp with a tacky film of toluene and roils of meshing polymers—beckoned the familiar green carpet, just like the one that had offered him those rare moments of comfort over the past few years, when his relationships had been faltering. Staring at the textures, he wanted only to stand upon it, move his bare toes, even as the floor transformed. He would close his eyes and drift off to a place of dreams and peace. He might step inside a cabinet, if one happened to be empty, and if he could connive it to open—

Close enough to touch the nearest door, his bare hand hovered centimetres from the surface. The smell, expelled with these sailors, from where they'd been dreaming, and the low roar of time, funneling through the booths, washed over him: he imagined a man, much like his father, stirring inside each cabinet, drawing cold liquid slowly into his lungs, a man utterly unaware of what had transpired since he went to sleep, unable to decipher present nor past when he would finally step free.

"Everything is changing," Crospinal said. He turned. His father had told him composites were encroaching on the pen, and must be held at bay, like darkness, but that wasn't true, either; composite was transformation, and transformation was inevitable. "This," he said loudly, to the gathered crew, who were all looking at him, "is endtime."

Highlights of physiognomies through the matt visors reflected fear and awe, but no more than he felt at hearing himself say such a thing. *Endtime?* He heard his father's voice. Now Crospinal put his bare hand flat against the door of the dream cabinet and felt the chill, like a shock travelling up his arm. Was the passenger inside dreaming of monsters? Were all dreams tainted now? Or was this father in a more pleasant place, where Crospinal used to go, when indications of struggles and questions of meaning and purpose and responsibilities were wiped clean?

When he removed his hand from the door, a tingling in his skin remained. Were these viruses from wherever the cabinets came from burrowing into his flesh? Crospinal turned to the girl. "Are you all right?"

The girl straightened, and nodded.

"Then take me."

To expedite their retreat, they would have travelled (she explained) down the *chute*, or *along* it, which, Crospinal deduced, must be the airless shaft he had drifted in, unconscious—the *pylon*—to be rescued by the men with the symbiotic animals on their backs. In a full uniform and helmet, the chutes were negotiable, but Crospinal had no arrangement for oxygen, nor would a fresh helmet mate with the damaged flange around the collar of his compromised unit, even if they had a spare helmet and the integrity of his uniform wasn't shot. So the group was forced to employ a secondary means of transit, where oxygen was consistent, and gravity held them down, bare feet, bare arms, and all.

Three people left the chamber where the dream cabinets were budding. Crospinal, the girl, and a shorter but broader boy, whose uniform conformed tightly, and who was lending a shoulder to assist the girl's hobbling progress. Crospinal knew this other was a boy because the visor was set clear, and his features were craggy and heavy. Like several people Crospinal had encountered since the pen exploded, though clearly not a *batch*, this boy seemed incapable of speech. Yet to be seen, Crospinal supposed, if this were truly the case. He had been wrong before.

Beyond the arch, as they departed the chamber, the metal rat and its patient remained. Crospinal did not hold the gaze for long, though he knew those red eyes followed him. Exposed by their stare, he worried that the scrutiny could undermine his newly budded determination.

The patient, he saw—the crew member on the floor—had rolled onto his side now, mitts clasped together, and was breathing regularly, tricot swelling.

The corridor extended for some distance, past the makeshift triage area, before becoming too narrow for any comfortable passage here; they slipped behind a bowed panel, into a crawlspace, transversing inside the wall. Pale green ambients in the composite swelled and proceeded them in fits and starts. There was the stench of dust, and recycling. This place was like a slipway between transfer tubes, where Crospinal had first ruptured the sleeve of his uniform, on his way back from the harrier, a lifetime ago. The day his father had died. He recalled where the shell of the world had split, the overnight damage, and the vision he'd had, dissolving into the wasteland outside. He marvelled, now, at this memory, and began to tell the girl what had happened, feeling that the events, and the correlations, must be important.

She stopped to listen, looking back over her shoulder. The boy, too. In this dim lighting, her visor had become translucent, as well, and Crospinal saw her face clearly again: her blue eyes darker now, her frown.

His head was thudding.

There wasn't much room in the crawlspace.

She didn't understand the point of his story.

Neither did he.

She said: "You're a pilot, Crospinal. You know that?"

He shook his head. Somehow his name had returned. This girl was trying to evoke the intangible. Perhaps she had succeeded.

"Paladins can't hurt you."

He almost said, *One broke my heart*. That pain could never be excised. When they walked again, light slid easily over the helmets.

"The rat told me I had died. Is that true?"

"Elementals don't have power over you, unless you give them power. You should avoid them. They seldom tell the truth."

The floor felt rougher against the soles of Crospinal's feet.

He hadn't made the recess fall, or the console and the people inside. He'd just stepped across the threshold tile as the world shifted, wanting to take the hand of the stricken boy, to help him.

Ahead, the other two moved shoulder to shoulder. Crospinal followed them. When they reached a juncture, a branch of darker tunnels, she raised the forearm of her uniform to touch it to a comm plate, mounted in a frame, and held it there, which was a futile gesture—Crospinal was about to tell her—since these sorts of plates were inert and did nothing at all—

Something came rushing from the darkness. Along the passageway, headed for them, bringing with it a glow—something *large*—hissed to a sudden stop. Crospinal, stepping back, saw a primitive machine, certainly a vehicle, with a teardrop-shaped body and three saddles, each big enough for a person to straddle. This was no elemental, no device with personality or intelligence, but an appliance, to serve, to take them from here to . . . someplace else.

They got on: Crospinal at the back (after a series of missteps), the girl in the middle, the silent boy in front. There were controls there, with which the boy fiddled. He held both forearms against the plate and the vehicle lurched forward.

A second later, accelerating through the wan slipway, Crospinal had to duck to stay out of the growing wind; no protective shield would rise before his face.

<hr />

More people waited, in fresh uniforms, but with no helmets on. They were watching the transit emerge from the aperture—into light—and pull into the landing, settling there with obvious deference, perhaps even trepidation. Crospinal dismounted awkwardly and stepped toward them. Their faces were similar, hair shorn, and he could not tell the gender, nor distinctions among them. From behind the two who had brought him here, he stared these people down, until they averted their gaze. They each held an arm out, slowly. A pattern of flickering gold lights shimmered in the air itself, and the whiff was ozone.

Crospinal was led past a hump in the floor, stepping off the platform and up to the rim of a large, bowl-shaped area, under a domed ceiling.

Arcs of small consoles, arranged in several rows, lined the slope of the basin. Thirty, thirty-five consoles, and at each stood a crew member with their back to him, in fresh uniform and blue helmet, sleeves deep into the holes. He stood there, gazing down, thinking for the briefest of moments that this could be a trap to conjure an angry manifestation, or maybe even his girlfriend. Instead, he saw apparitions, so faint he had to blink to bring them into focus, and even then, drifting aimlessly, they moved languorously past the features of the cluttered room, past the oblivious people. Were these phantoms compromised somehow, slowed? Certainly there were no frantic dogs, or any mercurial projections. No incessant chatter and worry and energy.

A crackle of brilliance from above made him look:

Where the walls curled in on themselves to form the ceiling, banks of dark gates angled out, washed in the growing light, as if they had arrived to watch over the proceedings. Large banks, like the one in the pen, with the same grey, null sheen. Tethered beneath each, in suspended thrones, was a father. A gathering of passengers, of sailors, connected.

The network of conduits bobbed toward the gates, but also fanned out, laterally, connecting the fathers to each other. There were ten in all. The ozone reek of their connections intensified, and Crospinal tried not to gag, or turn away.

"This is the cockpit," said the girl. "This is what Luella gave us. She said you would come."

Engines thumped in their distant haven. He took a step closer. "Luella told you?"

"Generations ago. Long before I was saved."

The name seemed to echo. At the farthest end of the cockpit, several more crew stood, hard to see how many, because they were blurred, crammed shoulder to shoulder, flickering somewhat in what could only be a haptic. Watching them, reacting and countering with scenarios and educations and images only they could see, Crospinal knew how absurd he must have looked all those times to his own father. The ghostly fractals, seen from the outside, where Crospinal watched, might be figments of an unhealthy mind.

"*Crospinal—*"

He had already started toward the crew.

THE SAILORS' HAPTIC

Vanished now from all but seemingly irremediable fragments of memories, scattered in recesses and crevasses, subsumed by the structure, juxtaposed and drifting through foetid back rooms, the other world once had *permanence*, and primordial history, never swayed by mere bursts of instructions or the whims of some remote generator. There had been a stillness, and patience, and the linear passage of eons. No engines turned over in unreachable depths, no landscape of false ruins, painted on lenses of the portholes. Toluene didn't dissolve chambers only to have them reconfigured and flash-hardened by mindless machines to suit the capricious agendas of an unfathomable power.

Yet a compression of time, and distances travelled, passing through flux lines of force and maybe back again, had brought distortions, and loops, and wiped the cortexes nearly clean, to lose coherency of the other world along the convoluted way.

Mountains of his father's fractured recollections were here, traces of them at least, their figments looming over the shadows of this haptic, joining memories of *stars*, from the first sailor Crospinal had met, in the sky station, and soft shards from other lives, all floating down, gleaned from the sailors tethered to the gates above, passed among them. Remnants of their world lurked in the bones of latent genealogies. Combined, they gathered momentum.

When a passenger woke, over the years of this or the years of that, they brought with them from their dream cabinet a tenuous network of recollections, memoirs so far out of context, so arcane and isolated, that only faint spheres of fragile logic could rail against the chaos. Even then, not for long. His own father had been fortunate and desperate enough to find, or maybe call into existence, *the pen*, connecting to a gate there, and raising his children. But Crospinal's father, in his solitude, could never rationalize nor arrange the ruins of his past into any form of tribute, just as much as he never really understood where it was that he had returned to life, or for what reason, not even within the information from the banks flooding into the back of his head.

But sailors were just men, ultimately, and men get sick and die, and the ethos they try so hard to build and sustain dies with them. Sons get older, and they wander off, bearing memories of their own, and echoes of their fathers'.

Fringes of the massive haptic lapped at his bare skin, sinking tendrils, hooklike, right into his scars. Crospinal already knew the impending immersion—without a functional uniform, or his dad to project him—would be nothing like entering the bland escapes from his childhood. Simple messages and haptic lessons he had taken part in as a boy had been succinct, and—from the sole source of his father's perspective—relatively *cohesive*. Where multiple spheres of shaky logic and viewpoints were brought together, memories of the lost world were cast down, to mingle, and a coherence had begun, a bastion, bringing the passenger's old world closer: this haptic would engulf Crospinal entirely.

He did not hesitate, stepping around and between consoles, around the entranced crew, faces hidden by visors, as if he, too, were an apparition. Walking was as slow as it had been at the bottom of the viscous water. The fabric of visions and recollections and ancient desires, woven together, more dense than any single passenger could relay, slowed Crospinal's progress, distorted time and pulled him irrevocably into an embrace he could never deny: here, at last, was human contact.

The floor before him was littered with concrete ephemera. Fragments, small metal tools, obscure forms: he kicked them as he stepped forward. Other artifacts fell from the ceiling, clanking as he passed.

He arched his spine, to shed his self, surprised by how readily he wanted to release his persona, shake it off, though flashes of identity persisted, like flakes of static composite, almost impossible to lose, each flash retaining a facet of his cognizance.

He knew he was walking through an area crammed with devices and consoles. He knew he might have died, several times over, and had been brought back to life. He knew there were fathers above him, and that they were linked together. He had facilitated the link, by entering.

Toward the end of the cockpit, in the haptic, lesser apparitions passed through him while the delirious fathers rustled overhead—

Elsewhere, a girl in full uniform and rare blue helmet called his name, the name his father had given him, shouting it in clear warning.

But he was dispersing as he went, like a cloud of polymers, helping to make up the walls and floors and furniture. Deeper in the mnemonic fray, his last thought was of being locked inside a dream cabinet, as it drained of chilly liquid, taking him from one algorithm to another. Or was he standing in the pen, in front of his father's throne, while colours and characters capered about like simple-minded fools—

There was, abruptly, an *isthmus*, upon which Crospinal stood. Hands behind his back.

Then, in the backyard of a small house, where he sat at a patio table, mug of whiskey between cold hands, looking up through the branches of a delicate oak at a dark sky, seeing breathtaking arrays of stars. The night was chilly and clear. He stared, unable to be moved by such sights. He'd be there soon, among them—

Wind pushed hair from his eyes. Standing on a strip of beach at night, the lights out to sea looking almost like another land, an intriguing and beckoning country he could never discern during the day. The beach was at the end of his street, between rows of buildings. More like a strip of debris and junk than a beach. There was a mattress before him, and foam on the rocks. An idle man, sitting there, in the dark. He looked at the lights again, out to sea, thinking of the family next door, in the apartment adjacent to his, who moved about frequently, always shuffling, moving, regardless of the hour. He heard the occasional brief shout, as if they somehow managed to surprise each other shuffling in the hallways of the tiny place. Never did he hear voices. Never the tones of talking, not from anyone in the family, not even the kid, who lived there, with his parents.

The boy.

Who seemed happy enough when they passed each other on the stairs.

Crospinal's meager contribution had woven in: ways to kill time; living with pain; apparitions as friends. Drifting past the crew now—their arms in holes, shuddering slightly, as if aware of his passage, and perhaps even who he was—past the last of the consoles, a thousand phantasms unravelling his fibres, picking him clean; he closed his eyes and was gone.

Nudged from one body, one scene, to another.

Once again he was walking, this time among a group of people in strange, inert garb, midway between the world of flux he had lived in and the lost world, lingering beyond.

Rows of dream cabinets, either side, open, and empty. They were called *stats*. Stats would soon be filled, and sealed.

The other men talked, but quietly, among themselves. They never talked to Crospinal, bringing up the rear, one glove resting on the rail of the dolly, maintaining its height. Talking sounds were a drone, the sounds most men made, pointless and dull, of no consequence, background to the thoughts that flitted like silver minnows in the dying pools of his brain.

He had not been sleeping well. His hands had started to shake. He felt as though he would never fill his lungs to capacity again.

He had a wife, and he would return to her after struggling through each day—trying to stay intact—often entering their apartment to a different kind of tension, one that was like tiny needles pushing against his skin. These days, the air inside his home passed right through his pores, through the holes that the tiny needles made in his flesh.

He and his wife would eat together, in silence. She never asked about his tremors or his day or showed any concern. Whenever he looked at his hands, flat on the table, he could not really discern the trembling either, yet he was convinced the shaking would soon break him apart. Incongruence between what he felt and what he saw was in no way comforting, serving only to add to his disconcertion and general state of discomfort.

"Boarding starts tomorrow." His voice sounded like blocks, falling. Wooden blocks. His tongue was wooden.

Clarissa. That was his wife's name. He recalled this now, like a sharp knock. The recollection brought her image into clearer focus. Nevertheless, Clarissa did not respond, nor even look up. Her hair was thinning. A whorl of flesh visible where the roots were grey. Flakes of psoriasis poised there.

Dinner this evening was a form of stew. Clarissa remained bent over her plate, and he watched her jaw moving, thinking of insects with mandibles, dissolving prey with their gastric fluid.

Or maybe Clarissa had already left by this point. Maybe he was alone in the apartment, sitting at the table, by himself. His bones were sore.

He tried again: "The stats are ready. The hub is full. Cortexes are beginning to think. Contract's almost up."

Nothing. A hiss of static. No, not static: next door, they were creaking about again. He heard the floorboards, the shuffling, and one of those rare shouts. Clarissa flinched but still did not look up. He watched his hands, inert either side of his bowl. He felt the shaking intensify but they appeared perfectly still.

Clarissa might have been crying.

Sometimes he would lay awake in the middle of the night, listening to the family. All hours, day or night. They had no routine. The boy was seven or eight, but Crospinal didn't know much about children, except that no child was going into a stat. The youngest passenger, other than the batches, was twenty four. A woman from Nairobi. He'd seen her at one of the conferences. She smiled a lot, in a nervous way. Her hands were very steady.

The oldest heading out was two hundred and seventy four.

Part of his job now was to guide the dolly, like he was doing. A cell in the palm of his glove adjusted the hover and equilibrium.

Concern gave him night sweats.

Startled, he looked suddenly about for his wife, his apartment—seeking the uneaten stew and red melamine table—but they had vanished.

Stats lined either side. Open stats.

The men in front of him were talking.

This load was fresh strings of polymers and scales of allotrope mesh. One of the last to the development area, in the north of the site, where they would be bombarded with instructions of light. Or rather, bombarded with a latency to *understand* instructions.

Dollies could almost guide themselves, like most low-functionals, but laden with raw materials, which sometimes developed ideas of their own. Even before composites were imprinted, they needed watching.

His foreman was a short, bald man who showed too many teeth too often, and who called what they did with dollies *chaperoning*.

Chaperoning, he would say, staring with his little eyes, *was a job for dumbasses*.

When he first brought up the tremors, and the sleeplessness, and the other unsettling sensations that were taking over, he was told simply by his foreman, *go home*. So he explained very carefully how he had been watching the pulses of instructions for so long now that he was able to decipher them, and that he could see individual polymers in the air, and he signed several forms, and reported to medical. He did not look in the development area again, keeping his eyes downcast. Though the light called to him on occasion and the other workers laughed at his fear. *There's visors for that shit, health and fucking safety. Why did they have to work with such retards anyway?*

Once, he had excelled at school, a good student, eager. Made it as far as second year of his Masters and, from there, getting cherry-picked for a pretty great job. There was a girl from childhood, and parents that seemed to *love* him.

Then he heard stories about the transponders, latent under the skin of the batches. He couldn't stop thinking about them. Ten thousand embryos, all tampered with. He felt there were beasts, searching for him.

Was he supposed to know as much as he did? While looking for his inlays, he ended up in hospital, bandaged to the elbow, with a nurse at the door. The tremors started then. They were difficult to hide, though at first he politely feigned belief when people told him they couldn't see the shakes. He asked so carefully, an impromptu poll, thin smile on his face, trying not to draw too much attention. Holding his hand out, asking.

"Shaking? No."

The problem was connected to the wires in his arms. He would have to get them out discretely. He didn't ask anyone about them, not the doctors, who clearly knew, and not his mother, when she visited, who did a pretty good job portraying concern.

The second time he tried to remove the inserts, the hospital put him on suicide watch, and he was kept in a ward for a month, sedated.

He was even more careful after that.

Though he was no longer consulted on matters of construction, he kept his job, and his option to take up a stat.

The tremors were getting worse.

He worked for a short while, then took more time off when the situation had not improved. He could not abide being alone. By this point, Clarissa was certainly gone. Guiding dollies, and checking optics in the massive compartments, seeing what was growing or not, and knowing that the other men were laughing at him, was still better than staying at home, listening to the floorboards creak next door and imagining the boy walking about.

Curtains of light would fall, like sparks, onto the tubes and buckies and complex grilles. Ozone made his head ache.

Once, a long time ago, when he himself was a boy, his hands had been so steady he could hold a brimming glass of cold water at arm's length, never spilling a drop.

He never did talk much, even back then. He had a dog. A white bitch, chosen out of sympathy, because she sat in the back corner of the kennel while the others in the litter approached and stood leaping against the mesh for the touch of his mother's fingers.

His father, when they brought the puppy home in a cardboard box, cowering in torn-up newspaper, would not acknowledge the dog. From his chair, with his glasses on his head, he scowled at the fuss. When his wife got down on her hands and knees with their son to encourage the unnamed pup out of the box, he told her to get up.

Don't be so miserable, she said.

His father did not reply, just glared, until they were seated around the table at dinner. (Canned corn; boiled potatoes; frying steak in a tepid pool of brown water.) The dog remained in its box on the mat by the back door, watching them, trembling. Though they had cut a flap in the cardboard, like a drawbridge for the pup to leave from, she remained inside.

The thing's sleeping in the basement. It's not allowed upstairs in the daybeds. And if it pees on the carpets, it'll live outside. I don't want to hear it barking, or whining. And don't expect me to walk it.

Much later, old enough to go to university on a scholarship to study at Tech Greene, he realized his father had been jealous of the attention the pup received, and despised it for that reason.

The dog led a miserable life, afflicted with hip problems, unsocialized, kicked once in a while by his father (who seemed, as years went by, to also lead an increasingly miserable existence).

Even in the hospital, when he spent most of his time in bed, dredging up memories, he couldn't remember what they had called the dog.

Not long after he took the job, he felt his life unravelling: his wife leaving him, the boy next door, walking the floorboards, the job itself going from lead, to staff, to chaperone—he thought about his dog more and more, unable to stop, until sometimes it seemed there were dozens of the poor creatures cowering inside him.

Clarissa wiped her mouth and looked up at him with cold eyes. He was surprised to see her but made no remark, in case she vanished again. His mouth hung open and he could not close it. Tremors shook him from inside. Clarissa didn't want to hear about the stats, or about how he was poisoned, or about the thousands of children frozen in the banks. She didn't want to hear about him floating off soon, into dreamland.

<hr/>

Like breathing for the first time, Crospinal gasped into a different moment of lucidity. Within the sailor's haptic, there were other people, standing, nearly touching. He was the only one in such a dishevelled state. He had this one instant to look up, and see the fathers, suspended above him, webbed to each other, before another wave of memories, another life, brought him under again.

Dieback began when *charlara fraxina* made the leap from trees of the genus *fraxinas* to other deciduous species. Perhaps the Latin name for the blight should have been reconsidered once *fraxinas* was no longer the sole victim, but priorities shift, and gaggles of scientists didn't have time anymore to sit around large tables classifying flora and fauna in a dead language. There were other issues to contend with. More pressing issues. Broad-leafed trees, in every country that could grow broad-leafed trees, had begun to sicken.

Ensconced within years of empirical accumulation, science mostly, dendrology toward the end, and memories of fieldtrips as a young, shy woman, to the taiga, and to the shrinking rainforest, mingled with a few paltry recollections of awkward relationships that didn't last very long. *Such promise as a child*, they would say. Award ceremonies, a published paper or two, followed by solitude, mostly, as an adult.

Passing through a forest of unreal proportions, trunks bigger than her torso, whipping past. The sky, when she looked up, like a semaphore of white flags flickering through the leaves. *Ash*, she thought, and motion slowed. Names were keys, connections to draw elements forth. Names brought souls and gave memories and dreams a dusting of true form. Names like *Crospinal*, and *Luella*, and *Richardson*, who had a daughter he loved so much he sometimes wished she had never been born.

He saw a flashed image, the capture of his hand, reaching, thin, naked arm rising up into the light.

<hr />

Moisture made it colder still. In winter, even the air froze, glazing the rocks and benches and grass with a coat of ice. Everything was grey. Kids wouldn't visit. *Weather was too bad*. That's what they'd say. *Roads were icy*.

Behind her, some confounded smart machine or other approached, no doubt sent by the administrators to coax her back indoors. She could hear the annoying attempts *to be heard*, the equivalent to a throat being cleared, had a person been sent. All these machines were able to move soundlessly, and the *imitation* of life, the false flaw they often tried to expose to a human to demonstrate a hollow concept of empathy, was most of the reason why she despised elementals.

She refused to look into the red eyes.

There would come a point in human history, she knew, when reproducing would be a bad idea.

She watched grey sky and grey land merge.

Everyone wondered, even in less dire times, whether bringing a child into the world was wise. But the wisdom of choosing *not* to have children had to become *explicitly* clear soon, even for those who didn't have much capacity for reflection. *Another generation could not be sustained.*

Even though she'd already had her own children, foibles and all. Both were born during her early twenties, just like her grandmother had done, but a bit of a scandal to have more than one, and at such a young age. Bright, lanky creatures, exhausting, selfish and mercurial, lying there with her after swimming, breathing heavily in half-sleep, salt in their hair, drying in the sun. Magnificent enough to take your breath away.

The swallowtails on this island were as big as her two hands together.

Perhaps the point of revelation had already passed, or was upon humanity now. All selfish reasons to have children (and what other type of reason could there be?)—for the sake of the couple; having reached that stage, another test to their bond, another step in their travels together, or maybe from a more desperate place, a futile attempt at throwing sand in the face of mortality, or even for the brief escape of coitus—were overshadowed by the fact that new lives could not be sustained. The gig was up. Growth, small joys, pain and love and fear.

The world was dying.

When her children got older, they lost their brightness, ensnared in a world that was dying around them, perceptions of themselves and their purpose suffering, fading, but with young families of their own, children born underweight, dangerously premature. . . .

Forests were gone.

Memories, cold as the cardiopelgic solution that would soon fill her lungs.

⁕

Shuddering, Crospinal came to, his own essences seeping back; the haptic had collapsed.

Crew were stirring, withdrawing.

Was his role to lead these people? To save them?

He felt winds in the cockpit, stilling, settling his thoughts. The sailors above eased, too, as if collectively catching their breath; they slept.

But there were legacies within Crospinal now, residues threading back through distance and time, back to where his father was from, and to lives that had played out there. He felt these threads flickering like tethers when he took a deep breath.

A shift had occurred while the passengers dreamt—

Crospinal blinked, and turned to see if the girl was still there in the entrance to the cockpit. Others, who had been immersed, turned also, groggy, glancing about.

A fundamental shift had occurred—

His father had wanted to prepare him, to accept these legions within, to accommodate them, but died disappointed.

In blue helmet and fresh uniform, the girl remained in the opening, in the same posture, making Crospinal suspect much less time had passed in the haptic than he had imagined. As he began toward her, Crospinal heard sailors above exchange dull, disturbed murmurs. Were they having nightmares?

But he did not consider for long, because controllers appeared, screeching in, swooping, getting louder and louder, sending mists of polymers from the surfaces around Crospinal as if the whole world was startled. A sailor shrieked. With his arm up over his face, ducking low, Crospinal ran toward the exit.

ENDTIME

It is not our eyes or ears, nor even our intellects, that report the world to us; but it is our own moral nature that settles at last the significance of what exists about us. In all respects each age has interpreted the universe for itself, and has more or less discredited the interpretations of previous ages.

—**Richard Maurice Bucke**

FOX AND BEAR

They huddled, three of them (though it seemed as if multitudes huddled, in turn, within the loose confines of his body), between fresh walls that gently shifted. The light that gave direction to the world surged from the ceiling in waves of brilliance, washing shadows from their faces that crept slowly back, a little slower each time. Beneath them, floor tiles formed, grilles taking shape. The air stunk of change and ozone and Crospinal had lost his tattered boots altogether: all that remained were two shreds of inert fabric, hanging from the attachment hooks, at the cuff of his uniform. The entire left leg was split to the hip, exposing his boney knee, and thigh, when he crouched, like now, to pray.

Moving his toes against the transmogrification, feeling the change against his bare skin, he ran through a brief list of sights and wonders and obstacles, but ended up mumbling half-finished words, overwhelmed by the volume and incongruity of the experiences that rose to his lips for pronouncement, none of which he could contextualize, now that he tried, feeling pressed for time and out of breath and haunted by the passengers he now hosted.

He lifted his face. His voice had stopped altogether. The idea struck him like a blow. The girl's visor was translucent. Staring into her eyes, he could tell she was just as afraid of him as she was of every other event unfolding in her life now. She had been expecting Crospinal—all crew had—but he was not who they expected.

Under a sudden focus, rare and crystalline enough for him to behold, crouching there—as two building machines scurried past, and toluene dripped onto his shoulders and arms—similarities close enough to jolt him back through time, as if thrown: he was stunned, before he made any pronouncement. He had wanted to reassure the girl but realized now that the distance between the illicit ceremony with Fox and Bear and when he had first left the pen was very short, mere days: the naming of the elementals was precursor to the end of his youth, catalyst for his straying, the beginning of his loss, and change.

They were coming back from the garden. Crospinal had destroyed a swath of growth. His sleeves were blue with the coating of fallen leaves. Fragments of branches clung to the Kevlar. Heading through the transfer tube, Crospinal in front, rocking painfully from side to side, grunting whenever his weight transferred. He was squat, bent, distorted by pain. His knees flared with white bursts, the way they always did, barking out criticism, taunting, complaining, while the two elementals moved quietly behind him and did not respond.

Perhaps, in the aura of the moments surrounding this memory, Crospinal had tested the guardians, falling from a hunched shelf, or straying out of range, in the round pool, pretending to ignore the crimson stare while he lay on his back under the enhanced water, shield steaming and bubbling, or maybe he'd stood before them, berating them, ostensibly for their silence and dimwittedness, but (he realized) more likely for their self-sufficiency and lack of doubt, which he had not recognized as a self-involved child. Inexpressive, inhuman faces angled down. When they stood and stared, their limbs were perfectly still.

Spells broke when two dogs raced past, chasing each other, happy that Crospinal was returning, safe, to the pen, to be by his father's side again, barking with a mad excitement: "Crospie, Crospie, Crospie!"

Making his frustration seethe.

They vanished down the tube.

Crospinal had been planning to give the elementals names since the year of disparate viewpoints. Before that, perhaps since birth, the nugget of the idea had been forming, unrevealed. This would be defiance against his father, against the world. Not because he wanted the miserable machines to have an identity, like his own; instead, he wanted them to share his burden of responsibility and the insecurities that accompanied it.

Naming, his father would say, *is the origin of all civilized things. Without a name, there is no distinction.*

And as his father dozed and mumbled, Crospinal hobbled out to the gardens for his exercise. He had become convinced he would go through with it, tired of inaction, palms sweating inside his mitts and loose bowels making his processor whine in anticipation. Driven toward this point with the aid of jabs shooting up his thighs, and from the look on his father's face when he was unable to complete the simplest of tasks.

This was the year of independent thinking.

Crospinal was . . . five?

When the dogs dispersed, recalled to his father to offer their report, Crospinal stopped walking. He breathed deeply to try to clear tension. Pivoting, in a lurch, he put one trembling mitt up, palm out. The red eyes stared but the elementals came on regardless, until he commanded them to *halt*.

Which they did.

Naming these companions in this refuge at what could only be endtime was an antithesis, an echo of his past, repeated once more in time. An attempt to counter or repair what he had done, to undo what could not be undone, or reintroduce it?

Crospinal put his hands (bare now) on the shoulders of the uniforms, one on each, and felt the violation against his skin, capillaries at work, the material fighting against the moisture on his palms.

"I hid from the next wave of my father's dogs," he told them.

(Controllers' alarms were still going off: another attack on the dream cabinets, the girl had said—*come, Crospinal, hurry, hurry!*

But he insisted they stop on the way back, coming through the crawlspace. Like he had stopped, that day, Fox and Bear.)

Within the frame of their helmets, both faces peered into his own. Marked with awe, and with elements of the fear he had earlier discerned, they were waiting for him to continue. They were waiting for him to guide them. Crospinal tightened the muscles of his jaw:

"Those red eyes," he said, "changed. First, I named *Fox*. I touched the alloy chestplate. Because he was no longer an *it*. His eyes *narrowed*. And then I turned to Bear, and I touched him, too, palm flat on his chest, and I told him his name, and it seemed to me those eyes changed just a fraction, a shift in radiance. Fox used to watch me the most, always staring, staying closest, hovering. I felt their power grow. If not grow, then *change*. I felt Bear *move*, and Fox, rising up, separating from me."

Crospinal turned toward the source of the distant alarms, where controllers shrieked. Someone had shouted. Another person. There'd been concussion, sending ripples through the flooring.

"Father discovered what I'd done. A dog must have watched, or one of his spirits, drifting through that tube. I don't remember how he found out. Perhaps I confessed in a prayer, or he gave me a pellet to say the truth, and I fell asleep.

"He never forgave me, though he claimed to. I think he gave up on me at that point.

"Fox and Bear took their names with them. They took their names, lifted from characters in a child's haptic, and never came back."

They looked at him. The boy was newly depilated. His forehead was thick, eyes bright. Behind their visors, they both had blue eyes, like him. The girl blinked. They were watching his face.

"Your name is Clarissa," he said, placing his free hand flat against her chest, just below the collar of her uniform, and energy tickled him. He had been that sailor, briefly, in the cockpit. He knew what it was like to be Clarissa, if only for an instant, knew enough that the yearning, the strangeness of *being alive*, the struggle, were bonds reassuring constantly between them across the worlds, across time, and he felt strands of her pass through his fingertips, into this other.

"*Clarissa.*"

The word, so quiet that the world trembled again, as if straining, incredulous to witness this event.

Something inside the broken tricot of Crospinal's fractured uniform clicked into place and started to rattle; he adjusted the plates with an awkward elbow as the girl tried to back away, but he held her. Had his father experienced this burst of hope while naming him, and naming his sister? Had names given them the ability to leave home?

Crospinal turned to the boy.

"And you are Richardson."

The boy, mute, continued to stare, as if unchanged, but Crospinal felt it.

Engines whined, altering arcane purposes. The alarms of the controllers had stopped, and he had not noticed when.

Inside the wall, a device clanked by, unseen, machines belonging to the crew, in no servitude to him, not knowing he was there, not caring if he named every human there was to name.

Could he grant invulnerability?

His own name had hardly prevented misfortune.

A quick, shuddering sequence of muffled explosions put an end to the ceremony: the three of them turned, faces lifted toward the disturbance. Even the walls had recoiled. Polymers rained down.

Batches had returned. A dozen or so, he was told later, by crew that had fought. They had attempted to access the new dream cabinets to prevent the sailors from emerging, though how these naked humans expected to tear sealed booths apart with bare hands—even if they did manage to get close enough—Crospinal could not conceive.

The regrouped attackers were reticent, though, and skittish, and by the time Crospinal, Clarissa, and the stout boy he'd called Richardson made it back to the chamber, outside which Crospinal had been drained of blood, the batches were already defeated, scattering back to the darkness from whence they'd come. Without the active console nearby, no manifestation or paladin could get close, or accompany the contingent, projecting apparitions about their feet.

Ambients in the walls of the station were much brighter than they had been; uniforms of the crew who had remained behind seemed to glow. Their helmets and tricots were reflective sheens. Fleetingly, Crospinal wondered if this display—the renewed attack, the brisk defense, the surge of lumens at this battle scene—were for his sake, because of the naming, but that was absurd.

The batches had done no real damage.

On alert, adrenaline levels elevated, the crew that had defended the dream cabinets watched Crospinal enter, Clarissa and Richardson behind him. The visors of the crew made them look like some beast neither human nor machine. As renewed gusts of acrid scents infiltrated Crospinal's sinuses, burning them, he put his hand over his face. *Smoke, real smoke.* With another tang underlying he could not identify.

The local controller, alone now, up by the ceiling, orbited in eccentric revolutions, quieter, though still clearly agitated.

Upon stepping over the threshold, Crospinal had actually seen the last batch, the last attacker—as stripped bare as himself, even more so, without a girdle—but darker, and sleek, moving with the same grace as a crow, or a rat. Had he or she fled when Crospinal showed up? There was an instant of eye contact, a jolt of what could only be *recognition*—

But Clarissa's breath, catching in the comm's speakers, caused Crospinal to cease his ruminations. He had been wondering if all crew began life as a batch, and if they were without torment, content in their condition. Turning, Crospinal looked where Clarissa looked:

In the rearmost chamber of the room, which was larger now, the dream cabinets were almost fully emerged. Lights around the rims of the doors flashed like the ones had back home, in the same patterns of yellow and red; he felt a rush of nostalgia, missing what he could never again possess, the past behind him now for good, no matter how jumbled.

Arrayed side by side, facing the entrance, the cabinets had been rearranged. Tiles at their base were almost totally resealed and hardened, and the green carpet had settled. As he began to turn away from the sight—unable to accommodate the continued rush of longing, those vanished afternoons in the pen, and the peaceful dreams he'd discovered in his own stat—he registered the body, the *corpse*, lying half-hidden on the soft green strip; his indulgences came to an abrupt halt.

He stepped closer.

One of the batches. A girl? A boy? With long hair, clearly dead, blood flowing from the ear, smeared across the cheek, dark and thick. But blood would not be assimilated, and a growing pool had formed, thickening now, coagulating.

Kneeling, he saw that the corpse had been, moments ago, a human around the same age as himself, during the year of long walks, or maybe younger, during disparate viewpoints. The haptic of accelerated decomposition—from life to nothingness—played through his mind as he rolled the body toward himself, almost stiff, and looked directly into the pale, bluish face. Drained eyes were a milky plastic.

His father's body had rotted while he was still breathing, as if death had been an afterthought.

He touched the cool, firm cheek. Batches were aspects of himself, of all people, reflections of a rudimentary persona that lurked beneath his exposed skin, beneath the veneer constructed from a father's lessons and teachings and prayers. Batches hid inside each crew member, and even inside the sailors who had passed through him and those who resonated there still.

When he moved his fingers into the black morass, touching the blood with his skin, he expected a reaction, exterior to him, a shock, but without mitts there was none. He wanted to weep, to say a tribute, thanks for surrendering life, or maybe an apology, but no words or strong emotions came and he was not sure if he should be grateful, or even if life, in any form, was a gift or a curse.

"Another console," Clarissa hissed, as if she had heard a voice Crospinal had not, speaking into the comm of her helmet. "Another console . . ."

She had followed him, and Crospinal looked up at her now. She did not even seem to notice the body of the batch, though the toes of her fresh boots touched it. "Crospinal," she said, "you have to get up now. They'll regroup, call the paladin. They know where we are. They know where the sailors are. If a paladin makes it as far as the cockpit . . ."

Now Crospinal broke into something almost like a sob. The first sailor he had been, in the haptic, the one with shaky hands, moved fingers again through the thick blood of the dead batch. No, skin did not react like mitts. Capillaries didn't hiss into action. "Paladins are ghosts," he said. "They're nothing." But he knew what paladins could do. He had seen Clarissa collapse in the hall. The metal rat had tried to heal the others, who had been stricken. And his own heart had been broken by a paladin, never to be the same again. They were ghosts that could change the world, transform a life. End it.

But so could crew.

And him, too: the console, the batches had plummeted when he stepped across the threshold—

Voices whispered inside him, and flickered.

The arms of the dead batch, lambent with illumination, were bent in an impossible pose, elbows almost touching, straight out, behind the back. Ambient glow on the dead skin appeared to be dancing, or searching. Blood was very dark. Leaning forward, Crospinal twisted the left forearm of the corpse wrist up, cooling flesh firm in his grip, a stiffening brought on by death and by the once-strong muscles and tendons he could never imagine rolling under any neoprene or spandex sleeve. These batches were some form of fabulous animal, vessels, without reflection or question, unless fathers took them or crew, and filled them with their incomplete knowledge.

He ran his thumb over the ridges of the cold transponder so hard the fibres under the skin distended and bulged like veins.

When he stood, the depression made by his thumb remained on the dead limb. Of the nearest crew, he asked what had happened, and the crew member said simply, facing Crospinal: "I killed it."

Craving evidence of humanity behind the visor, aghast, he saw only shadows. The statement of murder had not been confession, nor confrontation, but an offering, to be laid at Crospinal's feet.

I killed it.

For you.

He heard himself ask: *How?*

The crew raised a forearm, mitt closed into a fist, sheathed in the fresh sleeve—Crospinal put his hands up, mostly to protect his face, but when the crew member did not move again, he touched the neoprene, the uniform, clenching until the boy's mitt unfurled and capillaries hissed against his palm. A dark tube revealed, like piping, curving up and across the ridges of the boy's metacarpals, integral.

The brink he had stood upon, looking out across the impossible expanse— across clouds, no walls in sight, toward the mountains—used to be here somewhere, but configurations of the walls had changed, the opening sealed now. Parts of the floor shifted under his feet as he sought the aperture, small patches of grille uniting, regurgitated to join other patches and establish a pattern. Ambients flared, directing: a station was forming here, maybe the new console.

Controllers darted past to witness the development, swivelling toward Crospinal with evident concern, no doubt, but not pausing to interfere or speak. The devices might even have been the same ones he had passed, clustered, commiserating, not so long ago.

An area of composite had formed so fresh the veneer of linking polymers fractured when Crospinal tore at it, fingers still bloody from touching the face of the dead batch. Walls were hardly denser than smoke or the light that brought the materials here. Building machines stood by, thwarted, a dumb audience as Crospinal peeled aside a scale of the wall the size of his head, cracking the carbon and the bonding agents, letting a different light spill through the hole—not ambient, but warm, softer, like a caress: he smelled freshness that seemed to offer a modicum of relief, and release, so he resumed pushing at the scale with the heels of both hands, back and forth, until toluene flowed to repair, to break into molecules and try again, resume the intent, but he persevered at his labour until he was able to tear the piece off, stunned and breathless to be staring out over the vast core of the world once again.

Machines or great devices did seem to churn on the horizon, but the shapes he had previously imagined to be mountains now appeared to be a mere bank of fog, a hazy roil. There was a source of light out there, impossibly far away, an amber glow behind the haze. Perhaps, with residues of the sailors inside him, he would know a mountain if he saw one now, though what they might resemble would remain elusive to him, becoming clear only upon the trigger of absolute recognition.

He remembered his flight, literally soaring down, sure it had happened, and that he could do it again. Outrage was powerful, trapped inside his skin with the others, trying to burst free.

Clouds drifted, even below him, mists of polymers over a distant floor. Another garden, which he had not seen before, bigger even than the one he'd ridden the elemental through, sprawled in the middle distance. Greyness, scattered across darker pinpoints that might be hundreds, or thousands, of dead crows—

From within the huge chamber, a single data orb approached, moving so fast toward him a contrail spiralled behind. Stopping abruptly right before the aperture, before Crospinal's face, the orb hovered, either assessing the damage Crospinal had done to the wall or registering him. Crospinal's chest worked hard inside the battered tricot, like bellows from his father's ephemera. His processor whined. Was he being studied? He did not care.

Behind him, in the newly formed hall, a girl had began to cry. He did not turn. He could tell this was a girl by the tones, by the cadence of sobs.

With tentative fingertips, Crospinal reached out and touched the data orb, which did not back away: the surface was like his father's oil over a revolving skin colder and smoother than he had expected, almost a faint burning on his skin.

He said, "That crew member had a . . ." Searching for words. "A *weapon*. Here." Touching the inside of his own naked forearm, he was surprised, as the orb fell away, to realize it was Clarissa crying, and that she had been tugging at him, holding the hem of his tricot, as if to pull him back. He remembered now, Clarissa and Richardson, running after him as he fled the corpse, and the three fathers. "You all have that?" he asked her.

"Only sentries. Their sleeves—Crospinal, you know all this. You've done this before. Sentries are trained to fight."

He pushed her hand away, and tugged free.

"We need you, Crospinal. *We need you here*. Sailors are ready. Where are you going?"

Pipes bigger around in diameter than the harrier lookout, ringed by thinner tubes—some moving like netting, or veins in an arm—rose in formation to make vast, widening cones, webbing far overhead. The ceiling here, he imagined, could only be the outside perimeter of the world. Beneath him, the wall was mapped with striations and darker interstices. Staring down, he felt his outrage and dismay dwindling. His fists clenched and unclenched. Had the fathers been ready to emerge? He could have opened the doors, helped them out, brought them to the cockpit to tether them there. He could have helped the crew but the idea was abhorrent.

"You need to help us," whispered Clarissa, as if she had heard his thoughts. "We've been waiting. . . ."

He looked at the dried blood on his fingers.

You need to help us.

He was able to tear enough of the wall away to crawl through the opening. An expanse dropped toward the slow curve of the wall's base; Crospinal could not see the bottom for the roiling polymers. There could be no more death. All the while he had been staggering around the pen, useless, a battle had been fought. Killing each other, for years, and waiting for him.

He stepped up, precarious on the rim of the opening, and felt the warm breezes against his skin. Several building machines, which he had not seen before, were at work, an arm's length away, on the outside of the wall, relaying instructions of light. These, too, registering him, froze. He felt the crew members behind him, the two he had named, felt their expectations, their disappointment. If they followed, they would perish.

Letting go with one hand to reach down, Crospinal detached the flapping leg from his uniform and tugged if off altogether, which was excruciating; tendrils of the interface had pulled free from the muscles and nerves of his thigh. He removed the other leg more carefully, unhooking the clasps, one by one, and easing the connections from his leg before tossing it, too, over the brink, where it sailed away.

Clarissa and Richardson watched him, incredulous. Clarissa leaned on Richardson's shoulder. The run must have hurt her foot again, inflaming the wound. Neither were wearing helmets now, but Crospinal did not know when he had first noticed this.

"Leave," he said. "Go back."

Yet he knew they would follow. Turning carefully, he backed out, holding onto the rim of the hole, feeling for ridges or small crevasses in the wall with his bare toes, to begin the long descent.

ON THE LEDGE

"Before the first sailor stopped dreaming, there was only darkness. The empty world. Batches, dormant at the hub; paladins, watching over everything. Eons went by. But the world was passing through the tunnel, and when it came out the other side, paladins had changed. They didn't want to watch anymore, or maintain. They wanted to control. They brought one batch awake. And by one, I mean an *entire* batch. Four score, in all. A full year. The batches were just babies. As they grew, they were used like hands to shape the world in ways the world was not meant to be shaped. The network had also changed in the tunnel. Machines, too. When a batch got sick or died, the paladins woke another. For there were thousands, dormant down there. And they tried to prevent sailors from waking."

Crospinal sat cross-legged for the first time in his life. His hands were on his bare knees, rubbing them, the way he used to, but not out of pain, not to diffuse any pain. Skin now, on skin. "And sailors came awake?"

"One did."

Clarissa sounded like his father when he had lectured or prayed, or was pumped with nutrients, head full of visions. Though she was nodding at his question, Crospinal knew that Clarissa repeated what she'd been told, in hopes that the words might become truer each time they were relayed, that they might explain or validate. She did not truly understand why Crospinal was the way he was, and why he did not do what she'd been expecting him to do. She was certainly at a loss as to why she was here, on this ledge. Inside her, the essence of a passenger was beginning to stretch.

"You're not a batch anymore," she said. "Neither am I. We're *crew* now. We can't go back to the hub. We don't belong here."

"I'm not crew," he said. He showed his arms to her; the scars were inflamed. "You should return to the others."

"We were *both* batches." Clarissa persevered, getting desperate. "While sailors dreamed in their stats, the darkness was inside us. Inside *each of us*, Crospinal. But sailors have us now, we're safe, and they brought us into the light. We can change things. You can, Crospinal. You're a pilot."

Looking at the other thin scars, running the inside length of each white thigh, accompaniment to those scrawling his arms (where the metal rat, presumably, had straightened his femurs), Crospinal could imagine augmentations to the bone: titanium rods, or hafnium plates and minute medical screws. He imagined his thigh muscles re-stretched and pinned into place, tendons taut and stapled to his patellas, woven through with cremasteric fibres. Modifications, if nothing else, set him apart from the others. So many aspects altered since he had left the pen. Some added, some taken away.

Climbing down this far—thirty metres or so below the lip of the hole he'd torn in the wall—was arduous work, and slow, but not exceptionally difficult or, he felt, perhaps wrongly or stupidly, dangerous. Indignation carried him. Desire to keep moving steeled his grip. The polymers, if he leapt or fell, were surely there to absorb him.

Both Clarissa and the boy, Richardson, had followed his passage, as he'd predicted, coming headfirst through the hole, as if bound to him. Maybe they believed they could bring Crospinal back to the cockpit, when an opportunity arose, either by force or by convincing him that building crew, assembling sailors, and killing batches were paramount tasks. Maybe they'd been told to follow him.

Or maybe their names took away any choice.

Though Crospinal listened to everything Clarissa said, and was moved by her words, appreciating her attempts to convince him, he wanted nothing to do with such a destiny. Origins and circumstances of life were no reason for hostility. There were no sides to take. He would not bring the sailor's world back, not if it meant fighting batches and struggling to vanquish one another in the brewing hallways and chambers of this strange world.

Their mitts and boots had aided both as they descended by adhering to the composite; Crospinal had no such assistance. His uniforms had never performed that function anyhow. He climbed with his fingers hooked on cables and clawed tight into thin seams. They were bleeding now, a nail cracked, the palms of his hands blistered. His toes cramped from gripping meager features.

When he'd dropped to the shelf where they would rest, bare feet slapping hard, rebuilt knees articulating smoothly, he had to lean with the skin of his pale belly pressed up against the surface of the wall, the drop just centimetres away.

He spent a moment tugging at his girdle, trying to disengage the tendrils that bound what was left of his uniform to his body, but the connectors were still anchored firmly and he certainly could not have pulled his catheter free, not while remaining conscious.

Resting on this broader ledge now, Clarissa trembled. Inside, where she'd said nothing but darkness once spread—before thoughts, or a half-baked concept of awareness, before sailors passed through—Crospinal felt a strange calm. There were no weapons growing on Richardson's or Clarissa's sleeves. He had checked several times. He checked again now, as Clarissa waited for him to respond, or come around.

The corpse of the batch, like all biological matter, would take a long time to decompose. Most likely there were no worms, so far from a garden. No rats or crows, either. But decay would take even longer if the body was a crew member, lying dead, sealed inside a *jumpsuit*. If his father's body hadn't been blown away by the explosion, he would likely be mummified, preserved inside the sheath of Dacron and nylon for years to come.

Watching Richardson take a hit from his feedtube and swallow, Crospinal tugged with one hand at his own tightening collar, thumbing the broken attachment ridge, breaking a cable. Flakes of neoprene drifted away and dissolved on the faint breeze. His chestplate was loose, almost swinging free. There were only two bands of reinforcement connecting his collar to his girdle, through which unused conduits ran that could power a helmet, or the force that projected over one's head, though both options were inert to him now.

How could he disengage his processor?

A better question would be: *why*. Without it, he would not be able to live, at least not for long.

Looking out, Crospinal saw only distance, the bleary horizon. Below him, polymers continued to gather. A storm was brewing.

Having made a pest of itself when they first stood together on this shelf, asking repeatedly—*sotto voce*—if they needed anything, darting about, that they were *welcome, so welcome*, and they were the first visitors in *ages*, the local controller returned, hoping for further requests after, no doubt, directing a clean-up operation of its small station.

But the few pellets Crospinal had tried (and spat out) were stale and tasteless, the water tepid, so thick with enhancements that sediments remained even after the cup dissolved into thin air. No consoles, ill-formed or full. Crospinal got on his hands and knees and looked everywhere, murmuring, coaxing, while Clarissa and Richardson watched him. No uniform dispensers. *A bare bones operation*, as his father would have said. Which suited Crospinal fine. He did not trust, nor particularly wish to further test, his own abstinence from the supplies that the world had to offer.

Clarissa pressed her back firmly against the surface of the wall. She hugged her knees to her chest. "Luella told us to wait." She was crying again, quietly, breaths shuddering her body. "She told us you were coming."

She crumpled her face into her mitts, the capillaries of which began lapping up her tears.

Richardson watched, silent as always, sucking on his siphon. He had not long worn the jumpsuit and was on his first. The catheter still burned as it spiralled farther and farther up his urethra, supplying him with supplements and directives and even the seeds of an ability to process and understand language. Words bubbled in the boy's mouth, but Richardson was not yet ready to release them. He sucked at his siphon again. A battle ago, maybe two, crew members had trapped him as he rushed the cockpit. Held him down. Pushed his arms into a console and let the transponders connect him to passengers.

Before that, Richardson recalled nothing.

If he were able to release the words from his lips, they would say his name, firstly, and then they would say other names, which he conceived, lying here, as if whispered into his ear. He would name two crew, whose faces he could recall, and in whom he felt a kindred bond.

What Clarissa had implied, Crospinal was considering (as he had several times since leaving home). He wanted to raise his voice but did not. "I wasn't born in the hub. Neither was my sister. We were pulled from the womb. I've seen the cryonic pit, next to my daybed. I saw it every day. And I've seen haptics of me, babies too small for any uniform."

Yet other aspects of his life had been a lie, so why not his origin? Madness to consider. He would never let his childhood go. Without a foundation, even minimal, he would retain nothing, and be set adrift, once and for all, into the darkness his father had always tried to keep away.

"*Crospinal.*" She let her hands fall to the lap of her uniform. A plea, as if he was a kid in his year of growth. "We all came from down there. We can't go back, or forget what we've learned. *We can't go back.* We have to turn around."

Her emotions, though, eventually subsided in waves of release. She turned her face toward him. "Paladins are down there." Her blue eyes, moist, reflected desperation. "And not projections. Real ones, in their housings. If they find you, they'll *kill you*. They would see crew in a second."

Like shadows, or light on water, the other sailors flashed their lives across Crospinal's vision, too fast for details, though the effect left him giddy. Could Richardson and Clarissa see their spirits, too? Were they swelling in each of them? He raised his hands to greet these instances, or keep them at bay.

Richardson just watched. Intelligence burned in his eyes. A roll of flesh rose between the back of his head and his uniform, flattening only when he looked away—at last—and down.

Crospinal was distracted by the voices inside him. He could no longer understand their language. Time seemed to stutter.

"The sailor that chose you," Clarissa said, "was able—"

"My *father*."

"Your *father*." She struggled to persevere. "The passenger. He made two pilots. Luella, and you. Luella brought sailors together, took them from stats. She slung them, plugged them. She rescued us from darkness when we were sent to stop her. I remember looking into her eyes that first time. I remember blackness leaving me. Luella showed us how to call trains and cycles. Dispensers grew wherever she went. Objects fell from the walls. She knew everything, because she was also a pilot."

Crospinal closed his eyes and saw faint, stuttering images, hazy landscapes and scenes that could not possibly exist. *Mountains*, he thought. He opened his eyes again. "If she was hurt, why didn't a metal rat fix her?"

"A what?"

"An elemental. The smart machines. With red eyes."

Clarissa blinked. Finally, she said: "They're tempters, and detractors. They ask too many questions that can never be answered. When Luella was hurt, she went to sleep before elementals found her. But there are none left now, anyhow. They've been banished."

He looked out over the expanse, where once he'd imagined mountains, but he knew now that mountains were part of the sailors' dream. As if agreeing, those within him flittered.

"Why did you name me?" Clarissa whispered.

He turned to look her in the eye, met her gaze for a long while, his jaw working. He saw the struggle, inside. Reaching out—an action that surprised even himself—he touched Clarissa's face with his bare hand and, as his fingertips broke through the faint shield created by her collar, felt the electrostatic charge, like a tingling, and the fine hairs of her cheek, the bone under her warm, soft skin. She drew in breath sharply. She was crying, trembling. A fallen teardrop began to roll, whisked quickly away.

"There's nothing here," she said. "Where are you taking us?"

His fingers were still touching her face. Like everyone else, she was tormented by a past she could not recall. "Did Luella ever kill anyone?" he said.

Her blue eyes averted. She would not look at him. She moved away from his touch. "Luella converted when she could. Or she ended a life, if she had to. Batches are not like us. Seventeen stats rose from the floor when Luella was here. And when the batches came, most died, but some were saved, and converted. Like me. Even sailors were attacked, in their thrones, some who'd just come awake. They were torn from their gates and left to bleed. Memories were lost. You'd kill batches, too."

Out over the vista, clouds were clearing. He looked at the distant garden, visible now, and the hazy patterns of the floor. To walk to the horizon would take many days. "We all die soon enough. That's one thing I know."

"A batch lives for twenty years, until their year of transgression. Without a jumpsuit, without food, without thought. Attached to the hub. They are not like us."

Crospinal had never heard of the year of transgression; it sounded like a difficult one. He was thinking about the boy with the dead rats, who had bitten him. Was he a batch, far from the hub? And the men in the pylon, breathing through symbiotes: had they once been crew, and batches before that? The world was not as clearly divided as Clarissa had been taught. "And how long will Luella live?"

"Forever. She's in a stat."

"What about outside the dream cabinet?"

"A thousand years, maybe more."

Believing an untruth does not make it less of a lie. "And me?"

"Sailors can live for a thousand years. Have you forgotten? Until the year of miracles."

Crospinal frowned. "I've seen the world that sailors came from. When they went to sleep, nothing was like this, not like what we see." Watching faraway ridges, where a cascade of lights, flickering like sparks, meant the addition of yet another new feature, a hall or budding station, or perhaps their dissolution. "Something came into the world while they slept." Recalling the girder, fallen from the ceiling, smashing the cabinets back home, he added, "And it lives there," pointing down, at a slight angle, toward the horizon, "at the hub. Creatures found their way into their dreams."

Clarissa did not respond. Sobs shuddered her frame. Either she did not know what else to say or had run out of energy and hope of convincing Crospinal; she slumped now, as terrified of following him as she was of her inability to stop.

When he got to his feet, breezes moved over his naked skin. He filled his chest, held his lungs full, and adjusted the ruined waistband of his uniform.

"Farewell," said the controller. "Safe travels."

Two drones approached. Slow and steady, side by side, the blunt crafts came on, a crackling aura of energy roiling between them, wreathing their spinning forms. They were coming for Crospinal.

Above them, white helixes of lumens whirled, taking form, and as he raised his arms to greet the apparition, Richardson sat up, trying for the first time to speak, but his words were garbled.

In a blinding white uniform and radiant helmet, a figure of light appeared, reclining in a throne made of lumens. Legs open, high boots, sheathed arms snug and resting on the armrests. White mitts. The landscape beyond the projection was limned in brilliance; Crospinal, trying to shield his face with a bare forearm, could see nothing else. So bright because the source was *close;* some form of father was within range.

"Nice lecture, little brother," said the apparition. "You called?"

He could not see his sister's face through the glare off the visor, but he knew as she hovered before him that she was not happy with him. Beyond the representation of reflective polycarbonate, her expression was hardened, and cold. Wonder was gone. He knew this, like a kick to the gut. His sister's disdain washed over him.

"What have you done to yourself?" she asked.

Losing himself in the light, he did not respond. He thought she would have been happy to see him. She had other expectations.

"Father's dead," he said.

He wondered what her snort of laughter could mean.

"I heard. And I heard you went missing, stumbling off, half-cocked. I see those awful machines are looking out for you. What goes on in your head, Crospie? What the fuck goes on in there? You're a lunatic."

He was not surprised that drones had come for him. They had been watching him all along. Since he'd been born.

"The pen is gone," he said.

"The *pen.*" Luella laughed again, head back, visor flashing. "I can't believe you made it this far. You are an absolute reject. Talk about miracles. What do you remember, brother, about me? About when we were together?"

"Haptics. Us being bathed. The expression on your face."

She hesitated. "When I left, you weren't walking. You couldn't even talk. Your legs were bent and you slept in your little daybed. You should have been put down. Father wasted his life trying to educate you."

"Where are you projecting from? Down there?" He pointed. "Are you coming from there? Or are you inside the drone?"

"Look at you. Making demands. When I was four years old, *brother—four years old*—I was already a pilot. While you were half-baked and drooling."

He looked away.

"Don't worry about them," Luella said. "They're just having a nap."

Richardson and Clarissa were indeed asleep.

Had his first visit to the dream cabinet begun his downfall? Physical ability to enter—with his arms picked clean—and the yearning desires to seek solace beyond the hemisphere of his father's range, were dubious gifts. Maybe he didn't have the ability to fulfill a clear role in the world, like Luella had at a young age, but he had a yearning nonetheless.

Had that first visit undone what his father had been trying to achieve?

While he had dreamed, time crossed over itself. He drowned in cold fluid. Stealing away from the pen to climb the ladders of the harrier and invoke his girlfriend, or tucking himself into the oblivion of the stat, had changed him. He would never know what he might have become had he resisted. A sentry? A leader, like his sister?

A killer?

Waking groggily, tingling with dim euphoria, he pushed the cabinet's door open. He presumed each visit brief, an hour, maybe less, yet his stay might have been weeks, if not years, pulled into forgotten dreams.

Sailors could travel between worlds while they slept.

Why couldn't he?

Well-being started to diminish as soon as the soles of his boots touched the green carpet. Enough to go back to his dad, to his daybed, to his little corner.

Luella had been there. Passengers, too. Some of them, still asleep in their stats, drifted through the same way they drifted through him now. Others had woken, and were tethered, connecting. Maybe his father had joined. That's what dream cabinets could do. He had been inside, and *connected*. He knew this now, lifted by the drones, held aloft and barely conscious, while they hummed and strained and spun. His back arched, meager arms flung wide.

He had been connected.

From the ledge of fused polymers, the crew members lay inert, paralyzed by the paladin. Through slitted eyes they were still able to watch as Crospinal rose. The glare was powerful and pain was a throb that faded and surged with each slow heartbeat. Inability to resist the manifestations was one thing crew would always share with batches. Their heritage was undeniable: before a paladin, both were equally helpless.

Neither Clarissa nor Richardson saw Luella, not the way Crospinal did, sitting in her throne. They saw only the light, and Crospinal, transfixed, ascending.

For Clarissa, eyes watering, processor whining to transmute the waste she'd voided when the paladin made her drop and curl inward, this was a moment of revelation, of order, and even relief; she felt, in her fervour and pain, absolution.

Richardson, who was powerful and calm, knew the presence of lives within him, perhaps even more so than Crospinal. He managed to prop himself up. Shielding his face, with his body turned away—squinting through his fingers—no discernable impression betrayed his features. Since the jumpsuit was fitted, Richardson had witnessed and taken part in many struggles. He had seen and could recall wonders too innumerable for him to account or contextualize. This place, and this other human, whom they'd been travelling with recently, and who had initiated further changes, seemed hardly more remarkable than the litany of others. Before encountering the crew, Richardson recalled nothing. Not so long ago, he had been caught, pulled up from the formless black of existence in the hub. Now, when he fought or stood at a console, he watched batches coming in, attacking almost mindlessly, and he studied their faces as they skirmished. Even as he struck at them, to keep them away, he sought, as Crospinal did, familiarity, a common bridge.

Yet, new to motives, beyond the capacity of his burgeoning thoughts, Richardson nonetheless sensed, like his mentor, that a circuit was closing. Crew had waited a long time for Crospinal to appear. Now, watching him elevate—snared alive, naked and crackling with energy—he knew why.

Soon, Richardson would talk.

He would name people.

He would tell them a story.

<hr/>

"Stop fighting me!"

The bonds had tightened but could not fully hold him.

"Listen to me, Crospie. You were right about endtime. You were right *because you bring it with you*. You *are* endtime."

"What have you done with her?"

"You don't think I'm Luella?"

"I'm asking about my girlfriend. What have you done with her?"

"You're an idiot, Crospinal. How could you have a girlfriend? You should've stayed in the pen."

He felt heat spreading through his chest. The sailors inside darting about, as if seeking cover, or taking stations. Their voices hissed.

"From day one you were a failed experiment, little brother. A disaster."

Between them, the drones had taken him away from the wall. The abyss all around, the floor far below: he ceased his struggle, to listen, as the apparition commanded, and to breathe. What he heard were echoes of the sailors' lives. Their home might have been flawed, and alien, but lives were lives, replete with disappointment and pain and small joys, even here, at the end of the world, at the end of time.

"Empathy for you is a weakness. I don't know how you ever convinced any thing or any one to help you. Sit back now, brother, let me drive."

If this was Luella, something truly awful had happened to her since leaving home. He remembered Fox and Bear standing over them, their father smiling proudly, all hooked up—

With all his strength, and the strength of those dreaming within him, Crospinal twisted away.

The apparition screamed.

He could not be subdued. Because of what his father had done to him, because of his difference, he could not be subdued. He felt the threads of the others stitching through him, tightening, and he felt the crew, even flickers from Clarissa and Richardson, who were recovering now. The drones continued to move farther away from the ledge, and down. His body lurched sideways through the grip and the drones had to spread out to compensate. Crospinal dropped a metre or so before becoming buoyant again, bouncing in the invisible sling.

As a phalanx of data orbs rushed in, dozens of them from all around, to assess and add to the net, the projection of his sister vanished, replaced briefly by another, and then by one of his girlfriend, who appeared pained and beautiful, reaching out to him, about to speak, to confess, before she too vanished—

Lattices of support were failing. If Crospinal continued to struggle, they would have to let him go. With no choice but to descend—as quickly as they could, before the grip was fractured altogether—the drones whirred and spun and headed down.

Ambiguous projections stuttered around Crospinal's flailing body, belying anxiety from the source now that he had finally come into range. Crospinal was stronger than they had expected. He was a multitude. They could not hold him.

With a final twist, he broke free; for a moment, at least, liberated.

BATCHES

Darkness. He had known all along there would be darkness. And that he would end up there. More pervasive darkness in life than light. Certainly more in the reaches and recesses of the capricious world. If, indeed, the world was where he now found himself.

He understood nothing about his predicament, except for darkness. Had he been falling? Was this death? Then he was wrong about eternal oblivion.

The floor was cold and hard under him; he was seated upon ancient tiles.

A faint rustling—

The conversation about darkness had been with a *girl*. *A crew member*. Her face, the cast of her eyes upon him, and his hand touching her cheek: he could not imagine another chance to experience such wonders.

Then a faint glow—from quite close—bloomed. He recoiled slowly, blinking to see faces ringing him, brown and silent. Synchronous shadows moved across the bland expressions as the small lantern—a fibre of light (he'd seen these before, held them?)—was lifted higher, so they could see him better.

Batches. He remembered what these people were called. In this darkness, he was ringed by *batches*.

Another glow sparked, and another; the aura of the combined glows expanded:

He sat in a large, old room, the extent of which could not be discerned. Portions of smooth, metallic wall rose to his left, passing beyond the pale hemisphere of light. Detritus, fabrics, broken tubes and fibre clusters, strewn about; the smell of sweat, urine, faint smoke. He remembered his name—*Crospinal*—and a scattered series of vignettes that did not fit together in any satisfactory way.

There were actually twenty batches, maybe even more, in concentric rows, crowded about. Some younger, some children, all naked, with similar features: broad head; full lips; high cheekbones. Like his own. At least one toddler, dirty and naked, stared from the pack. In the year of growth, probably. Crospinal could not find any traits that distinguished gender: what he could see of the bodies was smooth, and equally grimy, highlighted by the glow. Identical. He was much paler than any, somewhat taller than the tallest, and a *whole* lot thinner.

Crouching at the fore, those with the lanterns (his father had kept a stash of these next to his throne for occasions when the ambients were dormant) caused harsher light as they leaned forward, fracturing their faces, chests, clenched hands.

The wall towered up, steady, indicating—

From the remaining dark, something was coming.

Crospinal had heard it, and he stepped back.

He was at the bottom of the hub.

Remembering the ledge now, and the cockpit, the face of the dead batch, he called out.

His voice was loud, yet swallowed abruptly: no echo, no answer. The batches did not flinch, nor change expression, though the glow quavered as one scratched at a stomach with the hand that held the torch.

"What's out there?"

They blinked and stared.

Had he been rejected by the apparition? Or had he escaped? He knew the figure had not been Luella's, but a projection, a lie, yet he was disappointed by her ire. If he had fallen—well, that wasn't even possible. Pointless to consider: the drop had been huge. He felt no pain in his body. He had once thought polymer clouds might catch him if he plummeted.

His chestplate flapped free. One of the straps detached in his fingers, so he tore the plate off altogether and tossed it before him. Still the batches did not react. Some shuffled, looked elsewhere. Already the material of his tricot was breaking down, reintegrating. He could smell the process. Crospinal felt his cool, bare chest, the minute bumps of his nipples smooth against the now-rougher skin of his fingertips.

"You can't talk," he said, addressing the batches. "Right? None of you. What's out there? A machine? A paladin?"

One of the smaller batches made a sound, a sort of nervous whine, like his father's dogs had done when Crospinal first began to stray.

He stood. Now the faces moved, a flicker of interest, watching him.

Crospinal touched his girdle, still anchored in place at his hips; then, around his neck, another vestige, his old collar. He held onto the loop of Kevlar with both hands, trying to remember enough details to form coherence. Images—his daybed; the blissful expression on his father's face when conduits opened up to let him have his dose; Luella's throne of light—he could not trust.

A corpse, sprawled at the base of a dream cabinet, killed by a crew member on Crospinal's behalf—

That sound again, a whiff that set his heart racing.

"Hello?"

Could Crospinal convince himself that he was one of these graceful, silent batches, who watched him so placidly? Feeling somewhat monstrous, he took a third step, hands splayed before him, unsure if he would actually *contact* any of them, should they not get out of his way. Hidden, the child whimpered again—

And a clear voice admonished: "*Stop making a fucking racket!*"

Crospinal was stock-still when the man stepped as if from nowhere into the gloom. Unlike the batches—unlike himself—he was large and broad, a head taller, with hair on his scalp and face, and more down his bare chest. A strange, soft fabric had been wrapped and tied around his waist. His arms, folding, were as big around as Crospinal's legs.

The batches, unafraid, parted at the man's approach. His skin, under the scrawls of hair, moving now into the light, was marked with dark symbols and glyphs. He put his hands on his hips (no girdle there) and said: "You need to rest more, and shout less."

He was not smiling.

"I don't want to stay here," Crospinal said. This was no apparition or projection. Though they shared a bond of sorts, he had not yet seen such a man.

"You've been out cold a long while. You're ill, boy. Rest." His voice was deep, slow. "Have you had some water, or tried to eat?" He pointed with a thick finger, but Crospinal did not look where he indicated. "You need to get your strength back. Go sit down. Sit back down."

"I'm not thirsty." Crospinal looked into the man's shadowed eyes but could not read them, nor discern their colour. Eyes were blue, though once or twice in his journey, there had been green eyes, hadn't there? He set his jaw. For most of his life there were no people *at all*. Except for his father. Were this man's statements—about being unconscious, and being ill—more lies? Crospinal sure didn't feel ill. He felt about as strong as he ever had. The passengers within had settled.

The man's expression lay somewhere between smug and patronizing.

"They were scanning," he said, "minutes ago. Looking for you, I presume. One of the cortexes, all the way out here in person, directing a small army. A paladin, you call them. On the move." Nodding his head, he smiled now, or grimaced, showing poor teeth that looked grey in the lantern's light. "Best remain here, with us. My friends here won't hurt you."

Crospinal stepped to the side, trying to pass, but the man blocked him with a strong, open hand, flat and firm against Crospinal's bare chest.

"You didn't hear me? I said don't go out there. They're looking for you."

Water here must be entirely unenhanced. The man's teeth were rotten. And for food? What did they all eat? There were no dispensers, no amenities. Uneven hair had never been depilated—at least, not in a very long time.

"Who are you?" Crospinal asked.

"I used to have a name, a few lifetimes ago. I used to have hundreds of names. But none of them are any use. Not now. They'd call me a sailor where you're from, but I'm just a man." Extending his free arm—

Flinching away, it took Crospinal a beat to realize he was not being reached for, and that the motion was merely to display the flesh of the man's inner forearm: even in the gloom—despite the darker marks—Crospinal knew there was no implant, no inlay there. He saw tendons move, the definition of muscle, but no inlay.

"You live here without tethers? Without a gate?"

"Same as you." The man lowered his arm and withdrew his hand from Crospinal's chest (where flesh, newly exposed, surged with warm blood). "But I live clean. It's not so hard, really, once you get past the worst. You adapt. Even down here. You know about this. You've been educated. If you can break free, leave all dependencies, you'll be in the clear, right? Shake them off." He stared Crospinal down. "Why are you here?"

Crospinal did not know how to answer. He said, "My father died."

The man narrowed his eyes, a faint smile still on his lips. "Are you talking about a god here? Or was your father a man, like me?"

"A man. I'm Crospinal. His son."

"He was probably all jacked up and fried out of his gourd. Did he raise you? Or did he catch you when you were older? How many years have you come around? I'd like to see your—"

Crospinal jerked back from what was clearly, this time, an attempt to clutch his arm. "Don't touch me."

"Shit, I'm not going to *hurt* you. I just wanna see. You're an interesting guy. I bet you've got great stories, if you could get them straight."

By now, the batches had begun to shows signs of disinterest, fidgeting, with soft grunts. Some must have dispersed when he wasn't looking; there seemed fewer. The dimming glow-sticks were lowered. One got down on haunches to inspect the skin of a grubby thigh. Another scratched at a temple.

Crospinal stepped back again.

"Your father was crazy. We all are. From getting here, I suppose. From too much dreaming. Maybe we were crazy when we went to sleep." He tapped his temple. "Most of us wake up basket cases, that's for sure. Heads filled with dope and broken memories, and we don't know up from down. Haunted. Your father should have known that it takes more than a little surgery and a few parlour tricks to make someone like you into a son."

Crospinal said nothing.

"I know what goes on. I spent time struggling out of a stat, trying to get oriented. I might even have worn a jumpsuit once, or had dispensers growing around me. Artifacts, falling from the ceiling. Controllers were happy to see me. Until a gate came along. I might have tried to continue with the mission, without ever knowing what the mission was." He laughed again. "I was like them once. Eating pellets of cytoprotection, antiflatulents, drinking water laced with antipyretics and immunoboosts. Recycling my sweat, my piss, my shit." He paused. "You know, I examined you—*Crospinal*—when you were recovering. When you were lying there, nearly dead. I learned a lot about you over the past few days."

Crospinal had been growing more and more tense; this last line—few *days*!—reverberated up his spine like a sharp wire. Looking at the faces surrounding him, suspecting ambush now, an impending attack, he saw only loose, blank expressions, disinterest. "I haven't been down here for days," he said. "And you don't know anything about me."

"You're wrong on both counts. I know you think you're equal, maybe even superior to me. I know you've got a shitload of damage done inside that head of yours. You were better off when you lived here, with us." Sweeping his arm to indicate the others.

Crospinal stared. His heart was pounding so hard his body shook. "If you're a passenger, why are *you* here?"

"Because everything is bullshit. You know that." He pointed at Crospinal's girdle. "Look, I hate to break the news, whatever you think your name is, but you're not even human. Did you know that?"

At his sides, Crospinal clenched his fists. He looked at the batches again.

The man said, "They don't understand anything except devotion. Like little puppies. The lucky fucks. Know what a puppy is, Crospinal? Like you would have been, if you'd been left alone. Now sit. You've been standing too long. Let's talk more after you rest. It's the least you could do." He came forward, almost touching Crospinal, and Crospinal had to step back again.

From a few centimetres away, the strong whiff of the man's scent was sweet and heady, and surprising appeal nearly dashed Crospinal's resolve.

"My friends here have been with me for a long time, since I arrived. I never tried to dress them up, though, or teach them anything. Intrusions leave me alone now. They're loyal. They live with me. They follow me. Look: I don't want to enrage you. I can see you're enraged. Try to stay calm, because we have a lot to discuss. You were quite ill. I want to ask you some questions. I want to pick your addled brain. So have some food, some real food, and rest a while." Indicating the area of the floor where Crospinal had previously sat, among the batches. Mere centimetres away, the man loomed.

"I'm not staying here."

"You'll get us killed," he hissed. "If you head out there, you'll get us fucking killed. Or you'll get my friends killed. I won't be impressed, either way." He rubbed at his face, where the hair grew, at his jowls. Darker marks on his skin, in this dim light, moved across his skin like creatures, images of creatures, with long limbs, stalking—

Crospinal drew in a sudden breath.

"Just," the man continued, right in Crospinal's face, "as you'll certainly get killed if you try to fight me." Clapping Crospinal's shoulder suddenly, his strong hand enclosing the knob of bone, a grip like metal. He pushed. "So sit the fuck back down."

"I don't want to stay here."

"Don't be a fool." (Among the batches, the youngest child whimpered.) "Where would you go anyway? Run around out there until you collapse? Then do it all again? What do you mean to accomplish? What is there to get done? You have a god complex. That's what your sailor gave you. Your *father*. Do you know what I mean?"

"No."

"Sailors are gods, right? Paladins are gods. Men had other gods once, but they got lost along the way, like everything else." He squinted. "All gods are selfish and vain. Gods demand worship. Gods demand prayer."

Crospinal tried to pull away.

"And prayer's a weakness. A sickness. People need to be careful about what they try to bring back." The man's grin exposed rotten teeth. "Light," he shouted suddenly, raising his hands, and the ambients in the wall behind Crospinal flared: they stood, blinking in the new glare, while batches ducked and moved about, seeking cover from the light. There were dozens of them in the vicinity, some standing nearby, others reclined or sleeping, naked and filthy, on the floor. All around was littered with shreds of heaped construction materials, carbon rods, scales of raw composite. Toward the wall, heaps of feces. He could see it now, their *toilet*. Unrecycled waste.

They were in a cove of sorts, opening up to a greater area that remained dark. The hub Crospinal had looked out over from the ledge opened up there, a vastness brimming with remaining night, like a weight, leaning in. Standing there, blinking, Crospinal again felt awed by the immensity of the world.

Within the dark, several very bright moving points of light glimmered, impossible to tell at what distance. He saw no walls, no hint of higher areas. The sight was wondrous and humbling—

The man had started laughing, breath sickly sweet. Within the cave of his mouth, a black tongue writhed. Ambients illuminated his eyes, not blue, nor green, but cataracted, and the marks over his body were not creatures at all but discoloured melanomas, crumbling dark patches of disease and dry skin. His scalp was blotchy; he scratched at it now, and there was blood. "I got some tricks," he said when he could speak again. "And that, my friend, is how you tell us apart. I'm the real thing. Let's see you try."

He circled now, pointing. "Your passenger fixed you because he thought that would make you his son. Fathers and sons haven't existed in a million years. We like to think we're smart, but we're not. We're pathetic and insane. Scrambled wrecks. It's a blessing to leave memory behind. Now, sit. Eat. I won't ask you again."

With his eyes still smarting from the light, Crospinal glanced behind himself again, saw the crude bedding, batches resting there, sitting or sleeping. Overhead was a local, lower ceiling, but arcing up, to blend into the vertical, and vanish upward. The active light from this cove faded long before the broader opening: he envisioned the bottom of the great wall, an illuminated pinhead where they had gathered, lost in the black cathedral of endtime's night. The sailors inside him were awake again, whispering from their hiding places, warning him, but Crospinal already knew the danger.

He walked back to the spot where he had woken, and sat.

Somewhere out there were Clarissa and Richardson, and the machines that had repaired him. Somewhere out there—

From the opening of a floor grille, lengths of old carbon rods grew; pierced on these, he realized now, were shreds of flesh. *Food*. No pellets here, no dispensers. But was this rat meat? Crow?

Hunkering down before Crospinal, still grinning, one hand flat on the floor, the man stared. His glazed eyes glittered and Crospinal wondered if he was able to see anything at all. Two fingers at the second knuckle were lost, nubs rounded and smooth. Crospinal knew he would never be able to leave this place, not as long as this man remained alive.

"Such a long time I've been here," he said. "I'm so happy you've come back."

"How did I get here?"

"I don't know." The man shrugged, dismissive. "I found you out there, and I carried you back. You were wedged between two floor plates crumpling together in some tectonic upheaval." Demonstrating with his fingers, pushing together. "Awash with toluene. Heart beat thin, almost nonexistent. I saw them, searching. But you're almost invisible, like me. The batches, well, they're idiots, to be honest, when it comes to initiative. I waited for a clearing, picked you up, and carried you here."

Crospinal was staring at a grotesque tumour dangling between the man's legs: wrinkled and olive-toned, it hung below the level of his garment and looked truly malignant. The man had paused but, realizing what had stricken Crospinal so, laughed again, grabbing and hefting the growth—which was loose, anchored in place by tendons. He *squeezed*. "Your old man never showed you his gear? Never saw him naked?" Bouncing what he held, gripping it. There was a shaft, the flesh darker and smoother than his knuckles. A hole at the tip of the shaft glistened with a drop of mucus. "Sometimes I think this is all that's left of the old world. Maybe that's what the sailors are searching for? Maybe this is humanity? All this talk about souls." He released the painful-looking tumescence. "Fuck it. But a surefire way of telling us apart. You don't have anything like this, boy, do you?"

"No." Something awful had happened to the man's genitals: before the catheter had corkscrewed into Crospinal's urethra, and the processor had bonded to his pelvis, his own penis had been as delicate as those of the batches around him.

But the man laughed and laughed for some time, finally subsiding into chuckles. Those lingering about settled down, curling on the floor, scratching themselves, drifting off into darker areas.

Crospinal leaned forward and snapped a carbon rod off at the base; the meat, dangling from the sharp tip, swayed. "You eat them," he said.

The man did not reply. His eyes glittered.

Crospinal raised the flesh to his face, sniffed, and pulled it free. The rod had been honed to a sharp point. Between his fingers, the meat felt dry, almost like the sole of a boot. He rubbed his thumb against it, never taking his eyes from the man, and tried to bite off a gobbet, but the meat was tough, so he pushed the whole piece into his mouth, awkwardly, with a knuckle, and chewed.

Sailors within began to sing.

Staring at the dark ceiling, he listened to creaking from next door. The noise had woken him. He could not recall falling asleep, yet it was 3:11.

Nor could he recall the transition from sleep to lying here, awake, listening. There had been a dream, a confrontation? Details were gone now. Muffled voices. After a moment, he touched the mattress next to him, to see if his wife still lived with him, but his hand fell upon nothing but a damp sheet.

The grace period, if it came at all, was at night, during times like this. He could not feel any tremors in his body. As if he was catching them unawares. Alerted now, they dashed back across time, and possibly space, to inflict him again. He held his hands up, watching them, but the room was too dark to see much of anything except the glowing red numerals of the clock.

Grinding his teeth, he tried to prep for the shaking to return, listening to the floorboards creak, and for the talking, imagining the boy next door roaming the cramped apartment, from his bed to the couch, to his parents' bed, to the dresser, and back to the couch. Were his parents even home? Who was talking? He seldom heard talking. He could visualize the furniture but had never stepped foot in the neighbour's apartment.

Why the fuck was the boy always awake?

Sometimes on the stairs, when he was returning exhausted from work—forcing his limbs to continue for just a bit longer until he could shut the door and lay on his bed, close his eyes, dream he was sailing the stars already—they would encounter each other, staring until he was forced to look away.

No one saw the shaking, except for the boy.

Floorboards creaked.

He had come to understand that the boy was trying to tell him something. About the one-way trip.

A warning.

Today, the last of the banks had been installed and activated. Ten thousand embryos, ready for their big chance. How often had he looked upon them, expecting the weight of potential futures, of myriad souls, to crash upon him and crush him, yet feeling very little from the innocuous tubes each time?

And all twelve gates were active. The last of the twelve cortexes achieved max right before his shift ended. Twelve minds would watch them all as they slept, would guide them through the galaxies. A crowd of psychologists and biotechs and selected press stood at the base of the housing and took readings and notes and wondered at the implications. A milestone, to say the least. This one had been a woman from Denton, a doctor.

They were ready.

As he hurried to get the dolly back to its dock, he was certain he felt the attention of this doctor, turning toward him. The cortexes would stay awake while passengers slept. They would stay awake while he slept. He even peed a bit into his suit, thinking for some crazy reason that he was already hooked up, but no co-worker, thankfully, noticed the wetness.

There were ghosts of the past and ghosts of the future everywhere. He was a receptacle; they would fill him, and the idea was terrifying.

His supervisor laughed when Crospinal told him, and called Crospinal a *fuckin' coward*.

As the tremors crept back, he had begun to fall asleep again, and the darkened room was turning upside down, so furniture became inverted. The bed, suspended from the ceiling. Crospinal had to push himself upward into the mattress, holding onto the crumpled sheet to prevent that, too, from falling.

"I live here," he murmured, convincing himself. "I live here, *I live here*," while, next door, the boy continued to move about, unhampered by any nocturnal inversions.

In sleep, breathing slowed. The room swung around, right side up. As his mouth slowly closed in relief, he had a dream of another boy named Richardson opening his, and speaking for the first time. Richardson had made it back to the cockpit. From there, he was sent by sentries to the chamber where the stats were now fully emerged. The corpse of the batch had been removed. A fresh sailor in full uniform and silver helmet was exposed; the door of a cabinet had opened. Richardson took part, holding the arm, helping the sailor down from the booth, his boots firm on the strip of carpet there. A chill washed over him from the stat, the slow breath of time. Dripping, on trembling legs, the sailor looked about, nonplussed. Richardson said his first words to the sailor, meant to reassure, to welcome, but the phrase came out in a language that did not yet exist, a whispering language of sibilant hisses and protracted clicks.

The sailor fell to his knees.

Then a wind swept the scene away, multitudes of faces rushing past, a sea of hopes and despair washing over him, none lingering long enough for him to recognize but enough to wake him again, slick with sweat—

3:47

Like red eyes.

Terrified of the coming day, he sat up, fully awake, until the glow of the ambients was just bright enough for him to see the forms of other people, sleeping naked all about. He frowned, wondering if he were remembering a dream, or entering into another one.

A carbon rod was clenched in both hands.

All was still.

Did he have the capacity to use the rod as a weapon? This was a test of sorts. Only one way to get away from the man who had held him down here.

Previously, he had swung a carbon rod, but had not connected; the batches, then, ran off. He imagined solid impact, flash-hardened carbon crunching a skull, life spilling out through a hole torn in a man's guts as the rod jammed upward, piercing intestines and diaphragm and juddering against the range of white vertebra—

Beyond the alcove, a great expanse of the hub was becoming visible in the growing light of a new day. Mists of polymers rose from the floor, commanded by the burgeoning lumens.

Had the man been real?

Crospinal could still feel the hard tap of a forefinger against his sternum, the thump inside his chest. The man's foetid breath, so close to his face.

Standing, he walked gingerly from the cove, stepping over the last of the sleeping batches into the larger expanse, the ceiling vanishing, swooping up to join the massive wall, which rose out of sight, swallowed by brighter areas higher in the world. He looked for the ledge where he last saw Clarissa and Richardson, but features were indistinguishable at this incredible distance, so he gave up.

At the horizon, clearer now, he saw no features.

He headed toward the open floor, taking big strides at first, picking up steam, leaving the batches and alcove behind, as the batches turned languorously and stretched, as if they, too, were dreaming. No sign of the man. The encounter seemed years ago.

At the bottom of the world, though, dwarfed on the ancient tiles, and feeling the inrush of time and the insurmountability of direction, Crospinal soon hesitated. An unknowable silence all around. The world poised, waiting. Had he been here before? From the people he was leaving behind there was a sort of peaceful, throbbing weight, settling over his shoulders, cast from them; they emanated the simplest of purposes, like a somnambulant heartbeat. He should sleep more. Go back with them, lie down. *Stay.*

He did not.

The carbon rod burned against his fingers. He clenched it *tight*.

A clear purpose would most likely elude Crospinal forever. But he carried within him a history, from sailors to batches, and even from elementals, too, who transversed the bays, watching over young children as they played in the pool, carrying within themselves colder yet no less complex questions about what sense life might possibly make. Any elemental, or lesser device with half an intellect—any living creature, humans of any sort, gazing upon sights such as the ones Crospinal had seen, and who felt the touch of fingers against their skin or uniform or plating—had felt this convergence, this moment of belonging.

Had he found what he was looking for?

The moment of peace and clarity was already diminishing.

He turned to look behind:

Distant batches were sitting, waking, knuckling their eyes. He saw one urinate, squatting.

From far away came a low hooting sound and a rumble, and he realized, looking for the source (again trying to evaluate just how *big* the world was), that he had not heard the engines in some time, nor felt their power, coming up through his reconfigured bones.

Crospinal resumed his walk.

Small patches of trees, larger and larger trees, on dried-out nutrient tiles. Between them, dry runnels must have once carried water.

Now, all the trees were dead.

A few moments later, on the far side of a gentle hump in the floor— revealing the expansive garden he'd seen from above, sloping away from him, also dead—he found the body of the man: eviscerated, flayed, torn asunder in every conceivable way.

HUB

A hundred batches, maybe more—an expanse of humanity as large as the body of water had been in his dream, certainly more people than he had ever seen before, all in one place—passed by. Two or three hundred bare feet thrumming at the floor in a ragged rhythm while he remained lurking among defoliated trees, ludicrously hiding behind denuded trunks for what seemed like ages. He felt the energies in his own feet, coming up his legs.

Who would he have been, if he'd never left the pen, if choices had been different?

Above the crowd, a massive drone—blunt, airborne—rotated nose down, driving the mass, or at least watching over them. *Paladins and drones and orbs.*

When he'd first struggled up the ladders of the harrier, every part of him had screamed with pain. Watching the icon of the hands over the controls as it shimmered into view, he'd shoved his arms all the way into the holes and clenched his jaw—

She materialized now, to stand before him in all her beauty—while he gaped. With a light smile, she said, "Hello, Crospinal."

His face itched where he had touched his cheek, then rubbed it, with the blood of the corpse. Both cheeks. Flaking off now, dried. He tried not to scratch or react for fear of drawing attention—though, when unable to resist the aggravation, he brushed at his face with the back of one hand and felt only his cool flesh, no crusty stigmata there at all.

At the site of the slaughter, Crospinal had tried to cover up the remains, but there was nothing in the vicinity of the man's devastated body except for bare floor tiles, withered fragments of ancient composite panels, and dead trees. The volume of gore would remain as he had found it for a very long time, at odds with the landscape, an incongruity of composition whose presence and chronicle was a mystery and an affront. Nevertheless, arranging splintered bones, shifting coils of still-warm intestines into heaped loops, as if to trigger some hidden mechanism, or at least rebuild the fleeting miracle of life—if only he could get the patterns right—he turned the skull (with a shattered parietal bone, brains spilling free), face up, and stared into the pulped eyeballs, haunted by the thought he might have done this carnage himself; his last thought, before falling asleep, had been of murder.

Sailors and batches hissed in his veins.

What Crospinal now believed, hiding in the copse, watching the receding exodus, with what was undoubtedly a paladin spinning above, was that the world and events of his past had not occurred, nor been arranged, the way he presumed. What he remembered fearing the most—that he would drift in darkness until the creatures came for him—would happen. All he could trust was the immediate moment: what he saw, the breath in his lungs. His interpretations were as unreliable as everything he had been told, everything he thought he'd learned, including the years of his father's advice, his lessons, and preparatory haptics.

Why *had* he come here?

The collar of his uniform slipped from around his throat and lay, writhing, at his feet. Whatever remained of a shield, if any shield remained at all, was now surely gone. No monitor scope, no comms.

In one hand, Crospinal retained the carbon rod. Had he bludgeoned the man with it?

What did he mean to accomplish?

Questions circled, the one constant in life.

A distant batch dropped to all fours and loped away from the group with an awkward, sideways gait, butt held high. Another lagged. Both sorts of stragglers dropped to the floor just as suddenly, twitching, only to get up and stagger back to take their places again. Did light feed them, like the walls and floors? Or their own flesh? Maybe they never ate, and lived for only a few days, despite what he had been told.

The flesh Crospinal had eaten sat in his stomach like an artifact. Sailors hummed quietly through his veins as he moved along the border of the dead garden in the opposite direction of the batches, staying within the spindly trunks for cover, though their cover was less than scant. Ironically, trees were tougher in death: they did not shatter as he passed or even as he grabbed at branches for balance. Between his toes, black tiles that had once sustained the root masses had crumbled to dust.

Soon, smoldering on the horizon, rose what could only be the source, or pen, of the paladins and batches both: an angular structure, heaving up from the floor, over which smaller drones and clusters of data orbs spiralled. Hazy with distant polymers, the mound grew quickly, as if approaching Crospinal at the same pace he approached it. He saw several large drones resting along the slopes on cradled facets, all streaming faint apparitions; shapes of light cascaded down the lower sides of the mound and spilled across the floor tiles before winking out. Some imagoes made it farther than others, as if attempting to escape, but all expired in brief flashes. Crospinal could not distinguish details. They were too vague, though he might have discerned the forms of people, or features of a face—an open mouth; narrowed eyes—rising, half-formed.

These were the paladins' dreams.

Chatter of the sailors became so loud he put his hands to his temples, expecting the cacophony could be heard from far away—the receding batches showed no sign of noticing, nor did the paladin, guiding the batches away, so minute now.

When he turned back, the mound seemed closer still. Filaments of light crackled from the peak—which appeared metallic from here, certainly non-composite—and shot up into the air. The pattern of features on the surface of the construction meant the formation was built more like the central pen, with grilles webbing polycarbonate girders.

Polymer mists directly above the mound were frantic with information gathering there. But this intrusion had been formed forever; a cyst at the core of the world, where struggles had gone on for so long they'd become symbiotic and inseparable.

Could this be the icon of his father's memories? Was this the mountain he tried so often to recall?

"Hey, Crospinal!"

For a second, he thought his name was being called by one of the voices murmuring in his head, but wheeling at a secondary, rustling sound, he saw movement behind a dead root mass: something low, shiny, and quick.

When the metal rat stepped into view, between two leaning trunks, its red eyes glowed in the already bright day. They stared at each other for a long while. Crospinal clenched the carbon rod tighter. The air seemed suddenly hotter, and the elemental wavered, as if projected. Not likely, though, with these dead trees all around, unless the image came from some device Crospinal had not yet encountered.

Nodding toward the distant procession, the individuals of which were now no bigger than the last joint of his smallest finger, he asked, "Where are they going?"

"They're being moved. All of them. That's the year of constitution. The year of delivery and the year of bad timing have already been moved. The cortexes are leaving."

"What?"

"Everything's changing, Crospinal. That's why I'm here. You need to come back with me. We've invested, well, a lot in you. I've been searching for days. You don't emit anything. You need to come with me, *now*."

"I'm not going anywhere." He frowned at the distant crowd, a blur that might not even be moving; they appeared to be climbing, as if the floor curved up, and were all on the inside of a massive sphere. When he turned back, to meet the fixed red eyes, he said, "What do you mean?"

"We have to go. I'll tell you as we travel back. I'm taking a big chance coming down here. I mean, if this shield dies, I'll be toast. They'll fry me in a second."

"I thought you might be a haptic."

"A *haptic*? *Shit*, no. That's all neurons and human energy bullshit. I'm *real*. I got a shield on. This is a force. They don't like us machines. Now let's go. I'll tell you everything you want to know once we get back."

"Just leave me alone, rat."

Rumbling shook the dead trees, but not from the engines. As if something equally hollow yet even more massive than the world ground gently against the other side of the floor. They both, elemental and man, looked toward the distant mound.

"We're not biotic, you know," the device said, after a moment. "So will you get that right? Look, Crospinal—"

A surge of frustration, or even anger: in sudden tears, he shouted, "I'm not going back! You'll tell me I'm sick, or that I died, or some shit like that. You'll tell me you've been looking for *years* and that I'm five hundred years old!"

"Keep it down!" Crouching low, the elemental became almost flat against the dried nutrient tiles. The shield wavered, curling over it, sheltering.

"Stop following me."

"Crospinal, you *are* ill. That's the thing. I'm telling you the truth. You really are. We want to help you."

"Just stop."

"*Listen to me*. This is important. I need to scan you. You've done a lot already, Crospinal, each time, but this one's gone off the rails—"

"Shut up."

"All right, all right, listen, Crospinal. *Listen*. All right. Just keep it down. The cockpit's doubled in size. The crew you named—Richardson, and the other one, with the girl's name, Clarissa—have brought back *twenty seven more sailors*. They're coming up fast now. Other crew are named. A structure's forming around them and the other pilot, the one like you, is awake again. She's coming back. The journey's almost over, Crospinal. We're so close. But they need you up there. You need to be well. You need to get better. You need to suit up."

"I killed someone."

The metal rat, silenced now, cocked its head. "Who?"

"Back there." He indicated with a nod the ridge where he'd found the remains. "On the far side of this garden."

"You mean the sailor? The first sailor? Tattooed and dismembered?"

"I don't know what tattooed means but, yeah, torn apart. I killed him."

The elemental stared.

"Well? Did I? Did I tear him apart?"

"Of course not, Crospinal. He's been there, well, since the beginning. Can we please go? I'll tell you later, I promise."

"Who was he?"

"The first passenger. The first sailor. There were no dispensers then. Us elementals were dormant. No one was set to wake up. No one had any idea what had happened. But he woke others and helped them find food and water, and ways to stay alive. He woke us. You were named after him."

"He had a name?"

"All sailors did."

"And his name was Crospinal?"

"Yes."

"You know what? Stop talking, okay? You've lied to me so much. You're a shitty fucking liar. He would have told me that Crospinal was his name when I said who I was. He would have told me."

Again the elemental paused. Delicately, it said, "Except he's dead, Crospinal. He's been dead for thousands of years. He can't tell you anything."

About to point out the fresh blood he'd smeared onto his face, the lesions he'd seen on the man's arms, the shreds of meat hanging from sharp carbon rods as he ate, Crospinal turned away instead, disgusted. The batches were no longer visible, nor was the paladin. A mist of polymers blew lackluster from the trees, catching on the bare branches and twinkling like grey streamers.

He walked away.

"Crospinal!" Following swiftly in leaps, the elemental would not be left behind. "You have no idea what you're doing. We've been trying to help you. Every generation. That's why we're here. We want to help you get better because you can fly this thing! With Luella. I need to bring you back. Please, Crospinal. *Listen.*"

The end of the garden was nigh. Fractals of apparitions from the paladins straggled as far as his feet now. Without stopping, he passed through the lights and they broke apart upon his shins. There were faces, stern and shocked, and forms of beasts that could never have lived in a corporeal world.

Quaking again: Crospinal felt the thrum, a familiar surge, pressure building in strength as the engines, wherever they were, turned over very slowly. And ceased.

"Shit," said the metal rat. "Aw, *fuck—*"

Through eruptions of light, haptics too virulent to contain, and mercurial projections, Crospinal watched the giant drones spinning slowly in their sloped recesses. They were as large as the pen. He remembered seeing them before, in the haptic the first metal rat had shown him. Being guided on the dolly. From where he stood there were three visible, and the limned outline of a fourth, against a nearly hidden facet. On another side, as he circled slowly, a greyer, calmer façade of the mound meant the paladin was gone. Had he just watched it leave? Was his girlfriend inside one of these, projecting out into the world? Glowing apparitions and the crackling lights they rode were hard to look at and caused the essences inside him to agitate.

He waded knee deep through haptics now.

The metal rat, running within the amalgam of lights, had to leap to clear the luminous carpet. "If you don't eat pellets, or don't drink water from a spigot, you'll revert. Everything will be lost. You understand that? It might be too late already."

Crospinal was only half listening. He actually felt a modicum of relief at the idea he might not have committed murder, though he had once contemplated it. Could he? Could everyone? Had that aberration been instilled in him as part of his education? That's all he wanted to know. Yet everything the metal rat said might be lies. He felt his heart slowing, his body grow less tense. He said without turning: "What about you, then, rat? Where do machines stand?"

The housings where the cabinets of the paladins were docked took up most of his field of vision, a massive formation that rose hundreds of metres above the hub floor. The remaining drones pivoted slowly, wreathed in their own light.

"Personally? I'm *a doctor*," said the elemental, jumping clear and dipping in again. "A *contrivance* from before this disaster unfolded. So I'm here, risking everything, to retrieve you from your unfathomable quest."

"The first sailor told me I'm not human. Is that true?"

"For goodness sake, Crospinal, you couldn't've spoken with him. He's long gone. He's dead. But I can assure you that you're human. *Please* stop walking. You'll get us both killed."

He did stop. Just for a bit. He was out of breath. "So, that's like, like a shield you have on? You're an elemental, wearing a sort of shield?"

"Yes. And it's depleting my batteries pretty quick."

"So go dormant. Conserve energy." Crospinal tugged at the girdle, which had started to sag now the collar was gone—the catheter stung, likes pins in his groin. Pulling free a length of gortex piping made the entire unit cant further on his hips. "How did he die?"

"Who?"

"You know. The other Crospinal."

"The first one? Shit, you know, I could just take you back. I could drop you in your tracks right now and get you carted away. Force feed you. Cram you back into a suit. But I want you to *decide*. I want you to make the right choice."

"*How did he die?*"

"He fell. He fell from somewhere up there, and he splattered where you saw him."

Projections and the entangled figures of light seemed to coil up his thighs. He pulled another strip of his girdle free—plastic rivets popped away—then rubbed his fingers to let the sheet of fabric drift away.

Voices added to the clutter and chatter in his head.

"You helped us long ago. In the year of naming. And now we want to help you."

"What did I do?"

"In the anterior passage, where the bridge once was, you gave two of us—"

The impact of the carbon rod chipped the tiny elemental right out from under its shield, out from under the apparitions, arcing the titanium body up with a resounding *thwack*. The machine's scream was delicate, high-pitched as it rose; before the device had been swallowed again by the paladin's dreams, let alone before it hit the tiles—as the shield leapt frantically to catch its host—he started to lope.

An arc of lightning from the nearest data orb, blackening the titanium frame and skin, sending the ruins skittering through the ghosts to rest immobile.

Crospinal dropped the carbon rod: clattering, it, too, was swallowed by phantasms.

Wading round an arc of the base through increasingly agitated projections, he faced another facet, exposed now, also empty, and dimmer because of the emptiness. The structure beneath was polymethyl, a web comprised of hard plastic beams like those behind the throne of his father, like the girder that had fallen on the dream cabinets he used to visit. He stared for a moment, overwhelmed by disparate and surprisingly moving fragments of his past.

Flanking the cradle where the huge drone had nestled, inlaid sets of consoles rose up, levels of them, meeting at a peak: a dais that would have been covered, had the paladin, like those adjacent, been docked. There were four score.

As he approached the consoles, a susurrus of voices from within egged him on. He was not struck by lightning, though orbs clustered over his head. He moved aside the cover of the lowest console, exposing the pair of holes.

The icon of hands, palms together, rose and spun before him.

Pushing his bare fists in, the energy was a soft explosion. He wondered if he would be annihilated for good, but he stood, sagging, the hum moving up his arms—

"Crospinal? Crospinal?"

For a second, he was back in bed. Clarissa had woken him. She had breakfast on a tray. A crepe; berries; coffee. It was his birthday.

But that was swept away, and when he woke this time, his girlfriend was with him, in her dark uniform and dark boots, her hair pulled back tight. She regarded him with such concern and affection he felt light enough to rise off the floor, transcend the world. He had found her. The image was so strong, clear. He could almost touch her. He wanted to drop to his knees, wrap his arms around her legs, rest his head against her forever.

"You came so far," she said.

Love was a force, pushing through him, like lumens, with information glorious and threatening both. He was barely able to speak. He was bursting with love. "How can you see me? You're the only one . . ."

"Of course I see you." A beatific smile, though her expression belied elements of resignation, fear, even a futility of events. (And her eyes, Crospinal realized, were . . . *green*!) "I always see you. You once belonged to me. I watched the passenger take you away. I watched you in the place the passenger found. You came to me when I called. Remember? Our visits?"

"Yes." He was falling into her eyes.

"I did what I could. I should have stopped it. But I was so proud of you. They wanted me to stop it, but I couldn't bear the thought. I got in trouble." Her smile faltered.

"Is this endtime?" He was trying to swallow a hard shape that had formed in his throat.

"Yes, Crospinal, it is." She reached for him, as if she had forgotten he was untouchable. "For better or worse. We've arrived."

"But the . . . the sailors? The crew?"

"They tried to return to a time and place that could never exist again. Reasons are flawed. We want you to thrive, Crospinal. Lead a good life."

"Paladins tried to kill me."

"No, Crospinal. Not you."

He gazed at her for a long while. Finally, with great difficulty, he told her how much he loved her.

"I love you, too," she said. "Always know that." Smiling, showing white teeth, she looked, for a moment, happy. "But you're on your own now. I can't take you with me. Not like that. You're free."

"I tried to—" What? What had he learned? What, indeed, had he tried to do?

When he lifted his fists free—as images rushed him—a shove sent him sprawling. Lying on his back under the carpeting of apparitions—for a moment startled by the vignettes and images of faces and bodies and landscapes that streamed over him—he did not rise until the thought that breathing in these strange projections without filters might be harmful.

He backed away from the mound, away from the paladins, away from the cascading images.

Rumbling, another paladin lifted off, streaming light as it rose.

And he saw batches, when the lights dimmed, dozens of them, standing at the consoles that had been uncovered, moving, coming awake. They withdrew their arms in a symmetrical pattern, and turned, climbing down. They were naked. Their faces were slack, void; their bodies thin and smooth. The giant drone waited, quaking the air, rife with the stench of ozone.

The mound was a gate, a font of knowledge.

Engines trembled again, a high-pitched whine, and the world stilled.

Under the diminishing lights from the paladin's dreams, a shift in the refraction of the floor revealed ranks of younger batches laying side by side, eyes closed. Children, infants, grey and curled with their mouths open, under the tiles—

He stood there, trembling, one hand outreached, for some time, culpable, if not for other deaths, then certainly for the death of the tiny elemental.

Younger than he and his sister had been in the first haptics, the infants beneath his feet were immersed, jaws moving, suckling. Thin conduits, up from the structure, visible beneath the floor, ran into the temples of each baby. He saw tiny inlays in their forearms, a darker insignia in the skin. One had a withered hand. Another, the enlarged head of hydrocephalia, adjacent to a third, legs curled by rickets.

These were his girlfriend's batch: the crippled, the rejects.

On his knees, he peeled aside the rough, translucent tile, and reached into the cold, cold fluid to snap the conduits free. He tore them clear away from the foundation. Somewhere, his girlfriend was watching over him, though he couldn't see her, and would never see her again. The sailors made a chorus of voices. He felt strong, alive, though saddened by what little he had learned. Icy liquid spattered him, dripping from his skin as he stood. He cradled two slowly twisting babies. They began to warm at his touch, and mewl.

⚉

A series of remote concussions shuddered the world. He smelled and heard configurations shifting. Far above were lights, flashing less and less. When he turned to look over his shoulder, he no longer saw the mound, but another paladin had angled out over the floor, driving away yet another year of batches.

Was the angry paladin inside this one?

He belonged to neither batches, nor crew.

Cradled against Crospinal's chest, one on each forearm, the infants, breathing by themselves now, sleeping, would soon need to eat.

Toward a series of columns, disappearing upward as far as he could see, he got a whiff of the pylon, the smell of the void, from the sky station. The old sailor, dying of cancer there, like his own father; the men that lived inside, absconded from this configuration of living altogether. Difficult to see the opening, or exit, for pylons were vacuums, illusions, like so much else. He hesitated. Was the world breaking apart? Composites and plastics both dissolving?

He had no means to feed himself, let alone the infants.

The stench of the vacuum was foul.

⚉

Before searching the time-scoured debris directly under the broad opening, which must have drifted from the void of the pylon, he placed the children down gently and, as he did so, felt his girdle cant, lurch, and finally dislodge. The processor was inert. Pulled from his urethra, where the suit had once seeded, the catheter slid, and he felt blood welling already, coursing down his groin and thighs. The blood seemed so hot. He didn't look, yet red droplets fell upon the infants and the floor where he'd laid them. Crospinal could not tell if the children were boys or girls or one of each. Their limbs moved sluggishly. They seemed ill-formed, and weak.

⚉

Symbiotes were easy to find. They waited sluggishly under the detritus, doing nothing to avoid Crospinal when he uncovered them. He wondered as he turned the smallest one over, and the legs clacked back against each other, if these beasts were part machine: their tiny eyes were red, unreadable, like an elemental's.

He placed the carapace very gently against the back of an infant's head, watching the legs wrap slowly around the thin neck and shoulders. The baby struggled feebly only when the longest limb, the tube unfolding, found the baby's mouth, and pushed inside.

The tiny chest filled, emptied, and filled again—

Then he did the same to the other child.

Finally, picking up the largest creature, he flipped it over and slung it in one motion, like he'd done this before, behind his own head. The legs were cool as they gripped him, and the carapace against the back of his head was not hard. He opened his mouth to let the tube seek his throat. A blue aura erupted from the mite. The legs gripped his haloed head.

Retrieving the children, lungs pumped full with cool air, he leapt up.

THE YEAR OF MIRACLES

He had vague intentions of retracing his steps, finding his sister and the cockpit—maybe even the pen if he searched hard enough—yet once he was floating, curled around the infants to keep them warm (while the symbiotes clicked and adjusted and hissed air into them), he found himself getting sleepy. In the formless black of the pylon, for an indeterminable amount of time, Crospinal faded in and out. Voices of the sailors were also fading. Were his passengers attempting to leave his body? Or were they feeling assured, finally, and merely quieting?

Blood from his groin drifted about him in perfect spheres. Though he could not see them as he dozed, the crimson globes were like worlds, planets, stars. Crospinal slowly passed between them and left behind a sparse trail.

Eventually, against his naked skin, the infants stopped moving. Their energies were spent. They knew nothing about what, if anything, they might be missing. Life to them had been a handful of hours—lungs just starting to work, now filled by an alien bladder, the discomfort and need of sustenance growing as they sailed without weight.

But Crospinal, for some reason, was no longer drifting.

He could not open his eyes.

After that, discomfort flared, and the thin wails of the infants grew louder, peaked, until they, too, were finally past. The three of them took slow, shallow breaths, the handful of hours thrown at them nearly spent. No questions had formed in the minds of the infants. There was silence.

He managed at some point, before or just after he had stopped drifting, to put one hand down, a massive effort, and lay it across a tiny body, holding it even closer. His skin, and the skin of the baby, was hot as real fire.

Then he slept again, or expired, and he thought for one last instant as he passed over a threshold into a place of light about the elementals that had watched over him as a child, his guardians, which he'd named Fox and Bear; it seemed as if he could see their red eyes again.

Calmness on the water. Overhead, constellations were visible, but wisps of clouds had begun to blow in. The shore was not far ahead, waiting. Creatures waited there, too. They waited for everyone, eventually, and took them, without regard. He did not fear death now. Lying, almost relaxed, mere dregs of life remained. The trembling returned to his limbs, one last time, and as he tried to quell it, he realized the boy next door was silent, and had been silent for ages.

He woke, exhausted, in the dark.

The fires of their skin had cooled.

A single sphere of light—one *star*—broken free from the others, resolved before his face. Were the shapes of land ahead the peaks of a coast? Dreams were memories, and memories were dreams. From the sailors that had travelled inside him, he knew about stars, and about a spine of green mountains at the end of the sea—

"Sir?"

One thing he had not known—and was surprised by—was that stars could talk.

Crospinal tried to respond but his lips and mouth were too parched. The creatures that waited for them all would not greet him, not just yet. One day, but not right now. Recalling the infants, and leaving his girlfriend behind in the hub, he understood how little time comprised a life, and how tenacious and wondrous and frustrating the interim between oblivions could be.

Lifting a hand, to hold it up to the night sky as he lay dying, and bid goodbye, he rapped the star with his knuckles.

"Shit," it said. "Sorry sir. I'm new to this. So sorry. I didn't anticipate your movement."

It's okay. He wanted to smile.

"And sorry for the profanity, too. I'm sort of, well, new to this. And *very* distressed. It's just that, well, I believe these are strange times. I'm getting no signals at all from network support."

It's going to be okay.

"You should be feeling a bit better, no?"

I am. My name's Crospinal.

"I, uh, took the liberty of hydrating you, and the, the infants—the *orphans*—when I realized no doctors were coming. Stanched your rupture, too, though I have only rudimentary help, I'm afraid. And one of the little ones has died, sir, the female, with the cleft palate. Her stomach was perforated. I couldn't do anything. We're not even supposed to help them, but I tried anyhow. She was very young and damaged, and I don't believe her batch, whatever their year was called, have the capacity to, well, *regenerate*. Not the damaged ones, anyhow. This situation is certainly not what I had been expecting."

Words of reassurance swam around Crospinal's head, though he could not express them.

"You were brought here by the strangest of humans. I've watched the footage. I've watched ten times!"

Now Crospinal managed to grin.

"I'm sorry, sir, if I've let you down. You had just two orphans with you? You were taking them somewhere? I don't claim to understand. The child's death was painless, I assure you."

"Light," Crospinal said, able to speak at last, and figuring out how to do so: ambients flared up the walls, then brightened, and brightened further, illuminating the area.

He was lying naked in a composite alcove.

Blinking, he got up onto his elbows.

The controller—concerned, unsure—stayed directly over the living child, who seemed pale, but peaceful, and suffused, like himself, with traces of life.

The other child was blue and cool.

So, this living child was a boy? Their bodies, in life and death, were identical. A very small food dispenser, which must have come up through the floor while they slept, gently rubbed the tiny lips of the boy with a milky pale pellet; the child responded.

Behind the dispenser, a water spigot craned its neck to watch.

And behind these devices, a porthole had opened in the wall, but he could see, even from here, that the view was opaque, uncertain.

"Are you ready, sir? The world has, well, *stopped*. On the other side of, uh, *fuck*, beyond these panels—"

Toluene was already seeping through. Polymers ran in darker rivulets, reconfiguring, recycling, as the controller hung there over the nursing baby.

"I'm ready," Crospinal said, and as these words came from his mouth, he believed them. *Or course he was ready*. One hand on the warm infant by his hip—the boy, chest softly lifting Crospinal's palm—and the fingers of his right hand around the small calf of the dead one, he cradled the bodies closer against his sides, and held them there so they lay full-length along his flanks.

The composite panel was almost fully dissolved now. Slanted columns of warm light fell across them, and breezes coming through brought scents that stirred his growing wonder.

Out there, the sounds of activity—

Creatures would have to wait.

Against his hip, the living child murmured, and gurgled, and swallowed.

The dead child, of course, was still.

Crospinal rose carefully and took a deep breath. He would name both, first thing, when he got outside.

ABOUT THE AUTHOR

Brent Hayward's shorter fiction has appeared in several publications. He is the author of the novels *Filaria* and *The Fecund's Melancholy Daughter*. Born in London, raised in Montreal, he currently lives in Toronto.

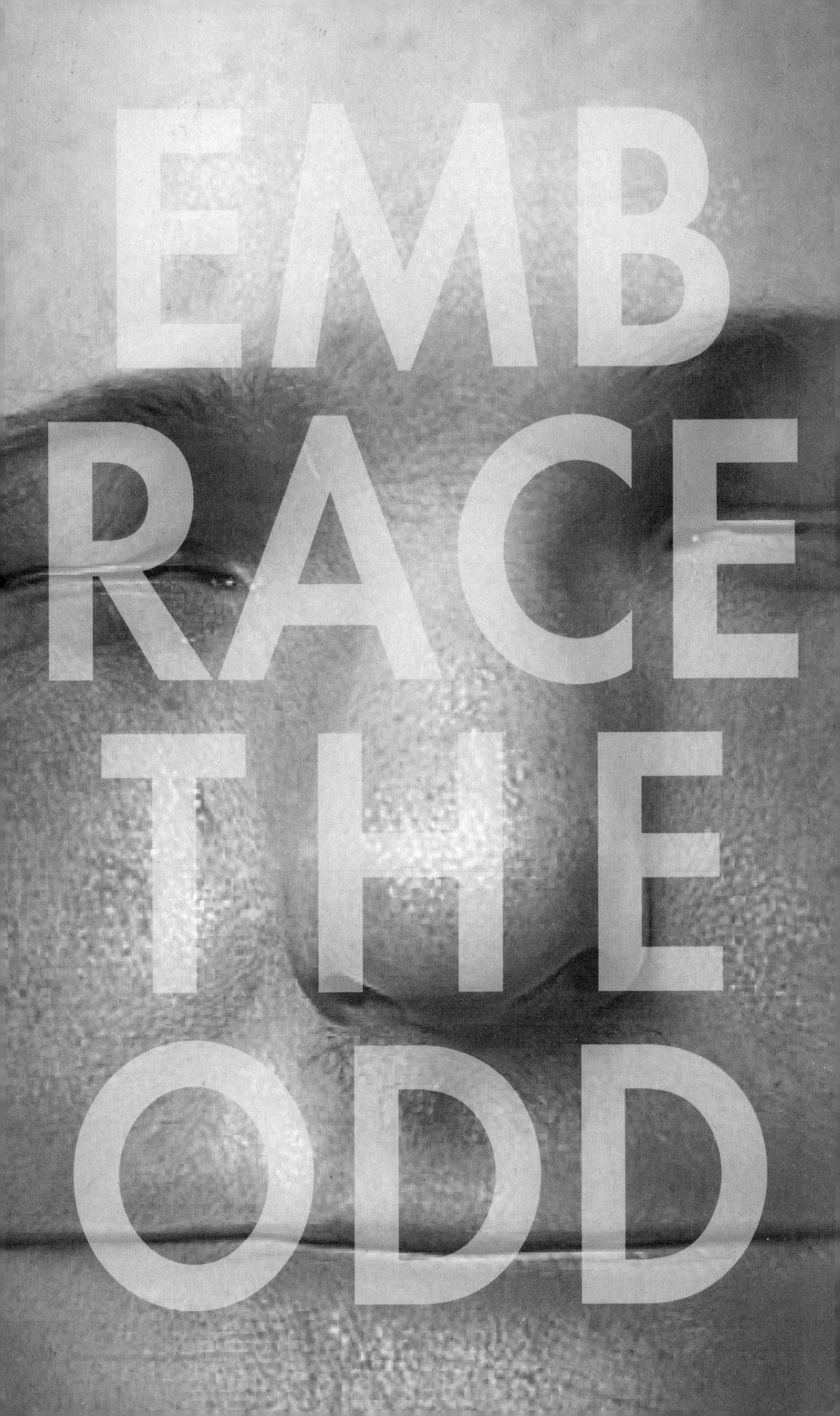
EMB
RACE
THE
ODD

FILARIA
BRENT HAYWARD

Four inhabitants of a crumbling world:
A drug-addled boy, living in dank recesses, sets out in an ancient car to find his ex, who has mysteriously vanished overnight;
A privileged girl, obsessed with the past, and exiled by her esteemed father, learns more about her long-vanished ancestors than she ever could have wished for;
An old man, on his hundredth birthday, deserts his quiet post as an elevator operator, climbing the great shaft in hopes of seeing the fabled topmost level before he dies;
And a fisherman, seeking answers to why his once-vibrant wife is now chronically ailing and wasting away, begins a quest to find and confront the god of all gods.

AVAILABLE NOW
978-1-92685-173-0

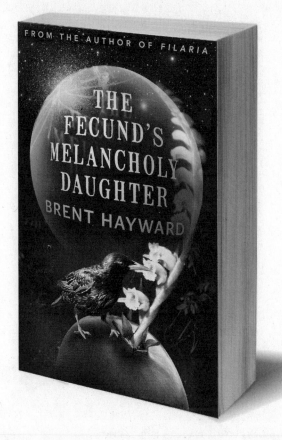

DAWN SONG
MICHAEL MARANO

A modern dark fantasy classic returns with this new, Special Edition of Dawn Song, the soul-haunting novel from a Bram Stoker Award-winning author with a deeply powerful—and prescient—vision. Set in Boston at the start of the First Gulf War, a larger, supernatural battle for Supremacy in Hell takes shape . . . but plays out on a personal scale as unassuming humans careen into the path of a beautiful, terrible Succubus who has come to Earth to do her Father's bidding.

In the iconic horror tradition of Clive Barker and Anne Rice, as well as of newer fantasy voices like Mike Carey and Tim Powers, *Dawn Song* is a dark meditation on Salvation, full of terror and tenderness.

AVAILABLE JULY 2014
978-1-77148-179-3

THE FAMILY UNIT AND OTHER FANTASIES
LAURENCE KLAVAN

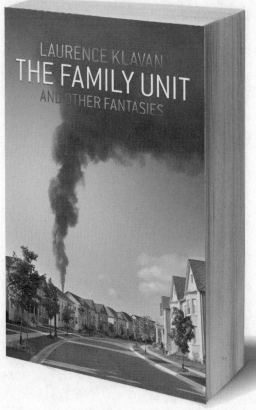

The Family Unit and Other Fantasies is the debut collection of acclaimed Edgar Award-winning author Laurence Klavan. A superb group of darkly comic, deeply compassionate, largely fantastical stories set in our jittery, polarized, increasingly impersonal age. Whether it's the tale of a corporation that buys a man's family; two supposed survivors of a super-storm who are given shelter by a gullible couple; an erotic adventure set during an urban terrorist alert; or a nightmare in which a man sees his neighbourhood developed and disappearing at a truly alarming speed, these stories are by turn funny and frightening, odd and arousing, uncanny and unnerving.

AVAILABLE AUGUST 2014
978-1-77148-203-5

WE WILL ALL GO DOWN TOGETHER
GEMMA FILES

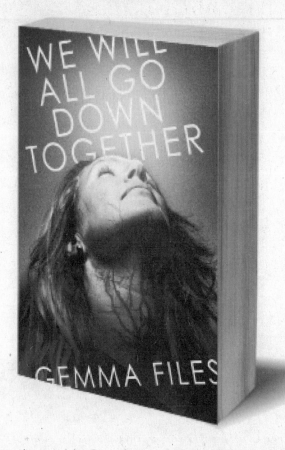

In the woods outside Overdeere, Ontario, there are trees that speak, a village that doesn't appear on any map and a hill that opens wide, entrapping unwary travellers. Music drifts up from deep underground, while dreams—and nightmares—take on solid shape, flitting through the darkness. It's a place most people usually know better than to go, at least locally—until tonight, at least, when five bloodlines mired in ancient strife will finally converge once more.

AVAILABLE AUGUST 2014
978-1-77148-202-8

THEY DO THE SAME THINGS DIFFERENT THERE
ROBERT SHEARMAN

Robert Shearman visits worlds that are unsettling and strange. Sometimes they are just like ours—except landlocked countries may disappear overnight, marriages to camels are the norm, and the dead turn into musical instruments. Sometimes they are quite alien—where children carve their own tongues from trees, and magic shows are performed to amuse the troops in the war between demons and angels. There is horror, and dreams fulfilled and squandered, of true love. They do the same things different there.

Robert Shearman has written four previous collections of short stories, and they have collectively won the World Fantasy Award, the Shirley Jackson Award, and three British Fantasy Awards. He is probably best known as a writer on the BBC TV series *Doctor Who*, and his work on the show gave him a Hugo Award nomination.

AVAILABLE SEPTEMBER 2014
978-1-77148-301-8

GIFTS FOR THE ONE WHO COMES AFTER
HELEN MARSHALL

Ghost thumbs. Miniature dogs. One very sad can of tomato soup . . . British Fantasy Award-winner Helen Marshall's second collection offers a series of twisted surrealities that explore the legacies we pass on to our children. A son seeks to reconnect with his father through a telescope that sees into the past. A young girl discovers what lies on the other side of her mother's bellybutton. Death's wife prepares for a very special funeral. In *Gifts for the One Who Comes After*, Marshall delivers eighteen tales of love and loss that cement her as a powerful voice in dark fantasy and the New Weird. Dazzling, disturbing, and deeply moving.

AVAILABLE SEPTEMBER 2014
978-1-77148-303-2

DEAD GIRLS DON'T
MAGS STOREY

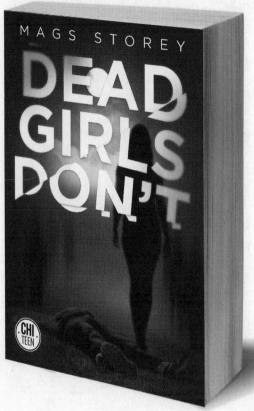

Liv might be in love with a serial killer. You'd think the fact she can talk to the dead would make it easier to discover who's really been slicing up her high school bullies. But all the clues have been leading back to Adam—the oh-so-hot fugitive she's been hiding in the funeral home. As the bodies pile up, she'll have to risk matching wits with the ghosts of her freshly-dead classmates—some of whom have deadly agendas of their own. Was the cute guy with the wicked grin really framed for murder? Or will Liv just end up the latest bloody victim at Rosewood Academy?

AVAILABLE OCTOBER 2014 IN CANADA; MARCH 2015 IN US
978-1-77148-306-3

FLOATING BOY AND THE GIRL WHO COULDN'T FLY

P.T. JONES

Things Mary doesn't want to fall into: the river, high school, her mother's life.

Things Mary does kind of want to fall into: love, the sky.

This is the story of a girl who sees a boy float away one fine day. This is the story of the girl who reaches up for that boy with her hand and with her heart. This is the story of a girl who takes on the army to save a town, who goes toe-to-toe with a mad scientist, who has to fight a plague to save her family. This is the story of a girl who would give anything to get to babysit her baby brother one more time. If she could just find him.

It's all up in the air for now, though, and falling fast. . . .

AVAILABLE OCTOBER 2014
978-1-77148-174-8

THE DOOR IN THE MOUNTAIN
CAITLIN SWEET

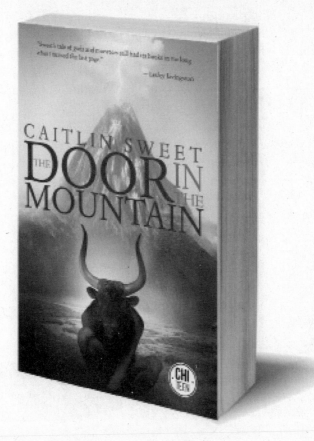

WE ARE ALL MONSTERS

Lost in time, shrouded in dark myths of blood and magic, *The Door in the Mountain* leads to the world of ancient Crete: a place where a beautiful, bitter young princess named Ariadne schemes to imprison her godmarked half-brother deep in the heart of a mountain maze, where a boy named Icarus tries, and fails, to fly—and where a slave girl changes the paths of all their lives forever.

AVAILABLE NOW IN CANADA; OCTOBER 2014 IN US
978-1-77148-192-2

CHIZINEPUB.COM

GET KATJA
SIMON LOGAN

Katja from Simon Logan's award-winning *Katja From the Punk Band* is back. Free and on the mainland, she emerges from hiding, only to find herself hunted by debt collectors, mad surgeons, and a corrupt detective, all of whom will stop at nothing to claim her for their own. And behind this scramble lies the twisted mind of an old adversary, desperate to have his revenge. Replete with dark humour, chaotic storytelling, and a fast-paced Industrial thriller setting, Get Katja is the latest novel from the author of *Pretty Little Things to Fill Up The Void*, *Nothing Is Inflammable*, and *I-O*.

AVAILABLE NOW
978-1-77148-167-0

WILD FELL
MICHAEL ROWE

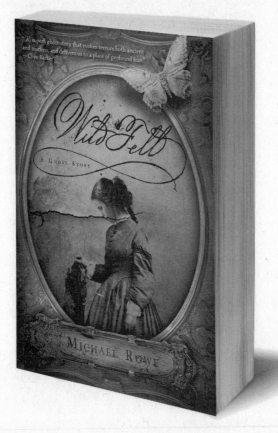

The crumbling summerhouse called Wild Fell, soaring above the desolate shores of Blackmore Island, has weathered the violence of the seasons for more than a century. Built for his family by a 19th-century politician of impeccable rectitude, the house has kept its terrible secrets and its darkness sealed within its walls. For a hundred years, the townspeople of alvina have prayed that the darkness inside Wild Fell would stay there, locked away from the light.

Jameson Browning, a man well acquainted with suffering, has purchased Wild Fell with the intention of beginning a new life, of letting in the light. But what waits for him at the house is devoted to its darkness and guards it jealously. It has been waiting for Jameson his whole life . . . or even longer. and now, at long last, it has found him.

AVAILABLE NOW
978-1-77148-159-5

THE 'GEISTERS
DAVID NICKLE

When Ann LeSage was a little girl, she had an invisible friend—a poltergeist, that spoke to her with flying knives and howling winds. She called it the Insect. And with a little professional help, she contained it. But the nightmare never truly ended. As Ann grew from girl into young woman, the Insect grew with her, becoming a thing of murder. Now, as she embarks on a new life married to successful young lawyer Michael Voors, Ann believes that she finally has the Insect under control. But there are others vying to take that control away from her. They may not know exactly what they're dealing with, but they know they want it. They are the 'Geisters. And in pursuing their own perverse dream, they risk spawning the most terrible nightmare of all.

AVAILABLE NOW
978-1-77148-143-4

TELL MY SORROWS TO THE STONES
CHRISTOPHER GOLDEN

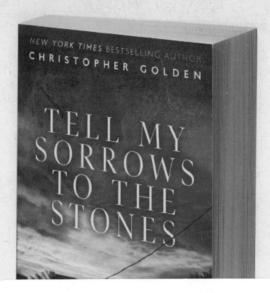

A circ... ...ectral
gunsl... ...es he
loves. ...places
that ...wood
actre... ...ssion.
A gri... ...for a
ghost... ...West
Virgin... ...story.
These... ...*ell My*
Sorro...

ALSO AV...